DIME NOVEL MORMONS

DIME NOVEL MORMONS

EDITED AND INTRODUCED BY MICHAEL AUSTIN AND ARDIS E. PARSHALL

EAGLE PLUME, THE WHITE AVENGER. A TALE OF THE MORMON TRAIL (1870)

THE DOOMED DOZEN; OR, DOLORES, THE DANITE'S DAUGHTER (1881)

FRANK MERRIWELL AMONG THE MORMONS; OR, THE LOST TRIBE OF ISRAEL (1897)

THE BRADYS AMONG THE MORMONS; OR, SECRET WORK IN SALT LAKE CITY (1903)

SALT LAKE CITY, 2017
GREG KOFFORD BOOKS

ISBN 978-1-58958-517-1 (paperback)
Also available in ebook.

Greg Kofford Books
P.O. Box 1362
Draper, UT 84020
www.gregkofford.com

Library of Congress Control Number: 2017931779

CONTENTS

CONTENTS

Frank Merriwell Among the Mormons;
or, The Lost Tribe of Israel

The Bradys Among the Mormons;
or, Secret Work in Salt Lake City

INTRODUCTION

During the first years of the Civil War three very similar novels about Mormons appeared in the United States, each featuring handsome heroes, villainous Mormon elders, and chaste young women who are kidnapped and taken to Salt Lake City as polygamous brides. In all three (spoiler alert!), the lecherous Mormons are defeated, the chaste young women are rescued, and the hero gets the girl.

Despite their many similarities, these books occupied very different positions in the commercial hierarchy of books. Captain Mayne Reid's *The Wild Huntress* (1861) was published by the New York firm R. M. De Witt as a cloth-bound, gilt-edged volume that sold for the princely sum of $1.25 (about $35.00 in 2017), while Theodore Winthrop's *John Brent* (1862) was issued by the prestigious Boston firm Ticknor and Fields (the same firm that published *The Scarlet Letter*) at the slightly less princely but still substantial sum of $1.00. Like most books published in the United States in the early 1860s, both novels would have been beyond the financial reach of many readers. Though most Americans knew how to read—thanks to the compulsory education movement that began in the 1840s—very few of them actually owned more than a handful of books, which were still considered luxury items and priced accordingly.

The third tale of Mormon perfidy, *Esther: A Story of the Oregon Trail* (1862) by Mrs. Ann S. Stephens, sold for a mere ten cents. *Esther* was a dime novel—volume 45 in the Beadle's Dime Novels series that began in 1860 with another book by Mrs. Stephens called *Malaeska: The Indian Wife of the White Hunter*. Dime novels did away with all the frills of book publishing—like covers. They were printed on cheap newsprint—looking more like small newspapers than novels—and they crammed 30,000–50,000 words into as few as fifteen pages of text, using multiple columns and achingly miniscule fonts.

Even though *Malaeska* had been published twenty years earlier as a magazine serial, when it appeared in this new format it sold more than 500,000 copies and changed the publishing industry forever. Between 1860 and 1920, somewhere around 60,000 dime novels were published in the United States with an average count of about 30,000 words and prices ranging from five to twenty cents. (The term *dime novel* was a brand name, not necessarily a price tag.)

Dime novels probably did more than any other kind of book to turn lower- and middle-class Americans into both book owners and book readers. They were so cheap that almost anyone could afford them, and they were so exciting that almost everybody wanted to read them. In an era without radio, television, movies, or the Internet they were the closest thing to mindless entertainment to be found. But they weren't mindless at all. Some of the best writers in the country were attracted to dime novels by the lure of high sales and regular work. The plots were often very sophisticated, and the reading level was as high as that found in volumes sold at ten times the price. Dime novels succeeded by creating new readers and by making highly entertaining and exciting stories the reward for literacy. It would be difficult to overestimate the impact this had on two generations of Americans.

Dime novels also took advantage of new developments in printing technology to remain inexpensive. Their prices actually went down during the nineteenth century. By the 1880s many of them were selling for a nickel. One reason for this is that most of the early novels were cast in stereotype plates so that they could be reused and reprinted often (usually as new titles), an innovation that had the effect of freezing certain kinds of portrayals—like the portrayals of Mormons—in time. The Mormons in early twentieth-century dime novels often acted and talked like characters from the mid-nineteenth century because most of the novels were written in the mid-nineteenth century and reprinted with new titles and new covers. Even new novels written at the time tended to use the same kinds of characterizations in order to enforce a sort of consistency across the industry.

And it wasn't just the Mormons. Though dime novels did a lot to promote literacy and book ownership they didn't do much for peace, love, and understanding. Their narrative formulas required spectacular villains and their style guides did not allow for depth or character development, so they turned to the most simplistic and outrageous stereotypes that nineteenth-century American culture had to offer. Just about everybody got the same treatment: Indians, African Americans, Chinese workers, gold miners, riverboat gamblers, and, of course, Mormons.

It's hard to tell just how many of these dime novels featured Mormons. They were not designed for long-term storage, and many thousands of titles have not survived in any form. Furthermore, title lists that we can reconstruct (often from the backs of existing issues) do not account for the common practice of reprinting the same material under different titles. After several years of searching, though, we have identified thirty-six dime novels (not including reprints) whose plots deal primarily with Mormons. I am certain that there are others, but even at twice this number, Mormon plots would account for around one-tenth of one percent of the dime-novel universe.

But the way Mormons were portrayed in dime novels was remarkably consistent over many decades and multiple genres. This consistency tells us that dime novelists were playing with common stereotypes that nearly all their readers recognized—indeed, these stereotypes worked their way into much of the more respectable literature of the day and influenced the way American culture has interacted with Mormonism ever since. These tropes were based on three things, perhaps the only three things that most Americans knew about

Mormons in the final decades of the nineteenth century: Danites, polygamy, and the Mountain Meadows Massacre. Whatever variation occurs in the dime novels comes from mixing these three ingredients into new concoctions.

Of these standard tropes, the Danites will probably be the least familiar to modern readers since they do not have any basis in actual history—at least as they are portrayed in the dime novels. Historically, the Danites (or Sons of Dan) were a short-lived group of Mormon vigilantes that were active during the Missouri War. Though we have no evidence that any such group existed after 1838, the group was a major aspect of Mormonism in popular literature for two generations, the stories operating under "the false assumption that there was a functioning Danite organization in Utah."[1]

As Rebecca Foster Cornwall and Leonard Arrington explain, Danites entered the world of nineteenth-century sensational fiction through Captain Frederick Marryat's 1843 novel, *Monsieur Violet*, a rambling travel narrative through the Southwestern United States with a section on the Nauvoo Mormons plagiarized directly from John C. Bennett's anti-Mormon exposé *History of the Saints* (1842). In the hands of dime novelists, these mythical Danites became a highly organized group of secret police, keeping the population of Utah in their thrall by murdering dissenters and tracking down runaway polygamous wives. They also planted spies across the country who fed a steady stream of information—and beautiful young maidens—to the Mormon prophet.

In nearly all of the Mormon dime novels the Danites (sometimes called the Destroying Angels) operate as a highly secretive parallel organization to the official Mormon hierarchy in Salt Lake City. Such a formulation connects the Danite myth to the contemporary anti-Catholic portrayals of the Black Pope—the head of the Jesuit order who secretly presided over a network of spies and assassins dedicated to wreaking havoc in the Protestant world. Both anti-Catholic and anti-Semitic stereotypes regularly infuse the dime-novel Danites, including a version of blood libel: new initiates sacrificing a Gentile as part of their induction. For example, in the 1890 dime novel *Keen Kit; or, The Border Detective Among the Mormons*, our hero is on the wrong end of such a ceremony as the hooded Danite leader announces,

> Brethren of the tribe of Dan . . . it is the custom of our secret order that every new
> member of our tribe be called upon to act as executioner at the first sacrifice that

---

1. Rebecca Foster Cornwall and Leonard Arrington, "Perpetuation of a Myth: Mormon Danites in Five Western Novels, 1840–90," *BYU Studies* 23, no. 2 (Spring 1983): 149. Cornwall and Arrington examine the portrayals of Danites in five novels: Frederick Marryat's *Monsieur Violet* (1843), Mayne Reid's *The Wild Huntress* (1861), Joaquin Miller's *First Fam'lies of the Sierras* (1876), Robert Louis Stevenson's *More New Arabian Nights: The Dynamiter* (1885), and Arthur Conan Doyle's *A Study in Scarlet* (1887). Though none of these were dime novels per se, they were all part of the general literary milieu of nineteenth-century readers and writers.

takes place after his having become a member of the tribe. We now have among us a newly-made member of the tribe, and therefore, according to our rules he must, upon this occasion, handle the sacred sword of the destroyers which is to cut the throat of the Gentiles whom we are about to offer as a sacrifice. (23)

Have no fear; Keen Kit escapes and routs the Danites, saving the maiden and all the rest.

The unsuspecting Gentiles in Thomas Hoyer Monstery's *California Joe's First Trail* (1884), on the other hand, aren't so lucky. California Joe was a recurring hero in Beadle & Adams's Half-Dime Library—novellas aimed at young boys that were both half the length and half the price of the publisher's standard fare. In this origin story, California Joe sets out with a wagon train to make his fortune in the West. He meets a mysterious stranger named Simplicity Fox who represents himself as a deacon in his church but is soon revealed as both a Mormon and head of the Destroying Angels (i.e., the Danites), a group of armed vigilantes who massacre wagon trains and kidnap women. Fox captures California Joe and compels him to join the Destroying Angels:

> Then the deacon made the prisoner repeat after him an oath of the most tre-
> mendous character, in which the man whom took it was obliged to call down
> on himself the vengeance of heaven, in this world and the next, if ever he dis-
> obeyed the order of the captain of the Lord's host or any of his officers. Even Joe,
> bold as he was, shuddered as the oath was repeated, and the circle of Mormon
> "Destroyers" round him at every sentence uttered a solemn "Amen," and re-
> peated the formula "*Damned be the traitor to time and eternity*," with a ghastly
> earnestness that left no doubt of their sincerity. (10)

As soon as this oath is complete, Fox tells Joe that he must now participate in the massacre of a wagon train. He is instructed to kill all of the men and boys, but spare the women to become polygamous wives. When the terrible deed is done (our hero shoots to miss, of course), the Mormons cast lots for possession of the women, but Joe, who is assigned advance-guard duty, takes his chosen woman and escapes with her to a nearby army fort where he surrenders and escapes the wrath of the Destroying Angels.

Novels like these helped the firm of Beadle & Adams tower over the world of dime novels from 1860 until around 1890. Then the market began to shift away from frontier fiction, and other New York firms like Munro, Frank Tousey, and Street & Smith moved in quickly with adventure tales, espionage thrillers, and—more than anything else—detective fiction. These new series featured the same characters solving different mysteries week after week. And their characters were modern: they rode on trains, drove automobiles, and had lots of bad-guy-catching gadgets. In 1897, Beadle & Adams closed up shop, leaving dime novels to the likes of Nick Carter, Frank Merriwell, Old Cap. Collier, and Old (and Young) King Brady—the detective-heroes of the remaining dime-novel publishers.

But readers' appetites for modern stories did not dull their appetite for dangerous Mormons. If anything, Mormons were featured even more prominently in dime novels published from 1890 until around 1920—precisely the time that Mormons were abandoning polygamy and doing their best to accommodate themselves to the modern world. A prominent theme in most of these later dime novels was that Mormons were only *pretending* to change—they were, in fact, more dangerous than ever! The new dime-novel detectives faced much higher stakes than their Western forebears ever had in combatting these new, more sinister Mormons. Along with the traditional tropes (kidnapped women, vengeful sons, spurned lovers), the new sleuths had to deal with Mormons plotting world domination and religious genocide.

Take, for example, *Old Cap. Collier in Salt Lake City* (1892). In this volume, the disguise-master detective Old Cap. Collier (George Munro's most popular character in the 1890s) is assigned by the US government to investigate a global human trafficking network that provides Mormons with new wives for their supposedly defunct harems:

> "For months we have received many complaints from foreign governments that women are being brought by Mormon elders or agents, and sold into slavery in Utah."
>
> "Yes."
>
> "More than that: it has been reported that girls have been abducted from Eastern cities, taken out to Utah and forced to become converts to Mormonism; becoming the slaves of the licentious elders."
>
> "I thought that the government officials out in Utah had broken up all of this?"
>
> "Outwardly it appears as if we had succeeded in breaking up the polygamous lives of the Mormons, but in reality, the same state of affairs exists under cover, that flourished in the days of Bringham [*sic*] Young. In fact, from the reports that come to me, the crimes committed are even worse." (4)

As Old Cap. Collier infiltrates the Mormon cabal and exposes the human trafficking scheme, he discovers a much broader conspiracy that involves massacre and political domination. In a secret meeting of the Mormons, their leader Elder Proud goes over the plan: "They would soon get together a formidable army," he announces. "The revolution would spread. The government troops would be unable to cope with them. Everything would be swept down before them. They would get control of the government and establish a Mormon republic" (42). A perfect plan—almost. They didn't count on the detecting prowess of the amazing Old Cap. Collier!

These types of detective dime novels exploited the fear that just beneath their seemingly reformed surface, Mormons continued to be the same old multiple-wife-marrying, dissident-killing, wagon-train-massacring miscreants they had always been, but now, with the power of a new state behind them—including the opportunity to elect senators and representatives to the national legislature—they could infiltrate and influence the nation in ways that a persecuted desert theocracy never could.

For this volume, we have chosen four full-length dime novels representing different aspects of the Mormon image in dime novels. The first of these, *Eagle Plume, the White Avenger* (1870), was the second dime novel (after *Esther: A Story of the Oregon Trail*) to feature Mormon characters. Like *Esther*, it was part of Beadle & Adams's original series, called simply Beadle's Dime Novels. This is the third of more than a hundred novels that Albert W. Aiken wrote for Beadle & Adams and other firms, and it is the basis for many of the Mormon stereotypes that pervade the industry. In *Eagle Plume*, Aiken introduces Danites into the dime-novel vocabulary along with one of the most popular anti-Mormon stereotypes: the singular avenger who has been wronged by Mormons and devotes his life to revenge. This figure recurs in many of the novels of this era and he survives to become Lassiter, the famous Mormon killer, in Zane Grey's *Riders of the Purple Sage* (1912). Nearly all of the anti-Mormon stereotypes of the nineteenth and twentieth centuries can be traced genealogically back to *Eagle Plume, the White Avenger.*

The second novel, *The Doomed Dozen; or, Dolores, the Danite's Daughter* (1881), was written by Prentiss Ingraham under the pseudonym Dr. Frank Powell. Ingraham was the most prolific of all dime-novel authors with more than 600 novels written under half a dozen different names. He is also the primary inventor of the Buffalo Bill mythos. He worked as a promoter for *Buffalo Bill's Wild West* show, and nearly all of his dime novels somehow involve Buffalo Bill Cody, usually doing superhuman feats of bravery and endurance. *The Doomed Dozen* is no exception. He weaves his story of revenge with the strangely named Satan's Pet acting in the role of the aggrieved avenger. The primary villain is the Danite chief, John Leigh—a thinly disguised depiction of John D. Lee, who was executed in 1877 for his role in the Mountain Meadows Massacre. This novel brings all of the standard Mormon tropes together in a single place: secretive Danites wearing hoods, a wagon train massacre, women kidnapped to become polygamous wives, murder, betrayal, and, of course, Buffalo Bill, who manages to set everything aright in the end.

Frank Merriwell Among the Mormons; or, The Lost Tribe of Israel (1897), the third novel in this volume, features the most popular hero in dime-novel history. Frank Merriwell was a star athlete at Yale and a world adventurer who was featured in the series Tip Top Weekly from 1896–1930. Merriwell was created to be a role model for young boys. He refused to drink or smoke (almost every issue has some reference to his abstinence), and he treats everybody with respect. Merriwell is one of only a few dime-novel heroes that survived after the dime-novel era in radio dramas, comic books, and motion pictures. *Frank Merriwell Among the Mormons* is one of the very few post-

Manifesto and post-Utah-statehood dime novels that actually accepts that the Mormons have abandoned polygamy and embraced some form of modernity. All of the action takes place among a breakaway sect of Mormons in a remote mountain village that has unlawfully kept to the old ways. So while this volume exploits all of the Mormon stereotypes that defined the dime novels, it does so in a way that relieves the Church of Jesus Christ of Latter-day Saints of responsibility for the actions of the villains.

The fourth novel comes from the immensely popular Secret Service series, which (due mainly to the innovation of color covers) replaced the Old Cap. Collier Library as the premier dime novel detective series. Secret Service had two detective-heroes: Old King Brady, the most famous detective in the world, and Young King Brady (no relation), his faithful sidekick. The Bradys actually made it to Salt Lake City twice—in 1903 in *The Bradys Among the Mormons* and again in 1906 in *The Bradys and Mr. Mormon*. In the first of these books, reprinted here, the Bradys are called upon by a US senator to investigate his prospective son-in-law, a Mormon from Utah who intends to run for the United States Congress. *The Bradys Among the Mormons* was written during the Reed Smoot hearings, and it echoes the concern of much of the country at the time—that the Mormons only pretended to abandon polygamy in order for Utah to become a state. Podmore (like Smoot) is a well-connected leader in the Church, and anxiety about his possible polygamist status sends the Bradys to Salt Lake City where, underneath the seemingly modern urban center, they discover a series of secret caves and tunnels where Mormonism is practiced as it was during the days of Brigham Young, complete with polygamy, Danites, and murder. *The Bradys Among the Mormons* was reprinted as late as 1920, keeping the nineteenth century's popular stereotypes of Mormonism alive well into the twentieth century.

All of these dime-novel portrayals had consequences for the relationship between Mormons and the rest of the United States. Dime-novel Mormons represented reality for millions of people, and the basic portrayals found their way into more serious (or at least more expensive) kinds of literature. We can trace back to these novels all of the Mormon images we see in Robert Louis Stevenson's *More New Arabian Nights: The Dynamiter* (1885), Arthur Conan Doyle's *A Study in Scarlet* (1887), and Zane Grey's *Riders of the Purple Sage* (1912). And in various ways, the key Mormon tropes of these novels have been found in popular literature ever since.[2] Understanding how these stereotypes were created and first employed can help us understand many things about the way that Mormonism has always functioned in American culture.

2. See Michael Austin, "Troped by the Mormons: The Persistence of 19th-Century Mormon Stereotypes in Contemporary Detective Fiction," *Sunstone* 21, no. 3 (August 1998): 51–71.

A Mormon Dime Novel Bibliography

Dime novels were generally published in series that were called *libraries*. Originally, publication was sporadic, but in time most libraries published a new novel every week (though publishers frequently reprinted old material under new titles without acknowledgment). From 1860 until the late 1880s, the various Beadle & Adams libraries dominated the industry. By 1890, though, firms such as Munro, Frank Tousey, and Street & Smith entered the market with more modern stories and new printing technologies (like color covers), leading to the demise of Beadle & Adams in 1897. The following bibliography lists novels by the original library they were part of. We have not included novels that I know to be reprints, though all issues of the Buffalo Bill Stories do reprint portions of earlier texts.

Beadle's Dime Novels (Beadle & Adams)

#45: Stephenson, Ann. *Esther: A Story of the Oregon Trail.* 1861.

#196: Aiken, Albert W. *Eagle Plume, the White Avenger. A Tale of the Mormon Trail.* 1870.

#312: Whittaker, Frederick. *Dick Darling, the Pony Expressman. A Tale of the Old Salt Lake Trail.* 1874.

Beadle's New York Dime Library (Beadle & Adams)

#41: Aiken, Albert W. *Gold Dan; or, The White Savage of the Great Salt Lake.* 1878.

#156: Burr, Major Dangerfield [Prentiss Ingraham]. *Velvet Face, the Border Bravo; or, Muriel, the Danite's Bride. A Romance of Border Mystery.* October 19, 1881.

#158: Powell, Dr. Frank [Prentiss Ingraham]. *The Doomed Dozen; or, Dolores, the Danite's Daughter.* 1881.

#170: Badger, Joseph E. *Sweet William, the Trapper Detective; or, The Chief of the Crimson Clan.* 1882.

#243: Cody, William F. *The Pilgrim Sharp; or, The Soldier's Sweetheart. A True Story of the Overland Trail.* 1883.

#311: Wilton, Mark. *Heavy Hand, the Relentless; or, The Marked Men of Paradise Gulch.* 1884.

#368: Willett, Edward. *The Canyon King; or, A Price on his Head. A Tale of the Wahsatch Range.* 1885.

#463: Manning, William H. *Gold Gauntlet, the Gulch Gladiator; or, Yank Yellowbird's Hot Campaign.* 1887.

#701: Holmes, Howard. *Silver Steve, the Branded Sport; or, The Man-Mystery of Moonstone.* 1892.

#758: Sims, A. K. *The Wizard King Detective; or, The Sharper Duke in Utah.* 1893.

Beadle's Half Dime Library (Beadle & Adams)

#73:   Wheeler, Edward L. *Deadwood Dick on Deck; or, Calamity Jane, the Heroine of Whoop-Up. A Story of Dakota.* 1878.

#205: Wheeler, Edward L. *Deadwood Dick's Doom; or, Calamity Jane's Last Adventure.* 1881.

#221: Wheeler, Edward L. *The Miner Sport; or, Sugar-Coated Sam's Claim.* 1881.

#240: Wheeler, Edward L. *Cyclone Kit, the Young Gladiator; or, The Locked Valley. A Strange Mountain Tale, of a Stranger Place and People.* 1882.

#376: Monstery, Thomas Hoyer. *California Joe's First Trail. A Story of the Destroying Angels.* 1884.

#387: Ingraham, Prentiss. *War Path Will, the Traitor Guide; or, The Boy Phantom.* 1884.

Beadle's Weekly (Beadle & Adams)

#72:   Wheeler, Edward L. *Bullion Bret; or, The Giant Grip of Git-Thar. A Tale of Silverland.* 1884.

#139: Aiken, Albert W. *Iron Dagger; or, The High Horse in Silverland. A Tale of Strange Adventures in the Mogollon Country.* 1885.

#261: Lewis, Leon. *The Sons of Thunder; or, The Rivals of Ruby Valley. A Romance of Nevada.* 1887.

#407: Ingraham, Prentiss. *The Texan's Double; or, The Merciless Shadower. A Revelation of the Mystery of the "Bravo in Black" in the Romance of "The Three Bills."* 1890.

#419: Ingraham, Prentiss. *Gentleman Jack, the Man of Many Masks; or, Buffalo Bill's Peerless Pard.* 1890.

Beadle's Boy's Library (Beadle & Adams)

#1:   Ingraham, Prentiss. *Adventures of Buffalo Bill: From Boyhood to Manhood.* 1881.

Old Cap. Collier Library (Munro)

#285: Aiken, Albert W. *Old Lynx, the Mormon Detective; or Saved from a Terrible Fate.* 1888.

#426: James, W. I. *Old Cap. Collier in Salt Lake City; or, "Piping" the Mormon Conspirators.* 1892.

The Boy's Star Library (Frank Tousey)

#147: Fenton, Walter. *Keen Kit; or, The Border Detective Among the Mormons.* 1890.

The Five Cent Wide Awake Library (Frank Tousey)

#184: Pad, Peter. *Chips and Chin Chin Among the Mormons.* 1874.

Secret Service (Frank Tousey)

#239: Doughty, Francis Worcester. *The Bradys Among the Mormons; or, Secret Work in Salt Lake City*. 1903.

#410: Doughty, Francis Worcester. *The Bradys and Mr. Mormon; or, Secret Work in Salt Lake City*. 1906.

Tip Top Weekly (Street & Smith)

#62:   Patton, Gilbert. *Frank Merriwell Among the Mormons; or, The Lost Tribe of Israel*. 1897.

Buffalo Bill Stories (Street & Smith)*

#38:   *Buffalo Bill and the Danite Kidnappers; or, The Green River Massacre.* February 1, 1902.

#215: *Buffalo Bill's Mormon Quarrel; or, At War with the Danites.* June 24, 1905.

#364: *Buffalo Bill's Waif of the Plains; or, At Odds with the Danites.* May 2, 1908.

#366: *Buffalo Bill Among the Mormons; or, $5000 Reward, Alive or Dead.* May 16, 1908.

*Authors are not listed in this series but internal evidence, including large passages of recycled materials from earlier dime novels, strongly suggests that all four were written by Prentiss Ingraham.

———————————

An early version of this introduction and bibliography appeared in Michael Austin's article, "Danites, Damsels, and World Domination: Mormons in the Dime Novels" in the Winter 2016 issue of *Sunstone* magazine. Neither the article, the bibliography, nor the current book would be possible without the near-superhuman efforts of Meg Atwater-Singer, the ILL librarian at the University of Evansville. Meg tracked down every source that we requested, often convincing libraries to photocopy or digitize original records that had not been accessed for more than a hundred years.

Semi-Monthly   Novels Series.

No.   **BEADLE'S**   196.

DIME NOVELS

EAGLE PLUME:
The White Avenger.

BEADLE AND COMPANY, 98 WILLIAM STREET, N. Y.
Am. News Co., 119 & 121 Nassau St., N.Y.

Albert W. Aiken. *Eagle Plume, the White Avenger.* Beadle's Dime Novels, no. 196. New York: Beadle and Company, 1870.

EAGLE PLUME,
the
WHITE AVENGER.

By Albert W. Aiken,
Author of "the Red Coyote," "The White Vulture," etc.

New York:
Beadle and Company, Publishers,
98 William Street.

{page}

(No. 196.)

{page}

CHAPTER I.
THE ADOPTED SON OF THE DACOTAHS.

On the west bank of the north fork of the Green river, lay the principal village of the Dacotahs—the warlike nation that roams from the great valley of the Salt Lake to the iron-like barriers of the Rocky Mountains.

'Twas in the pleasant spring-time; the snows of the previous winter, melting in the mountain gulches, swelled the streamlets rushing down to the plain.

The young grass was springing fresh and green on the broad surface of the prairie.

The braves of the Dacotahs were preparing for their usual spring hunt southward. The long scalping-knives were sharpened, the bows new strung with the sinews of deer or mountain elk, and those of the red warriors who were fortunate enough to possess a rifle or carbine, carefully polished it up with patches of deer-skin. All was bustle and activity in the Indian village.

By the river's bank, gazing upon the turbid and swollen waters, stood two chiefs. One, by the richness of his attire, the wolf-tails attached to his leggins—a mark of distinction only allowed to great braves—it was evident was a chief of note; and the eagle-plumes thickly braided in his long, dark locks, as well as the look of dignity and pride upon his thoroughly Indian face, confirmed this supposition.

His companion was not quite so tall, nor was his attire so rich.

The two were the chief of the Dacotahs, Hole-in-the-sky, and his brother, the Black-pan. {10}

The two chiefs were looking down the river anxiously, as though expecting some one.

"Wah!" said Hole-in-the-sky, breaking the silence, "Yellow Wolf is not a snake; he flies like the eagle, yet he comes not from the pale-face lodges by the Great Salt Lake."

"A moon has come and gone; the Dacotah chief will be here before the young moon comes," replied the younger chief, in a tone of conviction.

"Wah, it is good!" sententiously exclaimed the great chief; "then we shall know whether it is peace or war."

"And if it is war?"

"The Dacotahs will drive the white-skins into the lake! Wah-con-dah loves his red children; the valley of the Salt Lake is theirs. If the white-skins stay, they must pay tribute to the braves of the Dacotah."

"See!" exclaimed the Black-pan, pointing to two little black specks advancing from the southward; "the Dacotah chief comes."

Hole-in-the-sky bent his keen glance in the direction indicated by the out-stretched finger.

The two black specks were advancing rapidly across the swells of the distant prairie, and were looming up larger and larger every moment.

"Wah!" cried the chief, with an air of satisfaction; "it is the chief. And the other?"

"One of the white braves," returned the Black-pan.

The two horsemen advanced rapidly; one was a red-skin, the other a white. They rode directly for the two chiefs by the bank of the river.

Within a hundred paces of the two chiefs, the white man drew rein and halted; the red-skin continued on his course, and dismounted by the side of the chiefs.

The new-comer was a tall, muscular-formed brave, decked out in a complete deer-skin hunting-garb. He, too, wore the wolf-tails on his leggins, and well had he deserved that mark of honor, for the Yellow Wolf was one of the greatest braves of the Dacotah nation. Though young in years, he was equally renowned in the council-lodge and on the war-path; wise in deliberation, sagacious in thought, prompt in action, and untiring on the trail. Young as he was, he had won {11} a name among the braves of his tribe that few could match and all envied.

Thus it was that the Yellow Wolf came to be chosen by the Hole-in-the-sky as envoy to the lodges of the white braves by the big Salt Lake.

"My brother has come," said the great chief.

"Yes," responded the new-comer.

"My brother has been to the white lodges?"

"Yes."

"He has talked with the white chiefs?"

"Yes; the white braves are not like the chiefs in the mountains that dig in the earth—not like the white braves that carry short rifles" (the U.S. cavalry). "The braves by the big Salt Lake hate the pale-faces beyond the mountains," and the red-skin waved his long arm toward the east. "The white chiefs have many squaws—three, four, ten, twenty to each brave. The name of their tribe is Mormon."

The chiefs listened in astonishment to this strange tale. The custom of this new tribe of pale-faces was strange to them.

"Will the white chiefs pay the tribute?" asked the Hole-in-the-sky.

"No!" was the laconic answer.

"No?" echoed the great chief, an expression of astonishment appearing on his usually stolid features.

"No," again repeated the Yellow Wolf; "the Mormon chief says his warriors will not come east of the mountains—they will not disturb the hunting-grounds of the Dacotahs, but settle by the big Salt Lake. All they ask is a free passage through our country; if we refuse, they will fight their way through."

The eyes of the great chief sparkled with anger when he heard this bold defiance.

"Does the white chief know that the braves of the Dacotah are like the blades of grass on the prairie?—that they are the great fighting men of the big mountains? Wah! the braves of the Dacotahs will take the scalps of the white-skins and they shall dry by the lodge-pole of the red-men."

"The white-skins are many; they have big rifles, big as themselves, which shine like the yellow water when the sun {12} kisses it. The white chiefs are poor—no plunder—no blankets—no horses—very poor but big in courage. We fight them, gain nothing but scalps. Best fight the pale-faces in the mountains, who dig; they have many blankets—rich," replied the Yellow Wolf, sagely.

The great chief was silent for a moment; he attached great weight to the words of the Yellow Wolf, whom he knew to be as brave as he was wise. Why should the Dacotahs attack a foe on the west, from whom, as the chief had said, they could gain nothing but scalps, when they could pillage a foe on the east who was rich in all those worldly goods that were dear to the red-man's heart?

Besides, too, the chief remembered that, when first a young brave on the war-path, the Dacotahs attacked a big white lodge on the north fork of the Platte river; he remembered how the big rifles that shone like gold sent twenty of the Dacotahs to the happy hunting-grounds at a single discharge. He had little wish to again face the big yellow guns of the white-skins.

"Wah! my brother talks straight. The Yellow Wolf is a great chief of the Dacotahs; his tongue is not forked. My brother thinks that it will be better not to fight the white chiefs who are of the Mormon tribe?"

"Yes; the red warriors will make little now. Wait till the pale-faces get blankets, horses; then fight," said the wily savage; "is it good?"

"It is good," replied the great chief; then he turned to the Black-pan. "Summon my warriors to the council."

Black-pan at once departed on his mission.

"The Yellow Wolf shall tell the braves of the Dacotahs what he saw in the lodges of the white chiefs who have many wives; they will listen to his words and heed his counsel."

The young brave looked pleased at the flattering words of the great chief of his tribe.

The Yellow Wolf had no powerful relatives to aid him in his struggle for rank in his nation; alone, unaided save by his own skill and bravery, had he fought his way. The Hole-in-the-sky, the great chief of his tribe, was getting old, was childless; when he retired from the chieftainship his word would have great weight in deciding who should succeed him, and {13} to that honor, secretly in his heart, the Yellow Wolf aspired.

"How many warriors can the pale-faces bring upon the war-path?" asked the Hole-in-the-sky.

"The chief can not tell," answered the young brave; "the fighting men of the pale-faces are called the 'Destroying Angels;' they are of the tribe of Danites; their chief is a tall brave named Dan."

The Indian referred to that terrible band of men known among the Mormons as Danites—a troop of cut-throats who knew no law but that promulgated by the Mormon chiefs; they were the rod of iron used by the leading spirits of that strange horde, who sought to found a city of Zion in the great prairie wilderness—to bend unto their rule the "Chosen People," as they styled themselves, and to silence any uneasy spirit who dared to murmur at their decrees.

Their leader was a man who, whatever his real title had been, was known simply as "Dan." Assuming the name of the Israelite of old and pretending to have a mission from the Mormon prophet Smith, to act as an instrument of vengeance, a "Destroying Angel" to all obnoxious to the Mormons or scoffers at the Mormon faith, he was well fitted to head the ruffian band and execute the "Vengeance of the Lord" on all marked with the ban of the leaders of the new faith.

"Wah! the council shall decide whether the Dacotahs will have peace or war with the white braves." Then, as the chief turned to bend his steps to the council-lodge, his eyes fell upon the figure of the white man, who, still seated on his horse, had remained motionless some hundred paces from the Indians. The chief had noticed his approach with the Yellow Wolf, but the interesting intelligence brought by the young brave had for the moment banished him from his mind.

"Has the white chief come from the pale-faces to talk with the braves of the Dacotahs?" asked the Hole-in-the-sky.

"The white chief does come to talk with the red chiefs, but he is not of the tribe that have built their lodges by the big Salt Lake," answered the Yellow Wolf; "the Dacotah chief met him a long ride from the white lodges." {14}

"And he seeks the chiefs of the Dacotahs?"

"Yes."

"Good, he shall see them. Tell him that the red braves wait for him in the council-lodge." And the warrior turned upon his heel and walked toward the village. The Yellow Wolf went toward the white man, who, single and alone, had sought the lodges of the red braves.

And as the Indian is traversing the hundred feet or so of open prairie that separated him from the white man, we will take the opportunity to describe him.

He was a young man, not yet thirty, but bearing upon his face the marks of toil and care. The face, too, was singular; the cheek-bones were as high as those of an Indian; the piercing black eyes, the long ebon hair floating down upon his shoulders, the strange pallor of the skin, white, despite the prairie sun and wind, all made the face remarkable, once seen never to be forgotten. The firm, resolute chin, the massive forehead and the unyielding lines about the mouth told of a firm will and of daunt-less courage; but of the latter no better proof could be given than his presence in the great village of the Dacotahs—the deadly foes of the white man—alone, without even a single friend to aid him. Truly his courage was great or he valued his life but little. What motive, too, could it be that brought him into the fastness of the Indian country and caused him to seek the council-lodge of the red warriors?

In dress, the stranger was plainly attired in a rough woolen suit, big boots, a red flannel shirt and a slouch hat. His arms consisted of a long, wicked-looking rifle—one of the small-bore kind, carrying a ball of a hundred to the pound; a long, broad-bladed knife, something of the style made famous by the ill-fated Colonel Bowie, and a revolver of the old pepper-box pattern, while a Mexican lasso was coiled upon the horn of his saddle.

The stranger sat his animal with the ease of a practiced rider.

As the Indian came within a few feet of the horseman he straightened himself in the saddle to listen to the communication of the chief.

"Hole-in-the-sky big chief of the Dacotahs," said the brave, {15} pointing to the chief who was stalking toward the council-lodge. The Yellow Wolf spoke in English and quite plain, save the Indian accent.

The stranger simply nodded his head.

"The chief goes to the council-lodge; the braves of the Dacotahs will see the white chief; they will have a talk with him. Is it good?" asked the brave.

Again the stranger nodded his head.

"You come talk with Dacotah chiefs. Tell what for pale chief come to land of Dacotah." It was evident that the Indian was puzzled as to the motive that brought the white chief to the home of his red foes.

"Chief," said the stranger, in a harsh, powerful voice, "call one of your braves here, to take charge of my horse; the beast is restive."

The Yellow Wolf beckoned to a brave that, attracted by a desire to gaze upon the white chief, was near them. The Indian obeyed the gesture and approached.

The stranger dismounted and placed the bridle of his horse in the hands of the savage; then, from his back, he unslung the long rifle and laid it down at the Indian's feet; the revolver from his belt followed the rifle; then he drew the long, broad-bladed knife, and with a vigorous throw drove it into the prairie soil at his feet up to the haft.

The Yellow Wolf and the other Indian gazed at the strange movements of the white chief with interest and astonishment. All his weapons lay upon the ground; he was giving himself, unarmed, defenseless, into the hands of the Dacotahs.

"I am ready," said the stranger; "lead on, chief; conduct me to the council."

Then, with a firm, elastic stride, the tall white chief followed the Yellow Wolf, who led the way to the council-lodge.

The great chiefs of the Dacotahs were all assembled in the council-lodge, waiting for the white man who had traveled across the great prairies to hold a talk with them.

They did not have long to wait, for soon the Yellow Wolf lifted the skin that served as a door and entered the lodge, followed by the white. The Yellow Wolf took his place in the circle of chiefs, while the stranger remained at the door. {16}

The red chiefs were arranged in a semicircle, the great chief of the tribe, the Hole-in-the-sky, in the center.

The warriors for a moment looked upon the pale-face with inquiring eyes; they noticed that he was weaponless; they noted, too, the vigor and muscular build of his stalwart frame, and many of those seated in the half-circle mentally asked themselves, if they would be a match for the stranger in a hand-to-hand encounter.

"Yellow Wolf," spoke the great chief, in the Indian tongue, "tell the pale-face that he sees the great chiefs of the Dacotahs; let him speak; the ears of the red-men are open; they will hear."

The Yellow Wolf, who was the only one of the chiefs who could speak English fluently, arose, and in English delivered the speech of the Hole-in-the-sky to the white stranger. He listened attentively, and when the Indian finished, spoke. As the white spoke only English, being ignorant of the Dacotah tongue, of course Yellow Wolf was obliged to translate his speech to the council. This speech was as follows:

"The white chief has heard the words of the great fighting man of the Dacotah nation," said the stranger, speaking in the figurative language of the Indians; the gleam of the chief's eyes showed that he was pleased with the delicate compliment; "he will tell the red chiefs why he, a white-skin, seeks the lodges of the Dacotahs—the eagles who have flown from the great mountains to the broad prairie."

A gleam of pleasure now sparkled in the eyes of all the chiefs in the semicircle; it was evident that the stranger was creating a favorable impression in the minds of the sons of the wilderness.

"From my distant home in the East, where I have heard of the great nation of the Dacotahs, I have come to their home—come friendless, alone; I enter the council-lodge of the red chiefs, weaponless, defenseless—even as I came into the world. I am not afraid, because I know I am talking to great chiefs, men of mighty deeds, warriors whose actions are noted from the Snake river to the Colorado. I was born a white-skin; I am sorry for it; I would be born again, this time a red, and so I come to the council-lodge of the Dacotahs to ask the red warriors of that nation to take me {17} into their tribe, and to adopt me as a son of the Dacotahs."

A hum of astonishment pervaded the council-lodge as the Yellow Wolf translated to the braves the strange wish of the white chief.

Chapter II.
THE GANTLET OF DEATH.

THE council-lodge was hushed in silence, as the great chief, Hole-in-the-sky, rose to reply to the pale-face.

"The pale chief is unknown to the Dacotah warriors," said the Indian; "not a chief herein the council-lodge, but has bought his right to be present by some brave deed, some victory over the foes of his nation. We think the white chief is a brave man; will he prove to us that he is so?"

Gravely the chiefs nodded their heads in approbation of the words of Hole-in-the-sky.

"Let the warriors of the Dacotah put me to trial," replied the stranger; "if I show a white heart let them kill me on the spot."

"Wah!" said the great chief, in a tone that showed that he was pleased with the frankness of the offer; "my white brother speaks well. When a young brave of the

Dacotahs wishes to be a chief, we test his courage with the Gantlet of Death. Will the white chief submit to the trial?"

"Yes," replied the stranger.

"It is good!" said the chief. "Yellow Wolf" and he addressed the young warrior, "assemble all my warriors and people by the bank of the river, and prepare the torture-stake." The warrior at once departed on his mission. The chief then turned to his brother, the Black-pan, who was seated in the half circle. "The Black-pan will take the pale-faced chief to my lodge, and there let him prepare for the trial."

The Black-pan rose to his feet, and with a single gesture, beckoning the white to follow him, left the council-lodge. {18}

The Indian conducted the stranger to the lodge of the Hole-in-the-sky, and there left him.

Alone in the lodge, the stranger commenced to prepare for the trial. He stripped off the heavy woolen coat, girded the belt tighter around his waist, and cast the broad-brimmed hat upon the floor.

A look of determination shone in the flashing black eyes of the white-skinned stranger; the grim lips were compressed more forcibly together. The Gantlet of Death must indeed be terrible, if it could shake the iron nerves of the white man.

A half-hour elapsed before the Indians summoned the victim to the trial. The Yellow Wolf bore the message.

After delivering the summons, the brave looked at the feet of the pale-face, which were incased in heavy boots.

"Ugh! White brother no run; take moccasin."

And the warrior kindly removed his own moccasins and gave them to the white man.

"Thanks, chief," said the white. "I shall not forget your kindness, and perhaps some day I may be able to repay it."

The little act, coming from a savage, touched the white; he accepted it as an omen of success.

The Yellow Wolf conducted the white from the lodge. On the outside of the wigwam stood six warriors, waiting to act as escort to the place of trial. To these six, the Yellow Wolf resigned his charge. All proceeded toward the bank of the river, while the Yellow Wolf brought up the rear.

The inhabitants of the village—men, women and children—were gathered by the stream, close to where the torture-stake was erected.

Through the crowd proceeded the white man and his six guards of honor; behind them followed the Yellow Wolf.

Near the stake stood Hole-in-the-sky, surrounded by the principal warriors of the tribe. As the little procession passed through the scattered crowd, a young squaw detached herself from one of the groups, and spoke to the Yellow Wolf. The girl was barely eighteen, tall and finely formed, a handsome face though of dusky hue, a step as light as that of the mountain goat, and {19} as elastic; the flashing black eyes outshone in brightness those of the Rocky Mountain elk. In feature, she was strikingly like the young warrior known as the Yellow Wolf—a fact not to be wondered at, for she was his sister.

"Brother," said the forest-maid, "who and what is the white stranger?"

"A white chief that wishes to become a Dacotah," was replied.

"And why do they take him to the torture-stake?"

"To see if he is brave enough to be a chief of our nation."

"He is handsome as the mountain ash," murmured the girl, as she gazed upon the lithe yet stalwart form of the white, who was about to be proven by the torture-test.

What thoughts were in the mind of this young Indian girl? Many a young brave had laid his spoils of war and of the chase at her feet, and sued for her to come and share his wigwam; but to all she had said, "Not yet, not yet;" her heart was free; no son of the forest had yet caught her fancy; but now, as she looked upon the tall white chief, she paled and flushed like an April sky, under emotions that never before had thrilled her. How great he became, at once, in her eyes.

With admiring glance the "Red Fawn"—for so she was called—followed in the footsteps of the white man.

The stranger and his escort arrived before the torture-stake and there halted.

The great chief, Hole-in-the-sky, stepped forward and addressed the candidate:

"Will my brother be tied to the torture-stake, so that the warriors of the Dacotah may try their skill upon him?"

"I am ready," was the response.

Then, at a sign from the chief, two warriors stepped forward; they bore the white man to the stake and bound him securely to it, by two thongs of deer-skin, one passing around his ankles, the other around his chest and arms. At another signal from the chief, a tall brave stepped forward; he placed himself some fifteen feet from the helpless white; drawing the long, sharp scalping-knife from his girdle, he poised it for a moment in the air, and then, with a quick, powerful motion, he darted it at the prisoner. The heavy knife hissed through {20} the air and buried itself in the tree-trunk a few inches above the prisoner's head. Eagerly the Indians gazed upon the face of the white for some sign of fear, but the look was in vain; not a single muscle of the iron-like face moved. A hum of approval went through the crowd, for but few even of their own race—who were brought up from infancy to the sight—could behold the first knife-throw without a slight movement, if not of the muscles of the face, at least of the eyes; but the stranger had not as much as winked.

The chief made another signal, and this time the Yellow Wolf stepped forward in obedience to the sign. He, too, like the first chief, drew a knife from his girdle, and, after a moment's pause, cast it toward the torture-stake. His aim was better even than that of the first warrior, for his knife shivered in the stake within half an inch of the pale-face's head—so near that the sharp blade severed a lock of hair from the head, and the shining black curl floated lazily to the ground.

Again had the stranger stood the test. Had it been a marble statue, the face could not have been more rigid or shown less sign of fear.

Another hum of approbation resounded through the crowd.

And now, the final trial came, and the great chief himself, Hole-in-the-sky, took his place before the stake.

The chief drew his knife, and apparently without thought or aim, launched it at the prisoner's breast. As we have said, the thong around his body confined his arms to his side; the knife of the chief, thrown with all the strength of his powerful arm, had cut the lashing that passed around the breast, and struck the stake between the arm and the side, and there remained as though the pressure of the arm against the body held it in its place. Had the knife gone half an inch either side, it would have cost the stranger the loss of his arm or his life.

Again the white had borne the test without a muscle quivering.

The loud hum told that the Dacotahs were satisfied with the conduct of the white brave.

At a sign from the chief the two warriors unbound him.

"Tell the brave if he can run the gantlet and gain the council-lodge, the trial is ended," said the Hole-in-the-sky. {21}

This the Yellow Wolf repeated to the white, who then understood the service the young warrior had done him by proffering the light moccasins. He signified that he was ready.

The warriors, the women and children arranged themselves in two long parallel lines, the lines extending from the river half-way to the council-lodge. Through these lines the pale-face was to run. The etiquette of the ceremony required that none of the pursuers should leave their places in the lines till the runner had passed them. This, though it gave the runner a few feet start, yet placed a fresh opponent on his track every second. Should the pursuers succeed in capturing the pursued, they were the victors; but if the runner gained the council-lodge, then he was adjudged a brave.

Though the pursuers were prohibited from using weapons, when the runner was one of their own tribe, yet the free use of legs and arms was permitted, so that the contest was often productive of hard blows, terrible kicks, and heavy falls.

The lines were formed, the leading chief gave the signal, and, with the fleetness of the deer, the white bounded through the lines. With wild yells the Indians joined in the pursuit. On went the white man at a terrific speed, that left the fleet-footed savages far behind. For a hundred yards he ran at this tremendous pace; not a single Indian, as yet, had succeeded in even touching him; it seemed as if he would gain the council-lodge without even a scratch. He had reached the end of the lines, and now a hundred yards more and the goal was gained; but at the extreme end of the two lines was the fleetest runner in the Dacotah tribe, a tall brave who rejoiced in the name of Howling Wind. By his side stood the Red Fawn, the young Indian girl, the sister of the Yellow Wolf.

The runner had cunningly placed himself last in the lines so that, fresh, he could easily run down the fugitive, tired with the spin of the hundred yards.

On went the white over the little plain, close behind him came the Howling Wind; but the Red Fawn—where was she?

The terrific pace that the white had been running began to tell upon him; his breath came short and quick; despite his {22} efforts, his motion grew less swift, though still very fast. The brave was beginning to gain upon him. Where was the Red Fawn?

With bounds resembling those of the animal whose name she bore, the Indian maid passed the Howling Wind, and came almost within reaching distance of the fugitive. The brave, annoyed at thus being left in the rear, essayed a terrific "spurt," and came nearly abreast of the girl. A hundred feet more the council-lodge were reached; but even now the hands of the Red Fawn and Howling Wind were outstretched to grasp the runner! A yell of triumph went up from the Indians in the rear, when, suddenly, just as the hand of the Howling Wind was about to clutch the shoulder of the white chief, the Red Fawn stumbled and fell. Endeavoring to save herself, she fell against Howling Wind, and brought him to his knee. Profiting by the unlooked-for accident, with a few bounds the fugitive gained the council-lodge, and the race was done. The white chief had won!

The Howling Wind arose, looking daggers at the girl. She, with a peculiar, quiet smile upon her handsome features, withdrew among the women and children. Strange accident it was, that the Indian maid, whose foot was as sure as that of the antelope, should stumble and fall in the open prairie!

The chiefs and braves followed into the lodge, where stood the white chief.

"Wah!" said the great chief; "my white brother has done well. The braves of the Dacotah are satisfied. Can my brother use the warrior's weapons as well as he can his legs?"

"Let my horse and weapons be brought, and the chiefs shall see," replied the white.

Then all repaired to the open air. The horse and weapons were brought.

With his long rifle the white put a ball through the top of a slender pole, swaying in the wind, at a hundred paces. The savages gazed at this feat with astonishment.

Then, an unbroken horse being brought, the white mounted his steed, gave chase to the wild animal and skillfully captured it with a cast of the lasso. A murmur of admiration went through the savage throng at this performance, which was {23} much stranger to them than it would have been to a Comanche or Apache, whose forays were on the Mexican border.

"The pale-face is a great chief," exclaimed the Hole-in-the-sky, to the warriors that surrounded him, as the stranger, at a distance, was dismounting from his horse.

"Is the chief satisfied?" asked the white, as he approached the little circle of warriors.

"Yes," responded the chief, "the pale-face will be a great brave in the land of Dacotah." Then the chief turned to the warriors that surrounded him. "Are my braves willing to receive the white chief as a brother?"

For a moment there was a dead silence, then the Yellow Wolf stepped forward, and, as if answering for all, spoke:

"The pale-face is a great brave; he is worthy to be a Dacotah; the chiefs will be glad to welcome him as a brother. If the white chief would make his home with us, let him then take a wife or a mother from the women of our tribe, so that his wigwam shall not be empty. Is it good?"

A hum of approval greeted the words of the Yellow Wolf.

"The brave is as wise as the beaver," replied the great chief; "his words are good." Then the chief turned in the direction of the women and children, who, some few paces distant, gazed upon the scene. "Will any of the women of the Dacotah be a mother or a wife to the white chief?"

A moment of silence, and then forth from the throng stepped the Red Fawn! A pleased look appeared on the face of the Yellow Wolf as his sister stepped forward. The quick-witted brother already had guessed the love of his sister for the stranger, for the stumble of the sure-footed Red Fawn in the contest he knew was a device to impede the Howling Wind, and allow the white chief to win.

"The Red Fawn would dwell in the wigwam of a great chief; *she* will be the wife of the pale-face," said the girl, modestly, stealing a shy glance at the face of the stranger, to note if he was pleased with her preference.

A faint smile was upon the face of the stranger, as he gazed on the handsome, dusky features of the child of the prairie.

"The white chief accepts the maid for wife, and henceforth {24} his heart is Dacotah though his skin may be white!" cried the pale stranger.

And so, the unknown white man was received into the Dacotah tribe.

That night, when the moon shone clear over the prairie, decked out in the gayly-fringed hunting-shirt and leggins of a Dacotah chief, and with the long eagle-plumes braided in his black hair—the work of the Red Fawn—the white chief stood by the bank of the river. The Yellow Wolf was by his side.

"Will my brother tell the Yellow Wolf why he leaves his own nation and becomes a brave of the Dacotah?"

"For vengeance!" replied the white, his brows darkening. "Chief, I have a foe—a foe who has many braves to aid him. Alone, I am powerless; but now—" and the tone of the white was full of fierce joy.

"A hundred warriors will follow at the back of my brother, and the Yellow Wolf will be the first," said the young chief. "Where is my brother's foe?"

"In the Salt Lake valley—one of the 'Destroying Angels'—the tribe of Dan," returned the white, with fierce emphasis.

"Wah! their scalps shall dry in the lodges of the Dacotahs."

CHAPTER III.
THE CHIEF OF THE DANITES.

SOME six months after the events related, an emigrant-train halted for the night by the banks of a little creek some hundred miles from Salt Lake City. This train was composed of some twenty wagons, all containing Mormon converts, destined for the New Zion by the Great Salt Lake.

The emigrants were busy preparing supper. Apart from the rest, and seated by themselves, were some seven men, all fully armed with rifles, knives and revolvers. Seven stout, {25} muscular men were they, and of the seven, all but one bore the stamp of ruffian visibly imprinted on their faces.

These seven were the guides and protectors of the train, a portion of the famous "Destroying Angels"—the right-hand men of the Mormon leaders—the assassins, who acted as they were bidden.

The one among the seven who bore a face better than the rest, was the leader of the "Angels," the man known as Dan, and from whom the "Destroying Angels" were named "Danites."

Who and what this Dan was, no one had learned, not even the Prophet, whose chosen instrument he was. All that was known of him was, that about a year before the time at which we write, he had enrolled himself among the "Destroying Angels," and speedily became, by reason of his terrible courage and devotion, the head of that famous band.

In person, the Danite was tall; massive in form, yet not clumsy, but light and active as a cat. In face, he was fair to look upon; light-yellow hair clustered in little curls all over his head; a drooping mustache, of the same hue as the hair, shaded his lip; his eyes were of light-blue, approaching a gray, large and full, yet shifting and treacherous in their look; there were evil lines about the eyes and mouth that told of uncontrollable passions. A man was he with great capability for good, and still greater for evil.

"It 'pears to me, cap'n," said Red Dick, one of the burly ruffians by the side of Dan, who, from his bushy red hair and beard, had gained his cognomen, "that the elder, Higgins, is a leetle tuk arter that gal with brown ha'r, the one that rode in the fust wagon to-day. He were a-spyin' round the wagon 'bout all the time."

"Guess he wants her fur his sixth rib," said another of the party, with a laugh.

"He'd better look out, or he'll have somebody in his ha'r," said a third one of the "Angels," who, from his constantly wearing a dirty suit of gray, had got the name of "Grizzly Joe."

"Who's that?" asked Red Dick; "do you mean her brother?"

"No," responded Grizzly Joe; "I mean the young trapper, {26} Hank Baldwin. Hain't you noticed how he's stuck with our party? He's got his eye onto the leetle gal, now you bet."

"The elder'll be arter us to wipe out the Gentile, ef he hankers arter any piece of calico that the elder has got his eye on," said Dick, with a laugh.

"I reckon, ef it comes to that, we shan't git his top-knot without a right smart chance of a fight for it; that Hank's a Kentuckian, an' I b'lieve jist as lief fight as eat; he's old chain-lightnin' on the shoot," said one of the "Angels."

"An' that ain't all," cried Grizzly Joe. "There's the two Injuns, the Yellow Wolf an' Eagle Plume, they're big friends to Hank, an' any man that tackles him will have to tackle them, too."

"What are them air Injuns hangin' round the camp fur, anyway?" asked a fourth, joining in the conversation.

"They're chiefs of the Dacotah tribe, goin' to the city to see the Prophet, Young," answered Joe.

"Yes; but how is it that they and the trapper are such friends?"

"Wa-al, I hearn say that this Hank saved the life of the Yellow Wolf, up in the mountains, from a b'ar, an' that's how it come," replied Joe.

"That Eagle Plume looks as if he'd stand a tussle with Old Nick himself," said the fourth ruffian.

"That's so!" replied Dick, emphatically. "T'other feller, the Yellow Wolf, ain't to be sneezed at, either. I hearn say he was chief of the Dacotah Injuns now."

"Shouldn't wonder," said Joe.

The chief of the Danites had taken no part in the conversation; with a moody, abstracted look, he sat a little apart from the rest, and paid no heed to them. A strange fact had been noted in regard to the leader of the Destroying Angels, and that was, he was seldom seen to smile; a deep gloom seemed ever upon him. Men noted this, and wondered at it, and there were many in the Mormon settlement that whispered—for it was not wise to speak openly, and thus incur the anger of the terrible leader of the Danites—that it was the memory of some dark crime committed in the East, and which had caused him to fly to the prairie wilderness, that produced the shade ever upon his frowning brow. {27}

We will leave the Destroying Angels to their gossip, and their leader to his abstraction, and take a glimpse at another group, seated near a wagon at the other end of the encampment.

The group consisted of two men, and two girls just budding into womanhood. One of these men, about thirty years of age, was dressed in a rough, homespun suit. He was an Ohio farmer, who, lured by the specious promises of the Mormon Prophet, became a convert to the Mormon faith, had sold his little farm, and, with all his worldly goods, had dared the perils of the prairie wilderness to find a home, peace and rest in the New Zion, the city of Salt Lake. One of the young girls—the elder one, with light hair and blue eyes—was his wife, a wife of a few months only. The farmer's name was Stephen Miller. The young girl, of blushing, blooming eighteen, was his sister, Margaret by name, and it was to her that the "Angels" had referred in their conversation.

Margaret Miller, though perhaps not a beauty, yet was fair to look upon. Her face was little, round, and rosy with the blush of health. Dark-brown hair, bearing the rich gloss of the chestnut, was drawn back from the pure white forehead, Greek in its lowness and perfect in its outlines; the mild brown eyes—the eyes for faith and love—the little red lips, that formed the sweet, innocent mouth, displaying, when open, the even white teeth—all gave a charm to the face.

The last of the group was a young man, apparently about twenty-five, clad in the buckskin suit of a hunter. In person he was a little above the medium size, and his well-knit figure gave promise of great strength. His face was a frank and open one; the clear black eyes and pleasant smile gave token of a good, honest nature—a man whose friendship was worth the having, whose word carried with it his life; and such indeed was Hank Baldwin, the young hunter who followed the Mormon trail for love of pretty Margaret Miller, or, at all events, he appeared to have no other motive. Whether, in truth, he had some other motive besides the one we have spoken of, our story will probably tell.

"Three more days, and we shall be at our journey's end," said Miller. {28}

"Oh, I shall be *so* glad," cried Kate, his wife. "I expect we shall be very happy there."

"I hope so, wife," said Miller, fondly.

"And you, Margaret," asked Mrs. Miller, "will you not be glad to see the New Zion?"

"Why, Kate," answered Margaret, slowly, "you know I am not a believer in the Mormon faith, and if all they say in regard to it be but true—"

"Ah!" cried Miller, "but it's not true! Did not Elder Higgins tell us that the enemies of the true faith lied about it? and surely we should believe the elder, for he is a good man, and holds a high place in the church."

"To what reports do you refer, Miss Miller?" asked the young hunter, a quiet smile on his face.

"To the practice of polygamy," replied Margaret.

"Why, the elder assures us that it is all a falsehood!" cried Miller, hotly—"that it is not practiced by the chosen people, nor sanctioned by their faith."

"The elder has deceived you," quietly observed the hunter. "Brigham Young himself has many wives; even the elder has five."

"It can not be!" cried Miller.

"It is true, I assure you," replied the young hunter; "I have been in Salt Lake City and have seen with my own eyes."

"But, if it is as you assert," cried Mrs. Miller, "why do those who are deceived—as we shall be—why do they stay? Why do they not return to the East?"

"The prairie is wide, the path very dangerous," returned the hunter, "and the terrible Danites, the Destroying Angels, stand in the way. Once in Salt Lake City, it is difficult to leave it without the consent of the Mormon leaders."

"You must be deceived," cried Miller; "I can not, will not, believe that the elder would speak falsely to me."

"Time will show," said the hunter. "As it is, you have no choice but to go on; *now* you cannot return."

"As you say, time will show," replied Miller, a dim suspicion beginning to creep over him that, perhaps, the young man had spoken the truth, and that the elder had deceived him.

During this short convention, a man standing behind the {29} wagon near the group had overheard every word, and evidently the conversation had not pleased him, for his features were red with passion. He was a fat, oily-looking personage, a little below the medium size; his face was round like a full moon, and his little grayish-blue eyes resembled those of a pig; his short yellow hair was trained in soap-locks down the sides of his forehead. This was Elder Higgins, who was the chief in charge of the train.

Silently, behind the wagon, the elder shook his fist at the young Gentile.

"Ah! you son of Satan!" he muttered, "I'll fix you before we get to Salt Lake City, or my name ain't Higgins! The Destroyers must attend to him. He knows too much. What the devil does he want, following our train, anyway? He's after the girl, I know, but is that his *only* motive?" And the elder thought long and earnestly. "There's some mystery about this. I'll see Dan at once." And carefully the elder withdrew from his ambush, and crossing the encampment, approached the Destroying Angels' camp-fire.

"Dan, can I have a talk with you?" asked the elder.

Without a word Dan rose from his seat and followed the elder. When they were out of ear-shot of the rest of the encampment, the elder spoke.

"Dan, do you know the hunter Baldwin?"

"Yes," answered Dan, with his usual curtness.

"The Gentile knows too much; he dares to scoff at the saints—"

"Well?"

"He must be silenced!"

"A difficult job," said the Danite. "Why dos he follow our train?" he added, suddenly.

"Well, I suppose he's after that young girl, Margaret Miller, but I think he's after something else too. I think he is a spy, and that he has some mission of vengeance. Now, I've had a revelation," with a sanctimonious rolling up of the eyes, "and it commands me to give to the death the Gentile hunter."

"Has Margaret Miller any thing to do with the revelation, elder?" said Dan, quietly.

The elder coughed and looked a little confused. {30}

"I suppose then that you have noticed that the Gentile is partial to the girl."

"Yes," responded the assassin, "and I've noticed, also, that that fact don't seem to please you, over and above."

"Of course it doesn't," exclaimed the elder; "I don't wish to see the girl led out of the true path into the ways of sin. The Gentile must die."

"Very well, I'll attend to that matter, but it will be a difficult job, for he is not only handy with his weapons but he has two powerful allies in the Indian chiefs, his friends."

"Ah!" cried the elder, musingly, "that's bad. We mustn't offend the Indians if we can help it. The Yellow Wolf is chief of the Dacotahs, and we do not care to provoke them to hostilities. The chief now is on his way to see the Prophet in regard to a treaty of alliance. Could you not contrive, in some way, to separate the Gentile from the Indians and then strike him?"

"That depends upon circumstances," replied Dan. "If he should happen to separate himself from the rest of the camp, why, we'll fix him; but, it's not likely; besides, he's well armed and unless we bring him down by surprise he'll be apt to make a desperate resistance."

"Suppose I can manage to fix his weapons—wax the nipple of his rifle and remove the caps from his revolver?" asked the elder, with a cunning smile.

"Why, in that case we can settle him easily, and without creating an alarm; but, the main thing is to separate him from the rest."

"I've got an idea!" cried the elder, gleefully. "After we start on the march to-morrow, I'll make some excuse to engage him in conversation, and by that means contrive to lag behind the rest. You and your band can lay in ambush and so finish him. I think that scheme will hold water, eh?"

"Yes, and the crossing of the Green river will be a capital place for the ambuscade. The banks of the river are heavily wooded, and then, after we finish him, we can throw the body into the stream and that will remove all traces of the deed."

"That will do," cried the elder, rubbing his hands together with satisfaction; "he will disappear as utterly as if he had sunk into the earth." {31}

"And no longer interfere with your designs on the pretty Margaret, eh, elder?"

"It is our duty to bring all the young lambs within the fold," answered the elder, sanctimoniously.

"Particularly when the lambs are young, tender and pretty," said Dan with a sneer. "But, all right, elder; I'll smite him hip and thigh."

And so understanding each other, the two men separated; the Danite returned to his men, and the elder sauntered slowly back to the wagon of Miller. By the wagon he found Miller and his wife. Margaret and the hunter had disappeared—"gone for a walk," so Mrs. Miller informed the elder. He sat down by the camp-fire, and to the young farmer and his wife dilated upon the prospects of the desert settlement, the New Zion of the Saints, Salt Lake City.

Chapter IV.
What Happened Before the Moon Went Down.

Apart from the rest of the camp sat the two Indian chiefs, the Yellow Wolf and the warrior known by the name of Eagle Plume.

With the Yellow Wolf, our readers are already acquainted, but the other chief deserves some notice at our hands.

Eagle Plume was tall, muscular, and evidently possessing uncommon strength. He was clad in the usual Indian fashion, except that he wore no hunting-shirt, his body being naked from the waist upward, and gayly striped with war-paint, as was also his face. One peculiarity about Eagle Plume was, that, contrary to the Indian custom, he always wore the war-paint, and instead of being painted in alternate stripes as was the general custom of the savages, all of his body exposed to view was covered with paint. His hair, cut short across the forehead and worn long behind in the Indian style, instead of floating loosely down upon his shoulders was gathered up in a knot behind, braided in with which was a head-dress of eagle-plumes. All these little peculiarities gave {32} the chief a singular appearance. Across the lap of this chief lay a long rifle, one of the kind made famous by the American frontier-men, carrying a ball of a hundred to a pound, and certain death to bird, animal or man at a hundred paces.

"Has my brother found what he was in search of in the camp of the chiefs who have many squaws?" asked the Yellow Wolf, in the Dacotah tongue.

"The chief can not say; he thinks he has," replied Eagle Plume. "He will know when he sees the left arm of the white brave—"

"And when will my brother see the arm?"

"To-night." And there was a gleam like glittering steel in the chief's eyes as he spoke.

"Wah! it is good. Will Eagle Plume need the aid of the Yellow Wolf?" asked the chief of the Dacotahs, for the Yellow Wolf now held that position, the Hole-in-the-sky having died, and the Yellow Wolf having been chosen in his place, at his dying request.

"No; the chief thanks his brother, but he will talk to the white-skin alone," was the answer.

"Has my brother noticed the fat Mormon chief and the young hunter?" asked the Yellow Wolf.

"The Mormon chief is a snake in the grass; he would sting the heel of the young white-skin, but the foot of the Dacotah chief shall crush the snake," and the tone of the chief's voice was cold and calm.

"My brother speaks well," said the Yellow Wolf. "Suppose my brother has made a mistake and the brave he seeks to-night is not the one?"

"Then the Dacotah chief, like the wolf, will follow on the trail till he finds the right one, and then—" there was a fearful meaning in the unfinished sentence.

"My brother speaks straight—it is good," replied the Yellow Wolf. "The big Mormon chief has sent for the chief of the Dacotahs; he wishes a talk. In the Mormon lodges let my brother keep his ears and eyes open; then he will find what he seeks."

Let us now follow the footsteps of the young hunter and Margaret Miller, as they strolled along in the twilight up the bank of the little creek. {33}

"Mr. Baldwin," said Margaret, suddenly, "I have been thinking of your words this evening."

"In relation to the Mormon faith?" asked the young hunter.

"Yes."

"Do *you*, too, doubt my words?" he asked.

"No, I believe that you spoke the truth; but my brother has great faith in his Elder Higgins, who denies the report that the Mormons have more than one wife, and says it is nothing but a Gentile falsehood," replied the girl.

"Your brother will learn the truth, but it will avail him but little then; he will be in Salt lake City, in the power of the men whom he will soon grow to despise. Why, Margaret, do you know that I believe Elder Higgins has already marked you out for his victim, his sixth wife?" said the hunter, earnestly.

"He is deceiving himself then, for I cannot bear the sight of him, and sooner than be his wife I would die," cried Margaret, impulsively.

"I know that such is his purpose," returned the hunter; "in Salt Lake City you are utterly in his power, and as either he or the Prophet will have a 'revelation,' as they term it, commanding you to be 'sealed' to him, nothing can save you from him."

"Not even if my brother objects?" asked the girl, in astonishment.

"His objection will have little weight; there is but one law in yonder city, and that is the will of the Prophet. If your brother should be mad enough to attempt resistance to that will, the terrible Danites, the Destroying Angels, will make short work of him."

"Oh, this is terrible!" cried Margaret.

"It is the truth, and that truth it is best you should hear," earnestly replied the hunter.

"What can save me from this terrible fate?" asked Margaret.

"Margaret," answered the hunter, after a moment's pause, "your question prompts me to an avowal which otherwise, perhaps, I should not have made. Margaret, I love you."

A rosy blush tinged the cheek of the maiden at this confession. {34}

"Margaret, be *my* wife. I am only a poor hunter, but I can at least protect you from your persecutors. I am alone here, a Gentile amid the Mormons, but at my back are five hundred Dacotah warriors. Margaret, can you love me?" and his tone was low and pleading.

A moment he waited, and then answer came, the low "yes." With an exclamation of joy, he caught the blushing girl in his strong arms, and pressed her to his heart, while from her soft red lips he received the long-lingering kiss that proved that she was wholly his.

Hand in hand, in silent rapture, the lovers walked on.

The shades of night were gathering over the prairie, and darkness was vailing the earth.

"Had we not better return to the camp?" asked Margaret, pausing.

"Yes; for the darkness is coming on rapidly," replied the hunter. Then they turned, and retraced their steps.

"Henry," said Margaret, as they walked slowly toward the camp, "you have never told me why you are going to Salt Lake City. You do not wish to join the Mormons, why then do you seek their city?"

"I have two motives, Margaret. The first motive made me join the Mormon train, the second I found in the train; and even if I had not the first to send me to Salt Lake City, the second would probably have carried me there," and the hunter glanced meaningly at his fair companion, who blushed again up to her temples. She knew full well what that second motive was.

"And the first motive?" she asked.

"That requires some explanation; and in the first place I must reveal to you that Baldwin is not my name."

"What is the reason for this concealment?" she asked, in astonishment.

"Listen and you shall learn," he replied. "My right name is Hastings. My family lived in a small town in Illinois, located on the Mississippi river. My father died when I was quite a child, and my mother a few years afterward. I had a brother, some years older than myself, and a sister some five years younger. We were brought up by an uncle. When I was about twelve years old, my brother, who was then just {35} reaching manhood, went to Mexico; from that day to this I have never heard of him, and I know not whether he is alive or dead. When I became of age, I, too, left my uncle's home to seek my fortune. I joined a trapping-party bound for the upper Missouri, and that is how I became a hunter. My sister, who was a beautiful girl of seventeen, remained at my uncle's house.

"I was away from Illinois nearly four years, and of course, located as I was in the wilds of the Rocky Mountains, letters from my sister were out of the question. Well, at the end of four years, with a handsome little sum of money, the product of my skill, I returned to Illinois, went at once to my uncle's house, eager to hold my loved sister once again in my arms. Judge of my despair when I learned that, not two months before my return, she had been lured by the false words of a villain, and, trusting to his promises, had left her home and fled with him. My uncle and aunt had been almost heart-broken at the event, for they had loved my sister Ethel as though she had been their own flesh and blood.

"From my uncle I learned all that he could tell in relation to the affair. The villain with whom my sister had fled was named Luther Hardwicke—at least, my sister left behind a letter from him signed with that name. Then I pursued my search through the village. I found the ferryman who had carried my sister and her destroyer across the river. He remembered the circumstance, and said that this Luther had let fall a chance observation in regard to Council Bluffs which led him to believe that that was his destination. This was clue enough for me. I made my way to Council Bluffs. There I made inquiries, and found that a girl answering to the description of my sister had died some three weeks before. I sought the family in whose house the girl had died, only to have all my suspicions confirmed; the poor girl who lay in the cold grave was, indeed, my erring sister. She had been deserted, abandoned, penniless, by the villain who had lured her from her home, and but for the kindness of a gentleman who heard her sad story, and both pitied and aided the poor child, she would have suffered for the common necessaries of life. Struck to the heart by the desertion of him who had sworn to love and cherish her, she had literally died of a broken heart. The {36} gentleman who proved himself indeed a friend to the poor child, saw her buried, and had a little tablet bearing her name placed at the head of her grave; and then, as if he had only wanted to do the last kind offices to the poor child, proceeded on his way.

"At Council Bluffs of course I inquired eagerly as to the direction taken by Luther Hardwicke, for he had borne that name there too, and I learned that he had gone to join the Mormons. He had threatened that the Gentiles who had driven him from their midst—for the officers of the law were in pursuit of him—should rue it. I also gained another important clue as to the person of this Luther: on his left arm was the letter L in India ink. The descriptions as to his personal appearance were so varied, that it was evident he was using disguises at times, and perhaps always.

"Now you know, Margaret, what it is that brings me to Salt Lake City. I seek the man who bears on his left arm the letter L. I seek Luther Hardwicke, the murderer of my sister Ethel; and that the murderer—if I should happen to encounter him unawares, as it is probable I may—shall not be able to guess my object and by flight escape my vengeance, I have changed my name as a matter of precaution. Now, Margaret, you know all my history, and my purpose here in the midst of this Mormon horde; but be sure you do not breathe to mortal a single word of what I have told you, because, not for all the wealth and honors that this world can offer would I forego my vengeance on the guilty head of the destroyer of my poor sister."

"Do not fear," replied Margaret, gazing with a trusting look up into the manly face of her lover; "your secret will be safe in my keeping. But, have you any clue as to where or what this villain is?"

"But little," returned the hunter. "Cautiously have I inquired for the man with the letter L on his left arm, but as yet I have not succeeded in finding him. I have a dim suspicion that he is one of the band known as the "Destroying Angels"; it is but a mere suspicion, yet I am on the watch, and sooner or later fate will give him to my hands."

By this time the twain had reached the campaign.

"It is late; I must to rest," said Margaret, as they stood {37} by the wagon that served as her home for the present; "good-night, Henry," and with a farewell kiss, she parted from her lover and disappeared under the cover of the wagon.

Thoughtfully the young hunter walked through the Mormon camp till he reached its outskirts, where, beneath a cottonwood tree, were tied three horses; this was the bivouac of the Indians and the young hunter.

Carelessly the hunter cast himself upon the ground, his thoughts busy with the charming girl whose kiss even now was fresh upon his lips. How he thanked the lucky chance that had brought him to the rescue of the Dacotah chief, the Yellow Wolf, when the fierce mountain king, the grizzly bear, held the red warrior helpless upon the earth. But for that incident he would not now have been able to defy the power of the Mormons and make the pretty Margaret his wife; but now, backed as he would be, should the occasion call for it, by all the fierce Dacotah warriors, he felt that not even the Danites, the terrible Destroying Angels, would dare to snatch his bride from him. And then his thoughts turned on vengeance; and he asked himself if he ever would discover the wretch who had caused the death of his sister, and something within his soul whispered him that he would!

The two Indians were absent from the bivouac; the hunter had not seen them in his passage through the camp. They were probably on the prairie somewhere beyond the limits of the encampment.

So the young man stretched himself out in the shade of the cottonwoods, and fell asleep, his rifle by his side, and his belt holding his knife and revolvers unloosed, but placed within easy reach.

Twenty paces from where the hunter lay was another group of cottonwoods, and their shade also concealed the figure of a man. He was stretched at full length upon the ground, but was not sleeping. He was watching—watching earnestly the movements of the hunter.

Patiently the watcher beneath the cottonwoods waited. When the hunter remained motionless, and appeared to be slumbering, the watcher still stirred not, but patiently, for a half-hour longer, continued immovable. Then, with a snake-like motion, he raised his head and looked around. All was {38} still within the camp; all had retired to rest save the picket-guards posted on the outskirts of the encampment. Then forth from the shadow of the cottonwoods crept the spy, who proved to be Elder Higgins!

With catlike steps the elder stole across the open space between the two groves; then he paused by the side of the sleeping hunter.

Carefully the elder removed the revolvers from the unstrapped belt, then, with the rifle, crossed again to the trees that had sheltered him.

There he removed the caps from the weapons, and pressed wax down into the nipples; then he replaced the caps, and returning to the sleeper's side, carefully and cautiously restored the weapons to their place. He evidently was an adept in cunning and craft, and smiled over his achievement as he made his way to his own quarters.

As the elder climbed into his wagon, a singular muffled sound, coming apparently from the prairie, fell upon his ear. It sounded as if some one, choking, uttered a half-smothered gasp. For a moment the elder listened, but the sound was not repeated, and, as the elder knew that there was a picket posted beneath some cottonwoods from whence the noise apparently came, he felt no apprehensions.

Little did the elder dream that the dark angel of vengeance had spread his sable wing over the Mormon camp.

Chapter V.
The Letter L.

The light passed away and the morning came. Before the sun had risen, all the Mormon camp was astir; the fires were kindled, the breakfast prepared, for, prairie-fashion, the march commenced early.

By the camp-fire of the pilots stood the chief of the Danites, and the Mormon leader.

"Are the pickets all in?" asked Higgins of Dan. {39}

"Yes, excepting Ben Smith," answered the Danite; "he was posted in a clump of cottonwoods just beyond your wagon, elder."

"Why is he not in? Can he have fallen asleep?"

"I can hardly believe that," said Dan, thoughtfully. "He's one of the best men in the band. I've sent Grizzly Joe, to see what has become of him."

"Ah, here comes Joe!" cried Dan, suddenly; "now we shall know what has kept Smith."

"Yes, and he's alone," said the elder. "I begin to fear that something has happened to Smith."

Grizzly Joe came rapidly on toward the two men. The quick eye of the Danite leader saw that something indeed had happened, by the expression on Joe's face.

"Well, Joe," said Dan, as the ruffian came within speaking distance. "What keeps Smith?"

"He'll tell you himself," responded Grizzly Joe, in a voice that showed plainly that he was under the influence of some hidden terror.

"Where is he?" asked Dan, his brows contracting, for he saw that something unusual had happened.

"Under the cottonwoods, jest where you left him last night," replied Joe. "I thought it better to tell you quietly an' not alarm the camp."

"Why, what's the matter?" demanded Dan, following Joe toward the outskirts of the camp; the elder discreetly brought up the rear.

"Wa-al, I don't 'xactly know," responded Joe, dubiously, "but I think Old Nick himself was in the camp last night."

The elder stared at the "Angel" with astonishment, as soberly he stated his belief. Dan looked at the ruffian keenly, evidently under the impression that he was drunk; but, contrary to his usual custom, Grizzly Joe was sober.

The two gained the prairie; a few steps and they stood beneath the shelter of the cottonwoods, and there, right at their feet, with unclosed, staring eyes fixed in death, lay the lifeless form of Ben Smith, the picket-guard.

"Murdered!" cried Dan, springing forward.

"Yes, but by whom?" exclaimed the elder, gazing on the cor[p]se with fear-starting eyes. {40}

"Yes, and *how?*" cried Joe. "Thar ain't any wound that I kin see!"

Carefully Dan examined the body, which was that of a young man some twenty-five or thirty years of age, a good-looking fellow, though his face bore the lines of dissipation and crime.

The body lay on its back, stretched out at full length. Death had evidently been sudden and not very painful, for the features were but little distorted.

After a careful examination Dan spoke: "Smith was surprised sitting down here," and he pointed to the slight impression in the soft earth. "Whoever attacked him approached from behind, cast a cord or a lasso over his head, and dragged him backward, breaking the neck with a single jerk, for that's the cause of his death. Do you not see the traces on the ground where the body has been dragged?"

Closely the elder and Grizzly Joe examined the soil. It was as Dan had said—there were the plainly-defined traces where the body had been dragged along the earth.

"Ah!" cried the elder, suddenly, "I remember last night, just as I was getting into my wagon, I heard a sound like a man choking—a sort of muffled groan coming from this direction. I listened, but as it was not repeated, I thought it didn't amount to any thing, and so I didn't take any more notice of it."

"That confirms what I said," replied Dan; "the choking sound that you heard was the death-gasp of poor Smith."

"But, I cannot understand why he should have been killed, unless he had some secret enemy," added the elder.

"I don't think he had an enemy in the camp," replied the chief of the Danites; "and few men, too, dare to molest one of the Destroying Angels," and a grim smile was upon his face as he spoke. "But the manner of the death puzzles me. I don't think there's a man in our camp expert in throwing the lasso. If there were any Mexicans now among us—"

"The two Indians!" cried Joe, suddenly.

"They are Dacotahs," replied his chief; "their lasso is nothing but a lariat. If they were Comanches or Apaches now, why, I should suspect them as having a hand in this work. Besides, they could have no object in killing Smith. Who- {41} ever did this deed throws the lasso in the Mexican fashion, and from a considerable distance, because it isn't reasonable to suppose that Smith would let anybody get very near to him, even in the darkness."

Just at this moment, Joe, who had knelt down by the side of his murdered comrade, gave vent to a sudden exclamation:

"What's the matter?" demanded Dan.

"Smith's coat and shirt-sleeve have been slit from the wrist to the shoulder—the left arm."

"Well?"

"An' on the fleshy part of the arm are two knife-cuts, makin' the letter L," cried Joe.

Astonished, the elder and the Danite chief examined the arm; it was as Joe had said. Plainly visible on the arm were the two knife-cuts forming the letter L.

The features of the chief of the Destroying Angels seemed hardened into stone as he gazed on the strange sight.

"Whoever did it, left his totem, as an Injun would say!" cried Grizzly Joe.

"This is the strangest thing of all," said Dan, slowly, as he rose to his feet. Then a sudden light flashing into his eyes, while a visible pallor whitened his face, he exclaimed:

"'Twas Baldwin who did this deed!"

"No, that's not possible," returned the elder. "Last night, for a certain purpose, I kept my eyes on him, and I left him fast asleep when I came to my wagon, and that was the time I heard the noise, which now I am sure was the death-gasp of Smith. So you see it *couldn't* have been him."

It was evident that a deep feeling of uneasiness had taken possession of the Danite's mind.

"What shall we do with the body, cap'n?" asked Joe.

"Take half a dozen of the men and bury it quietly; tell them to keep their mouths shut and not blab the affair all over the camp." The Danite chief ground his teeth together fiercely. "I'll find out this midnight prowler before we reach Salt Lake City and he shall have my life or I'll have his. But this letter L! It is very strange!"

The elder and Dan walked slowly back to the camp.

"By the way," said the elder, "I fixed the Gentile hunter's weapons last night." {42}

"You did?"

"Yes," and the elder gave vent to a cunning laugh. "I stole to his side while he was asleep and plugged the nipples of his rifle and revolvers, then put the caps back again. When he wants to use them, they will be about as much use as a broomstick. He'll have his knife, though; of course I couldn't fix that."

"We won't give him a chance to use it. Now, what's the programme you've laid out?" asked Dan.

"Simple as falling off a log. It will be about an hour before we cross Green river. I'll get into conversation with him and lag behind. When you reach the river, you let the train pass on, and ambush yourself and a few men in the bushes on the bank of the stream; then, when we cross, why you can pick him off his horse with a revolver shot, and tumble him into the river. The sound of the shot won't be apt to reach the train, for they'll be too far in the advance. Don't you think that will work?" and the elder laughed gleefully.

"Good as grace before dinner," replied Dan.

———

Chapter VI.
The Spider and the Fly.

Breakfast being eaten, the wagon-train again took up its line of march across the prairie.

The train had proceeded some twenty minutes, when Elder Higgins rode up to young Baldwin and requested the favor of a few words with him.

"Willingly," replied Baldwin.

"Just slacken the pace of your horse a little," said the elder; "let the train pass, because what I have to say to you is very important, and I don't wish any one to overhear our conversation."

"Just as you please," replied the hunter, pulling up his horse.

So the two halted until the train passed them. {43}

Now, the young hunter was by no means thrown off his guard. He knew that the elder had guessed his love for Margaret Miller, and that he would not be sorry to have him out of the way. He knew, too, the character of the man by his side, and that he would not hesitate at any means to achieve his ends.

Therefore, when the train passed, he watched quietly to see if any of the Destroying Angels remained behind, too, as he had an idea that they would do. But they went on with the train. When he noted this, it was with little fear that he remained behind, confident that it was with the elder alone he would have to deal.

After the train had passed, the elder spoke:

"Mr. Baldwin, as what I have to say may take up some little time, suppose we dismount, and walk under the shade of those cottonwoods?" and he pointed to a little clump of trees some hundred feet from them, to the left.

"Certainly," replied the hunter, but, ever on the alert, he swept his watchful eye around the horizon, to note if there was danger visible, but the rolling prairie showed no sign of life, save in the fast-disappearing wagon-train.

The two men dismounted, tied their horses to the trees and sat down beneath the shade, the hunter carefully placing his rifle by his side. The Gentile, as the Mormon would have termed him, little guessed that his weapons were harmless—that treachery had done its work, and that he was alone on the prairie, defenseless.

"You are not a believer in the Mormon faith, I think, Mr. Baldwin?" began the elder.

"No," replied the hunter, shortly.

"Ah, I thought so. Mr. Baldwin, as you are well aware, the wagon-train that you are traveling with is composed of Mormons—the believers of the true faith—the seekers after purity and virtue in the New Zion," with a sanctimonious snuffle.

"Yes, I am aware of that fact, too," replied the hunter.

"As I have said," continued the elder, "you are a Gentile, an unbeliever and a scoffer at the true faith—"

"No," interrupted the hunter, "you are wrong there. Never in my life have I scoffed at any one's belief, no matter whether {44} I have thought the faith worthy or not. Each man is his own judge on *that* subject, and I do not profess to tell my neighbor what or how he shall think."

"Ah!" and the elder drew a long breath; "but you stated certain things concerning our religion, that I had denied."

The hunter looked at the elder with a sort of half-smile upon his face.

"Oh, I see now, elder, what you are driving at," he said. "You have found out, by some means, that I told Miller that the Mormons practiced polygamy. You have sharp ears, elder, and long ones."

"Take care, young man," cried the elder, sharply, "how you revile the Mormon faith."

"I haven't reviled it. I merely said what you know to be true, though, for some reason, you see fit to deny it," said the hunter, coolly. "As long as I travel with your train, I shall hold my tongue in regard to my thoughts about your religion: though now, between ourselves, elder, I have no hesitation in telling you that I don't think a great deal of the Mormon religion nor of its professors."

"Take care, young man," again cried the elder. "Those that revile the chosen of the Lord shall suffer!"

"Well, as regards that, I have serious doubts whether fellows of your kidney *are* the 'chosen of the Lord;' and, as to the suffering, I do not fear your threats; if your Destroying Angels molest me, they shall find I can protect myself," and the young hunter slapped the butt of his rifle meaningly.

"I spoke not of earthly vengeance," the elder said, with his usual canting snuffle. "I am not a man of violence."

"Yes, but like many another coward, you use a tool to do the work your heart prompts, but your hand shrinks from," replied the hunter, with calm deliberation.

"Then you will still persist in journeying with our party?" said the elder, rising.

"In your party, no; with your party, yes. The prairie is free; I can camp where I like, and who dares say nay?"

"We shall see!" cried the elder, untying and mounting his animal. "I understand why you linger about the camp. You would devour one of the young lambs of our flocks; but beware that you are not stricken with the vengeance of the Lord {45} in the attempt!" and with this parting shot, the elder put spurs to his horse and galloped off.

For a moment the hunter looked after the Mormon with a disdainful smile.

"The vulture!" muttered Baldwin. "No, I am wrong—not a vulture, a crow; that suits him better. He threatens, does he? Well, the Angels may 'fix' me, but it shall take several to play that game of life or death."

Slowly the hunter mounted his horse, and followed in the trail of the wagon-train.

Higgins, the elder, had disappeared across the swells of the prairie.

<hr>

Chapter VII.
The Secret of the Waters.

The river—quite a stream here, where the Salt Lake trail crossed it—came rolling calmly down between banks fringed with cottonwoods—those everlasting adjuncts to southern and western rivers—and alders. Just by the ford, the bushes and trees grew densely, so that the ax of the emigrant had been called into play to clear a passage for the teams.

Just below the ford, the stream spread out into a broad, deep pool.

After leaving the young hunter, the Mormon elder pushed his horse into a sharp gallop, and by the time he reached the ford, he had left the hunter so far behind that he was not visible, being hidden from view by the swells of the undulating prairie.

The elder crossed the stream—the water of which reached to the breast of his horse—and halted upon the opposite bank. With a quick and searching glance to the rear, he satisfied himself that the hunter was not in sight; then he cast his eyes around him; all was still; no signs of life appeared in the tangled underbrush that fringed the course of the stream.

"Can Dan have misunderstood my intentions?" muttered the elder to himself, a scowl wrinkling his brows; but, as if {46} in answer to his thought, the tall form of Dan rose from his covert in the bushes.

"Ah!" cried the elder, in glee, the frown upon his face giving place to a smile of satisfaction. "You are here all right. I was afraid that you had misunderstood me, and that the cursed Gentile would escape."

"No fear of that," replied Dan; "he is following you?"

"Yes, close behind me. Remember, I've fixed his weapons so that they are harmless. I'll ride on at once, for he's likely to come at any moment, and if he saw me halting here he might suspect something. Fix him as quietly as possible," said the elder.

"Don't be alarmed," replied Dan. "If the sound of our shots reached the train, they would imagine we were after game; they wouldn't have any suspicions."

"Where are the two Indians?" asked the elder.

"'Way on, ahead of the train," said the Danite.

"That's good!" cried the elder. "If they had any idea of our purpose, they might give us considerable trouble."

"No danger; we'll settle this impious meddler before he's an hour older," said Dan, with a grim smile.

"All right. I'll ride on; be sure and don't fail," cried the elder, putting spurs to his horse.

The Danite sunk back to his hiding-place, and the Mormon, borne swiftly on by his quick-limbed beast, disappeared in the distance.

Concealed in the tangled underwood by the bank of the river, was Dan and four of his best men, namely, Red Dick, Grizzly Joe, and two others, whom we have not before mentioned in our story, known as Tom Ewens and Dave Gindar. From this warlike array, it was plain to be seen that the Danite leader did not hold the prowess of the Kentucky hunter lightly.

The five were ambushed in the thicket close together; from their hiding-place they commanded a full view of the ford.

"Wa-al, capt'n," said Dick, as the Danite leader resumed his former position, "what's the bill of fare? Shall we all fire together, or how?"

"No," replied Dan, "I will fire first. If I miss him—which {47} is not likely—you will fire next; if you miss him, then Joe and the rest, all together. But I don't think it will require more than one shot. Use your revolvers, boys; they won't make quite so much noise as the rifles," said Dan.

Then, to the listening ears of the Angels came the sound of horse's hoofs rapidly approaching the ford.

"That's our bird!" cried the Danite, coolly drawing his revolver from his belt and cocking it. The rest of the band followed his example. And so, crouching in their ambush, like the tiger preparing for his spring, the Destroying Angels, revolver in hand, waited for their prey.

We will now return to the young hunter. After the departure of the elder, he leisurely followed on his trail. As he rode along, he thought of the interview that had just taken place. The more he thought, the more puzzled he became.

"Could it be possible," he said to himself, as he proceeded slowly on his way, "that this Mormon elder thought that any words or threats of his would turn me from my purpose, and make me leave the train and give up pretty Margaret to him?" He shook his head in doubt. "No, no!" he cried; "I do not think that Higgins is such a fool as that. What, then, *can* be the object of this? Is it to separate me from the train, and then have the Angels ambush me at some convenient spot and wipe me out? Is *that* their game? Well, let them come on; I'm ready for them," and he loosened one of his revolvers from his belt as he spoke.

The hunter now urged his horse onward at an increased pace. Soon the yellow gleam of the Green river appeared before him, the surface of the water reflecting the sunbeams that danced upon it, and shining like so many diamonds, through the openings in the shrubbery that grew along the banks.

At the moment he reached the bank of the river, a sudden thought flashed across his mind. "By Jove!" he cried to himself, "this is the very place for an ambush, if they mean me harm!" and, as his horse entered the water, he quietly cocked his rifle. His keen eye swept along the bushes that fringed the opposite bank, but no sign of life met his gaze.

The hunter reached the middle of the river; the water {48} touched the breast of his horse, and washed the feet of the rider.

Crack! and the little, sharp sound of the explosion of a cap broke upon the air. No report, however, followed it, the revolver of the Danite—for it was he who had fired at the hunter—had missed fire. With an oath, he dashed it to the ground.

Quick as the flash of the lightning Baldwin brought his rifle to his shoulder, leveled it at random at the thicket before him, and pulled the trigger. The explosion of the cap alone followed: *his* weapon, too, had missed fire.

Crack! crack! two quick reports rung out on the air. One bullet grazed the shoulder of the hunter, tearing the hunting-ing-shirt [*sic*] the other came within an inch of his head; as yet he was unhurt. Drawing a revolver from his belt, he leveled it at the thicket before him; five times he pulled the trigger; five times the caps exploded, yet the chambers hung fire! Dismayed at this, the hunter mentally asked himself if some malicious demon had not laid a spell upon his hitherto trusty weapons.

Then, from the bushes before him, rung the loud laugh of the Destroying Angels, as they beheld his fruitless efforts, and from their covert in the tangled underbrush the assassins rose to their feet. They leveled their revolvers at the horseman; death stared him in the face from each shining tube.

"Ha! ha! ha!" grimly laughed the Danite leader, "your weapons are useless, your life is ours."

The only reply the hunter made was to hurl the revolver in hand full at the head of the Danite. The missile went whiz through the air, within a foot of the head of Dan, and struck Red Dick, who was standing a little behind him, right between the eyes, and laid him out flat on his back. A howl of rage escaped from the lips of the ruffian, as he fell.

Quickly the hunter leaped from his horse, and sought safety in the river. The Mormons emptied their revolvers at him as he disappeared. That he had been hit was plain, for here and there on the yellow surface of the water the stains of blood could be seen.

Eagerly the villains watched the water; each moment they expected to see their victim, writhing in the throes of death, {49} rise to the surface. Long they watched and long they waited. Calmly flowed the river, its quiet waters undisturbed by the convulsive agonies of a dying man.

The murderous wretches were puzzled.

"What has become of him?" growled Dick, whose natural beauty had not been at all improved by the couple of black eyes that the blow from the revolver, hurled by the hunter, had given him. Eagerly he had watched, revolver in hand, for the man to rise to the surface, intent on paying back the blow he had received with interest; but, Red Dick was doomed to disappointment, for the body of the hunter appeared not to his anxious gaze.

"I am sure I hit him!" said Dan, with compressed brows, evidently in doubt as to the fate of the man.

The horse of the young Kentuckian had returned to the other bank, and was quietly grazing on the prairie-grass.

"Hit him!" cried Joe. "Sartin you did, cap! See the blood-stains on the water."

"But, what can have become of him?" said Dick, savagely.

"Possibly he was killed outright and his dead body has sunk to the bottom," replied Dan.

"That's so, of course!" cried Joe. "Just like a man when he drowns, he always sinks—he don't float."

"I'd like to see him dead though, so as to be sure of it, cuss him!" growled Dick.

"So would I," said the Danite leader. "If he was a good swimmer, he might have swum down the river when he sprung from his horse—"

"What! under the water?" interrupted Dick.

"Aye."

"Blazes! so he might. I never thought of that," cried Red Dick.

"'Tain't likely, cap," said Joe. "It's plain that he was badly hit, and bleeding like a stuck pig. He wouldn't have strength to swim fur."

"Perhaps not; yet the blood may come from a flesh wound. At any rate, we'll make sure. Some of you cross the river, and search along down the bank; we'll go on this side. If he has swum down under water, he'll have to take to the bank somewhere," said Dan. {50}

So, in obedience to his commands, Dick, with two more of the Angels, brought forward their concealed horses, crossed the river, dismounted, and scouted carefully along down the opposite bank. Dan and the rest of the party did the same on the other bank.

The search was fruitless, though the assassins traced the stream down a quarter of a mile.

Reluctantly the men retraced their steps to the ford.

"Well, capt'n, are you satisfied that he's gone under?" asked Dave.

"Yes," said Dan; but his tone was far from being one of conviction.

"What shall we do with his horse?" asked Dave.

"Well," said Dan, thoughtfully, "it will not do to carry him back openly to the train, because these two Indians will recognize him; and when they discover that the trapper is missing they'll be apt to have a suspicion that we know something about his disappearance, and had a hand in it. We'll camp to-night somewhere near Snake Cañon; so two of you had better take the horse and *cache* him there, and then smuggle him into the camp to-night. To-morrow hitch him to one of the wagons; mixed in with the rest he'll not be noticed."

Following the instructions of their chief, Grizzly Joe and another of the men started off with the horse.

Dan, after a long, parting glance at the yellow water, as though with his eyes he would penetrate through the turbid stream and drag to the light the secret that the dark waters concealed, turned his horse's head to the west and gave the signal for the advance.

Over the swells of the rolling prairie the Destroying Angels followed their leader. Suddenly, a hundred yards or so before them, a large white wolf sprung from the shelter of a little clump of bushes, and sped away over the prairie.

The path the men were following led them right past the clump. As they rapidly approached the bushes they saw, to their astonishment, a man extended on the ground, half concealed by the shrubbery. The man was evidently dead, and had attracted the blood-scenting wolf, which the approach of the band had frightened away. The wagon-train, too, had {51} passed the spot not an hour before; evidently, the body had not been there then, or else the men of the train would have given it burial, not have left it to be devoured by the prairie-wolves.

All these thoughts passed rapidly through the mind of the Danite leader, as he galloped toward the body, and now, as he came nearer, a feeling of horror seized upon him, for he fancied he recognized the dead man. His fears were true—an hour before the man had been alive.

"Jim Dent!" cried Dick, in a tone of horror, as they dismounted by the body. A cry of terror from the rest of the band answered him. 'Twas true indeed; before them lay the bravest of the Destroying Angels, a good-looking, black-haired fellow; and though his eyes were now closed in death, and his features paled by the dread summons he had received, yet they were as calm and peaceful as though he were sleeping.

"Who can have done this?" cried Dave, as he knelt by the side of his dead comrade.

"I don't see any wound," said Dick, examining the body.

"Look at the neck," said the Danite, in his usual quiet, cold tones.

Carefully the Angels examined the neck of the dead man; no wound was there, nothing, save a slight red mark as though, for a moment, a grip of iron had encircled the throat.

"Nary wound," said Dick, after a careful search; "only a little red mark round the neck."

The little red mark told the tale to the leader. He recognized the traces of the fatal lasso; he remembered the appearance of the body of the picket-guard, found that morning. It was plain to him that both had perished by the same hand! What could it mean? Was it some foe who had sworn to exterminate the Destroyers one by one? And if so, who and what was he that he was able to traverse the pathless prairie, strike his blows of vengeance quick and deadly as the lightning, and like that leave no clue behind.

A feeling of terror crept over the soul of the bold, reckless Danite; it might be his turn next: how could he fight this invisible foe? {52}

A cry of astonishment from Dick, who was kneeling by the body, attracted his attention.

"Well, what is it?"

"The left sleeve has been cut open, and on the arm two slashes with a knife make the letter L," replied the man.

A second time had the secret foe left his sign.

Chapter VIII.
The Spot of Blood.

Astonishment showed itself upon the faces of all the crime-hardened band as they looked upon the body of their slain comrade, for now it was plain to all that he had fallen by the hand of some secret foe.

Terror had taken possession of the leader of the terrible band; though he showed it not in his face, yet the terror was in his soul—a secret terror, one he could not fight against.

A strange circumstance the Danite had noticed in regard to both murders. It might be nothing but a mere coincidence, a chance, and then again it might be by *design*, and if it was by design, the Danite felt he was a doomed man. What he had noted was this: both the men slain had black hair, both were nearly alike in general appearance, both young men; and if the Danite's locks had been ebon instead of golden, the three men, he and the two slain ones, would have looked enough alike to have been brothers.

Gloomily the Danite looked upon the body at his feet; silently he asked himself how long it would be before he, too, would be lying in the cold embrace of the grim king of terrors.

The unknown danger frightened him. These silent, deadly blows, given apparently without warning, against which there was no guard, inspired him with a dread that he could not overcome, that he could not account for.

"What do you think of it, capt'n?" asked Dick. {53}

"The man has been approached from behind, snared with a lasso and strangled," replied the Danite.

"That's the reason thar ain't no mark, or blood about him," cried Dick.

"Yes, but I can not understand how he could allow any one to approach near enough to lasso him in broad daylight. Look and see if you can discover any other trails besides that left by the wagon-train," said Dan.

Carefully and eagerly the men scouted over the prairie, but their search was useless; no trail was there save the broad one left by the train.

One by one they came back and reported their failure to their leader, who, gloomy, motionless and abstracted, had remained by the side of the murdered man, gazing into his face as though he expected there to find some clue to the terrible deed.

"Boys," he said, at length, "for the first time the Destroying Angels have met a dangerous foe; each time he has appeared it has cost one of our band. If we knew this foe the danger would cease, for we would crush him—but he who strikes from behind and in the dark, I can not tell how to fight. The first thing is to discover who and what he is; then we can tell how to deal with him. It is very plain to me that be our enemy man or demon, he acts single-handed and attacks but one man at a time; so, henceforth, boys, hunt in couples; let no man go anywhere alone, but always with a comrade. In that way, I think we can bother him; and mind, boys, don't breathe a word of this outside of our band. It's very plain it's a fight for life and death between us and this unknown enemy. We must find him out and kill him, or he'll kill us, one by one."

"What shall we do with the body, capt'n?" asked Dave, solemnly.

"We shall have to leave it as it is," replied Dan. "We haven't any tools to dig a grave, and the train is too far off for us to procure any from it. Now, boys, to saddle; and remember, keep in couples if you don't want to share his fate," he added, swinging himself into the saddle.

The rest of the band followed his example, and soon they were off in full gallop over the plain, leaving the body of their {54} dead comrade to the mercy of the gaunt wolves of the prairie.

Return we now to the wagon-train, winding its slow way like a huge white serpent across the prairie.

The foremost wagon of the train was the one belonging to the young Ohioan, Miller. In the wagon were Mrs. Miller and Margaret, while Miller rode by the side of the horses, in close conversation with the elder, Higgins. The two women were talking together.

"You took quite a walk last night," said Mrs. Miller, mischievously.

"Yes," answered Margaret, casting a side-glance from under her long lashes at the face of her companion.

"I hope you enjoyed it," said Mrs. Miller, with a smile of interrogation.

"Yes, I did," demurely returned Margaret.

"Mr. Baldwin is a very nice young man."

"Yes, I think so," said Margaret, in the same quiet tone.

"Much nicer than the elder."

"Do you know, Kate," said Margaret, impulsively, "I almost hate that man?"

"Yet he loves you!"

"Loves me!" and Margaret's lip curled in scorn.

"Yes, he told my husband so last night, and wished to get him to aid his suit."

"What did my brother say?" asked Margaret.

"He told him that you were free to make your own choice, and that he should not attempt to control your feelings on the subject," replied Mrs. Miller.

"Why, Kate, I would rather die than be his wife," cried Margaret, the color mounting to her cheeks, and a gleam of anger in her eyes.

"Mr. Baldwin is a great deal better than dying," said Mrs. Miller, archly.

"Do you think so?" asked Margaret, with a smile.

"Yes; don't you?"

A silent bend of the head was Margaret's reply.

"The elder warned your brother against this young hunter; he says that he is a bad man and a Gentile."

"Well, I am a Gentile too, but the elder is eager enough to {55} marry me. I suppose he thinks it is a duty he owes to his church," said Margaret, scornfully.

"Oh, Margaret!" cried Mrs. Miller, with a shake of the head, "I'm afraid that you're in love with this handsome young hunter."

"I am," replied Margaret, frankly; "nay, more, I am engaged to be married to him."

"Well, well!" exclaimed Mrs. Miller, in astonishment. "Why, I didn't suspect that you had gone as far as that."

"Yes, he asked me to marry him last night, and I consented."

"Well, I wish you joy," said her sister-in-law, earnestly; "but where has Mr. Baldwin kept himself to-day? I've not seen him since we started this morning."

"Neither have I," returned Margaret. "I suppose he does not wish to excite remark by being too attentive."

Just at this moment, the Indian chief, Eagle Plume, rode up alongside of the wagon; behind him came the other Indian, the Yellow Wolf.

"Will the little white squaw talk with the chief?" asked the Indian, speaking English very plainly.

Though the maiden at first shrunk from the hideously-painted savage, yet his gentle manner, and the mild look of his full black eyes, that seemed strangely familiar to her, half banished her fear.

"Yes," she replied, "if the chief wishes to speak, I will listen with pleasure."

Lightly the chief swung himself out of the saddle, gave the bridle of his horse to the Yellow Wolf, and climbed into the wagon. The two girls made room for him, and he sat down upon the seat by the side of Margaret.

"The white squaw has a brave heart—good," said the chief, sagely. "Did the white squaw see the young hunter, who is not a Mormon, this morning?"

"Yes," replied Margaret.

"Ah!" eagerly cried the savage, and by the quick flashing of his eye, it was plainly to be seen that he was deeply interested. "When?"

"At the camp—before the train started—early this morning," said the girl. {56}

A look of disappointment was visible on the face of the red chief.

"Wah!" he exclaimed, slowly, "you have not seen him since?"

"No;" and Margaret wondered at the question. She could not comprehend the interest the savage took in her lover.

For a moment the chief was silent, apparently in deep thought. Then again he spoke.

"Did the hunter say he would hunt to-day?" asked the savage.

"No; he said he should not. He told me he would ride near our wagon all day," and a slight blush appeared upon her face as she caught the meaning smile of Mrs. Miller.

A puzzled look was on the stolid features of the Indian.

"He said he would ride near the wagon, and yet you have not seen him since you started?" questioned the chief.

"No; he rode by us a little way, and then the elder, Mr. Higgins, spoke to him; then he stopped his horse, the wagons passed by, and since that time I have not seen him."

"Wah!" and the eyes of the savage glistened as he uttered the exclamation; "with the elder, ah!" Then the Indian made a sign to the Yellow Wolf, who drew near with the horses.

"Good-by," said the chief, abruptly, as he sprung from the wagon to his horse's back; and then the two chiefs drew off a little to the left, and apparently commenced an earnest conversation.

"What a strange creature!" said Mrs. Miller, in astonishment.

"Yes; and how well he speaks English—as well as a white man," replied Margaret.

"It is really strange," responded Mrs. Miller; "and why is he so anxious to know about your husband—that is to be?"

"That of course I can not guess," said Margaret, with a smile at the term; then she happened to glance down at the seat by her side, that the savage had just left, and at the glance she started as though bitten by a snake.

"Why, Margaret!" exclaimed Mrs. Miller, "what's the matter? What made you start so?" {57}

"Oh, Kate, look there!" and she pointed to the wagon-seat. A single glance, and Mrs. Miller knew the cause of Margaret's sudden movement. On the smooth board that formed the wagon-seat was a drop of blood-red, clotted gore. "How could that get there?" cried Margaret, half in fright.

"Why, simple enough; it came from the Indian's knife. Didn't you see that he had a long knife in a scabbard by his side?—and the drop of blood probably leaked through the end of the scabbard," answered Mrs. Miller.

"Yes; but how could the blood come on his knife?"

"Why, he has probably killed some game this morning, and used the knife to cut it up."

"But it looks like human blood," said Margaret, with a shudder.

"Why, you silly girl, just as if all blood didn't look alike; you can't tell the difference," replied Mrs. Miller.

"Yes; I suppose what you say is true; but someway, the moment I saw it, it seemed to bring Henry before my eyes, wounded and dying. I know it's very silly of me to think of such things."

"I'll clean it away, dear, and then it won't annoy you." Then bustling Mrs. Miller removed the little drop of blood that had fallen, as she suggested, from the knife-scabbard of the chief. Yet, strange to say, though the blood dropped from his knife, the Indian chief, that morning, had killed no game—no deer, antelope, or buffalo had fallen beneath the shot of his rifle. Whence, then, came the blood—animal or human—that that morning had stained his knife?

The two chiefs rode on together in earnest conversation.

"He lagged behind the train with the Mormon chief; you remember when the chief rode up?" said Eagle Plume.

"Yes; it was just after that that one of the Mormon braves left the train to shoot at a wolf; you followed him," replied the Yellow Wolf.

"Yes; the brave has not returned," said the other.

"The white wolf has eaten him!" observed the young chief.

The two chiefs looked at each other meaningly. It was evident they perfectly understood each other. {58}

"Just before we came to Green river, the Danite chief and some four or five of his braves detached themselves from the train, and remained behind. After we crossed Green river, I missed them altogether. The Mormon chief has come, they have not."

"Ugh!" cried the Yellow Wolf, suddenly. "I remember now, I heard the sound of shots. I thought it was the whites after game."

"The white hunter is the game they sought; I am afraid they have been successful."

"Look!" cried Yellow Wolf. Dan and his Destroying Angels were riding across the prairie, toward the train. The Indians turned their keen eyes upon them.

As the Angels approached, the Indians noted the face of Red Dick, and the injury he had received.

"The white hunter has been ambushed," half whispered Eagle Plume.

"Yes, surprised, or he would have left more marks behind him," responded the Yellow Wolf.

"He may have escaped; his horse is good, his hand sure."

The Destroying Angels joined the train. Dick explained that he had been accidentally kicked by his horse, which appeared reasonable to all.

Then an antelope happened to appear far to the left of the train. The Indians noted it, and at once gave chase; pursued and pursuers were soon lost in the distance.

Once they were out of sight of the train, the warriors gave up the pursuit, and struck back again toward the trail of the wagons.

"My brother has made two trials?" the Yellow Wolf asked, as they rode swiftly over the prairie.

"Yes."

"Has my brother succeeded?"

"No!"

"No!" responded the Yellow Wolf in astonishment.

"No; the totem was not there. The man I seek is still alive!"

"Wah!" exclaimed the Yellow Wolf, thoughtfully; "that is bad. What is this man like?" {59}

"That I cannot tell, except that he has black hair, and is not quite as tall as I am."

"But he bears the totem?"

"Yes; there is no doubt about that," answered Eagle Plume.

"In time then you will find him."

"Yes. I have aimed too low; my bird is higher in the tree. I shall succeed next time," said the chief, in a cold, determined tone.

"Eagle Plume is not a child; he has the cunning and the bravery of the pale-face and Indian combined; he can not fail."

The other bent his head to the compliment.

"Where shall we ride?"

"To the ford of the Green river; it is the only place on the trail fit for an ambuscade. If the Mormon chiefs have trapped the white hunter, it is there that they have laid their snare," replied the elder chief.

"Good. In a few minutes we shall know."

"And if the white hunter has fallen beneath the knives of the Mormons?" asked Eagle Plume.

"Then the Mormon braves shall fall beneath the knives of the Dacotah warriors; one by one shall they fall, like the leaves of the forest, and their scalps shall hang and blacken in the Dacotah lodge, to show the vengeance of the Yellow Wolf."

———

Chapter IX.
THE FOOTPRINTS BY THE RIVER.

SWIFTLY the two warriors rode toward the wagon-trail; the trail once reached, they bent their course to the ford. Once there they dismounted, and carefully scouted over the ground. A few minutes' search and they discovered the spot where the Angels had lain in ambush.

"You see—one, two, three, four, five!" and the Yellow Wolf pointed to the traces of the ruffians. {60}

Then the chiefs crossed the stream; they noted the hoof-prints of the hunter's horse where he had left the river, eaten off the grass, and then again returned to the stream.

The shrewd instinct of the savages told them what had happened.

"He was ambushed as he was crossing the stream," said Eagle Plume.

"Yes, the hoof-prints were made by his horse coming from the stream, but he again entered the water."

"Probably the hunter fell into the stream; naturally the animal would return to the bank."

"But he again crossed the water."

"The Angels came for him; let us look on the other bank."

Then the two Indians recrossed the ford; they followed the trail, and soon noted where the two Angels with the riderless horse had left the others and struck off to the south.

"See!" said the Yellow Wolf.

"Yes, the hunter is—"

"In or by the river—let us look!" cried the younger Dacotah chief.

The two Indians carefully scouted down the stream, one on each side. They soon saw the traces where the Angels had been on a similar errand. Then the truth flashed upon them; the hunter had been attacked, had taken refuge in the river, and the Angels had been searching for him. It was plain, then, that the ruffians had not killed him outright.

An idea entered the minds of the two chiefs at the same moment. If the hunter had sought the water for safety, he would be more likely to go *up*-stream than down. So, speedily they retraced their steps; they passed the ford, and by the borders of the stream above it they sought for traces of the presence of the white hunter.

Carefully and earnestly they scouted along the river's bank. A hundred feet above the ford, the elder chief came upon the overhanging bank, from which the alders grew down, washing their leaves in the river. A sprig of alder, from which some of the leaves had been stripped, caught the keen eye of the lynx-eyed observer. He bent down and examined it; the twig had evidently been grasped by a human hand; another {61} glance revealed to the eyes of the Indian a little drop of blood on one of the leaves of the alder-bush: he had struck the trail—in frontier parlance, had "lifted" it. He signed to the Yellow Wolf on the opposite bank—that warrior immediately crossed the river.

Carefully the warriors examined the alder-twigs.

"He has been wounded," said Eagle Plume, pointing to the little spot of blood.

"Yes, he found shelter under cover of these bushes."

"He must have taken to the bank here somewhere; he is not dead."

Carefully the warriors proceeded up the stream: not a bush dipping its leaves in the running waters, not a blade of grass growing on the bank, escaped their searching gaze. A hundred feet or so beyond, the bank sloped more to the stream, and in the shrubbery that fringed it, the Indians came to a little open space; in the open space they found ample evidence of the presence of the hunter—the blades of grass here and there had been crushed by his feet and were sprinkled with drops of his blood; the crumbling bank, too, showed where he had emerged from the water.

The work of the two warriors was easy now—it was but to follow the footsteps, and thus trace the hunter to his refuge.

"He was not wounded bad," said the Yellow Wolf, pointing to the print of the hunter's feet; "you see, he walks straight."

"Yes," and then Eagle Plume swept his eye over the country before him, in the direction that the footprints went. His glance fell upon a little clump of timber some hundred yards or so from him—one of those little clumps known to the prairie-men as "islands." Toward this island of timber the footsteps tended.

"He is there," said the older chief, indicating the island by a sweep of his hand.

Swiftly the two Indians walked toward the little timber-clump, following the plainly-defined footprints.

They arrived at the refuge, but no motion within gave sign of life.

Eagle Plume parted the bushes with his hands and looked {62} in; a little open space met his eyes; in the center of that space lay, motionless, the senseless form of the young Kentuckian.

Silently and sorrowfully the two Indians knelt by his side.

———

Chapter X.
An Elder's Wooing.

Elder Higgins had noticed the approach of Dan and the Angels, and eager to learn if they had succeeded in their mission, he reined in his horse until they came up to him.

"Well?" he asked, impatiently.

"It's all right," answered Dan; "we've fixed him."

"Thank you—thank you!" cried the elder, joyfully.

"We shot him as he was crossing the ford of the river, and he tumbled into the stream."

"Very good, Dan. Now there is one other service that you can do me; I'll pay you handsomely for it," said the elder.

"Something private, then?"

"I'll tell you to-night, after we halt for supper. I haven't exactly made up my mind yet which is the best way to fix it. I can tell then," replied the elder.

"Well, let that pass now. Elder, two of my men have been killed."

"Two?" cried Higgins, in astonishment.

"Yes, the one last night that you saw, and another one this morning, killed not an hour ago and left on the prairie—both killed the same way, no mark of violence, except a red line around the neck."

The elder became thoughtful.

"Do you think these Indians have had any hand in it?" he asked.

"I don't know what to think," returned the Danite, gloomily; "two of my best men have been killed outright, apparently without even a struggle for their lives. When I think {63} the matter over, it seems as if the very devil himself must have had a hand in it. I say, elder, you had better be careful; it may be your turn next."

The elder's rubicund cheeks became white.

"I can't understand it," he said, and his lips trembled as he spoke. "I think I shall put some of the men on guard around my wagon to-night."

"Yes, you had better; but, if it is the Devil, it won't make much difference to him; he'll take you, guard or no guard," said the Danite, grimly.

"Don't be foolish!" exclaimed the elder, testily, but he trembled as he spoke, "our foe is a man."

"Well, if he is, he's got the courage and shrewdness of the Devil," returned Dan; "but, man or demon, I'll hunt him out. It is my life against his."

"Keep good watch to-night; you may discover him," suggested Higgins.

"Yes, my eyes won't close in sleep to-night, you may depend upon it," said the Danite leader, an air of determination in his manner.

"Well, I'll see you to-night about the little job I want fixed."

"I'm your man," returned the Danite.

The elder spurred up his horse, and again resumed his place by the side of Miller. The Danite, moody and abstracted, rode on a little apart from the train.

For once in his life, all the bravado of his nature was silenced. In his heart he cursed the unlucky chance that he placed this terrible foe upon his track, for he felt a presentiment that these two terrible blows, each one of which had cost a human life, was intended for him; the unknown foe as yet was striking in the dark, but light might come at anytime. The singular mark left on the arm—the two knife-cuts making the letter L—puzzled him.

"What can it mean?" he cried, moodily, to himself, as thoughtfully he proceeded on his way. The face of the young hunter would come up before him. Why he could not tell. He had certainly never before met the man, and yet there was something familiar in his face, voice, eye. Who {64} was he? But what had all that to do with that mysterious sign on the dead men's arms—the letter L? Yes, what? The Danite turned his thoughts back to former years. "No," at length he muttered, "the name is not familiar to me. *That* man could have had no interest in my past life. Stay!" he cried, as a sudden thought flashed upon him, "the name may be a false one! If so, what act of my past life would place him upon my track?" And the leader of the Destroying Angels thought long and earnestly. "It is useless, I can not guess; besides, what matters? He's out of the way; all I have to fear is this secret foe; he alone is dangerous." And so, with his mind busy with plans to outwit the invisible foe, whose blows alone were seen, the Danite rode moodily on.

When the train made the noon halt, the two Indians again joined it; when questioned as to their success in the hunt they said "nothing."

In the afternoon the train was again in motion. Higgins rode by the side of Miller and once more endeavored to get the young farmer to press his suit with his sister. Miller, although he frankly told the elder—whom he regarded as a bright and shining light of the Mormon church—that nothing would please him better than to have his sister marry him, yet he would not force her inclinations but should leave her free to choose for herself. With this answer the elder had to be content, but he resolved that that very evening he would propose to the pretty Margaret and endeavor to persuade her to become his wife; for a suspicion had taken possession of the sanctimonious scoundrel's mind, that without the girl's consent it would not perhaps be as easy to get her "sealed" to him, on their arrival in Salt Lake City, as he had thought. Margaret was very pretty, and there were men higher in power in the Mormon church than he; if she should happen—as was extremely likely—to catch their fancy, the elder felt that his chance was very far from being the best in the world. Like a beautiful ox or ass, she was liable to seizure and appropriation by any one of those above him in authority.

If Margaret should refuse to become his wife—as the elder was pretty certain that she would—then he had a scheme by which she might be won, and in carrying out that scheme, he needed the assistance of the Destroyers. {65}

So when the train halted for the night, the elder, after supper was over, took advantage of a favorable moment to approach Margaret and request the favor of a few minutes' private conversation.

The poor girl was ill at ease; she had not seen her lover since the morning, and his continued absence alarmed her. She felt sure that harm had come to him, and she looked upon the elder as the author, or at least the instigator of that harm. She went with him, then, with the same reluctance that she would have felt had a hyena offered to be her escort.

When they had walked out of hearing of the rest of the camp, the elder spoke.

"My dear Miss Margaret," he said, "I presume it is not unknown to you that I have taken a great interest in your welfare. You are a young lamb exposed to the wicked snares of this world. I, as a shepherd of the Chosen People, feel it my duty to bring you into the fold. My position in the church, of course you know; I am high in favor with the Prophet and rich in worldly goods, but richer still in the knowledge that I am an humble instrument in the great cause," and the canting tone of the Pharisee came out loud and strong. "I have spoken to your brother and he gives me his sanction. Miss Margaret, I would ask you to leave the Gentile faith and become one of the Chosen People. It is not good for man to be alone; therefore I would take you for wife and thus secure your eternal welfare."

To the pure young girl, brought up in the simple Christian faith, reared from child to girlhood under the truthful teaching of the good old minister, the pastor of the little Ohio village—a man kind and simple in heart as a child—preaching the "Word" with love toward all men, Jew or Gentile, Christian in heart, thought and deed—the phrases of the wily Mormon seemed like idle mockery, and each word that he spoke increased her loathing for him.

"Mr. Higgins," she said, slowly, "I am sorry that you have spoken in this way to me; I do not love you, and I must reject your proposal."

The Mormon elder looked any thing but pleased, although he had anticipated that his suit would be unsuccessful.

"Take time, my dear young lady, to consider the matter; {66} be not hasty; you can hardly know your own mind as yet," he said, in his smooth, oily accents.

"Time will not change my mind, Mr. Higgins," she replied coldly, annoyed that he would not take no for an answer.

"Ah, you don't know that, my dear young lady," he rejoined; "time does a great deal. And, as you do not love any one else, why, you may learn to love me."

"Suppose I do love some one else?" asked Margaret, provoked at his manner.

"It is not likely," he replied, coolly; "you may think you love some one, it is natural for a young girl to think so; but young ladies of your age seldom know their minds."

Margaret's eyes flashed fire at this cool, insolent remark.

"You may be certain, sir," she said, quickly, "that I know mine, and I am not likely to change."

"Ah, my dear child, we all change in this world. To give you an illustration: take the young hunter that has been traveling with our train, this Kentuckian called Baldwin; report says that he was in love with a certain young lady belonging to our party, and the foolish child probably thought that he really did love her and that she loved him; yet this morning, when he was mildly told that the course he was pursuing was wrong, and that if he continued in it, would probably bring down upon his head the vengeance of the Lord, he wisely gave up his purpose, left our train and started for the East."

The elder watched the face of Margaret keenly as he uttered this false tale, but, save a slight compression of the lips and a quick flash of the eyes, sign of emotion she showed not. The elder was disappointed. He had expected a passionate outbreak; the cool silence disconcerted him.

For a while they walked on in silence, the elder not exactly knowing what to say, for the girl's manner puzzled him.

As for Margaret she did not believe a single word that the Mormon elder had uttered. In her own mind she was fully satisfied that if the threats of the Mormon had compelled her lover to withdraw from the train, he was hovering near, and at the proper time would come and rescue her from the power of these bold, bad men.

Just as the elder had made up his mind to renew the conversation, Margaret turned suddenly around and announced {67} her intention of returning to the camp. Of course the elder could not very well object, and he was compelled to retrace his steps with her.

"You will think over what I have said, my dear Miss Margaret?" he asked in his blandest voice.

"It is useless," she replied, firmly. "I have already told you that I cannot love you and therefore can not be your wife."

The Mormon bit his lips; he was getting angry; but he kept back his passion although it was difficult to do so.

"This is your final answer, then?" he asked.

"Yes," she answered.

"You will not change?"

"No."

For once in his life the fluent-tongued elder was at a loss for words; bitterly in his heart he cursed the fair girl at his side, and he mentally swore that she should be his, if not by fair means then by foul.

The two reached the camp again. The elder conducted Margaret to the wagon of Miller, and with a bow left her and strode away to seek the chief of the Danites. He was too angry for words; he felt that he could not trust himself to speak, for his policy now was not to excite her suspicions until after he had played his next hand in this game of life, and that hand he felt sure would be a winning one.

———

Chapter XI.
The Elder Plays a Desperate Game.

The elder found the Danite just preparing to post his sentinels for the night. Contrary, however, to his usual custom, he placed them in couples instead of singly; he was taking the first move to checkmate the invisible demon that had already destroyed two of his band.

The elder accompanied him on his rounds till all the men were posted. {68}

"There," said the Danite chief, as he left the last couple, "if I lose a man to-night, it's the Devil I'm fighting against, and nothing human. Now, elder, I'm at your service."

"You know, of course, that I feel a very deep interest in this young girl, this Margaret Miller."

"That is, you want to make her your sixth wife," said Dan, bluntly.

"Exactly," replied the elder; "but the foolish child—"

"Prefers the young hunter to you?"

"Yes, I'm afraid so," said the elder, with a shake of his head.

"Well, how can I help you?" asked Dan.

"That's just what I'm going to speak about," replied the Mormon. "Of course you are well aware that there are many in Salt Lake City higher in the church than I am. Now, if this young and pretty girl goes into Salt Lake free, some of these men may take a fancy to her. I shall be powerless to resist, and so, though I have got the Gentile hunter out of the way, I shall lose her after all."

"That would be ugly."

"I should say so. Now, Dan, you are the only man who can place this girl in my hands."

"I?" and the Danite looked at the elder in astonishment.

"Yes, you," returned the elder, "if you will do so. And if you will aid me, I'll give you a hundred dollars."

"It's a bargain!" cried the leader of the Angels. "Now your plan?"

"It's very simple. You know my house in the city is remote from all others, being in the outskirts of the town. To-morrow night we make our last halt, for, on the following noon, we reach the city. Now, after we halt for the night to-morrow, let you and two or three of your men, disguised as Indians, burst into the camp, seize the girl, carry her off with you, bandage her eyes, put her in my house in Salt Lake, and the thing is accomplished; she's in my power, and I'd like to see anybody save her," and the little pig-like eyes of the elder sparkled as he unfolded his plan.

"It's a good idea," said the Danite, thoughtfully.

"Yes, I think it will work," responded Higgins, rubbing his hands together gleefully. {69}

"The dash will have to be quick."

"Of course. Arrange matters so that no one can interfere with you. You can seize the girl and be off before any one can even attempt resistance. No one will suspect the plot."

"And I'm to have a hundred dollars?"

"Yes," responded Higgins.

"It's a bargain. I'll carry off the girl for you," said the ruffian.

"Let the dash be made about nine o'clock. I'll call Margaret out of the wagon on pretense of wishing to speak with her. Then you can make a rush from the timber, fire a shot or two; I'll pretend to be hit, and tumble over; then you can carry off the prize."

"All right; you can depend upon me," replied the Danite, and so the pair of rascals separated.

The elder sought his wagon to rest for the night, while the Danite leader, rifle in hand, stole slowly and cautiously from picket to picket, intent on surprising the mysterious assassin. All night long the leader of the Destroying Angels kept his ceaseless vigils; his eyes closed not in slumber; the trusty rifle left not his grasp; his watchful ear caught every sound that floated on the still prairie-air; but, when the gray tints of the morning broke through the eastern skies, Dan was no wiser than he had been the day before as to the identity of the foe who had stricken to the death two of his assassin band.

When the pickets came in, Dan noticed that Dave Gindar looked pale and careworn; he, with one other, had been stationed on the prairie to the north of the camp.

Dan took the young man aside and inquired if any thing had happened during the night to alarm him. Dave at first seemed reluctant to answer, but after a little urging he spoke.

"Well, capt'n," he said, slowly, "if you must know, I think the devil or one of his imps was around my post last night. You know Bill was on guard with me. Well, he can't hear any more than a post. I guess it was about twelve or one o'clock; it got as dark as thunder, and it was hard work to keep sleep away. Just about that time I heard a slight noise {70} to the rear of us, between our post an' the camp. Of course I didn't expect danger from that side, but I just turned my head to listen."

"What was the sound like?" asked Dan, earnestly.

"Why, 'bout what a small dog might make stepping over the ground. I shook Bill, who was half asleep, and we both got up and went to where the noise was."

"And you found?"

"Nary thing; and then I heard the noise again, only this time it seemed to come just from the very spot that we had left; so Bill and I went back again, but there wasn't any thing there or any sign of any thing. Well, capt'n, as I'm a living man, I heard that slight noise, now in front of us, then behind us, then on the right side, then on the left side, for nigh an hour; it sounded just as if some creature was prowling around, waiting to get a chance to spring in upon us. Bill couldn't hear any thing, and said I was a fool and was dreaming it all; but, capt'n, I was wide awake. Then, about twenty or thirty minutes arter the noise stopped, I got kinder sleepy and was wishing that morning would come, when something inside of me said, 'Turn round.' I don't know exactly how it was, but it seemed just like a voice. Well, I turned round, an', capt'n, as I'm a living, breathing man this minute, right afore me, about ten yards on the prairie, was a dark figure. It looked nigh onto ten foot high, an' it had something in its right hand which was raised up just as if it were a-going to throw it at me. I leveled my revolver at it, though I mought have known that it wa'n't no use to fire at a spirit, an' just as I were a-going to pull the trigger, the dark figure sunk right into the ground! I tell you, capt'n, I shook just as if I had the ague. I made up my mind, though, to see if the thing left any thing arter it; so I went to where it stood, but there wa'n't a thing to be seen there."

The Danite chief listened attentively to Dave's story. He did not believe in the spirit part; but he was convinced that the man had seen the unknown enemy in the very act of casting the deadly lasso, which had already taken the lives of two of the band, and that accident alone had saved him from their fate. Then he noticed, too, that Dave's hair was black and curly. This invisible demon, then, struck only at men {71} whose personal appearance resembled his; that is, would have resembled his, had his hair been black instead of yellow.

"Come," he said to Dave, "show me where all this happened."

Dave led the way to the post he had occupied during the night.

Carefully the Danite chief examined the ground; at last his search was rewarded, for, on a little bare space of sandy loam, he found the full, clean impress of a human foot—a foot unshod by either boot or moccasin; not the foot of an Indian, as the Danite had expected to find, but the foot, evidently, of a white man—a delicate, finely-formed foot, not the broad, splashing one of the savage.

The Danite pointed to it.

"You see," he said, "your spirit leaves foot-prints. Try your revolvers on the next one, and if your aim be true, you'll find a body."

Once again the train was on its last day's march but one, and the hearts of the wayfarers grew glad as the journey grew short, and the city of the saints—the New Zion—the Mecca of the Mormon faith—drew near.

At noon, as usual, the train halted. The two Indians scouted out over the prairie, as if in search of game.

Half an hour or so afterward they returned, bringing with them a strange Indian.

The stranger chief was a tall, muscular-looking brave, oddly attired; his leggins had been made with the wrong side out, and were streaked with paint; his chest was bedaubed with war-paint, as was also his face; a red blanket was wrapped around the upper part of his body; his hair was quite short for an Indian, worn long behind and cropped across the forehead, in accordance with their custom; in it, feathers were thickly braided. There was quite a striking resemblance between the strange Indian and the Dacotah chief, Eagle Plume.

The elder, as captain of the train, approached the strange Indian.

"Big chief—found on prairie—come see Mormon braves," said the Yellow Wolf, introducing the stranger.

"Ah, does my brother speak English?" asked the elder. {72}

A grunt from the stranger answered the question in the negative.

"What nation?" asked the elder.

It was evident that the savage understood the meaning of the question, for he drew himself up proudly and replied:

"Ute!"

The elder started. The tones of the Indian's voice were strangely familiar to his ear. For a moment he gazed at the savage in astonishment, and evidently bewildered; but the savage looked at the elder without moving a muscle.

"It's very strange," muttered the elder, to himself. "I can swear I've heard that voice somewhere before. Chief," he said, addressing the stranger, "do you *understand* English?"

The savage nodded his head, as much as to say "yes."

"Ah!" The elder hesitated for a moment, and looked the savage straight in the face, with a puzzled expression. "Has my brother ever been in Salt Lake City?"

"Ugh!" the guttural grunt from the savage signified that he had.

"Oh!" and the brow of the elder grew clear again; he remembered that a delegation of Utes had visited Salt Lake City some time before, and it was there that he probably had heard and seen the fellow, for the savage's face, as well as his voice, was familiar to the elder.

"My brother is going to Salt Lake?"

Another grunt from the Indian conveyed the intelligence that he was going.

The elder, satisfied, left the group, for, by this time, quite a little knot of people had gathered around to look at the strange chief. Among the rest came Mrs. Miller, and Margaret. When the tones of the Indian's voice fell upon the ear of the young girl, she, like the elder, started in astonishment. She fixed her eyes searchingly upon the features of the dusky chief; a few moments she gazed, and then a smile of joy came over her face; for, despite the war-paint daubed upon the face—despite the altered fashion of the hair, her keen eyes discovered the truth: Love discovered the truth that hate passed blindly by.

With a beaming smile upon her lips, and new hopes spring- {73} ing fresh in her heart, as the Indian turned away with the other two, Margaret returned to the white-topped wagon, which was her home for the present.

Again the train proceeded on its way; the strange Indian, mounted behind the Yellow Wolf, following leisurely in the rear.

That night the cunningly-contrived plan of the Mormon elder for the abduction of pretty Margaret was to be put in execution.

During the afternoon march, the elder and the Danite leader had arranged all the details of the scheme. How the Mormon longed for the shades of night to come, that they might shut him and his prey out from the gaze of the world!

The train was halted for the night, as usual—the last night of the march, for the morrow would bring them to the City of the Wilderness—the Promised land for the Chosen People.

The train was "parked" for the night, the pickets, as usual, thrown out, the supper was prepared and eaten, and the emigrants began to prepare to retire for the night. By nine o'clock the entire camp was hushed in slumber.

It had been arranged that Grizzly Joe and Red Dick were to play the part of Indians, and carry off Margaret; the rest of the gang were to fire their weapons, and act as though they thought the camp surrounded by the red-skins. In the confusion, the two emissaries could easily escape, and when they were missed in the morning, all would imagine that they had fallen into the hands of the Indians.

All was favorable for the elder's plan.

Having seen that the bogus Indians were ready, concealed in a convenient thicket, the elder went to Miller's wagon. The family had not yet retired, but were seated on the ground by the team. The elder joined the circle; a short conversation followed, then the Mormon gave the signal—a slight cough—for the attack.

Joe and Dick, disguised as Indians, sprung from their concealment in the thicket. With a single blow they stretched Miller out on the ground, then Dick seized Margaret in his arms, and ran swiftly toward the two horses that stood by the little thicket. In a second, both he and Joe were in the saddle {74} and in full gallop for the open prairie. The elder shouted for help, and discharged his revolver in the air; the pickets, also, as had been arranged, fired their pieces, and came running into the camp, as if every red warrior of the Great American Desert was at their heels.

The camp was a Babel; the emigrants, expecting a terrible Indian attack every moment, gave themselves up for lost; the shrieks of the women and children mingled with the prayers and curses of the men.

The three Indians, who sat their horses like statues—for the stranger chief had procured a horse during the excitement—and waited, rifle in hand, for the attack, were about the only cool ones in the camp.

As no attack came at last, the excitement ceased; then, and not till then, did Miller discover that Margaret was missing.

The elder was loud in grief. Miller besought the Danite chief to send a force to rescue his sister, but the chief of the Angels refused.

"I have but a few men," he said; "the Indians may renew the attack at any time; for the sake of one shall I leave all helpless and unprotected?"

The emigrants, fearing for their own safety, protested loudly against endangering the whole train, and so Miller was forced to yield. The elder, however, consoled him, by assuring him that the moment they reached Salt Lake City, he himself would see a large force dispatched to rescue the helpless girl from the hands of the brutal savages. And all this while the elder was laughing in his sleeve at the apparent success of his plans.

———

{75}

Chapter XII.
The Three Friends.

Carrying the senseless girl in his arms, and closely followed by Joe, Red Dick spurred his fleet, powerful horse over the prairie.

On went the two ruffians for a mile or so, without a halt; then they reined in their steeds. Dick bound a bandage tightly over the eyes of the still senseless girl, and they again rode swiftly on toward Salt Lake City.

The emigrants' halting-place was only some thirty miles from the city, so that four hours hard riding brought the party to the house of the Mormon elder.

Margaret of course came to her senses long before that time but she did not for an instant dream but that she was a prisoner in the hands of the Indians.

Dick rapidly explained to the servant in charge of the house the wishes of his master. He, accustomed to obedience, at once conducted the captors and the captive to the room that the elder had designed as the cage for his lady-bird.

Stout bars were upon the windows, which looked forth upon a little thicket that hid from view the distant country.

The bandage was removed from the captive's eyes and she looked upon her captors. At a single glance she recognized them, and at once realized her position. She was not in the hands of the red savages—no, worse, in the power of the Destroying Angels!

"Now, little gal," said Dick, in his rough way, "jist make yourself comfortable hyer; don't try fur to git out, 'cos you'll only git badly treated if you do."

"Why has this outrage been committed?" indignantly demanded Margaret.

"Ax us no questions an' we'll tell you no lies," responded Dick, with a grin.

And with this consoling observation the two ruffians withdrew. {76}

Margaret sunk upon her knees in the agony of despair. Poor girl, her fate was, indeed, a hard one. She was helpless in the power of the Mormon elder—the man who, a coward at heart, crushed the weak and trampled upon the defenseless.

The two Angels had ridden fast across the prairie, but, fast upon their track came the three Indians, Eagle Plume, the Yellow Wolf and the Ute chief.

From the first these sagacious men had suspected that they were not following the trail of red warriors. The mode of attack was so unlike the Indian in character, the manner of their flight so foreign to the ways of the savages, that they at once suspected the plot: and then, the hoof-prints of the horses showed that they were shod with iron, something rare for the horse of the prairie Indian. The three were fully satisfied that the abductors of Margaret had white skins and not red.

Strange to say the Ute chief seemed most anxious in the pursuit, as he came first on the trail, while behind him followed the Yellow Wolf and Eagle Plume.

When the pursuers arrived at Salt Lake City, they were only some thirty minutes behind the two abductors, with their prey.

Near the city they lost the trail, as it was impossible to distinguish it from the numerous other hoof-prints leading into the town.

The three halted and held a council.

"Brothers, what do you think?" said the Ute chief, using most excellent English, although in the Mormon camp he had denied all knowledge of the tongue.

"The girl is in the hands of the Mormons," said Eagle Plume, slowly.

"That is plain," said the Ute chief. "Probably these two men are acting for Elder Higgins, but as we have lost the trail—"

"We can find it again," cried Eagle Plume. "When the elder comes to the city he will seek the girl. We will watch him and he will lead us to her."

"My brother speaks straight," said the Yellow Wolf in approval.

"Yes," replied the Ute chief; "he himself shall reveal to us the prison of his victim." {77}

And so, ambushing themselves in a clump of timber, the Indians waited for the approach of the wagon-train and the Mormon elder.

In due time the train arrived. As it passed the hiding-place of the Indians the Yellow Wolf spoke.

"Let my brother of the Eagle Plume follow the steps of the Danite chief; we will watch the Mormon brave."

"So be it," laconically replied the elder chief.

So into the city rolled the train, and after it came the three Indians.

Higgins and the leader of the Angels made their report to the Prophet of their journey, and then returned to the street.

"I'm going to see my beauty," said the elder, with a grin. "Will you come?"

"Yes, in an hour or so," answered the Danite.

"I expect the little beauty will be terribly angry, but I think I can tame her."

"At least you'll try," said Dan, with a cold, chilly laugh.

"Yes."

And so the twain parted—the elder to seek the prison of Margaret Miller, the Danite on his way to the head-quarters of his assassin band.

The house of the elder where Margaret was confined—for he had two, the other in the heart of the city, where he kept his five wives—was fully a mile from the house of the Prophet.

The reader will bear in mind that at the time of which we write, Salt Lake City had just been founded and was not the flourishing place that it is at the present day.

The elder at last arrived at the house, entered it, and went at once to the room where Margaret had been placed.

The two Indians, who had tracked him step by step, followed him to the very door, and then, as the closing portals shut the portly figure of the elder from their sight, they commenced a survey of the adjacent premises. The barred window of the room where Margaret was confined first caught their attention—the Yellow Wolf pointed it out to his companion.

Then the little clump of timber that fronted the window received their careful examination.

"From the trees we can look into the room," said the red chief. {78}

"Yes," replied the other, "let us see."

And with the agility of monkeys they ascended the tree; the foliage concealed them from view. As the chief had said, from the tree they commanded a view of the room. In the room was—as they had suspected—Margaret Miller!

The elder had just entered the room as the two Indians gained their position in the tree. Margaret had risen to her feet at the entrance of the Mormon, in indignant surprise.

"You are doubtless astonished at seeing me, my pretty dear," said the Mormon, insolently.

The hot blood of the girl tingled in her veins at his insulting manner.

"Perhaps, sir," she said, restraining her passion and speaking with cold dignity, "you can explain why I have been brought hither?"

"Of course I can, my dear," returned the elder, with a leer that made the heart of the young girl sink with terror. "In the first place I've had a revelation that commands me to take you for my wife."

"Your wife!" cried the maiden, hotly; *"never!"*

"Don't be in a hurry, my dear. Just wait till I ask for your consent, before you either refuse or give it. In this case I think we can get along without your opening your mouth at all."

"You will not use force?" cried the girl, in utter amazement, her pure mind unable to understand such baseness.

"Not if you consent willingly, my dear; of course not," said the Mormon, with a chuckle.

"And if I do not consent?"

"Why then, my dear, I'm afraid I'll have to do without it."

"Then it was you who had me carried away by these men?"

"Exactly! You see I knew that you didn't know what was good for you, so I thought it better to put you where you would not be able to act like a foolish child, and refuse the worldly advantages I offer you."

"Oh, but you will suffer for this when some one learns the truth!" cried Margaret, with spirit.

"I suppose you refer to the young hunter Baldwin, eh?" said the elder, with a sneer. "Allow me then to have the {79} pleasure of informing you that he is dead. He was drowned in the Green river the day before yesterday."

"You are wrong in what you say," said the girl, quietly, "for I myself saw him alive and well yesterday."

The elder stared at her in amazement.

"You are dreaming, girl; I tell you he is dead!" cried the elder.

"And I tell you, that it is you who are dreaming when you say that he is dead, for he is alive!" she said, firmly.

"Well, if you choose to believe it, do so if you think proper; but I tell you that he is dead; still it doesn't make much difference, for alive or dead he would not be able to aid you," and the lip of the elder curled scornfully as he spoke. "Now, my dear, I'll give you just one hour for reflection; at the end of that time you'll consent to be my wife or it will be the worse for you." And with this pleasant, parting salutation the elder withdrew.

Margaret's heart sunk within her. Was she indeed wholly in this man's power? Could nothing save her from the fate she dreaded far worse than death?

Mechanically she walked to the barred window and looked out upon the little thicket. Suddenly a face appeared before her eyes, half hidden by the leaves of the tree. 'Twas the Ute chief. He made a sign of encouragement, and then the face disappeared again amid the leaves.

Overcome with joy, Margaret sunk upon her knees and thanked heaven for the aid that thus, at the eleventh hour, had come to save her.

What of the Danite chief? After repairing to his headquarters and leaving commands for his men, he took the road that led to the house of Higgins.

Dan had no suspicion that his footsteps were tracked; but it was so, for Eagle Plume had dogged him like a bloodhound.

The Danite entered the house, and Eagle Plume sought the little thicket as a place of ambush. In the thicket he found the Yellow Wolf and the Ute chief.

A short consultation took place between the three. The two Indians told what they had seen from their ambush in the tree-top. {80}

"Wah!" said Eagle Plume at length; "we should be inside the house not out of it."

"How can we gain admittance?" asked the Yellow Wolf.

"I will knock at the door; the servant will come; one knife-thrust and the admittance is ours."

"Good; we will go," said the Yellow Wolf.

"Yes, for they might murder the poor girl and we on the outside would be none the wiser for it," cried the Ute chief.

All three proceeded to the door. Eagle Plume knocked once, low and cautiously, as he had noticed the Danite leader do.

The door was opened by Grizzly Joe. Perceiving the face of the savage he would have closed it again, but the attempt came too late, for the iron fingers of the chief had clutched him by the throat, stifling all groans, and the straight, powerful thrust of the scalping-knife, driven home by the strong arm of the savage, had let out his life in one deep, gaping wound.

Laying the body down in the passage-way, the chief bent over it for a moment, knife in hand, and then rising, led the way cautiously through the narrow entry, the Yellow Wolf and the Ute chief following.

At the foot of the stairs the three halted.

"You can find the room where the girl is confined," said Eagle Plume to the Ute chief; "go up there at once. We are more than a match for all that are in the house; the Yellow Wolf and I will remain below. A warning of danger will call us to your side. When all is safe for our escape I will let you know; do not attempt to move till then," said the chief, warningly.

"Be satisfied, I will not."

So, cautiously up the stairs went the Ute chief, while the other two Indians remained below.

The Ute chief, proceeding with caution, soon stood before the door of Margaret's prison. A key was in the lock, the chief turned it and entered the room. Margaret looked up expecting to behold her persecutor; her joy knew no bounds when she saw who it was that had entered the apartment.

"Henry!" she cried, and joyfully sprung into his arms. {81} As our readers have doubtless guessed, the Ute chief was the young hunter in disguise.

"You know me then, Margaret?" he asked.

"Yes; I knew you when you first came to the Mormon camp in this disguise; I recognized you at once; but tell me, what is the meaning of it?" and the young girl looked fondly into the face of her lover as she spoke.

Briefly, then, the hunter told of the attack made upon him by the Destroying Angels at the ford of the Green river.

"When the balls whistled around," he said, "I saw that I had but one chance for life, and that was to seek refuge in the river; so down into the water I dived, receiving a shot in the shoulder as I did so. I am a capital swimmer, so once under water I swam upstream as long as I could and then came to the surface close to the bank; taking a long breath I again swam under water still further up; this time I came to the surface right under some bushes that overhung the stream and they concealed me nicely. All this while, the Angels were watching the ford below, for me to reappear. Then at last they scouted down the stream in search of me. I did not dare to leave my ambush, for I expected each moment to see them return and search up the bank. At last they did return, but it was only to gallop off after the train, giving me up as dead. Then I essayed to leave my hiding-place, but I found that I was quite weak from the loss of blood from the wound in my shoulder, and it took all my strength to lift myself from the water. The bank once gained, I felt that my strength was fast leaving me. I noticed beyond a little cluster of bushes, and had just strength enough to walk to the clump and then I fainted. When I came to myself, I found my two Indian friends, the Yellow Wolf and Eagle Plume, bending over me. Under their simple treatment, I soon found myself quite strong again, for the wound in my shoulder was but a slight one. They procured me my disguise and suggested it, for I felt that I could not remain away from the camp and from you. Last night after the supposed Indian attack I found that you were missing; my Indian friends and myself at once followed on the trail and tracked you here, and, thank Heaven, we have come in time to rescue you from the power of these villains." {82}

"I shall owe my life to you," said the girl, earnestly.

"I've no doubt that when I ask for payment you will cancel the debt," said the hunter.

Margaret answered the question by again casting herself into the arms of her lover.

Chapter XIII.
The Story of the Danite.

Eagle Plume and the Yellow Wolf watched the Ute chief—or Baldwin, as we should call him—ascend the stairs. When he disappeared, the first-named turned to the Yellow Wolf:

"My brother, we must find some place of concealment where we can overhear all that goes on without being seen."

The Yellow Wolf nodded his head in the affirmative.

"Let us look."

They quickly discovered a dark recess under the stairs.

"It is good," said the Yellow Wolf, with an air of satisfaction.

And so the two chiefs hid themselves away in the gloom of the recess.

In the main room of the lower floor sat the Mormon elder and the Danite leader.

"Have you seen the girl yet?" asked Dan.

"Yes, about an hour ago," answered the Mormon.

"Well, how does she bear her captivity?"

"The girl has got a good deal of the devil in her," returned the elder. "She defies me."

"She does?"

"Yes; I shall have to use force with her, that's very plain."

"That's ugly," said the Danite.

"I've got a little scheme that I think will work. I'm going to drug a glass of wine and send it up to her; if she drinks she will fall asleep, and then I'd like to see any thing {83} or anybody save her from me," and the Mormon monster chuckled with delight as he spoke.

"You plan well, elder," said the Danite.

"Yes, I generally succeed," he answered, complacently.

"Well, I've always heard it said that the devil helps his own," said the leader of the Angels, sarcastically.

The Mormon laughed.

"Ah, Dan," he said, "you and I must be his chosen children, and a nice pair we are. By the way, this girl has got a strange idea in her head."

"Indeed? What is it?" asked Dan.

"Why, she believes that the young hunter, the Kentuckian, is still alive."

"The devil she does!" cried the Danite, in astonishment.

"Yes, she says that she saw him yesterday."

"Yesterday?"

"Yes, she is positive about it. Are you sure that you killed him?"

"Well, I saw him tumble off his horse into the river, and I'll swear he was hit, for the water was stained with blood," answered Dan.

"But, did you see his dead body?" asked the Mormon.

"No, of course not," replied the Danite; "don't I tell you that he tumbled off his horse into the river, mortally wounded, and of course his body sunk to the bottom."

"But, are you sure that he was mortally wounded?"

"Well, as sure as any man can be. I'll swear the ball from my revolver hit him, and I don't generally have to fire twice at the same man."

"Yet she declared that she saw him yesterday alive; she has no motive to tell a falsehood about the matter; by some means he must have escaped," said Higgins.

"It's not impossible," returned the Danite. "I've been in as tight a fix myself in my time, and yet got out of it."

"You think, then, that it is probable he may be alive?" said the Mormon elder, uneasily.

"Yes; if the girl says she saw him, you may depend upon it she did," replied the Danite, positively. "I say, elder, it will be an ugly reckoning for you to settle if the hunter is alive and calls you to account for this little business. Do you {84} think the girl is worth an ounce of lead or a slash of a Bowie-knife?" and the Destroying Angel smiled grimly as he put the question.

The Mormon elder grew pale at the very thought. Bravery was not one of his virtues—that is, if he possessed any virtues, which is doubtful.

"Well, I don't know," he said, slowly; "a pretty woman, to a man who cares for such things, is sometimes worth a great deal more than the mere risk of personal danger. I don't doubt that you've often risked your life for something of that sort."

"Yes, you are right," returned the Angel, "I have. It was a woman who made me what I am now, the leader of the Danites and the destroying sword of the Prophet."

"How was it?" asked the elder inquisitively. "I have never heard you speak of your past life; how was it that you came to leave the States?"

"Oh, it's the old story. I was clerk in a banking house in New York. I got into bad company, robbed my employers, was detected and obliged to fly. I came West; got in with a lot of gamblers, but nothing seemed to prosper with me; where other men won, I could only lose. Then I took a step downward, and joined a band of counterfeiters and horse-thieves. For the first time in my life I was successful. I became the head of the band; we operated in the river counties of Kentucky and Ohio. For five years we succeeded in baffling all the efforts of the officers of justice to capture us or break up our band; but, at last, the citizens organized a vigilance committee, and then it was all up with us; they hunted us down like wild beasts; the band was dispersed, and again I was obliged to fly for my life; this time, however, I had considerable money. It was a narrow shove for life, for descriptions of my personal appearance were circulated all over the country. I was obliged to disguise myself, but that was easy enough. I bought a bottle of hair-dye, and by the use of it turned my hair from its bright yellow into a deep black. Of course that entirely destroyed my identity. Why, I put up at the same tavern with the men who were in pursuit of me, eat at the same table with them, and heard them speculate upon the chances of capturing me. Finally I reached {85} a small town on the Mississippi river. I hadn't exactly made up my mind where to go, so I resolved to remain there a few days. During my stay in the town, I became acquainted with a young girl; she was about as pretty a creature as I ever laid my eyes upon. As was but natural, I took a fancy to her. She loved me, and at last consented to fly with me. I took her to Council Bluffs; in a short time I became wearied with her; she discovered that I was not exactly the angel that her fancy had painted me to be, and at last her tears and complaints made me angry. I resolved to get rid of her. As chance would have it, just as I had formed that resolution, a stranger whom I was fleecing at play one day accused me of cheating; I gave him the lie and a fight followed. My life had taught me to be quick with my weapons, and so I shot him dead on the spot. This was a little too much even for the citizens of Council Bluffs to stand; there was talk of a vigilance committee, so, to use the western saying, I 'lit out.' All this time, mind you, I had kept my hair black; but shortly after I left Council Bluffs I met one of my old partners from the Bluffs, who told me something that made it necessary again for me to change my name and personal appearance; so I shaved my head clean, and of course, when the hair grew out again, it was yellow, its natural color."

The Mormon elder had listened to the story with interest.

"What was the news you heard that caused you to do this?" he asked.

"I'll tell you," the Danite answered. "When I fled from Council Bluffs, of course I left the girl that I had brought with me, there, glad in fact to get rid of her. A short time after my flight, she—poor, weak fool—pined away and died. A gentleman, passing through the Bluffs when she was on her death-bed, in some way heard her story and went to see her. This man took a strange interest in the girl, looked after her as carefully as if he had been her own brother—she died in his arms; the man, they say, was almost wild with grief, and, by the body of the dead girl, he swore a terrible oath that he would hunt me through the world until he had avenged her death."

"Well, he did take a strange interest," said the elder.

"Yes; this threat of the stranger was the news my old {86} partner brought, and he advised me to look out for the man, for it was evident that he was in earnest. I came to Salt Lake City, joined the Destroying Angels, became their captain, and then I felt powerful enough to defy the malice of any one man, even if he were half devil."

"You have never seen this man?"

"No," replied the Danite; "but I have a presentiment that these two blows, each one of which has cost one [of my] men his life, were intended for me, and came from this man. I have noticed that both the men slain had black hair, such as mine was—and with such hair I was probably described to this person."

The elder gave a nervous shudder.

"It would give me the horrors to know that I had such a bitter, unrelenting foe on my track!" he exclaimed.

"Well, the feeling is not a pleasant one," returned Dan; "but why this stranger took such an interest in the girl puzzles me."

"Perhaps he was some distant relation of hers," suggested the elder.

"Oh, no!" cried the Danite; "the girl came of Kentucky stock. She had two brothers; the elder went off when a boy, and as he was not heard of afterward, was supposed to have died in foreign lands; the other was a hunter in the Rocky Mountain region. I have come to the conclusion that it was only one of those strange whims that sometimes seize upon men."

"What makes you think that these deaths are the work of this avenger?" asked the Mormon.

"Why, from the peculiar manner in which they have been killed," answered the Danite; "there are no marks of violence on the bodies, except a little red ring around the throat, and a couple of knife-slashes forming the letter L."

"I don't exactly see how, from such marks as these, you can lay the deed to the hand of this person," said the elder.

"Is it not plain that the men have been strangled to death?—strangled by a noose cast over their heads—and is not the lasso the national weapon of the Mexican?" asked the Danite. "This person, I was told by my friend, had but just come in from Santa Fé, and probably was a Mexican or Texan, in which case the lasso would be his natural weapon." {87}

"Yes; that is true," said the Mormon, thoughtfully. "It's a most mysterious occurrence. But how could he follow our train, and know the exact moment to spring upon his victim?"

"That's what puzzles me," said Dan, his brows darkening. "As I have said, it seems more like the work of a demon than that of a man."

"And what can be his idea in marking the bodies on the arm with the letter L?" said the elder.

"I cannot guess," answered Dan, shortly; but in this he lied, for, in his own heart, he had guessed the meaning of that mark—he knew the terrible warning conveyed.

"By the way!" cried the elder, suddenly, "that hunter Baldwin was a dangerous man; could he have had any thing to do with these mysterious murders?"

"No," returned the leader of the Angels, thoughtfully; "it is only one of those strange coincidences that sometimes occur in this world. I confess at first I suspected the hunter, but now I am satisfied that he had nothing to do with it."

"Well, it's strange!" cried the Mormon.

"Yes, it is; and the strangeness is what makes it so terrible. If I could see this foe that is striking such deadly blows at me, he would lose half his terror; but, as it is, I am acting in the dark. At first, I thought these two Indians—Eagle Plume and Yellow Wolf—had something to do with it; but the foot-print in the sand, that this secret demon left when in the night he hovered around our camp, was never made by the foot of an Indian. Besides, these red-skins have no motive."

"That's true," said the elder.

"I think, however, that, here in the city, I am safe from this man, or devil—whatever he is—that is tracking me so closely. He will hardly dare to come here."

"I gave the girl an hour to reflect upon her position," said the elder; "the time is about up. I guess I'll visit her, and see if she hasn't made up her mind to accept my offer."

"And if you find her still obstinate?"

"I'll try a nice little bottle of wine; that'll fix her," said the Mormon, with a chuckle.
{88}

"Well, I wish you luck. Take care that she don't cost you more than she's worth."

"What do you mean?" asked the elder, rising.

"Why, if the young hunter *is* alive, and learns the fate of his lady-love, he may seek vengeance upon you."

The Danite evidently desired to frighten the Mormon.

"I'll risk it," the elder replied with the air of a bravado, though his cheek grew a shade paler as he spoke.

"You may need help—just call on me," said the Danite, with a sarcastic smile.

"Help?" cried the elder. "Well, I think I can manage a single woman without calling in the aid of the Destroying Angels."

With this parting remark, the elder left the room and ascended the stairs to the prison of Margaret.

Arriving at the door he laid his hand on the lock; he saw, to his utter astonishment, that the key had been turned; the door, that he had felt certain he had locked behind him on leaving the room, was now unlocked. The elder was puzzled.

"The devil!" he muttered; "could I have been careless enough to have left it this way? I thought sure that I had locked it. I can't understand it."

A moment he remained in deep thought.

"It's all right, anyway," at last he said; "she couldn't have got out of the house, even if she had escaped from the room."

Then the elder opened the door, and entered. A single glance around the room reassured him. Margaret was seated by the little table exactly as he had left her upon his former visit.

The dull eyes of the elder did not notice the joyous gleam of the girl's dark orbs, the brightened color of her handsome face. All he saw was that she was there, in his power—at his mercy.

"Well, Miss Margaret," he said, casting glances of admiration upon her that made her blood tingle with anger in her veins, "the hour that I gave you for reflection has elapsed. I hope you have made up your mind to walk in the broad, straight path of righteousness, and forsake the evil ways of {89} the Gentiles!" and the elder devoutly rolled his eyes upward as he spoke.

"No, sir; I have not changed my mind in the least," answered the girl.

"I am sorry for it," returned the Mormon with a shake of the head. "I am sorry to see one so young wedded to the ways of Satan. Oh! young girl, let me take you by the hand and lead you in the path of grace;" and the elder advanced toward her as she spoke. A noise behind him stayed his footsteps; but, on looking around, he saw it was only the door of the little closet in the room that had swayed open a little.

Margaret had risen to her feet at the movement of the elder, yet, strange to say, she did not seem to be much alarmed.

"I have given you my answer, sir," she said; "and if you are a gentleman, you will be satisfied with it."

"Can you doubt that?" he asked, reproachfully. "Do you not see that I am actuated solely by a desire for your welfare, carnal as well as spiritual? Perverse girl, you are walking in the path of evil; you are a brand in the fire of iniquity; shall I not pluck you forth and save you from the fire eternal? Yes! I have had a revelation that commands me to make you my wife, and one of the chosen of Zion. Let me place upon your lips the seal of our faith, in a pure and holy kiss."

And with outstretched arms the Mormon elder advanced to the shrinking girl. Just as he thought his triumph secure—just as he was about to clasp her in his arms, he felt a hand of iron grip him by the throat; a second more and he lay on the floor beneath the knee of an Indian—whom he recognized as the Ute chief, and who held a glittering knife close to his throat. {90}

———

Chapter XIV.
Fate.

After the elder left the room, the leader of the Angels remained for a while in gloomy abstraction; his thoughts were busy with schemes to capture and destroy the terrible foe that he felt certain was following remorselessly on his track.

The entrance of Red Dick interrupted the Danite's meditations.

"I say, capt'n," said the ruffian, "have you see'd Joe any whar?"

"No," answered Dan.

"Yes hain't sent him off anywhar?"

"No," a second time answered the Danite chief.

"Wa-al, I can't find him round anywhar."

"Can't find him?"

"No, neither hide nor ha'r."

"He surely would not leave the house without orders!" exclaimed the Danite.

"That's jist what I thought, but I can't find him," returned Dick.

"Have you looked to see if the outer door was unfastened?" Dan asked.

"No, capt'n, I hain't."

"Let us see at once, then."

The two left the room and proceeded to the outer door; close by the door, lying on his back on the floor, they found Grizzly Joe—dead.

The two men looked at each other in terror.

"Who can have done this?" cried the leader of the Angels.

"The devil himself I should think!" said the burly ruffian, in a subdued tone.

"See if the door is locked!" cried Dan.

Dick obeyed the order.

"No, capt'n, it's unlocked!"

"The man then who did this deed has evidently escaped; {91} and to kill Joe so quietly, without even a struggle to alarm the house, I cannot understand it," said the Danite, slowly.

Dick knelt down by the side of the body.

"One straight poke settled poor Joe, an' on the throat, capt'n, there are marks as if he had been choked."

"Look on the left arm!" cried Dan, a dim fear beginning to take possession of him, that the invisible foe had again been at his deadly work.

Dick whistled in astonishment.

"What's the matter?"

"Why, the sleeve has been slit open from the wrist to the shoulder, and on the muscular part of the arm two knife-cuts make the letter L."

Cold drops of sweat stood on the forehead of the leader of the Destroying Angels; 'twas the third time he had heard that announcement—the third time that the secret foe had marked his victim! The blows were coming nearer and nearer; the Danite had a presentiment that the next one would be aimed at his own life. The now desperate man mentally asked himself if there was no escape from this invisible demon.

"What do you think of it capt'n?" returned the ruffian.

"I don't know what to think," returned Dan, moodily.

"P'haps the elder may know something about it," suggested Dick.

"No, it is not likely. How Joe could be killed without even a struggle I cannot understand."

"Why, they caught him by surprise and put a knife into him afore he had time to holler; it must have been a powerful big feller, and as strong as a bull, to have given him this dig."

"Remain here and keep your eyes on the door while I see the elder. This matter must be explained; we must discover this demon or he'll murder us one by one."

Saying which the Danite went up-stairs and left Dick alone with the body—a position he by no means relished, for, like all bullies, he was superstitious and at times cowardly.

"Blazes!" he muttered to himself as his leader disappeared up the stairs, "if I stay hyer what's to prevent the fellow what give Joe this ugly poke from coming and giving me one too? Keep my eyes on the door, he said. Wa'al, I kin do that outside as well as in, so I'll jist git out; if any one tackles {92} me thar, I shall have room to either fight or run as the case may be—I ain't goin' to stay here no longer, that's flat." So the prudent ruffian opened the door and placed himself as a sentry outside. Scarcely had the door closed behind him when the two Indians emerged from their hiding-place under the stairs and noiselessly and with extreme caution followed in the footsteps of the Danite chief up the stairs.

We will now return to the Mormon elder, whom we left prostrate on the floor, held down by the knee of the Ute chief.

The astonishment and terror of the elder at his sudden downfall knew no bounds, and the glittering knife put close to his throat, coupled with the threatening eyes of the Indian, did not tend to lessen his fright.

"Utter a single sound, you infernal villain, and the knife is in your throat!" hissed the savage.

The elder opened his eyes still wider in astonishment. The few words revealed all to him; he knew why the voice and face of the Ute chief had seemed so familiar to him; he knew now—too late—that the Ute brave was the hunter Baldwin in disguise; he uttered a suppressed groan; he knew that he was fully in the power of the man to whom he had shown no mercy, and it was not likely that mercy now would be shown him.

Baldwin's sudden appearance is easily explained; he had heard the elder coming up the stairs and unwilling to risk a contest until he knew the number of his foes, had taken refuge in the closet; from that convenient ambush he had been able to spring upon the Mormon elder unperceived.

"You are the hunter, Baldwin," murmured the terror-stricken elder in a whisper, afraid to speak loud lest the terrible knife should enter his throat and put a stop to his talking forever.

"Yes," said the hunter, "I am the man whom you and the Destroying Angels attempted to assassinate, and I am an avenger now of my own wrongs and those of this outraged girl."

"No, no!" murmured the elder; "I had nothing to do with it, I assure you."

"You lie!" said the hunter, sternly.

"No, no!" said the elder, fearing his last hour had come; "I did not injure you." {93}

"No, you were too cowardly to expose your precious person, but you paid others to attack me. The Destroying Angels only carried out your orders; they were your tools, you black-hearted villain," and the quivering Mormon felt the keen point of the steel prick his throat, and his usually red cheeks were as pale as a sheet.

"Oh, spare me!" he moaned. "I will do any thing for you, only spare me!"

The hunter gazed with contempt on the white face of the trembling wretch.

"Will you swear never again to persecute this girl with your attentions?" demanded the hunter, sternly.

"Yes, yes," replied the elder, willing to swear to anything, willing to do any thing to save his body from harm.

"You promise never again to molest this young lady, or to mention what has taken place here to-day?"

"Yes, yes; I will do any thing you wish." The elder thought he saw a chance for life.

"Now, then, I am going to let you up; but, mind, if you utter a single sound to alarm the house, I'll drive my knife through your foul body," said the hunter.

"I won't speak above a whisper," replied the elder, humbly.

The hunter rose to his feet; crestfallen, the elder followed his example. He saw that his prey was about to escape him; he could only prevent it at the risk of personal damage, and that risk the elder did not dare to encounter.

The hunter saw that triumph was within his grasp; by the aid of the Mormon— that aid which he should force him to grant—he and Margaret could easily escape from the house.

"Now," said the hunter, but his speech was cut short by the sudden opening of the door and the entrance of the Danite chief. The chief of the Angels comprehended the situation in a moment. With the spring of a tiger he dashed upon the hunter and bore him to the floor. Taken by surprise Baldwin did not have a chance to use his knife. The Danite's grip was like that of a vi[s]e; powerful as was the hunter he was no match for the leader of the Destroying Angels; the elder, too, lent his assistance; he procured a small {94} piece of rope from the closet, and the two bound the hunter's arms tightly behind him; Margaret, woman-like, had fainted at the beginning of the struggle.

The hunter lay upon the floor, bound; and the Danite leader stood by him with a grim smile. The elder bore the fainting girl and laid her down carefully upon the bed; the tables had turned and she was again in his power.

"Who is this fellow?" said Dan, for he had not recognized the hunter.

"Why, the hunter Baldwin!" exclaimed the elder.

"Ah!" cried the Danite, "so it is! You escaped me the other day at the ford of the Green river. I hardly fancy that you will be able to repeat that operation a second time."

The hunter replied not to the taunt.

"By the way, I believe you are in search of a certain man, who, you think, is one of the Destroying Angels; is it not so?" asked Dan.

"Yes," coldly replied the hunter. "How knew *you* of it?"

"What is the reason that impels you to seek this man?" questioned the Danite, without replying to the hunter's question.

"Why should I tell *you?*" asked the hunter.

"Because I can aid you in your search," replied the chief of the Angels.

"You?"

"Yes, I!"

"Do you think I am a fool?" said the hunter. "I know very well that alive I shall never leave this place. You wish my death; I am in your power; I must suffer."

"And you are content, eh?" said the Danite, with a sneer.

"Because I can not help myself."

"Granting what you say be true—that you will never leave this place alive—which is likely, what matters it whether your secret is known or not?" asked the leader of the Angels.

"True," answered the hunter, "it does not make much difference; and in that case, I may as well hold my tongue as speak."

"Perhaps," said the Danite, slowly. "But I had an idea that it might be some gratification to you to see the man you {95} are in search of, even though your mission was fruitless. Besides, you may escape from our hands; I don't think it likely that you will; but still, you may. Some strange chance may aid you; you will then know all you seek to know, if you speak now."

The hunter looked at the Danite keenly.

"Why are you so anxious to learn my secret?" the hunter asked.

"A whim of mine, that's all; all men have strange fancies at times, you know," answered Dan. "You seek a man who bears on his left arm the letter L in India ink?"

"How did you know that?" asked the hunter in unfeigned astonishment.

"Never mind," replied Dan. "Enough that I *do* know it. Do you not seek such a man?"

"Yes," said the hunter, "I do."

"I'll make a bargain with you," cried the Danite. "Tell me why you seek this man and I'll show him to you."

"Here?"

"Yes, here."

"Then, listen, for it's a bargain. The man who bears on his left arm the letter L pricked in with India ink, I seek because he is the heartless villain who robbed me of a sister, and broke her heart by desertion," said the hunter, in a low, deep voice.

The Danite started as though bitten by a snake; he looked at the hunter earnestly.

"What was your sister's name?" he asked.

"Ethel," answered the hunter.

"Ah!" and again the Danite started; "your name then is not Baldwin?"

"No," replied the hunter, "my name is Henry Hastings. And now," he continued, "fulfill your promise; show me the man that I have tracked across the prairie."

"Look at me," said the Danite.

"Well?" questioned the hunter.

"I am the man you seek!"

"You?"

"Yes, I! I am Luther Hardwicke; I confess I did wrong your sister," said the Danite. {96}

"You are lying!" cried the hunter.

"No, I speak truth; you are in my power, therefore I do not fear you, and so I speak freely. You have trailed me as the sleuth-hound tracks its prey, and the path has led you to your death. You think I am deceiving you; see!" Then the leader of the Angels stripped off the hunting-shirt that he wore, rolled up the left sleeve of the flannel shirt, and exposed his arm bare to the elbow. "See!" he cried, "the mark you seek!" and there, plainly imprinted on the arm in blue, was the letter L. "Will you believe me now?" cried the Danite. "Again I tell you I am Luther Hardwicke, the betrayer of your sister, Ethel Hastings, and your executioner."

Triumph swelled the voice of the leader of the Destroying Angels as he spoke.

"Luther Hardwicke, horse-thief, betrayer of innocence, murderer, you have spoken the words that seal your doom!" cried a loud voice, intense with hate.

All turned; in the door-way, knife in hand, stood the Indian, Eagle Plume, while close behind him came the Yellow Wolf.

"The Dacotah chief! What mean you?" questioned the Danite, thunderstruck at this sudden appearance.

"You are wrong; I am not a Dacotah, but a white man like yourself. I am the so-called Mexican in whose arms your victim, Ethel Hastings, died. I am the man who has followed on your track like an avenging demon; three of the Destroying Angels have fallen beneath my knife, mistaken by me for you; on each dead ruffian have I left my mark, the letter L; to hunt you down I became a Dacotah, but now my mission is ended. Devil that you are, your last hour has come! I am the elder brother of the girl you murdered—my name is Edwin Hastings—prepare for death!" and then, with the bound of the tiger, the avenger sprung upon the Destroying Angel. A single knife-thrust—vain was the attempt to parry the terrible blow—and Luther Hardwicke fell dying to the floor; a few convulsive motions and the guilty soul of the bold, bad man, the leader of the Destroying Angels—the Danite chief—fled from the earth to meet its Judge.

Calmly and grimly Edwin Hastings watched the death-throes of the leader of the Angels. {97}

The elder, Higgins, had looked upon the scene with speechless terror.

Margaret by this time had recovered her senses, and seeing the two men, and her lover free—for the Yellow Wolf had unbound him—she knew that she was saved.

Warm was the greeting between the two brothers who had been separated so long, but whom a common cause had brought together.

Eagle Plume, or Edwin Hastings, as we should call him, made preparations for an instant departure.

The elder was locked in the room that had served as the prison for Margaret, for both the brothers disdained to strike at the life of such a cur as he had shown himself to be, and he was warned that if he gave an alarm, within, at least, two hours, it would be the worse for him; then by the door leading from the rear of the house the party gained the open air.

In the city they procured their horses, and in an hour after leaving the house of the Mormon elder, the little party were in full gallop over the prairie eastward.

"Will not the Angels attempt a pursuit?" asked the younger Hastings.

"Let them, and they will be met by all the red warriors of the Dacotah nation," was the stern reply of the adopted son of that tribe.

But the Mormons did not attempt a pursuit. Higgins was only too glad to have the entire matter hushed up, for he dreaded the vengeance of the Dacotahs.

The Yellow Wolf and Edwin Hastings accompanied the young hunter and his promised bride to the Missouri river, opposite Council Bluffs, and there turned their horses again toward the prairie. During the journey, Edwin Hastings had told how, in returning home from New Mexico, he had accidentally met his sister abandoned by her destroyer, and of his oath of vengeance and search for the villain; how he had become one of the sons of the Dacotah tribe to aid in the search.

"Will you not come home with us, brother?" Margaret asked, as they were about to part.

"No, my home is there," and Eagle Plume—to give him {98} his Indian title—pointed to the west, where the setting sun tinged the clouds with ruddy light; "the Red Fawn waits for her lord by the shadows of the great mountains; my heart now is red; I am a Dacotah warrior, and I will live and die on the prairie. Good-by!"

And the two chiefs soon disappeared in the distance.

Henry Hastings and Margaret were married, and soon settled down in the pleasant Illinois village—Hastings' early home—that nestled on the bank of the great Mississippi.

Miller and his wife settled contentedly in Salt Lake City; Miller became Mormon throughout, and wives were "sealed" to him; and though Kate, his first wife, made no complaints, and seemed contented, yet her cheek is paler far than when she dwelt, the wife of a poor man, in the Ohio village.

The Mormon elder, Higgins, attained to a high position in the church, and became a shining light for the young men of the New Zion.

Years after the time of our story, when the Prophet, Young, became embroiled with the United States Government, and war was expected, he sought the aid of the powerful tribe of Dacotahs. His treaty of alliance was rejected, solely through the influence of two great warriors, the Yellow Wolf and Eagle Plume.

THE END

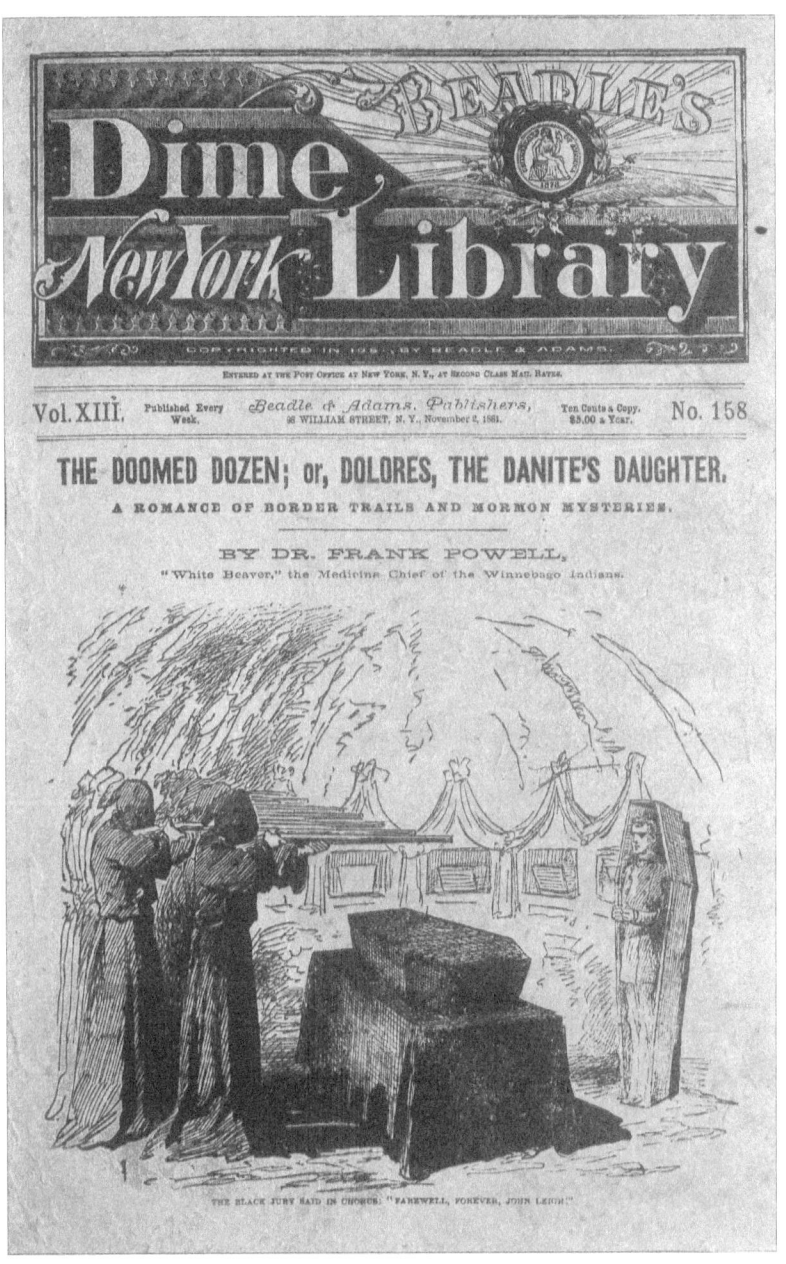

Dr. Frank Powell [Prentiss Ingraham]. *The Doomed Dozen; or, Dolores, the Danite's Daughter. A Romance of Border Trails and Mormon Mysteries*. Beadle's New York Dime Library, no. 158. New York: Beadle & Adams, 1881.

THE DOOMED DOZEN;
or,
DOLORES, THE DANITE'S DAUGHTER.

A Romance of Border Trails
and Mormon Mysteries.

By Dr. Frank Powell,
"White Beaver," the Medicine Chief of the Winnebago Indians.

[Illustration: The Black Jury Said in Chorus: "Farewell, Forever, John Leigh."]
{2}

Chapter I.
The Suicide's Daughter.

"Dolores, I love you."

The words were breathed forth with impassioned earnestness from the lips of a man.

They were addressed to a young and beautiful girl, whose face betrayed no pleasure at the utterance of her companion, but rather pain.

The two were standing in the conservatory, opening from a parlor furnished with a luxurious elegance that indicated the home of wealth and refinement.

The man wore the undress uniform of a captain in the army, and his face was noble in expression, resolute and handsome, his form above the medium h[e]ight, and indicative of strength and activity.

The lady was youthful, scarcely eighteen in fact, attired in a dark silk, with long train, that fitted her faultless form to perfection.

Her face was exquisitely lovely, and of an Italian type of beauty, that was in fine contrast to the blue eyes and golden hair of her companion.

"I am sorry, very sorry, Captain Moncrief," was the low reply.

"Sorry! sorry that I love you, Dolores Moultrie?" he asked reproachfully.

"Yes, Captain Moncrief, for yours is a hopeless love, and, knowing your noble nature well, I am sorry to give you pain, for you and I can never be more to each other than now we are."

She spoke firmly and looked him squarely in the eyes, though her face was very pale, and her lips quivered slightly.

"Will Miss Dolores Moultrie kindly inform me why we cannot be more to each other than the friends we now are?" he asked with a tone of sarcasm.

"Why will you not take my word that we must remain friends, and not force me to say more?" she asked pettishly.

"I will tell you why, Dolores.

"One night, now ten years ago, I saw a woman spring from the deck of a Sound steamer, with a child in her arms.

"Her pale, sad face, when I saw her in the cabin, had touched me, and seeing her take her little girl by the hand and go out upon the after deck in the storm, for it was blowing hard, I followed her.

"I heard her words:

"'God forgive me! but it is better so; yes, better so!'

"Then, ere I could prevent, she seized her child in her arms and sprung into the tempest-lashed waters.

"I called loudly for help, tore a life-preserver from the rack overhead, and bounded after her.

"The officer on duty heard my cry, saw my act, and ordered the steamer stopped immediately and a life-boat launched.

"I had, in the mean time, reached the drowning woman and her child, and fastened the life-preserver around the former, while I took the latter in my arms, at the same time loudly hailing the boat, to show where we were.

"The woman seemed determined to die, and was unconscious when taken into the boat; but the little girl did not mind her ducking in the least.

"While I was changing my clothes in my state-room the stewardess came for me and said the lady was conscious and wished to see me.

"I obeyed her request, and found her dying.

"But she had strength enough to beg me to care for her child, gave me her purse of money, and that is all I knew of her, other than that I could see that she was a lady.

"I pledged my word to care for her child, and carried her to my mother's, and she took the little girl into her heart and her household.

"Dolores, I was then just twenty, and had graduated a week before at West Point.

"That was ten years ago, and in all that time the image of that little girl has been in my heart, and now you tell me that we cannot be more than we are, friends.

"No, no, Dolores Moultrie, I love you, and if you have not, while I have been on the frontier, fallen in love with another, you shall be my wife."

"Would you have me marry a man I do not love, Howland?" she asked calmly.

"No, no, not that, not that; only I was vain enough to think you did care for me, for when on leave at home, each time you have treated me so kindly. You do not love me then, Dolores?" he asked in almost piteous tones.

"Only as a brother, Howland," she faltered.

"Ah, Dolores, I have deceived myself most cruelly."

"I owe you my life, Howland, and never can I forget you; yet never can I be your wife," she said firmly.

"So be it, if you say truly that you do not love me."

"I do not love you, Howland."

He bowed his head an instant, his form quivering with suppressed emotion, and then taking her hands he drew her toward him, pressed a sudden, impulsive kiss upon her forehead, and said:

"That is my farewell to love, Dolores; henceforth we are friends only."

"Yes, friends only."

He made no reply, but turning away, left the conservatory and walked hastily across the lawn.

As he departed, another approached and joined Dolores, whose face was white, and whose lips were quivering, while her tiny hands were clasped close together.

Chapter II.
The Secret.

The one who approached Dolores, when Captain Howland Moncrief left her, and, unseen by the maiden, glided out from behind the heavy velvet curtains in the parlor, where she had been hiding and heard all that was said, was a stately woman, with a cold, proud face, and the air of one born to refinement and riches.

Dressed superbly, and sparkling with diamonds, for it was near the dinner hour, Mrs. Marmaduke Moncrief swept up to where Dolores stood, the very picture of despair, and said in a soft, velvety tone that had in it not one atom of sympathy:

"Dolores, my sweet child, you have done well, for I heard all."

She kissed the maiden as she spoke, and lowered her eyes before her gaze fastened upon her, as Dolores replied:

"I did as you demanded, madam; I sacrificed myself and gave pain to your son, that your ambitious views regarding him might be gratified."

"Dolores, you forget yourself," said the lady, sternly.

"No, Mrs. Moncrief, I do not forget that I have no claim upon you, and that I came to your house with only my name, and not even knowing whether I have a right to that.

"No, no, madam, I have lived on your charity for ten long years, and, in your way, you have been very kind to me.

"But I sinned in loving your son, and for that sin you have punished me.

"Now I will no longer than to-morrow burden you with my presence, for I can teach, I've music lessons, paint, and in many ways earn an honest livelihood, while the little money my poor mother had in her purse will support me until I can make sufficient to support myself.

"I thank you, Mrs. Moncrief, for all you have done for me, and one day hope to repay it."

"Dolores, are you mad?" cried the woman, evidently frightened at the determination of the maiden.

"No, madam, I am sane," was the haughty reply.

"But you cannot, shall not, leave this house."

"Pardon me, but I will do as I please in this matter, having acted to please you in one that was a more important step."

"But Howland will not permit you to go."

"Captain Moncrief has no claim upon me, madam."

"Oh, Dolores, I beg of you not to leave me, for Howland will be furious," and it was evident that the lady feared her son's just wrath, should he know that his mother, to have him marry her choice, a silly young heiress, had urged upon Dolores to refuse him, telling her that she was but a charity child, and none knew who her parents were.

But Dolores Moultrie, for such she had said was her name, had a proud heart and iron will, and that night, when all was quiet, crept out of the elegant mansion, carrying with her only a small valise in her hand, and going forth into the cold world friendless and alone, determined never again to cross the threshold of the house of Mrs. Moncrief, who so bitterly had made her feel all that she was, as soon as she knew that her son had learned to love the little waif whose life he had saved and whom he had begged his aristocratic mother to care for, for his sake.

CHAPTER III.
MOTHER AND SON.

CAPTAIN Howland Moncrief sauntered into the breakfast-room, a cloud upon his brow and a haggard look in his eyes, for he had slept little during the night, the pain at his heart of unrequited love being with him more than a passing emotion.

He had not seen Dolores since their parting in the conservatory, as she had excused herself from dinner on the plea of indisposition, and he started at the rustle of a dress in the hall.

But it was his mother, and, though she tried to look cheerful it was evident she did not feel so.

He greeted her affectionately, and at the same time asked:

"How is Dolores, mother?"

"I have not seen her this morning."

"Indeed!"

Stepping to the bell-rope, Captain Moncrief gave it a decidedly hard pull.

"Benson, send Judith to Miss Moultrie's room and ask her, with my compliments, how she is feeling this morning, and if we are not to see her at breakfast?"

The servant obeyed, but Judith soon returned with the startling statement that:

"Miss Dolores was not in her room, and the bed had not been slept in."

At the same time she handed the captain a note.

He took it with trembling fingers and white face, and read, as the girl left the room:

"Captain Howland Moncrief:

My Dear Friend—After all your kindness to me in the past, it is a poor return for me to steal from your home in the night like a guilty creature; but I do so for the wellfare and happiness of us all, as I cannot longer remain beneath this roof.

"As we will never meet again, you may ask your mother why I leave.

"With a heart full of thanks for all that I owe you, and wishing you a life of happiness,
            "Your friend ever,
                    "Dolores."

Twice he read the letter aloud, and then said:

"Mother, what does this mean?"

His voice was low, earnest and stern, and Mrs. Moncrief felt that she had gone too far; but she was determined to have it out, and said coldly:

"It means that in return for our devotion to her she has left our home for some one's protection she doubtless likes better."

"But whose protection, mother?"

"She had many admirers, and I intended to marry her off well; but she has chosen differently."

"Mother! not one word against Dolores; do not dare to cast one aspersion upon her, or I will leave this house forever.

"I told you that I loved her and intended making her my wife; but alas! she refused my love, and she has left this house.

"Now, I ask you, mother, what does it mean?"

She saw that her son was in deadly earnest, and she went into tears, while she cried:

"Howland, my son, my love for you prompted me not to encourage her ambitious hopes, for what is she, who is she, but a nameless beggar?"

"Silence, mother! not one word, I say, against that girl; I took her from the waves, when she was drowning, and I pledged her dying mother that I would be a brother to her—"

"A brother, yes, my son, but you wished to make her your wife."

"True, and would have done so had she not refused my love.

"By heaven! but I believe you caused her to do so, for Dolores was no hypocrite, and up to yesterday certainly showed that she cared for me."

"But, Howland, I have other views for you, {3} and I have already pledged you to Judge Ortelle for his daughter Ada."

Captain Howland Moncrief said something, *sotto voce*, that sounded very much like:

"D— Judge Ortelle and his daughter too."

But aloud he said:

"I am my own master, mother, and shall place my love where I please.

"You would have me marry a silly bundle of frills and false hair, paint and powder, because she is an heiress to millions, rather than a noble girl who is poor.

"But I choose otherwise, and I tell you frankly, as you have driven Dolores Moultrie from your home, I go also, to return only when you have brought her back."

The mother pleaded earnestly, but Howland Moncrief left the breakfast-room and the house, and half an hour after an expressman called with a note to his *valet* to pack up his baggage and join him at a hotel.

In despair Mrs. Moncrief knew not what to do, for she dearly loved her son; he was the idol of her worship, and ordering her carriage she sought him at the hotel.

But he would not yield; said his leave of absence was about up and he would start West that night to join his regiment in Wyoming; but that when Dolores Moultrie was again in the Moncrief mansion he would return.

"But, Howland, what shall I say to Judge Ortelle and Ada?"

"Tell him to go to Jericho and take his brainless daughter with him," was the rude reply.

And thus the mother and son parted.

The son to go West to join his command in the Indian country; the mother to bury her ambitious hopes of trebling her son's already large fortune, and to set to work to find and bring back Dolores Moultrie to the home from which she had driven her.

Chapter IV.
A Wolf in Sheep's Clothing.

Upon the return of Mrs. Moncrief to her elegant, but now desolate home, she found awaiting her a gentleman whom she had met in society, and the very one whom she had selected for Dolores to marry.

He was a man of courtly manners, passed forty evidently, though he appeared younger, had a dark, intelligent face, and though a favorite in society, none seemed to know his antecedents, and his own word was taken for it that he was a Western cattle king, and possessed vast wealth.

Mrs. Moncrief, a dashing widow herself, and an artist in making her fifty years seem but thirty-eight, had "set her cap" for this stranger, Mercer Aldrich.

But he was not to be caught, the widow soon saw, by any one on the shady side of forty, his penchant being for young girls of twenty and under.

Failing in her own matrimonial scheme, Mrs. Moncrief masked her batteries and opened on him for her "darling niece" as she called Dolores, and as she led people to believe she really was.

This bait Mercer Aldrich eagerly caught at, for, from the very first he had seemed strangely drawn toward the young and beautiful girl.

As she swept into the parlor, after her return from the unpleasant parting with her son, Mercer Aldrich saw that she had had something to worry her, and, in his courtly way, bade her tell him if he could serve her.

Impulsive always, Mrs. Moncrief told him that Dolores had left the house, and gave as a cause that she had been persecuted by Howland in his attentions, and not loving him, had fled to escape from him.

"Now, my dear Mr. Aldrich, my son has gone, thinking I am to blame, and I do hope you will find Dolores," she said, entreatingly.

"Willingly, madam, and upon condition that I may claim the right of you to make your niece my wife," was the calm reply.

"And I give that permission, sir, for already I believe that Dolores loves you."

The man seemed pleased, and promising to at once strike the trail of the fugitive he took his departure.

But days passed away and no tidings came of the missing Dolores, or of Mercer Aldrich, and Mrs. Moncrief had almost begun to despair.

Not that she wished Dolores back again; only if she could prove to her son that the maiden did not love him, and had really loved another [line obscured] longer blame her, and become a willing tool in her hands to dispose of to Ada Ortelle.

"Dolores has but a few dollars, and all her jewels and presents, given her by Howland, she left, so if Mr. Aldrich can only find her in poverty, be good to her, and ask her to marry him, she will do it through spite."

Such was the argument of the ambitious woman.

One day she received a letter from Mercer Aldrich, and it read as follows:

"My esteemed Madam Moncrief:

"I have at last to report to you that I have struck the true trail.

"After leaving your home, Miss Moultrie was robbed in the cars of her pocket-book, and had to dispose of some article of jewelry, or dress, to enable her to advertise for a position as governess.

"An answer readily came, and she started West with a gentleman and his daughter, a maiden of fifteen.

"They go to some frontier fort, where the gentleman has an Indian Agency.

"I will follow, and I pledge you that before very long, you shall hear that Dolores Moultrie is Dolores Aldrich.

"I will write you again.

"Wishing you health and happiness, ever devotedly,

Yours,

"Mercer Aldrich."

Hardly had Mrs. Moncrief finished reading this letter, and was congratulating herself upon its contents, when Benson the butler brought a card in, and said:

"He's in the parlor, m'am, and he's pretty enough to be a girl.["]

Mrs. Moncrief took the card and read:

"Arnold Aubrey,
                    "Colorado."

"Who is he, Benson?"

"Dunno, m'am; but he's pritty as a picture."

Mrs. Moncrief swept into the parlor with the air of one who meant to awe Arnold Aubrey of Colorado.

But her dignity and elegance did not have that effect, for the person answering to that name calmly arose from the most luxurious seat in the parlor, and said in the coolest tones:

"Good-morning, madam; I am on the track of a villain of whose whereabouts you can perhaps inform me."

"Sir!"

It was all the astonished woman could say, and she bent her gaze in anger upon the one who faced her.

What she saw was a youth, apparently not over nineteen years of age, and with a face so womanly in its beauty that she almost thought it was a young girl in disguise.

His hair fell in golden curls upon his shoulders, his eyes were dark blue, full of expression, and his other features perfect in formation.

His slender, graceful form was clad in a dark-blue velvet coat and vest, and a pair of black broadcloth pants, which were stuck in the top of handsome boots, upon the heels of which were gold spurs, and in his hand he held a gray sombrero with broad brim, while he wore kid gloves white and spotless.

Such a person seemed out of place in the very streets of the city, and who he was and what his business with her might be, Mrs. Moncrief could not comprehend.

Hearing her indignant exclamation at his words he said in his cool, polite, yet off-hand manner:

"My dear madam, do not get angry, for I am not accusing you of being the friend intentionally of a scoundrel, for I am convinced you do not know his character; but you must know that he is a wolf in sheep's clothing."

"To whom, sir, do you refer?" she said frigidly.

"Why, to Mercer Aldrich the Danite, madam."

The lady was shocked, for the fair-faced youth made a bold charge against the wealthy Cattle King.

"Mr. Aldrich a Danite?" she almost gasped.

"Surely, sir, you are not mistaken?"

"No more than I am in my intention to one day take his life," was the stern response from lips that did not look like they could threaten.

"Merciful Heaven! pray tell me what you mean, sir?"

"I mean, Mrs. Moncrief, that I have the honor of your son's acquaintance, and meeting him, as I came East, and telling him who I was seeking, he made me come to you and ask regarding Mr. Mercer Aldrich, who, from my description, he was confident was the Mormon captain known in Utah as John Leigh."

"No, no, Mr. Aldrich cannot be that wretch." [line obscured]

[". . .] Aldrich is one of his aliases, and I have been on his track a long time West, until I found he had come East to get proselytes to his Mormon creed.

"Will you kindly give me his address, madam?"

It was a terrible blow to Mrs. Moncrief to have to acknowledge, even to herself, that Mercer Aldrich was other than he represented himself, and she said coldly:

"Mr. Aldrich has gone West, sir, and there you had best seek him; but I warn you he is no man to be accused falsely of the crime you lay upon him."

"I know him, madam, and that he is one of the most cowardly devils that disgrace the western country.

"May I ask for his address in the city?"

Reluctantly Mrs. Moncrief gave it, and with a polite bow Mr. Arnold Aubrey bowed himself out, sprung into a waiting carriage and was driven rapidly away, leaving the mistress of the Moncrief mansion in no very amiable frame of mind.

Chapter V.
Friend or Foe.

A bivouac on the prairies, and on the overland trail to the far West, is the change of scene from the parlors of Mrs. Moncrief's elegant mansion.

A range of hills a few miles beyond, which the wagon train had hoped to reach by night, but failing to do so, had camped on the banks of a small stream, with its fringe of willows and cottonwoods, that wound its way across the level plain.

A semicircle of "prairie schooners," as the wagons are called on the western border, each end resting on the stream, the horses and mules lariated near by feeding upon the rich grass, and half a dozen camp-fires, with a score or more of people gathered around them, preparing their evening meal, formed a picturesque scene for the eye of an artist to fall upon.

Suddenly the quick eye of the guide detected a dark object coming across the prairie, and then another, until five horsemen came in sight.

It was a locality where it was necessary for men to be on their guard against Indians and train robbers, and the little party were soon ready to meet friend or foe.

But a hail from the horseman in advance that they were friends caused the answer from the captain of the train that they might come on.

A moment after they rode up and dismounted, and he who appeared to be the leader asked:

"Is this the wagon-train of Captain Harmon?"

"It is, sir, and I am Captain Harmon," said a kindly-faced, portly gentleman, stepping forward.

"My name is Aldrich, sir, and I believe you have an old friend of mine under your charge; Miss Dolores Moultrie, I refer to."

"Ah, yes; Miss Moultrie, here is a friend of yours," the gentleman called out, and then he added:

"You are welcome, sir, to my camp; Aldrich, you said your name was?"

"Yes, Captain Harmon; Mercer Aldrich, and I am a Colorado cattle man, who met Miss Dolores while visiting in the East."

Just then Dolores advanced, accompanied by a young and beautiful girl of fifteen; but in his changed attire in the city, to his border costume, handsome though it was, she did not at first recognize him.

"Why, Miss Dolores, have you forgotten an old friend?" he asked, reproachfully.

"Mr. Aldrich!"

"Yes, at your service, Miss Dolores."

She extended her hand, for though she did not like the man, she was glad to meet, far out on the plains, one whom she had met in the home around which still clung so many kind remembrances.

After greeting him, she said, pleasantly:

"Captain Harmon, this is an old friend whom I met in the city, Mr. Mercer Aldrich, though I believe he lives out here."

"Yes, Miss Dolores, in Colorado; I had gone home, but receiving a letter from your aunt that you were going West with Captain Harmon's train, I determined to see you, so, with my cowboys here, sought to head you off." [line obscured]

{4} ["... Mon]crief, know that I had come West?" asked Dolores, coldly.

"Oh! he would not lose sight of you, and was anxious to know how you were getting along.

"I believe you are a governess to the captain's daughter?" and Mercer Aldrich gazed admiringly upon the little beauty, Hortense Harmon, who, with her father, had walked back to the fire, leaving Dolores to entertain her visitor.

"Yes, and my pupil is as lovely in character as she is in face, and I feel that I can be happy out here."

"I hope so," said the man, earnestly, and being called to supper, while the cowboys looked after his and their horses, he joined the captain's men around the camp-fire.

A man of brilliant conversational powers, Mercer Aldrich soon charmed all by his anecdotes, and witty stories, and after supper was over, took up Hortense Harmon's guitar and sung for them in a voice full of pathos, and even Dolores regretted when the hour for retiring came, for, though she had always shunned the man at home, there was in him such a change on the plains, and he being the only link present to connect her with the happy past, she felt drawn toward him as she never had before.

The next day he continued on the march with them, and the next, and he had quite won over every one in the train, excepting Dolores.

As for her, in the bright glare of daylight, she saw marks in his face that she did not like, and she felt confident that his genial, courtly manner was not natural to him, and she began to dread him.

One evening, several days after Mercer Aldrich had joined the train, there rode into camp a horseman.

He was splendidly mounted and thoroughly armed, and possessed a face and form that would attract attention among a thousand men.

A face that was strikingly handsome, resolute and perhaps reckless, a form over six feet, straight as an arrow, and clad in buckskin, and long dark hair falling far down below his shoulders, he was the very type of a prairie hero.

The guide of the train recognized him at a glance, and sung out in cheery tones: "Boys, it are Buffalo Bill!"

Dismounting, he greeted the guide kindly, and was presented by him to Captain Harmon, to whom he said:

"Pardon my intruding on your camp, captain, but I am a Government Scout, and learning that a man answering to the description of John Leigh, the Danite, had lately joined your train, I ran in to have a look at him."

"You are welcome, Mr. Cody; but you have been misinformed, for no such person has joined us," answered Captain Harmon.

"I am glad to hear it, and must be wrong; but did not a party of horsemen join you lately?"

"Yes, sir; but they were known to us, one being in fact an old friend of a lady of our party, and the others his companions."

"Ah! that accounts for it, but let me urge, sir, that you double your guards from this on to Fort Bridger, which I believe is your destination, for dangers will lie thick in your trail."

"I thank you, Mr. Cody; but you will remain with us all night?"

"No, thank you, for I am bearing dispatches and must not tarry; but I will join you at supper."

A few moments after supper was announced and the handsome young scout was presented by Captain Harmon to Dolores and Hortense, and also to Mercer Aldrich.

"Buffalo Bill! indeed I am glad to meet so famous a borderman," said Mercer Aldrich, as he grasped the scout's hand.

But, from the moment of meeting the ranchero, Buffalo Bill kept his eye upon him, striving to recall where they had met before, for the face of Aldrich seemed to come back to him like a troubled dream, and he muttered:

"I feel that I have met that man before, and under circumstances of an unpleasant nature.

"But where? where?

"Bah! I must be mistaken, for he is, I believe the captain hinted, the acknowledged suitor of that handsome Miss Dolores, and therefore must be all right, for she could not love a bad man."

And, as Buffalo Bill rode on his lonely trail across the prairies that night, the face of Mercer Aldrich the ranchero still haunted him; but not until days after did it flash upon him who he was.

Then he cried suddenly:

"By the Holy Rockies! that man is John Leigh.

"Fool! fool that I was not to know him, because he had cut his beard and hair off.

"I will at once— No, no, it is too late now for whatever devilment Leigh intended, it is already done," and with gloomy face Buffalo Bill continued on his way, for a dread of evil rested on his heart.

Chapter VI.
The Threat.

Onward toward the setting sun went the Harmon train, dragging its slow length along over prairie and hill toward its destination in the Territory of Deseret, now Utah, the land of the Mormon.

And each day did Mercer Aldrich linger with the train, evidently held there by the fascination of Dolores Moultrie's beautiful eyes; and each day he grew more in favor with all in the train.

His comrades, whom he called his cowboys, spoke of him as a noble-hearted man, and the wagon men guide[s] and hunters of the train were willing to swear by him, while Captain Harmon also seemed greatly drawn toward him.

But with both Dolores and Hortense it was different, for both of them, without divulging their feelings the one to the other, seemed to fear the man, and the former constantly avoided him.

One night, when the train had gone into camp in a pleasant grove, Mercer Aldrich asked Dolores to walk with him to the summit of a hill near by and enjoying the sunset scene.

Fond of the beauties of nature, and with no ready excuse for not going, she arose and accompanied him, and in watching the fading glories of the setting sun, glancing upon mountains of gold, purple and crimson clouds, she was fully repaid for her walk.

But at last the rosy hues died away, and she said:

"Come, let us returne [sic] now, Mr. Aldrich."

"One moment, Dolores, while you hear what I have to say," he said eagerly.

"But tell me while we retrace our way to camp," she urged.

"No, hear me now, and let me know my fate.

"While I believed that you cared for your cousin, or rather Captain Moncrief, for you have told me he was really no kindred of yours, and he loved you, in my belief, I breathed to you no word of my love; but now when I know that you are free to listen to me, I throw myself in entreaty at your feet, Dolores, pleading for one little word of love from you, one atom of hope to which I can cling and know that I am not to leave your side forever."

He ceased speaking and gazed earnestly into her face, awaiting reply.

She had stood, with her eye bent on the western horizon, and not on her pleading lover, and her tiny boot tapping the earth with almost impatience.

Not once had she by word or gesture, interrupted his passionate appeal for her love, until he stood waiting her response.

Then in her soft voice she answered:

"Mr. Aldrich, believing that you mean what you say, I feel sorry to have to tell you that I can never love you, that our friendship, such as it has been, must end here forever."

"Ha! you love another then?" he said angrily.

"I do not acknowledge your right, sir, to question me," was the cold reply.

"But I take the right, Dolores Moultrie, and ask you if you love another."

Her face flushed with anger; but she replied haughtily:

"You should be content, sir, with the knowledge that I do not love you, and, if you do not permit me to pass you, and return to the camp, that I will even lose respect for you."

"By the God above! girl, you shall rue these words," he hissed.

"No threats, sir, for I have a protector in Captain Harmon."

"I fear not Captain Harmon, or any one else, Dolores Moultrie, and again I say to you that the woman who casts my love beneath her feet will rue it to her dying day."

He stood aside and permitted her to pass on to the camp.

Swiftly she went along, his words causing her real alarm, and had arrived within a short distance of the camp-fires, when she glanced back and saw him standing where she had left him, his form relieved against the sky.

And, as she looked, she heard a long, shrill whistle given.

Instantly there was a slight stir in the encampment, and a moment after four horsemen dashed by her, one leading an animal which, even in the twilight she recognized as the steed belonging to Mercer Aldrich.

"It was a signal from him, and his men are going to join him.

"Oh, Heaven! can that man really mean his threat against me?" she muttered, and quickly she ran on to camp, and dropped down beside Hortense, who wondered at the emotion of her beautiful governess.

CHAPTER VII.
SNAKES IN THE GRASS.

IT was a beautiful spot in which to camp, and both Dolores and Hortense who had ridden on ahead with Revolver Nick, the guide, flattered themselves upon having selected the prettiest encampment of the long and weary march.

Behind them towered lofty hills, at the base of which glided a crystal stream, and before them stretched away a plain, knee-deep in juicy grass for the stock.

Revolver Nick had argued that it:

"War a pretty place fer a meetin'-house, but no kinder place fer a camp as hed ter be guarded from inemies, both pale-face and red."

But his arguments were overruled and the train went into camp, the horses were lariated out on the plain, the guards placed, and long before midnight the sounds of music and laughter died away, and nothing broke the deep silence that darkness had cast upon the scene.

The guards leant half-asleep upon their rifles, the horses and mules had tired of feeding and had dropped down to rest, or stood drowsily with heads bent.

But one in the camp tossed uneasily, for somehow a presentiment of evil had been upon her ever since two weeks before she had heard the threat of Mercer Aldrich.

Strive as she would she could not drive his stern, sinister face from her mind, and something told her that he would meet her again.

Rising, because she was unable to sleep, she dressed herself and stepped out of the tent, and stood gazing upon the calm scene.

Soothed by its quietude she laughed at her fears, and was about to return to her tent, when a form startled her by gliding up to her side.

"Why, Hortense! how you startled me."

"Forgive me, Miss Dolores, but I could not sleep; I have a weight on my heart, and seeing you come out, I dressed myself and followed you."

"I too have that feeling, Hortense, a feeling of coming evil; but see, are not those men coming yonder through the long grass?"

She pointed quickly out upon the plain, and Hortense saw the dark forms too, and said:

"There is a guard stationed just there, I think, and they must be some of our people, and—"

She never finished her sentence, for there came a flash off on the plain, a cry of pain, and up from the grass-covered prairie sprung a hundred forms, and wild war-whoops echoed back from the hillside, as they dashed upon the surprised camp.

Clasped in each other's arms the maidens shrunk back for shelter behind a huge tree while around them waged the fierce battle, for the train men knew they fought for their lives.

And thus crouching, more dead than alive, they saw Revolver Nick fall, fighting bravely against a score of painted savages; then came a cry that Hortense knew too well came from her father's lips; a cry of pleading, not for himself, but for his child, and a pistol-shot was the answer.

And thus it went on, the fight surging away from them toward the wagon, and they gave up all hope. {5}

But suddenly up to them dashed a slender form, and he held in his arms a bundle, while he said quickly:

"Come, throw these Indian toggeries around you and come with me.

"Hasten, or all will be lost."

They were paralyzed with fear and did not move, and instantly he threw a blanket over the shoulders of each and a head-dress of feathers on them, and said, earnestly:

"Come, for God's sake, for these are not Indians, but John Leigh's Danites, and your fate will be worse than death.

"Come!"

His words sent a chill of horror through them, but roused them to action, and, springing to their feet, they quickly followed him toward the shelter of the hill.

"My father! oh, my father!" cried Hortense, pausing in an agony of grief.

"Died like the brave man he was; but come, for they'll not *kill you*."

There was a significance in his tones they could not fail to understand, and they darted along by his side with a speed they did not believe themselves capable of, and each moment the rattle of firearms and cries of combatants grew fainter and fainter in the distance.

At last their strange leader paused for a moment and listened.

All was silent behind them, and he said sadly, and yet with triumph in his tones:

"Those snakes in the grass have finished their red work, but you two, who were their intended victims, have escaped them.

"But come, for you are not yet safe."

And once more they continued their rapid flight.

Chapter VIII.
The Flight.

"Here we halt," and the unknown guide of the two maidens, and whom they had trusted themselves to without the slightest doubt of him or fear that he might be one of their foes, stopped in a small canyon.

It was dark there, for the foliage of over-hanging trees kept even the starlight from penetrating the spot; but their guide bade them remain quiet an instant, and disappeared from their side as silently and mysteriously as he had approached them in the camp.

Several minutes, which seemed more like hours to them, passed away, and he did not return.

What could it mean?

Who was he?

Certainly not one of the train men, for both maidens knew all of them well.

Had he led them there to the better get them in their power?

In their grief at the fearful massacre, which still was before their eyes in all its horrors, they were almost crazed, and knew not what to do.

But Dolores at last said, calmly:

"Cheer up, Hortense, for if it comes to the worst, I have this."

"It is a pistol," whispered Hortense.

"Yes, one which once saved the life of Captain Moncrief, and he gave it to me, and it may serve us both."

"But how, Miss Dolores?"

"If I see that there is no hope, Hortense, I will kill you and then send a bullet through my own heart."

The young girl shuddered, but made no reply, for death then seemed to her less terrible than life.

"Come, my horse is ready."

It was the voice of their strange preserver and he was by their side when they believed him nowhere near them.

Silently they followed him through the canyon until they came into a valley.

Here stood a fine large horse, who gave a low neigh at the sight of his master.

"One of you must ride behind the other," said their guide.

"And you, sir?" asked Dolores.

"Oh! I am used to trotting over the mountains, and will go on foot; but Comrade will carry you both with ease."

With a strength that surprised the maidens he raised them to seats upon the back of his patient horse, Dolores being in the saddle, and at once set off on a rapid walk down the valley, the animal following like a faithful dog.

All through the night he kept up his untiring pace, over hills, along valleys, and across plains, until the daylight dawned, and the maidens saw before them a broad, swiftly running stream.

But, without hesitation, their guide plunged in and, holding his belt above his head, swam to the other shore, followed by his horse.

Still keeping on, he held his way up into the mountains, until he halted before a rocky cavern.

"Here we can rest for awhile," he said, and he lifted the tired maidens to the ground.

But in spite of their grief and fatigue they gazed upon him with unfeigned admiration, for in years, now that they saw him in the daylight, he seemed but a youth; in fact, it was the same young man that had called upon Mrs. Moncrief in her city mansion, and denounced Mercer Aldrich; but now his dandy costume had been changed for a hunter's suit, far more fitting the wild life he was leading.

He saw their earnest gaze, and, as if to put them at their ease, and pitying them in their grief and helplessness, he said, softly:

"You can rest here without fear, while I look us up some breakfast, for you look tired and hungry."

"No, no, I am not hungry, I am not tired, I am broken-hearted, for my poor, dear father is dead," groaned Hortense.

"It was all that villain Leigh's work, and I wish I could have overtaken you a little sooner; but I could not, and only got there as they made the attack.

"I saw you two hide by the tree and determined to save you, and only wish I could have saved your father, miss; now, lie down on my blanket and rest."

He spread his blankets upon a bed of soft grass near, gave them a drink of water from his canteen, and, mounting his horse, rode away in search of game for breakfast.

But ill-fortune seemed to dog his steps, and it was long before he could kill a deer and retrace his way to the little cavern in the mountains.

At last he reached there to find no trace of the maidens.

He hailed, and no response came, and, dismounting, he picked up his blankets, which lay just as he had placed them.

Throwing them across his saddle, again he called aloud.

This time there came an answer, for a bullet whizzed by his head, and half a dozen forms darted out of the cavern upon him.

Chapter IX.
The Danites.

THE sun had soared to quite a h[e]ight above the horizon, the morning after the attack upon the encampment, as a horseman rode along at a rapid pace, following the trail left by the wagon-train.

One glance at his horse was sufficient to show that he had been urged hard, and upon the rider's face was a look of anxiety, and he constantly kept his gaze fixed upon the trail far ahead of him.

It was Buffalo Bill, the scout, who was thus following the track left by the train, and, having delivered his dispatches at the fort, for which he was destined, when he first came upon the party under Captain Harmon, he had determined to head them off ere they could cross the Green river, and warn them of the danger they would meet by following the direct course to their destination.

He had crossed their trail as he had expected he would, and pressed on at a hard pace, even for the splendid horse he rode, and knew that ere long he must soon come in sight of the white tilts of the wagons.

But instead he saw a smoke rising from the timber in his front, and cautiously he approached, to suddenly rein his horse back, while a cry of horror broke from his lips.

"Too late! too late!"

The cry seemed wrung from him by mortal grief, and springing to the ground he stood with uncovered head upon the spot, gazing spellbound upon the fearful, sickening scape.

And the sight that met his gaze was fearful indeed, for the dead of the train lay about him, mutilated almost beyond recognition.

Here was Revolver Nick, his knife still grasped in his hand, and around him were others of the train.

There lay the body of Captain Harmon, and near him were several women of the train, the wives of emigrants, who had seemed to fly to him for a protection he could not give them.

Beyond, trainmen, emigrants and hunters lay thick, and all dead, with here and there a woman, and now and then a child that had fallen before the merciless bullets and knives of their foes.

All had been rifled of their money and valuables, and many of their clothing, while the smoldering fires showed where the wagons had been burned, after being despoiled of all the murderous band could carry with them.

"Strange that not one dead man of the attacking party can be seen," muttered Buffalo Bill.

"This looks like Indian work, as does also the scalpless heads; and yet I don't believe it.

"I will see.

"Yes, here is a tomahawk, and here a bow, and this moccasin has come off a wounded foot.

"All Indian signs, especially carrying off their dead; but paint and feathers don't make red skins."

So saying Buffalo Bill looked around until he found the trail leading away from the fatal encampment, and a low call brought his horse to his side, while he muttered:

"Ironheart, there are two that I do not find here, old fellow."

The horse gave a low neigh, as though understanding what was said, and Buffalo Bill continued:

"Those two not being here are alive, and it will be better to look after the living than tarry here to bury the dead, so we will jog along, Ironheart."

The scout then threw himself into his saddle, and the rest having refreshed his horse he set off at a quick pace along the trail left by the murdering band.

"They came across the prairie, and retreated this way after their hellish work.

"Oh Heaven! but a fearful retribution shall follow this red deed," and Buffalo Bill's face was white and stern.

Suddenly he drew rein, for his experienced eye had detected some sign.

"Ah! here is where they branched off to bury their dead, and they have covered up their tracks well; but I shall soon see what secret the grave will tell."

With an instinct that was remarkable he followed the faint trail, and soon halted by a spot where his scout's eye told him the ground had been disturbed.

Leaves, blown from the forest lay about in piles, as though left there by the winds; but beneath those was soft earth, and Buffalo Bill's knife soon manufactured for him a wooden shovel which quickly threw out the dirt.

It was not a long task, as he worked unceasingly, and a body was soon revealed.

"In full war paint and feathers, *but a pale-face*," he muttered, as he rubbed the dusky cheek of the dead.

"And another, and another; well, the train made a good fight of it, and rid the earth of a few of these devils.

"But alas! they went under at last.

"Yes, they are all white men, not one red-skin here, and, as I thought and feared, *they are Danites.*

"Now, to the rescue of those two whom they have spared to make Mormons of them."

With a muttered curse he again sprung upon his horse, and once more followed the trail.

But soon it branched off, the main force going to the right and a smaller one to the left.

An instant did Buffalo Bill hesitate and then he made up his mind which course to pursue and he followed the smaller trail.

It led him down the valley and then up into the hills again, and he was about to give his horse rest before attempting the climb, when he heard ringing shots not far away, and with the speed of the wind he rode in the direction from whence came the sound.

Chapter X.
An Unexpected Ally.

When the men in the cave dashed out suddenly upon the youth who had saved Dolores and Hortense from the massacre of the train people, only to have them fall into the power of the party who had so swiftly trailed him, they expected to see him surrender to them, and at least thought they held him at their mercy.

But with a cry to Comrade, that sent him spinning around, as though on a pivot, the youth drew a revolver in each hand, and merrily they rattled forth deadly music to his assailants.

He saw rushing upon him six or more men {6} who looked like Indian warriors, for they were so rigged out and painted hideously; but well he knew that white faces and black hearts lay beneath the red paint, and his every shot was sent with an unerring aim that showed he meant to give no mercy, and ask none.

But seeing that his foes, after several of their number had fallen, quickly retreated back into the shelter of the dark cavern, he gave a cry to Comrade, and with a bound the splendid animal began a rapid flight, while shot after shot rattled harmlessly after him.

But ere he had gone a hundred yards the youth suddenly reined up, for before him he saw a horseman coming rapidly toward him.

It was Buffalo Bill, and the two came to a dead halt, and each with a revolver leveled, sat regarding the other.

"Well, who in the name of the Rockies are you?" asked the scout, gazing upon the handsome youth, as he coolly sat on his horse, his revolver thrown forward and a quiet smile upon his lips.

"Up in the mining country the boys call me Satan's Pet.

"May I ask your handle, pard?"

The reply was so cool, the manner of the youth, whom Buffalo Bill felt certain had just escaped from some dread danger, was so indifferent, that the scout laughed lightly and replied:

"On the prairies I am known as Buffalo Bill."

"Buffalo Bill! put it there, pard, for I have heard of you North, South, East and West," and the youth lowered his revolver and rode forward, with extended hand, while he added:

"And rumor don't lie in saying you are the handsomest man that ever put on a buckskin suit."

Bill flushed at the unexpected compliment, and said pleasantly, as he grasped the extended hand:

"And I have heard of you too, little pard, and now I look you squarely in the face I guess neither your friends or foes have lied about you."

"Friends I have none, and as for foes, all men seem foes to me," said the youth, while a look of deepest sadness came into his beautiful eyes.

"Don't say that after this pard, for I am your friend; but what's the trouble up the anyone?"

"Trouble enough; John Leigh's Danites butchered a train, and though I saved two of its members, and left them up at a cavern in he hills, while I looked up gain, I came back to find them in the hands of those devils, and they nearly got me too, and I know they want me."

"Doubtless, from what I have heard of your trailing the Danites."

"I have had cause," was the sad reply.

"Who were the two you saved?"

"Two young ladies."

"Ah! the captain's daughter and her governess?"

"Yes."

"Well, the party that have them is not large, so let us return and see what we can do to rescue them; but I should have thought you would not have left them?"

"I could not help it, for I had only Comrade here to carry them both, and traveling all night, felt certain I had gained some seven hours' start, and could rest for five;

but they followed me rapidly, and how at night I can not understand, for I covered my trail as well as I could."

"I can tell you."

"Indeed."

"Yes, they had bloodhounds, for I saw their track."

"By Heaven! that is it then; as soon as they missed the maidens they struck out after them."

"What are those ladies to you, may I ask?"

"Nothing."

"Then why did you serve them?"

"To serve myself, for I learned that Leigh was organizing his band, and felt he would attack the train, and he was the one I wanted, and if I could join the emigrants, I knew that was my best chance to meet him; but I was too late, and seeing the maidens saved them."

"Had you joined the train before you might have been massacred."

"True, but not until I had killed John Leigh the Danite leader," and the youth spoke with a savage earnestness that told the scout how deep was his hatred for the man.

"Come, let us go back up the canyon and see what can be done, and we'll doubtless surprise those fellows, as they'll think I'm scared off for good," and the youth laughed lightly.

"I am your ally, little pard, so lead on," was the pleasant remark of Buffalo Bill, and side by side they went back up the canyon toward the cavern.

Chapter XI.
Caught in Their Own Trap.

When the two allies arrived in sight of the entrance to the cavern they saw that the escape of Satan's Pet, as he said he was called in the mines, had created an excitement that had not subsided.

White men painted as savages were bending over fallen comrades, shot down by the daring youth, and three were preparing to mount horses led out of the cavern, as though to go in pursuit of the enemy who had dealt them such severe blows.

"I'll tell you what you do, sir; open on them with your rifle and run them back into the cave, and they'll think I have returned, for they did not notice I carry only revolvers, I am certain," said Pet, addressing Buffalo Bill.

"A good idea, and we can keep them besieged there until night, and then, as they come out, follow and make a dash to rescue the young ladies."

"We need not wait until night, for yonder cave is one of my haunts in these mountains, and there is another entrance which they do not suspect, and I will go there and see if I cannot steal the girls out."

"I hate to have you go alone."

"I am generally alone; I told you I had no friends, and besides, you must stay here and keep them in the cave.

"Now let them know they are not forgotten."

Buffalo Bill raised his Colt's repeating rifle* and with the flash a man fell dead in front of the cavern entrance.

Back, pell-mell into the cave went horses and riders, and only the slain were left without.

---

*at that time the only repeating rifle in use.

A boyish laugh broke from the lips of the youth at the sudden stampede of his foes, and he cried gayly:

"That's the music; just sing them the same song each time they appear, and I'll be back in an hour or so."

He left his horse lariated out with that of the scout's, and hastily disappeared in a canyon that led further into the hills, while Buffalo Bill, protected by the bowlder, kept his eye fixed upon the cavern.

Once he caught sight of a form moving far back in the shadows of the cave, and instantly his eye ran along the sights and his finger touched the trigger.

A smothered cry followed the shot, and the scout knew that his aim had been true.

At last he came to the conclusion that the occupants of the cavern were preparing some surprise for him.

He could hear their horses moving about on the rock flooring, and their voices were echoed back to him in earnest conversation.

Presently out of the cavern, riding in a group, dashed six horsemen at full speed.

Then Buffalo knew that their plan was to charge upon him *en masse*, each man trusting to luck not to be the one who got the rifle-shot, and feeling confident that their weapons at close quarters could quickly put the youth to flight, for it was evident that they believed that their foe guarding the cave was none other.

But they had not taken into consideration the deadly aim of Buffalo Bill.

Hardly had their horses given half a dozen bounds before they saw their mistake, for one man and two steeds had gone down under the scout's fire, and a forth shot broke the arm of a second rider.

A narrow canyon, with steep sides led to the shelf upon which the cave opened, and feeling that it was safer to retrace their way to the cavern, than keep on for a hundred yards under that fatal fire, they drew rein to go to the right about.

But during the temporary check the unerring rifle poured in its fire, and in wild terror they started back to their retreat.

But suddenly the three men left, reined back their horses with cries of terror, for out of the cavern bounded a slender form, a revolver in each hand, and instantly he opened upon them.

With horror they beheld the very one they believed had been firing upon them from over the bowlder, and, as another horse went down beneath his aim, they darted to the steep side of the canyon, and deserting their animals, clambered up the embankment.

But Satan's Pet was determined not to let them escape so easily and sent another shot after them which brought a man tumbling back into the canyon, just as Buffalo Bill came dashing up toward the youth, who cried out in his cheery tones:

"Four from six leave two."

"Well, what discovery did you make in the cavern, Pet, for I see that you did indeed flank the devils?"

"Yes, but the girls are not there."

"Not there?"

"No, they did not come with this party, but kept on with the larger force, contrary to what we thought; but I don't give up their trail."

"Nor I; but have you searched the cavern well?"

"Oh yes; they found the girls asleep doubtless, and sent them on after the main force under Leigh, while eight remained to capture me on my return.

"Well, they didn't do it, for six of the eight are now only coyote meat; now what do you say do?"

"Report to the commandant of Fort Bridger that the Danites have two maidens captive, and have doubtless carried them on to Salt [Lake] City, and that they have massacred all the train people."

"No, there are not troops enough at Fort Bridger to do us any good, and, though we know that these fellows are all whites in Indian garb and paint, we must be certain who their commander is, so we will go to Salt Lake City if you say so."

"It would be taking great risks."

"True, but I have been there often before, and we can do more to save the girls than an army can."

"I am ready, little pard."

"Good! then we will play Injun too, but your handsome mustache will have to come off.["]

"I care not; tell me your idea?"

"I know a weed that will make big Injuns of us, as far as skin goes, and we can rig up suits out of these, and I speak the Ute tongue like a native."

"And so do I."

["]Then to Salt Lake we go as renegade Utes," was the determined reply of Satan's Pet.

Chapter XII.
Hope and Despair.

Utterly prostrated with grief and fatigue both Dolores and Hortense at last sunk into deep slumber, lying upon the blankets spread for them by the youth who had so cleverly rescued them from the camp during the massacre.

How long they were unconscious in dreamless slumber, they knew not; but they awoke with a start, to behold bending over them a tall form, with painted face and feather headdress, while near by were full a dozen horsemen.

At once they gave themselves up for lost, and clung to each other with the energy of despair, while Hortense said pleadingly:

"Spare us."

"You are in no danger, for if I were to harm a hair of your head, it would be the worse for me," was the reply of the pretended savage in perfect English.

"Oh, sir, you are not then an Indian and you will be merciful," cried Hortense.

"Certainly, miss; I was seeking you, for the chief knew that you had escaped the—well, from the encampment, and I had orders to find you and carry you to him."

"Who is your chief?" coldly asked Dolores.

"It must remain a secret until you see him, miss; but who, may I ask, brought you here?"

"That too must remain a secret, sir," was the calm reply of Dolores.

"As you please, miss; but we shall soon know.

"Come, you must go with me, and I advise you to give us no trouble."

"We will go, for we are in your power. Come, Hortense, keep up a brave heart, for the end has not yet come."

Cheered by the example of Dolores, the younger maiden wiped her eyes, conquered her emotion, and said calmly: {7}

"I am ready."

At a motion of the man who appeared to be the leader two horses were brought forward and the saddle arranged for them, and telling the greater part of his followers to remain in the cavern, and "Capture that fellow, whoever he may be, and take him alive too," he mounted his own horse, and placing himself between the maidens he rode away from the cavern.

Having reached the regular trail, by which the force under the chief had gone, he sent a messenger on ahead to report his capture of the maidens, and then rode on in perfect silence, refusing to answer any of the questions put to him by Dolores.

At length the messenger returned and said to the leader something in an unknown tongue, and once more the party went on in silence.

At night they went into camp in a pleasant spot, and a rustic arbor was built for the fair captives and every attention was shown them; but a silence was kept which none of the Danites, as the maidens knew them to be, would break.

Early the following morning they again resumed their march, and the shadows of night were again upon them when they came in sight of the glimmering lights of Salt Lake City.

As they passed into the town all hope seemed to forsake Hortense; but Dolores felt a ray of hope which she could not account for, and said quietly:

"Hortense, before the massacre, I had a presentiment of evil, and it came upon us most cruelly; now I feel a hopefulness that I trust will bring succor to us."

"But who will know our fate, now that youth is dead?" sighed Hortense.

"I am not certain he is dead."

"But they remained there to kill him."

"True, yet I do not believe that he was caught in their trap, and I intend to hope and not give up to despair, and you must do the same."

"I will try: but oh! how fearful to be in this hateful city."

"It might be worse, Hortense. Ah! we are stopping here, and if this house is to be our quarters, they certainly will be pleasant."

The party of horsemen had now turned into a yard and drawn rein at the door of a comfortable house.

Lights gleamed from the windows, and several servants were visible, as though expecting the arrival of visitors.

Lifted from their saddles by the man who had captured them, for they were too fatigued to spring to the ground, though they hated to have him touch them, they were ushered into a large, pleasantly furnished room, where a table was spread for tea.

Adjoining it was a bedroom in which, to their utter amazement they found their trunks of clothing which had been with the train.

"Young ladies, the chief assigns you these quarters, and he hopes you will be comfortable.

"The servants will supply your wants, but will also be your guards, so that escape will be impossible.

"After you have rested for a day or two, the chief begs me to say that he will visit you," and the man, still in the Indian garb and paint, was bowing himself out of the room, when Dolores again asked:

"And who is this chief?"

"Lady, I only obey orders given me, and have received none to tell you who he is," was the polite reply, and the maidens were left to themselves and their grief, alone, friendless, and wretched in the home of the Mormons.

Chapter XIII.
The Masked Visitor.

Several days passed away, and no change came to the captives in their Mormon prison, for the house was nothing else.

They were made most comfortable, the servants being most attentive, and the table was well supplied; but the hearts of the maidens were full of grief, and they dreaded the coming of every day, the setting of every sun.

Poor Captain Harmon had expected a happy life upon the border, and, a man of some means he had loaded his train down with all that he would need in his new home to add to the comfort of himself and daughter.

A widower, he had only Hortense to love, and to advance her education, he had advertised for a competent governess to take charge of his daughter, and Dolores Moultrie had been the applicant, and from the first the captain and Hortense had been drawn toward her with the deepest affection.

And how had the end come?

Back in the hills lay the massacred people of the train, and in the heart of the Mormon city were the daughter and governess, and no one to aid them.

The unknown fate of the youth who had come to their aid on that fearful night was also a cause of grief, and altogether the lonely girls had only sorrow to hug to their hearts.

Upon the evening of the fourth day of their captivity, Dolores and Hortense sat in their room, talking over for the hundredth time their hopes and their fears.

Suddenly the door opened and the servant woman entered.

Hers was a cold, emotionless face, and they had never liked her, and Dolores said impatiently:

"Well, what is it?"

"The chief begs to see Miss Moultrie alone," was the response.

Dolores turned pale, but remained perfectly calm, and said:

"Now, Hortense, we will know what is to be our fate."

"Do not leave me long," pleaded the young girl.

"I will not; but if you hear me call come to me."

She passed into the next room with all the dignity she could assume, and pausing near the door remained standing.

Upon the other side of the table stood a tall form, a cloak thrown around his shoulders, and clad from head to foot in deep black.

He wore his hat and his face was hidden by a black mask, and gloves of the same sable hue covered his hands.

"Miss Moultrie, I believe?" he said, in an inquiring, but polite tone.

"I am Dolores Moultrie, sir," was the cold reply.

"You were in the train, which the Indians attacked back in the foothills of the Escalante Mountains, I believe?"

"I was in the train, sir, which the Danites, your tools doubtless, disguised as Indians, attacked and cruelly put to death all but two of us," was the fearless reply.

"You are mistaken, Miss Moultrie, they were Indians," he said, hastily.

"I am not mistaken, sir, for I know a wolf's skin from a wolf."

"Ah! well, we'll not discuss that matter, other than to say that, knowing so much, you will doubtless see the necessity of our never allowing you to spread such a disagreeable story concerning the massacre where the United States soldiers can hear of it."

Dolores saw at once that she had made a sad mistake in making known that she knew the murderers of the Harmon train were not Indians, and she remained quiet, biting her lips to hide her chagrin.

The masked visitor seemed to read her thoughts, and continued:

"I have come, Miss Moultrie, to offer you a compromise out of your difficulty."

"There can be but one compromise, sir," was the haughty reply.

"And that is?"

"The release of my young friend and myself."

"But where can you go?"

"Anywhere, so it is away from this hated spot."

"The father of Miss Harmon is dead, and you, her governess, have no friends upon whom you can call for aid, so I beg you accept a compromise."

"Name it, sir."

"You are here among the Mormons, and—"

"Alas! I know that but too well."

"You will find the Mormons not so black as they are painted—"

"They could not be worse," was the fearless retort.

"You mistake them, for there are many noble men and women among them."

"Their creed differs from yours, but they are a God-fearing people, and there is one of their number who esteems you most highly."

"Ha! do I know any of them?"

"You do."

"His name?"

"First hear my proposition.

"He is rich, stands well in rank, and would make you his wife."

"Never!"

"Do not be hasty."

"I say never!"

"But you do not know to whom I refer."

"I care not, I will never so debase myself."

"It is better to be a Mormon's wife than the bride of Death," was the significant reply.

"I differ with you, sir."

"What! you would rather die than become a Mormon's bride?"

"Yes."

"You cannot mean it."

"I do, with all my heart."

"Perhaps your sweet young friend will not think as you do."

"Villain! would you break the heart of that poor child?"

"Oh, no! there is many a girl as pretty who has been glad to become a Mormon."

"She will not."

"I shall ask her."

With a bound Dolores reached the door between the two rooms, and looking the man firmly in the face, said, fiercely:

"Dare to intrude here, and I will send a bullet through your coward heart."

He laughed lightly and moved forward, but suddenly halted, for she drew from her pocket her trusty pistol and leveled it at his heart, while she cried in ringing tones:

"Come on, and you die!"

Chapter XIV.
Mysterious Intruders.

The bold attitude of Dolores Moultrie took the masked visitor all aback.

He halted with the promptness of a soldier on parade, and seemed very uneasy.

It was evident that he had not believed her armed, and a glance at the weapon showed that it was by no means a toy pistol, but one that would do deadly work.

Feeling his danger, and that it was not a pleasant position to be in, he determined to extricate himself as best he could, and said calmly:

"Very well; for the present you can have your own way, and I will decide your case, instead of that of your young friend."

"As you please, sir; you know that I consider death preferable to being bound by hated ties to a Mormon, and Hortense feels as I do."

"But you will not be allowed to die."

"That we shall see.["]

"If you will become the wife of the one to whom I refer you shall be the queen of his household, and your life shall be made a happy one."

"Never!"

"Then a fate worse than death shall be yours, as I will sell you to the Ute chief for squaws."

The cruel words came out harsh and sneering, and Dolores grew sick at heart, and buried her face in her hands, momentarily forgetting herself.

And it was for her a fatal act, for, with the bound of a panther the masked visitor was by her side, and her pistol was wrenched from her grasp, while into her ears sunk the dismal words:

"Now, my beauty, you are in my power."

Maddened at her helplessness, she suddenly raised her hand and tore from his face the black mask.

Instantly the sinister face of Mercer Aldrich was revealed.

With a cry of horror Dolores started back, just as Hortense darted into the room, having heard the angry voice of the man as he sprung forward and seized the pistol.

"Mr. Aldrich!" cried the young girl in amazement.

"You too are in this hated place?"

"Hortense, that man is a traitor, and to him we owe all our misfortunes, for he is I now know, none other than John Leigh the Danite," and Dolores gazed upon the man before her with a look his eyes dare not meet.

"No, no, he cannot be what you say he is, Miss Dolores; he was so kind, so good, and poor papa liked him so much."

"Hortense, he was a snake in the grass when in our camp, and he is now our bitterest foe," was the fearless response.

"Are you what Dolores says?" asked Hortense, who found it hard to believe what [s]he had heard.

"Miss Moultrie seems to know me, and I see no reason for denying further, and there- {8} fore tell her plainly, that I am the one she is to marry," was the calm, shameless reply.

"By my own hand will I die first."

"I have heard those threats before, Miss Moultrie, and those who made them thought better of them afterwards.

"I will leave you now; but the third night from this I will return and carry you to the Endowment Home to become my wife."

Without another word he resumed his mask, yet why they could not then understand, and left the house, and Dolores and Hortense were again alone with their grief, the former seeming the more cast down, as she no longer had possession of her pistol with which to protect herself.

For some time they sat in sorrow, utterly silent, for they knew not what to say, and then the door opened and they were startled by seeing an Indian enter.

They feared that already had their trouble come upon them, and gave themselves up for lost; but the red-skin intruder said in broken English:

"Want see Dora; chief sent for her."

"For me?" gasped Dolores.

"No, wait squaw, Dora."

"Ah! he means the servant woman, Dora," said Hortense.

"Yes, is her here?"

"Yes, I am here," and the cold-faced woman came from the adjoining room.

"Chief send this," and the Indian held forth a slip of paper in his hand.

She stepped forward to take it, when with a panther-like spring he was upon her, his hand upon her throat, and in a tongue that was certainly not Indian, he cried:

"Here, miss, I do not wish to hurt her, so take this rope and tie her."

It was Dolores that he addressed, and, though startled at his sudden act she seemed to realize the situation, and with a skill and firmness that was remarkable, she quickly bound the woman's arms, while the supposed Indian held her in his firm gripe.

"Now, a gag in her mouth to prevent music, and all will be well," was the quiet remark, and both maidens started, for they recognized the voice of the apparent Ute warrior.

"You are—"

"'Sh—! don't speak names here, miss," said the man breaking in upon the words of Hortense.

Then he added:

"I am only an Injun; now, my ugly Mormon female guard, I guess you'll rest quiet for awhile."

As he spoke he raised the woman in his arms and carrying her into the adjoining room rolled her unceremoniously under the bed.

As he was about to return to the front chamber he beheld through the open door a tall form enter.

Instantly he darted back, and his hand sought his knife, for he recognized the visitor as a Mormon captain, and knew that his life was in danger were he seen there.

But that instant Hortense came into the room and said earnestly:

"Oh, sir, fly for a Mormon officer is here."

"So I saw just now," was the cool reply.

"But you will go?" she entreated.

"I came here to save you, and my ally and myself had our plans well laid, but with that fellow there it will be impossible to-night."

"Then go now and another time aid us, for knowing that we have friends near we will have hope to cheer us."

"I'll go but you may rest assured that you have friends near; good-by."

She seized his outstretched hand, and asked earnestly:

"Pray tell me who you are?"

"That old hag under the bed has only her mouth, and not her ears stopped up, so it wouldn't be healthy for me to speak my name here, so I'll give you the handle my pards call me by."

"And that is—"

"Satan's Pet."

Hortense started, for that name she had often heard around the camp-fire at night, connected with wild stories of border life and adventure which poor Revolver Nick and the train hunters had to tell.

But ere she could reply the strange visitor, with the stranger cognomen, glided from the room, and hastily she returned to the chamber in which she had left Dolores.

To her horror she found her gone. The room was without an occupant.

Chapter XV.
Faith in a Foe.

The stranger who had entered the room and startled the two maidens, causing Hortense to run quickly to warn the one who came to aid them, was a man of striking appearance.

He was tall, well-formed, dressed in a suit of black corduroy the pants stuck in top of boots, and wearing a black sombrero encircled by a silver cord.

His face was beardless, resolute and handsome, though his dark eyes held in them an expression of recklessness.

"Pardon, lady," he said raising his sombrero from his head.

"But I come as a friend, not a foe."

"Alas! I look for no friends here, sir: but your voice seems familiar, though I recall not your face," said Dolores.

"I am the one who brought you here, Miss Moultrie, and I do not wonder, in my then disguise, that you do not remember me."

Dolores started back at his words, but he continued quickly:

"Miss Moultrie, I pledge you my honor—"

"A Danite's honor!"

"I wonder not at your sneer; but I pledge you my honor that I mean you well and have come to save you from our chief, Major Leigh."

"I thought you were his hireling."

"You are severe, Miss Moultrie; but I cannot blame you after all you have suffered; but I have come to serve you if you will only trust me."

There was an honesty in the man's tone that Dolores could not doubt.

She remembered he had been kind to them in bringing them to Salt Lake City, and his face was not a treacherous one, and she said:

"Alas! I know not what to say."

"Trust me, for you cannot be worse off than here."

"True, I will trust you."

"Then come with me."

"Whither?"

"If you fear, do not come."

"And Hortense?"

"Must remain."

"I will not leave her."

"You can return for her."

"No."

"Then I will leave you, and, in the power of John Leigh, I say may God have mercy upon you."

She was alarmed at his impressive words and cried:

"Where would you have me go?"

"To the home of the head chief."

"Ha! Why?"

"To escape John Leigh."

"One may be a evil as the other."

"Not toward you, Miss Moultrie."

"Why not toward me?"

"Trust me and you will find out."

"I will."

She threw around her a shawl and passed out of the door.

There she halted and asked:

"You pledge yourself that I shall not be separated from Hortense?"

"Yes, I give you my pledge that you may return within the hour."

"Enough. I will go with you."

He drew her shawl around her with a courtly manner that could not offend, and drawing her hand through his arm, led her out of the yard, just as poor Hortense came back into the room to find her gone, and in an agony of grief threw herself down upon the sofa.

Utterly worn out by her violent sobbing she at last sunk to sleep, but started up at a touch on her arm.

It was Dolores that stood before her white as a ghost, her hands cold and trembling, and her whole manner indicative of having passed through some terrible ordeal of mental excitement.

"Oh, Dolores! why did you leave me?" cried Hortense, springing up.

"I could not help it, child, and I went for your good and mine," was the reply in a voice that had lost its music.

"Well, Dolores?" asked the young girl.

"Do not ask me to-night: to-morrow I will tell you all, but not now, not now."

"And I have to tell you, Dolores, that the one who visited us in Indian costume was the youth who led us from the camp that fearful night."

"Ah! that then was his voice: now I recall it."

"Thank God he is safe."

"Yes, and he came to save us, and—"

"Hortense, where is that woman?" suddenly interrupted Dolores.

"In the other room, lying where Satan's Pet left her."

"Satan's Pet?"

"Yes that is the name he gave me as his own."

"Strange; how often we have heard that name; but the woman, Hortense—"

She paused quickly, for the door opening into the yard slowly opened, and in stepped the same dark-faced visitor with whom Dolores had left the house a couple of hours before.

At sight of him her face again paled, and she asked, faltering:

"You here again?"

"Yes, Miss Moultrie, for one of my spies reported that he saw an Indian warrior enter this house, seize, bind and gag your female guard, and place her in the adjoining room.

"Is she there now?"

"She is."

"Then, as the door is ajar, she has doubtless seen me and heard what has passed, and I must carry her away with me.

"If asked regarding her, you need simply say that she left the house by that door."

There was a strange, grim smile upon the face of the speaker, and as he ceased speaking he gave a low call.

Almost instantly two men, heavily bearded and rough specimens of manhood, entered and saluted their officer.

"The woman lies in the other room; go and bring her here."

The two men silently obeyed, Dolores and Hortense looking on and wondering what new horror was to be brought before their eyes.

With the woman in their arms, her eyes wildly and fiercely glaring upon all in the room, the men returned, and stood waiting a second order from their officer.

"To doom with her!"

It was all he said, but the woman seemed to understand what was meant, as she writhed fearfully, and in vain tried to cry out as the men bore her away.

"There are some secrets that must not be known, Miss Moultrie, and the grave alone keeps them," he said, calmly.

"You would not—" began Dolores.

"You need have no fear of the woman now, and, if you are threatened by John Leigh, you know your escape. Good evening, ladies."

He bowed politely and departed and once more the maidens were alone, and Hortense cried, eagerly:

"Now, Dolores, we can escape from here, for that lynx-eyed woman has gone."

"Gone, and alas! to a sad fate I fear; but, Hortense, calm yourself, for we need not attempt to escape, as it would be useless; but go to sleep now, for we are safe."

"Safe!"

"Yes."

"What mean you, Dolores?"

"To-morrow you shall know all, but not to-night, not to-night."

Chapter XVI.
A Strange Story.

With the sunlight of the following day some of the gloom passed away from the hearts of Dolores and Hortense.

The woman, Dora, had been asked for by the other servants; but they were told, and truthfully, that she had left the house, and more regarding her the maidens could not tell.

Word of her disappearance was at once sent to John Leigh, and he soon put in an appearance, but could elicit no other information from either Dolores or Hortense than they had given the servants.

Cursing her for a traitress, and with a threat to Dolores that he would keep his word at the appointed time, the Danite leader left the house, having placed another woman in the place of the one who had so mysteriously disappeared, and one who, judging from her almost savage face, would be a she-dragon to guard them, for not in a single feature was there an atom of goodness or heart.

"Why do you smile, Dolores, at the threats of that wretch?" asked Hortense, noticing the look upon the face of Dolores after the Danite had departed.

"I will tell you, Hortense, and to do so, must first make known why I left you last night," and, as though some painful memory {9} swept over her, called up by her words, Dolores turned deadly pale.

"Did you notice the man who came here last night?"

"No, indeed, for I darted out to keep that Indian, or rather Satan's Pet, for I know him by no other name, from coming back in here."

"Well, he was the one who captured us at the cavern, and brought us here, and his name is Elmo Vane, and he is a captain of one of the bands of Danites."

"He did not treat us unkindly, Dolores."

"No, for the man has some heart; but he acts from a motive in serving us."

"He will serve us then?"

"Yes."

"And you know his motive?"

"I do; but let me explain:

"He came here last night and urged me to accompany him, saying it was for my good.

"Strange to say I trusted him, and I went where he led me.

"It was to a large house in the principal part of town.

"We entered the garden, ascended a piazza noiselessly, and he bade me gaze into a room in which shone a bright light.

"Hidden by the foliage of the trees near by I obeyed, and I beheld a man of fine presence slowly walking to and fro, his hands clasped behind him.

"There was that in his face that made me feel I had seen him before, and I seemed fascinated in gazing upon him.

"But, strive as I might, I could not recall when and where I had seen him before, and yet each moment that I gazed upon him, his face looked more and more familiar.

"My companion, Captain Vane stood by in silence, and I seemed to forget his presence until presently he called me away.

"Silently I followed him to a rustic arbor in the garden, and then I asked him why he had brought me there?

"'To see that man,' was his reply.

"'Who is he?'

"'My chief.'

"'But who?'

"'The chief of the Danite Legion.'

"'Ha! that man is then the wicked leader of the Danites?' I exclaimed.

"'He is the head chief, and next to our prophet, but he is not a wicked man at heart.'

"'He cannot be otherwise and be a Danite,' I answered.

"'Ah! Miss Moultrie, you do not know us all; you cannot read our thoughts, and know our hearts, to understand why we are what we are.'

"He spoke so sadly, Hortense, that I almost pitied him, and said:

"'I do not think you are vile at heart, or the chief whom we have just seen, for his is a noble face.'

"'True, and in many respects he is a noble man.'

"'But what motive had you in bringing me here to gaze unseen upon him?' I asked.

"'Were you in trouble is he not a man you could appeal to for protection?'

"'If he were other than he is—a *Danite*.'

"'I see I shall have to force you to appeal to him,' he said, impatiently, and after a pause continued:

"'Miss Moultrie, do you remember your parents?'

"I started at the question, Hortense, and answered:

"'Why do you ask, sir?'

"'I will tell you why; some years ago the head chief whom you just saw, saved my life.

"'I was crossing the plains, our train was attacked by Indians, and they in turn were attacked and defeated by Danites under our Prince, as we now call him.

"'I was then but twenty, and the Prince took a fancy to me and that is how I became what I now am.

"'Trusting me, the chief sent me East on a special mission of his own, and it was to find his wife and child.

"'He had left them, it seems, infatuated by the Mormon creed, as many men have been, and, his wife refusing to follow him into the Mormon church, had also refused his support after he had deserted her.

"'Finding that Mormonism was not all he had believed and hoped, he determined to secretly give it up, and to carry out this plan sent me to look up his wronged wife and child.

"'Armed with their names, and knowing where they had lived, I sought them out to find that the poor wife had taken her own and her child's life, driven to despair by her husband's desertion of them, for she had devotedly loved him.

"'This sad news I brought back to him, and from that day the head chief became a changed man.

"'He took the leadership of the Danite League, and seemed wholly imbittered with the world in general.

"'One day ago I found out a secret, which I have not divulged to the chief.

"'I picked up a leather case of letters, and in it I found that which I was determined to divulge to you.

"'The letters were addressed to Major Leigh, and also to him under the name of Mercer Aldrich and other *aliases*.

"'He had been sent on a proselyting tour to the States by the Prophet, and knowing something of the head chief's history, had, while there, accidentally found that his daughter was not dead, having been saved at the time of her mother's suicide, and left to the care of her preserver.

"'Knowing that the head chief is a man of vast wealth, and that he has no children here, and has received permission from the Prophet not to marry, Major Leigh determined to make this daughter of his leader his wife, and thereby get possession of the property he knew that she would possess, as soon as he brought her to Salt Lake.

"'Failing to win her by fair means, he intends doing so by foul, and this is why I brought you here, Miss Moultrie, to claim the head chief's protection, which is justly your due, as *Mark Moultrie, the Danite chief, is your father!*'"

CHAPTER XVII.
FRIENDS IN DISGUISE.

WHEN Dolores made the startling announcement to Hortense Harmon, that Moultrie the Danite chief was her father, the young girl seemed to be struck dumb with amazement.

But seeing how deeply distressed her friend was, she put her arms around her neck and said kindly:

"Don't care if he is, Dolores, for he does not know you are living, and he need never know it."

"Yes, Hortense, he must know it."

"What! will you tell him?"

"Yes."

"But why?"

"I will tell you why, my dear girl; this young Danite captain told me that the power of Major Leigh is fearful, and he wields an influence over the Danite League that can drive them to any evil.

"He is determined to make me marry him by Mormon law, and will then make our marriage known to my father, who will have to acknowledge him as a son, for the Prophet, who he says stands in awe of Leigh, would compel him to do so, even though he knew this wretch had forced me to marry him.

"Captain Vane has but half a dozen men in the League that he can depend upon as true to himself, and he says otherwise he would aid our escape from here, but that under the circumstances it would be worse than madness to attempt it."

"Oh, Dolores, how sad is our lot; my father dead, and yours—"

She paused, and her face colored; but Dolores bravely finished the sentence:

"And my father worse than dead, for he is Moultrie, the Danite."

Hortense sighed, and wiping away the tears that dimmed her eyes, Dolores continued:

"The captain, therefore, thinks it best for me to make myself known to my father—"

"But, can you prove that you are his daughter, Dolores?"

"What a little lawyer you are, Hortense; yes, for I have here with me his own miniature likeness he gave my mother, and a few other trinkets which that fiend, Leigh, saved from the flames; then I have changed but little since I was a child, in expression of face, and he would know me."

"And can he save you from this Major Leigh, whom you say is all-powerful?"

"Yes, for Leigh could not force me to marry him if I was under my father's care."

"And poor me, Dolores?"

"Don't think, Hortense, that I would desert you; if you cannot go with me, I will remain with you, and, if it comes to the worst, we can die together."

"Brave, good Dolores! I love you so much," and the affectionate girl again twined her arms around her neck.

Dolores kissed her affectionately, and continued:

"Of course I dare not make known to my father where I got my information regarding him, as it would compromise the Danite captain, and their law is that making known the secret of a superior, and breaking their oath to know no friendships, outside of their League, is punishable with death.

"I must, therefore, not let it be known that he told me; but he promised to send a messenger here to-night, who will secretly guide us to the head-quarters of my poor misguided father."

"But the she-dragon, who sleeps in our room?"

"He has prepared for her by giving me a small bottle of chloroform, which I can stupefy her with to-night."

"Good! and I don't care much if she never wakes up."

"Don't be wicked, Hortense."

"It's catching; it's in the air, Dolores."

"Well, to-night we go together from this place."

"And what then?"

"I will make myself known to my father; tell him we were taken captives when the train was attacked, and that Major Leigh wished me to become his wife, though I will not say that he knew who I was, or that he had ever seen me before, and with this secret held *in terrorem* over the Danite major, I may be able to escape his persecutions, until—"

"Until what, Dolores?"

"Until we can escape, for I shall never remain in this horrid place, had I ten thousand kindred who were Mormons."

"Nor I."

"And I will let my father think that I knew he was here, a Danite chief."

"And he will protect you, Dolores, you think?"

"Yes, Hortense, he will protect us, for a father, be he what he may, cannot be so vile as not to protect his child from a fate worse than death."

"God grant that he does; but what about our young friend, who has risked his life to come in here to rescue us, Dolores?"

"You mean Satan's Pet?" asked Dolores with a s smile.

"Yes."

"He will know where we are, and, if he has formed a plan of escape for us, he can aid us there as well, if not better, than here."

"True, and I believe he is one to carry out what he undertakes, Dolores."

"He certainly looks it; but how strange that a youth with his wonderful face, for it is really beautiful, should lead the life he does!"

"Strange indeed, Dolores: there is some mystery in his life, I think."

"I feel sure that there is, Hortense. But see, yonder come two Indians that look strangely like those who captured us."

She pointed out of the window, and instantly her eyes fell upon the two warriors. Hortense said quickly, and in a low tone:

"Dolores, that is Satan's Pet! see, do you not recognize him now?"

"Yes, it is the same young Indian who paid us a visit last night."

"It is indeed; but who is his companion?"

"That I cannot tell; but he is a splendid looking man, be he white-face or Indian."

The two individuals referred to were in full Indian costume, and certainly looked like thorough Indians.

They came along the street with an indifferent air, it seemed; but as they drew near the house the maidens saw that their eyes were fixed intently upon them.

The larger of the two held his bow in his hand, and an arrow in rest, and suddenly, with a light pull upon the head of the missile he sent it with unerring aim into the sill beneath the window, where it stuck quivering in the wood.

Around the head of the arrow was a piece of paper closely wrapped, and in an instant it was in the hand of Hortense, while the missile was drawn out and hastily concealed.

The pretended Indians passed on, and eagerly the two maidens bent over the slip of paper and their eyes devoured as they read.

Written in a bold hand was the following:

"The Danite means you harm, and to-night he will bear you away to his camp in the mountains.

"Be ready to fly with us, and have no fear."

This was all. {10}

"Oh!" what shall we do?" cried Hortense.

"If the messenger from the captain comes first, we will go with him to my father; if they come first, we will accompany them.

"It is but a lottery both ways, Hortense, and I cannot understand how these men can rescue us from the dangers with which we are surrounded."

Hortense sighed, and the two determined to bide their time and see what the night would bring forth.

Chapter XVIII.
Hope.

WHETHER the Danite captain felt that what he did to save the maidens, must be done quickly, or the major would act, neither Dolores or Hortense knew; but certain it was that his messenger came early, shortly after dark.

It had been agreed between the captain and Dolores that the messenger should come to the house and ask if Major Leigh was present, and this should be the signal for her to get rid of the woman and at once take her departure with Hortense, and they would find their guide awaiting them outside.

It was just after dark that such a personage appeared: a tall man, wearing his hair and beard long, and dressed in the uniform of the Danites.

The female guard was on the alert and met the man at the door, in answer to his knock.

"Well?" she said shortly.

"I are seekin' the majer; are he heur?" asked the man.

"You mean Major Leigh?"

"Yas, who else?"

"You gave no name," said the woman in a surly tone.

"Majers must be thick in these heur parts thet yer doesn't know who I means."

"He is not here."

"He rid down this heur way late this arternoon an' ther guard told me I were likely to find him heur, as this were his bird-cage fer gal-kernaries."

"He is not here."

"So yer told me jist now."

"Look for him elsewhere."

"S'pose I has ter; good-night, says I, ter be perlite, tho' yer is as cross as a settin' hen."

The door was banged in the face of the man, and to soothe her ruffled temper Dolores called the woman over to her and said kindly:

"Here is something I guess you do not often see out here?"

As she spoke she handed her a bottle of cologne.

"What is it?"

"Perfume."

"Oh, yes; no, I have not seen a bottle of cologne for many a long year.

"I have mostly forgotten how it smells."

"You may have it if you wish, for I have more."

"I can't be bribed, young woman," was the sharp reply, as the bottle was pushed aside.

"I meant not to bribe you, for I know that would be impossible.

"Take it, for I know you wish it."

"Thank you."

"And Hortense, get me that bottle of perfume, please, among my traps, and I will put some on the lady's handkerchief."

Hortense passed into the other room, and soon returned with a small bottle marked "perfume."

"It looks precious," said the woman.

"It is; just smell it and see how delicious it is."

The woman took a long breath and drew in the intoxicating scent, and then another, after which Dolores said with the utmost coolness:

"Give me your handkerchief, Hortense."

The young girl obeyed and received it back again with some of the *perfume.*

Then Dolores poured some upon her own handkerchief.

"It is sweet, isn't it?" said the woman and she inhaled another long breath of it.

"Yes, very; now let me have your handkerchief."

"It isn't very clean."

"Never mind, the effect will be the same," and, as if by accident she dropped the bottle, and the contents saturated the piece of soiled linen.

"Quick! don't lose the perfume of it," cried the maiden, and the woman held it to her nose.

But only for a moment, for her hand dropped in her lap, and her head drooped forward.

But Dolores was not satisfied yet, and held the handkerchief a moment more to the nose of the woman, while she motioned to Hortense to quickly get their wraps and their bundles, which the young girl had hastily put together when she was pretending to find the perfume.

A moment after the two stepped out of the house into the darkness, and Dolores leaned an instant against a tree, while she said nervously:

"A moment more and I would have been under the influence of the chloroform, too; but the air revives me, so let us see where the guide is."

"I am here, Miss Moultrie."

Both maidens started back as a tall form glided up to them.

But they recognized the messenger who had pretended to be in search of Major Leigh, and Dolores said quickly:

"You come from Captain Vane?"

"I am Captain Elmo Vane, Miss Moultrie; I am glad my disguise was so perfect as to deceive you; but come, let us hasten, for Leigh may arrive at any moment, and I would hate to be compelled to take his life."

Dolores glanced at the speaker in surprise, and he continued in a low tone:

"Rather than see you again in John Leigh's power, I would kill him in his tracks, be the consequences what they might."

"Thank you," said Dolores softly, hardly knowing what to say, and she continued:

"Captain Vane, this is my fellow unfortunate, Miss Hortense Harmon."

The young Danite bowed politely and rapidly led the way along the road, having taken from the maidens their bundles.

All the way to the home of the Danite chief Dolores seemed nervous and sad, for she felt that a fearful ordeal was before her, as she would rather have her father dead than what he was.

At last the garden was reached, and fully acquainted with the surroundings, the Danite captain led the way to the little arbor, and said:

"Miss Harmon and myself will await here until you call for her: then I will leave; but be certain not to speak of my being here[."]

"I shall not betray you, sir, and believe me I shall ever appreciate your kindness; farewell."

She held forth her hand, and grasping it warmly he said softly:

"We shall meet again, Miss [Moultrie]; especially shall we if you need a friend."

She was nearly uttering the words, "I hope not;" but the latter part of his speech checked them, and she merely bowed, and said:

"Hortense, I will soon call for you, and have some hope for your poor little heart."

"There is the door, Miss Moultrie; the one to the right of the window."

"Thank you, sir," and trembling like a frightened bird Dolores Moultrie went forward to the mansion to meet face to face the father who had deserted her mother and herself long years before, and had given up the creed of his people for the strange belief of the Mormon.

CHAPTER XIX.
THE DANITE AND HIS DAUGHTER.

WITH limbs that barely supported her, Dolores ascended the steps to the piazza, and hesitated at the door, as she glanced in through the window.

There as upon her former visit, she beheld the form of the Danite chief pacing the room, in the same meditative mood he had seemed in then.

She gazed upon his clear-cut features, stern mouth and deep-set eyes, and then upon his tall form, clothed in black, and said softly:

"Yes, he is indeed my father."

Twice she attempted to rap on the door, ere she found strength to do so, and then drawing a vail over her face, gave a sudden knock.

"Come in!" said a low deep voice.

She opened the door and the man had turned about and faced her.

He seemed surprised at the entrance of a woman, and bowed with courtly grace.

"I believe you are Colonel Moultrie the Danite chief?"

Her voice as she spoke was hardly audible, but he to whom her words were addressed heard them, for he answered:

"Yes, I am Moultrie the Danite; how can I serve you?"

"I have come to seek your protection."

"Indeed? from whom?"

"From one who persecutes me."

"Who are you, may I ask?"

"A poor, unfortunate girl who is friendless."

"Then you need a protector; but who is so vile as to persecute you?"

His tone was kind, though his manner was stern.

"One who holds high rank in your command."

"Ha! it is Leigh, I'll lay odds on it."

"It is Major Leigh."

"He is a bad man to oppose in his whims, for he is backed by the Prophet; but prove that he persecutes you and I will protect you."

"He wishes me to marry him."

"Ah! and you have your eye on some one else?"

"No, I do not expect ever to marry."

"Tell him so."

"I have."

"Refuse him decidedly."

"I have, but he means to force me into a marriage with him."

"He is capable of it; but has he any claim upon you?"

"None; I have, on the contrary, every reason to abhor and hate him."

"Indeed?"

"Yes, for he it was who attacked the train of which I was a member, and oh God! my heart sickens at the fearful massacre that followed."

"I have heard of this; the emigrants were opposed to our religion, and were forcing themselves into our valley to settle, and refused the warning given them, fired upon my men, and we had to protect ourselves."

"You have been misinformed."

"So it seems, for Major Leigh led me to believe, if I heard aright, that there was not one escaped, and I find you here."

"Yes, and there was one other."

"Ha!"

"A young girl, and we were brought here and have been occupants of Leigh's town house, until he got ready to force me into a marriage with him."

"By the Mormon Prophet! but he shall not do this."

"Oh sir, from my heart I thank you; but let me tell you that those emigrants did not intend to settle in Utah, but in Wyoming, in the vicinity of Fort Bridger, and they formed but one half the train; the others were government men, and train men, all under command of the newly appointed Indian agent, Captain Harmon.

"We were not warned off, received no admonition of attack, and the massacre left but two of us to tell the story."

"This is far different from Leigh's report of it."

"I tell you the truth of it, and, if the Danites meant to fight for their rights, why were they all painted and costumed like Indians?"

"Were they?" and the chief raised his eyebrows in surprise.

"To a man."

"This shall be looked to, and I shall give Major John Leigh to understand that I am the chief of the Danites, and he but my officer," was the stern response.

"And I will not be given up to him?"

"Upon my honor no!"

"Heaven I thank thee!" and advancing to within a few feet of the Danite, Dolores continued:

"Look in my face, sir, and see whom you have saved from that man's power."

She dropped her vail, and her beautiful face, now flushed with intense excitement, was revealed to him.

The light fell full upon her, revealing every feature, and her faultless form, and the man stared at her as though an apparition had suddenly arisen from the grave and stood before him.

At last, in husky tones, he cried:

"In the name of God, I implore you, tell me who you are?"

"*Your daughter.*"

"No! no! no! that cannot be, for I have no daughter."

"You had one?"

"Yes, a wee little girl in the long, long ago; had she lived, she would have looked like you."

"I am your daughter."

"I tell you *no*, for she died; her poor mother, {11} whom I cruelly deserted for this accursed—no, no, no, I will not say that, for I am a Mormon, and once a Mormon, ever one.

"I left her, my beautiful young wife, and our little daughter, and in grief and despair she took her own life and the life of her child, and the sin lies on my hand and heart, and not hers.

"Yes, I am the guilty one."

"I tell you *I* am your daughter; my mother, your wife, sprung with me into the sea; she died and I was saved."

"No, no, no, that cannot be."

"I am your daughter, Dolores."

"*Dolores!* yes, that was her name."

"See, here is your miniature likeness I had round my neck on that fearful night my poor mother died."

She handed him a gold medallion in which was a painted likeness of himself.

"Great God! it is the one I gave to my poor child.

"But how came you by it?"

"Father, look at me, and tell me if I am not Dolores?"

"She was a child, and—"

"And that was years ago. I have grown to womanhood since, and tell me, do I not look as my mother did then?"

"Good God! yes you are my child, my Dolores."

He drew her toward him passionately, but almost instantly sprung back while he cried in bitter tones:

"But you, my pure, beautiful child, can but feel polluted by the touch of such a father."

"Father, hear me!

"Had I found you cold of heart, as you are said to be, I would have almost hated you.

"Finding you sympathetic with my grief, though you knew me not, I was drawn toward you, and oh, I have so longed for a mother's and a father's love in all these long years."

Again he drew her to his broad breast, and, Danite leader though he was Dolores Moultrie felt that in him she had one to love her and to protect her and poor Hortense, whom a moment after she called into the room, where her lone heart, too, was made glad by the welcome she received.

Chapter XX.
DIAMOND CUT DIAMOND.

MAJOR JOHN LEIGH was in a towering passion, and the half dozen men who rode up to the town-house with him, leading two horses with side saddles on them, were really frightened for their lives.

He had dismounted at the door of his dwelling in town, and which he had used as a prison for Dolores and Hortense, and to his rap on the door no answer came.

Pushing it open he beheld the female guard lying back in an easy-chair, apparently asleep.

One vigorous shake, and she fell to the floor.

Then his nose was made sensitive of a peculiar and overpowering fragrance filling the room, and he cried out savagely:

"She has been chloroformed, by the holy Prophet!"

Vigorously he shook the unconscious woman until he aroused her from her stupor, and she was fairly terrified when she beheld the livid, furious face peering down upon her.

"Fool! where are my captives?"

The woman glanced stupidly around her, but made no reply.

"Idiot! dolt! where are those maidens I left for you to guard?" he shouted.

"Gone."

"Curse you, am I blind?"

"Where are they?"

"That is what I asked you, thou accursed hag of Satan."

The woman put her hands on her ears as if to shut out his profanity, but he dragged them rudely away, and asked, in ringing tones:

"How long have they been gone?"

"How long have I been under the influence of this drug?"

"It is now ten o'clock."

"Then they have not been long gone, for I relieved Matta in her watch."

"You had better have let her remain on duty, you silly fool, than allowed them to trick you so."

"It was the perfume."

"What perfume?"

"They gave me."

"It was chloroform; and as soon as you were under its influence they left.

"But, they can have no one to aid them, and must be near; ho! Danites!"

The men sprung forward at his call, and he cried:

"Dash through the town, and give my orders for the capture and restoration to me of two maidens found alone."

Away rode the men, and bidding the woman tell them on their return to await him there, Major Leigh mounted his horse and rode rapidly to the home of the Danite head chief.

He found Moultrie alone in his room, pacing to and fro, as was his wont, yet not wearing his habitual look of sternness.

"Ah! Major Leigh, is there news?" asked the chief, calmly.

"Yes, chief, for two captives have escaped."

"How can captives escape from our power, Leigh?"

"Only through treachery, sir."

"Do you suspect the traitor?"

"I do not."

"Who were the captives?"

"Both of them young women who escaped from the emigrant train we fought in the Escalante mountains."

"I understood you that none escaped."

"So I believed; but two women were afterward brought in by my men."

"Well, what was your intention regarding them, Leigh?"

"One, I confess, sir, I desired to make my wife, and the other, too, when she grew to womanhood."

"Ah! would they be willing, think you, to accept the hand that shot down their kindred?"

"It would be a better lot for them than others that might befall them."

"Well, you are your own master, Major John Leigh, so can do as you please, so you do not force a woman to become your wife.

"That I would resent, sir; is there aught else to communicate?

"Nothing, sir, only I would like a general order issued to have them returned to me when taken."

"Send your couriers to report such an order to the outposts, then."

"Thank you, Chief Moultrie."

"And, Leigh, let me beg that you be more careful in your scoutings with your command."

"How mean you, chief?"

"You failed to see, or, if seeing, to report, that a large band of Indians had been seen of late within a few leagues of the city."

"Ah! I had forgotten it; they were but a hunting party of Utes."

"I will warn their chief that they must not hunt so near; they must keep on their Reservation, or we will regard them as foes."

"I will so instruct them, sir."

"And remember; be careful to have no collision with United States troops, or emigrants, as in that affair the other day, for we are not prepared to fight as we would wish."

"True, sir, I will have care."

"Good-night, Major Leigh."

The Danite officer bowed and retired. When he was gone the Danite chief rung a silver bell.

In a moment a servant appeared in answer.

"Tell Captain Vane I would see him."

The young captain, whose quarters adjoined those of his chief, soon appeared.

"Vane, set a trusty spy on the movements of Major Leigh, with orders to report to me daily."

"Yes, chief."

"And place several of your own men that can be thoroughly trusted at the South Pass."

"Yes, chief."

"And hold yourself in readiness for special duty with a score of your very best men and horses, for I may need you."

"I will obey, chief."

The young officer bowed and withdrew, muttering:

"He little knows that I brought them here; but I believe he intends to keep their presence a secret, fearing to allow the Prophet to see his beautiful daughter."

And the Danite chief muttered to himself:

"I can trust Vane for he is as true as steel. I see danger ahead, from that lynx-eyed Leigh, but I will meet it boldly and neither he or the Prophet shall win the prize."

Chapter XXI.
The Allies Scent Danger.

Upon his return to the house to meet his waiting men, Major Leigh gave a few orders to his servants, and mounting dashed away, followed by his Danites.

As they disappeared up the street, two men stepped out from the shelter where they had been concealed, and one said:

"Well, the birds have flown, and they have not gone with Leigh either."

"That's true, Bill; but who have they gone with?"

"You've got me there, Pet. They had evidently just gone when we arrived and had to hide at the coming of Leigh. My stars! but how mad he was: he could have bitten a ten-penny nail in two."

"He could that, Bill; but those girls had no friends, so where have they gone?"

"I give it up."

"They got our note, for I saw them read it."

"Yes, Pet; but they may have found out that that devil Leigh was coming to carry them off, and so left, hoping to find us."

"Then we must look for them, Bill."

"That's just our little game."

"Well, which way first?"

"I'm off the trail."

"And I."

For a moment they stood in a quandary, not knowing which way to turn or what to do.

Then Satan's Pet said quietly:

"When devil Leigh rode away he went down toward the Danite chief's."

"Yes."

"Well, he may have gone to put the guards on the path, so let us go there and see if there is any excitement going on."

"I am with you, Pet."

Off they went to the house of Moultrie the Danite chief, and while Buffalo Bill crouched in the shadows of the foliage, Satan's Pet went into the house garden, being well acquainted with the surroundings.

"If you want me, Pet, sing out," said the scout in a whisper.

"Oh, I'll call, never fear, if there's trouble."

Creeping forward the youth soon gained a position near the piazza, and climbing a tree with the agility of a monkey, he peered over the blinds into the room.

He saw the Danite chief pacing to and fro, and just as he looked in walked Captain Elmo Vane.

The conversation between the two he heard and it set him to thinking.

Still keeping his perch on the limb of the tree he saw the Danite officer depart on his mission, and then, as he was about to leave his point of observation, he was amazed to see two female forms glide into the room from a door on the further side.

He gave a low whistle of surprise, but from his position he could not see them, but merely heard the chief remark:

"It is late, you had better retire now."

"And I'll retire, too," he muttered, and at once dropped from the tree.

Retracing his steps to where he had left Buffalo Bill, he hastily informed him of all he had heard and seen, and the two then sat in silence, in a worse quandary than ever.

"I'm afraid it[']s a case of out of the frying-pan into the fire, Pet," said the scout after awhile.

"You mean their being in the power of the Danite chief?"

"Yes."

"I do not think so, for he is not as wicked at heart as is Leigh, though he is a bold, stern man."

"How can he have gotten possession of them?"

"I am off the scent; let me see, I guess he had spies who told him of Leigh's little game, and he brought them there to protect them."

"And marry them himself."

"A better lot than to be Leigh's wives."

"Six of one, and—"

"No, Bill, the chief is not a marrying man, and he is different from that black-hearted Leigh."

"You seem to hate Leigh fearfully."

"By the God above; but I have had good cause."

The words fairly burst from the lips of the youth, and he spoke with almost ferocity in his tone.

But an instant after he said in a quiet way, and with his off-hand air of indifference:

"I'll be in at his death, Bill, for I have sworn it."

"You could have killed him to-night."

"No, I am not ready yet; I wish to talk with him before he dies; there is something I must find out." {12}

"Well, we won't find out the mystery about those girls if we sit here."

"True; but I'll tell you how I'll find out."

"How?"

"What kind of a girl would I make for looks?"

"A beauty."

"Nonsense."

"I mean it, little pard; few girls have your good looks."

"Thank you, Bill, but I will tell you a good plan."

"Go ahead."

"You remember when we were near the Endowment Home this morning?"

"Yes."

"We heard the Danite chief wanted a housemaid."

"That's so."

"I'll be the very girl for him."

"You!"

"Why not?"

"It strikes me you wear pants and not petticoats."

"I can easily change the rig; come, we'll go over to Jew Abrams, our Hebrew friend, and I'll buy a feminine outfit, and go and apply for the situation the first thing in the morning.["]

"It will be a great risk."

"I like to take desperate chances, and I'll do it, while you remain at Jew Abrams and be a good Injun."

"Good Injun's dead Injun," laughed the scout.

"That's so; well, be your own handsome, brave self, and I'll turn up with news. Come!"

They set off at a swift pace for the abode where they made their quarters when in town, and the Jew told Satan's Pet, that:

"I haf te clothes dat makes you just so same as a leetle gal."

Chapter XXII.
The Messenger from Fort Bridger.

The home of the Prophet was the most pretentious mansion in Salt Lake City, and the master of Mormonism, and all that its name signifies, sat alone in his room, the morning after the escape of Dolores Moultrie and Hortense Harmon from the power of Leigh the Danite.

His was a face that would have been kindly but for a certain sinister expression hovering about the mouth; but it was bold, resolute, and intellectual in spite of its sensuality.

Before him on his table were innumerable papers, letters, and what appeared to be legal documents, while upon a black-board at hand was drawn a map of the surroundings of his capital, its approaches, and the natural and artificial defenses.

His brow was contracted into a frown, as he sat there, and the pen he held in his hand was dry, showing that he had been toying with it, instead of using it.

Presently with an impatient gesture he threw the pen aside, and said:

"That wild reckless Leigh will get me into serious trouble yet, either with the [United] States Government, or the Utes.

"Unless he knew them as foes it was all wrong for him to make that attack, and he had no good reason that I can see for believing them to be enemies.

"This wiping out the whole party does no good, for a body of men and women cannot die by violence, and strict investigation not be made.

"I must keep an eye on Leigh, or tell Moultrie to do so, for he is too rash and fond of killing— Well?"

"A United States officer to see you, sir," and a Danite orderly saluted his Prophet.

"Some complaint, doubtless, of which Leigh is the cause; bid him enter, and send at once for Major Leigh."

The Danite retired, and a few moments after a tall, splendid-looking young man, clad in the full uniform of a captain of cavalry in the United States army entered the room, and saluted the Prophet politely.

"Be seated, sir, and allow me the pleasure of knowing whom I address," said the Prophet with courtesy.

"My name is Howland Moncrief, sir, and my rank that of captain in the American army.

"I am here, sir, with a message from General Duncan of Fort Bridger," was the matter-of-fact reply, yet delivered in a courtly manner.

"Well, Captain Moncrief, I may say that I have heard of you, sir, and am glad to meet so gallant an officer."

Howland Moncrief bowed.

"Now tell me how I can serve you, your general and the United States Government?"

"In scouting the other day I came upon a scene of horror, sir; scores of men, women and children massacred and mutilated, and left unburied."

"Yes. I heard of it, and have just sent for my scouting officer to ask the particulars; he will be here soon, and you can hear what he says. Oh! here he is now.

"Major Leigh, my honored guest, Captain Moncrief, of the American army," said the Prophet, as John Leigh the Danite entered.

"It was evident that Major Leigh intended to be most courteous to the Prophet's guest, for he started forward with a smile and his hand extended; but his manner changed at the frigid air of the young officer, who did not offer his hand, but said, with a cold, meaning smile:

"Major Leigh and myself really require no introduction, as we have met before."

"Indeed, sir, where, may I ask?" and the Danite bit his lips with vexation.

"In various little encounters, sir, for I was detailed by my Government to especially watch the movements of Leigh the Danite."

The major made no reply, but his face paled, and the Prophet came to his rescue with:

"Major, Captain Moncrief is sent by General Duncan at Fort Bridger to inquire regarding a massacre that took place in the region of the Escalantes some days ago."

"Ah yes; you refer to that Indian massacre of the train?" was the calm reply of the Danite.

"I refer, sir, to a massacre of a train, but whether by Indians, or—"

"Or what sir?"

"Or Danites—"

"Captain Moncrief, I cannot permit, sir—"

"Major John Leigh, permit me to finish my sentence, sir; I was remarking that whether the massacre was by Indians or Danites, I had come here to find out."

"And your opinion, sir?" asked the Prophet calmly.

"The *signs*, sir, point to Indians as the perpetrators; but unfortunately all were slain and no one can tell who were the base and cowardly fiends."

"I had formed my opinion, sir, for I came upon the fearful scene, while on a scout, that they were Indians, in fact they could be nothing else, and I sent word to your commander to that effect.

"I then followed the trail, sir, but lost it in the Uintah mountains, for it divided into a score of trails leading among the head waters of the streams that flow into the Uintah river. Returning to the scene of the massacre, I discovered that the dead had been buried, and the marks indicated that it had been the work of troopers."

"Yes, I buried them, and then set to look to find the trails; but they had been so gone over I failed, even with my best scouts, to discover the traces I sought.

"As your opinion points to the Utes, I shall have to so report it, and the general will make an expedition at once into their country, for the captain of the train was his friend, and the newly appointed Indian agent, whom we were expecting, and with him, we learned that he had his young and beautiful daughter."

"It was a very sad affair, Captain Moncrief, and so express my feelings, please, to your general.

"You will remain our gust for awhile, I hope, sir," said the Prophet.

"Thank you, no sir; I am anxious to return and make my report," and saluting the Prophet, but taking no notice of Major Leigh the Danite, Howland Moncrief took his departure, leaving behind him a most uncomfortable feeling in the hearts of the Mormon leader and his *aide*.

Chapter XXIII.
The Prophet and His Pet.

"Well, John Leigh, what does this last rash act of yours mean?" said the Prophet sternly, when Captain Moncrief had gotten beyond earshot.

"Indians."

"Indians what?"

"I say it means Indians," was the cool reply.

"What Indians?"

"The Utes."

"John Leigh, you reported to me a massacre in the Escalante mountains and that not one escaped: what does it mean?"

"I reported to you, Prophet, that a massacre had occurred in the Escalantes, and that not one of the train had escaped."

"Just so."

"Did I report who had done the killing?"

"You led me to believe that your band had been attacked and—"

"You are all wrong, Prophet; my band was attacked by this same train, that is, were beaten off, they fearing we were road-agents; but this same train, while encamped, was met by Utes, who massacred them all; so was my report, if you will remember."

"I am glad to know that such is the case, and that I misunderstood you.

"The United States Government is ever ready to press us hard; but though I am ready to meet them if they drive us too hard, I will not permit acts of deviltry like this massacre, and so understand me, John Leigh."

"Oh! you make it plain enough, Prophet; now to tell you a bit of gossip."

"Well, sir."

"You granted my revered chief, Moultrie, absolution from marriage, I believe?"

"I did."

"You had your reasons?"

"I did. He is a woman-hater, though a thorough Mormon in belief; he is a man who has known deep sorrows, and prefers to be alone."

"A woman-hater, you say?"

"Yes."

"Then why has he two fair ladies residing with him?"

"What?" and the Prophet looked amazed indeed.

"Why, as a woman-hater, and a man who has absolution from marriage, does my revered chief have the right to keep two lovely housekeepers?" said Leigh, with a sinister smile.

"By no means."

"Yet he does."

"No, he has a maid-of-all-work there."

"And two beauties."

"John Leigh, what do you mean?" asked the Prophet, sternly.

"Just what I say, sir; I saw two ladies there myself this morning, though they did not see me.

"One of my spies told me that he saw two ladies enter the chief's grounds last night, and, with a field-glass, I looked into their room from a high elevation, and saw that I had been correctly informed."

"This is strange. Let me know that old Moultrie is deceiving me in this style, and I will deprive him of his rank."

"In that case, I come next, I believe, Prophet?"

"Yes, of course; but, mind you, no trumping up stories to get the place."

"Do you think I would do a wrong to get promotion, Prophet?" asked the Danite, in an injured tone.

"I think that you are a villain, John Leigh; in fact, I know it, yet I cannot help regarding you kindly; but I will withdraw my affection from you if I ever catch you in any one act of deviltry you know would not be sanctioned by me."

"It's catching before hanging, sir," laughed the Danite.

"True, but I may try to see how the old adage works."

"And that is?"

"Set a thief to catch a thief."

"Ah! forewarned is forearmed."

"You have just caught old Moultrie, or pretended to have done so."

"I have caught him, and I will bring the two fair ladies before you, if you wish."

"No; simply watch him, and when you have discovered proof, I will accompany you to his house and unmask him then and there."

"It shall be done, Prophet; and if I catch him you will grant a favor I ask?"

"I think your promotion will be favor enough."

"No, Prophet, for I have another to ask."

"Name it."

"Will you grant it?"

"Yes."

"Then I will tell you what it is when we catch the old fox." {13}

"Silence, sir, for Moultrie is your superior officer."

"Ah, I beg your pardon, Prophet."

"You are a graceless dog, I fear, Leigh."

"Perhaps not so black as I am painted, Prophet," and with a salute John Leigh the Danite departed, leaving the Prophet meditating upon the charge made against Moultrie, his colonel of cavalry.

Chapter XXIV.
JUDITH.

LITTLE dreaming that when he had spies on the movements of John Leigh, that worthy, through one of his secret service men, had already discovered the secret which he wished unknown, that is, the presence of the maidens in his house, Moultrie the Danite Chief sat in his half-sanctum, half-office, meditating as to the best plan to be adopted for the safety of his lovely daughter and her young friend.

For them to remain in Salt Lake City he knew would bring sorrow upon them, and he did not doubt but that the wonderful beauty of his daughter would at once cause the Prophet to demand her as his wife.

Knowing well the abhorrence that Dolores had shown against the Mormon faith, he knew that it would break her heart to meet such a fate.

And lovely little Hortense would be another prize for the Prophet's eye, he felt assured.

If they should escape this honor then some other personage of less importance would sue for their hands, and the end would be even more wretched.

There was but one course for him to pursue, and that was to carry out his original intention and get the two maidens out of the city.

Having decided upon this course he was about to send for Captain Vane, and make a clean breast of it to him, depending upon his valuable services to aid him out of the trouble, when the door opened and the servant ushered in a young girl.

"Mrs. Barney, sir, has sent this girl up for Eliza's place, and says she can be fully trusted," was the servant's remark.

"Come in and let me see you," and at the invitation the applicant for "Eliza's place" entered the room.

She was a young girl apparently of eighteen or twenty, with red hair, freckled face, that was by no means homely, and a figure that many a belle might be proud of.

"What is your name?"

"Judith, most howly Prophet."

"A Jewish name on an Irish girl," muttered the Danite, while aloud he said:

"I am not the Prophet, but simply one of his officers."

"I thought yez was afther being that same, yer riverence."

"Which, the Prophet or his officer?"

"Divil the loikes o' me cares which?"

"Where did you come from?"

"I was afther being a convert from ould Oirland, God bliss ther grane sod."

"You came over with Elder Broadcastle's party?"

"I did thet same; he convarted me ter H'athenism in the ould sod, and I got me passage paid over, an' now I'm riddy for worruk or marryin'."

"Ah! what kind of work?"

"Divil the loikes o' me cares, yer riverince, fer I kin cook, wash, iron, swape, and be house-gal in general."

"You will be most useful then, and, Eliza, I will—"

"Don't call me Eliza: me name is Judith, av yer plaze; Judith O'Hara, of the ould sod, which was me father's name 'afore me."

"Well, Judith, I will engage you, for my girl was called away by sickness in her family.

"Go into the kitchen, now, and tell Tom to set you right."

"Oh, I'm all set right, now, yer riverence; and I kin dress hair, too."

"Dress hair; we don't eat hair, here, Judith."

"Who says yez is ter ate it; I says dress it, ther hair o' yer riverence's head."

"Ah! but I take care of the little I've got myself."

"But ther ould lady's."

"I am not married, Judith."

"Oh, ther divil! I thought yez all had harems in this woild land."

"No, not all of us; but Judith, I hope you are not given to talking outside, about the affairs of a house in which you serve?"

"Divil a talker am I; no, yer riverence, I hev a mouth that niver talks."

"Well, Judith, see to it that it continues so, and if you are asked who forms my household you are not to know."

"I'll be dumb as a parish praste."

"Then go into yonder hallway and knock at a door at the further end, and see if the young ladies need your services."

"The young ladies; oh, the sly look of yer face; will, will, yer riverence, I'll do as yer says, av it's ter marry mesilf," and the newly-engaged servant went to the door indicated, and knocked.

"Come in," said a sweet voice.

"Oh! thet's music through ther kayhole," muttered Judith, and she entered the room.

It was not very bright in there, for the chief had sent word to have the blinds closed; but Judith saw the two maidens seated upon a sofa, chatting earnestly together.

"I'm ther new gurrel, miss, and his riverence sint me to say if yez was afther wanting anything."

They started at seeing a stranger enter the room, for they knew the chief's house-girl had been called away, and seeing it, Judith put her finger on her lips, and advanced on tip-toe, while she continued in a whisper:

"I'm Judith; that is, his riverence is afther belavin' I am; but, before you, ladies, *I am Satan's Pet.*"

They gazed on the pretended Judith an instant, and then saw that it was indeed their young preserver, and their sad faces lighted up with a smile at his wonderful make-up as an Irish girl, while Dolores held forth her hand and said, kindly:

"This is another plot on your part to serve us."

"It is, for here you are in danger."

"I had hoped we would not be, and hence we came here."

"No young girl is safe herein this town, so you must leave it, as already Major Leigh knows you are here."

"Ha! he has found that out?"

"Yes, for I heard him telling one of his spies, as I passed, to keep an eye on the house, and if the ladies left it to at once follow them, and if they attempted to leave the city, to all his comrades, arrest them, and carry them to his mountain den."

"But my—that is, Moultrie, the chief, will protect me."

"If he can; but if he saved you from Leigh, the Prophet, once seeing either of you, would claim you for his wives."

"Then we are indeed lost," groaned Dolores.

"Your only plan for safety is to leave this place."

"And where go?"

"My ally has a kinsman living near the mines, and we will take you there and leave you with his family until you can decide what is best."

"Who is your ally?"

"Men call him Buffalo Bill."

"Ah! he is that splendid-looking scout, Hortense, who visited our prairie camp one night, and said he had heard John Leigh, the Danite, was with the train."

"Yes, I remember him, and your having known Mercer Aldrich in the East, allay the scout's suspicions regarding him."

"True; and he is in Salt Lake City?"

"Yes, he came here with me, disguised as a Ute chief."

"Well, I do not fear to trust myself with you and Buffalo Bill, nor will Hortense, so we will have a talk with my—Moultrie the Danite chief, and decide what to do."

"Remember, I am Judith here; but I will be Satan's Pet when needed," and the supposed Irish girl withdrew, and sought the kitchen, where she set to work with a will at her duties.

Chapter XXV.
The Plot.

When Captain Elmo Vane came at the summons of his chief, he found him in a somewhat impatient mood.

"Vane," he said, "I wish you to do something for me, and make no botch of it."

"I shall endeavor to do as you desire, chief."

"Well, to begin with, I have a confession to make."

"If it is to tell me you have two young ladies in your house I already know it, sir."

The Danite chief started.

How had this closely kept secret leaked out?

"Well, sir, may I ask how you got this knowledge?" he said sternly.

"I got it from a spy who was set to watch your house, and you, by Major Leigh."

"Indeed!"

"Yes, sir, he is one of my secret service men, and one I fully trust, and he told me that the major had put him as a spy upon your house, with orders to arrest any ladies who left it, and attempted to escape, and that they were to be arrested and carried to his den in the mountains."

"Aha! I wonder if the Prophet knows this" said the chief thoughtfully.

"The major came directly from the Prophet's quarters, sir, when he put his spy on duty."

"Then what is done, must be done at once."

"Yes, sir."

"This spy, as your secret service man, though, need not report—"

"Pardon me, chief, but he must do as the major orders; his duty to me is in warning me, so that I can plot against his commander."

"Ah! this is indeed a land of spies and mysteries; you think he would do his duty as the major orders?"

"Unquestionably, chief."

"Then we can expect no aid from him?"

"None."

"And his orders are to arrest any ladies leaving this house?"

"Yes, chief."

"Then I am in a quandary."

"Can I help you out?"

"That is just what I want you to do."

"Well, sir, let me understand the case."

"It is this; you once went East on secret service for me."

"Yes, chief."

"It was to find my wife and child, or to learn their fate?"

"Yes."

"You came back with sad tidings."

"That your wife and child were dead."

"Yes; but it was but half the truth."

"Indeed!" said the captain with mock surprise.

"Yes, my child did not die, her life being saved, and she is now in this house."

"In this house?"

"Yes."

"You surprise me, sir."

"She surprised me, Vane."

"A glad surprise."

"Indeed it was, and a sad one too; but I am content so that she lives."

"It seems she was driven to seek a support for herself, became a governess in a family coming West, and they were with that ill-fated train that was massacred in the Escalantes."

"But she escaped?"

"Yes, she and her fair pupil, and they are the two beneath my roof."

"She knew I was a Mormon, heard my name, and to escape persecution came to me, and she shall have my protection even against the Prophet himself."

"It would be better to save trouble, sir, by having her leave the city," suggested the captain.

"Just my intention; I have a brother who is a miner in Colorado, and a man of wealth, I believe.

"He has a wife, but no children, and I intended sending the poor girls there for the present, for he would gladly receive them, and you were to go as their escort."

"Why not carry out your plan, sir?"

"I dare not."

"Dare not?"

"Yes, for that spy would report their leaving, and that would spring the trap on me."

"We might bribe the spy, or carry him along."

"No, no, for if Leigh has placed him on my movements, you may be certain he has others watching him."

"I declare I believe you are right, chief."

"Then what shall we do?"

"I must think, sir."

"Bedad let me tell yez."

Both men started at the voice so near, and into the room stalked Judith, the new girl, her arms akimbo.

"What means this intrusion?" said the chief sternly.

"It manes the good of yez."

"My good?"

"That same, begorra." {14}

"Woman, did you hear what was said?" sternly asked the chief.

"Bedad I'm not dafe."

"This is a dangerous country to eavesdrop in, as you may find to your cost."

"It's 'avesdroppin' does a wurruld of good betimes, yer riverince, an' my overhearin' yez hilps yez out o' thrubble."

"How so, woman?"

"Yez was after bein' in a quandary?"

"Yes."

"Will, hear the loikes o' mesilf talk; yer say, ther spoy will be after catchin' yez av yer l'ave ther leddies go out of ther house?"

Neither officer spoke a word and Judith continued:

"Av thet is after bein' ther Mormon of it, ther Irish of it is thet yer kin change ther females inter min."

"What?"

"Driss thim same darlints up in breeches an' thin who ther divil knows thet they is gals?"

"By Heaven, you are right; Judith you are worth your weight in gold," cried the chief grasping the hand of the supposed woman.

"Av ther Prophet w'u'd only think so, yer riverince, I moight be afther bein' ther belle o' ther Bayhoive."

For the first time since he had known him, Captain Vane heard the chief laugh, and seeing the advantage gained, Judith continued:

"Av yez wants ther leddies ter go ter Colorady, me partner an' mesilf will be afther takin' thim."

The chief now glanced upon the supposed woman with suspicion, and said:

"Captain Vane, here, is to be their escort."

"You may nade him, and I kin be afther takin' thim there gintale."

"Woman, I almost fear that you are one of Leigh's spies."

"What think you, Vane?"

The young Danite officer, who had begun to see his pleasant duty as escort fading away, was willing to condemn Judith at sight, and answered seriously:

"There is no telling, chief, who are spies upon us."

"Then, although we take her suggestion, regarding the metamorphosing Dolores and Hortense into young men, I think we had better secure her, until all danger is over."

"True, sir."

"Bedad, but yez is a foine pair o' Mormon hathins thin."

"I am sorry, my good girl, but the safety of these ladies, and ourselves, just now, demands that we seem unjust to you.

"If we find out we have wronged you, I will make such ample payment for my mistake as will reward you."

"Be afther callin' ther ladies, an' say av they won't give me a good character."

"But they do not know you."

"Bedad, yez might be wrong; jist call them, av yez plaze."

The chief walked to the door of the room, in which sat Dolores and Hortense, and called to them to come with him.

"My daughter, this is Captain Vane, my special *aide* and friend; Miss Harmon, Captain Vane."

All then bowed as though they had never before met.

Then turning to Dolores the chief continued.

"My child, I have been plotting with the captain, here, how to get you away in safety.

"I intend sending you to my brother, Lyman Moultrie, in Colorado, where you will have a warm welcome; but your presence here is known, and spies are set on the house to prevent any ladies from leaving it; but this good woman, who was eavesdropping, came to our rescue with the suggestion that you disguise yourselves as Danites, and—"

"A good idea, sir."

"But I fear this woman, who volunteers to accompany you to Colorado, may also be a spy of Leigh's, who can thus get you into his power."

"Bedad, am I, Miss Dolores?" said the supposed Judith.

"No, I'll vouch for it she is not a spy."

"And I," said Hortense.

"But your hearts may run off with your heads," suggested Captain Vane.

"Colonel Moultrie, I will cease my masquerading, for I am not what I seem, but one who came to this house in disguise to save your daughter and Miss Harmon."

In amazement both the Danite chief and the captain gazed upon the supposed woman, and the former cried in a hoarse whisper:

"In the Prophet's name, who are you?"

"Men call me Satan's Pet," was the cool reply.

"Satan's Pet! that deadly foe of the Danites?" cried the chief, while Captain Vane dropped his hand upon his revolver.

"Yes, the foe of John Leigh and his old band known as the Danite Dozen."

"We all know you, and also remember that there is a price set on your head," said Captain Vane.

"I am worth it, so you had better take me," was the fearless reply.

Chapter XXVI.
Unmasked.

"Father, this young man is our friend, for he it was who risked his life, and led us from the train, that awful night of massacre, and he has again taken desperate chances to come into this place and save us," said Dolores, with some spirit.

"From my heart I thank him; but may I ask why you hold this deep interest in Miss Moultrie and Miss Harmon?" asked the chief.

"Yes the interest I have in them is their misfortune, in having fallen into the hands of such hellhounds as Leigh and his Danites."

"Ha! you speak boldly; remember I am the Danite chief," sternly said Moultrie.

"I do not forget it, sir, I assure you; I know that you, and your *aide* here, are not the class of men that are Leigh and his Danite hounds.

"Those are my game, and I have dogged their trail for two long years, and will never leave it until John Leigh and his Danite Dozen are wiped from off the face of the earth which they pollute with their vile presence."

All were struck with the intense manner of the disguised youth, and they seemed to forget his make-up as an Irish girl, when they met his flashing eyes.

"This is a bold threat," said the chief.

"It is not an idle one."

"Then you never met these ladies until you saw them the night of the massacre?"

"I never did, sir."

"I believe you, and I will trust you; but I advise you to leave Salt Lake too, as men are constantly on your trail to win the reward offered for you."

"I know my danger, sir; but this is by no means my first visit to Salt Lake City, and it shall not be my last."

"And you propose to have the young ladies dress up as men?"

"Yes, sir."

"And thus leave this house in company with Captain Vane?"

"No, sir; you are under watch now, as is also the captain, and were he to leave with them you would at once bring suspicion upon them."

"True."

"When they are found to be gone the captain and all his men must be here to answer at roll call."

"Then what?"

"The Prophet will believe his spies were misinformed."

"Ah, yes."

"And that these ladies, in their disguise as men, may leave unsuspected, it would be a good idea for you to send to your different officers to come to your quarters to-night, under some excuse for consultation, regarding this late massacre, we will say, and then their riding off will prevent the spies holding the slightest suspicion."

"You are right indeed."

"And more, sir, they must have two of your best horses for speed and bottom, and we will need too—"

"*We?*"

"My ally and myself; our animals are hidden away in the mountains, for we came in disguised as Utes, and on foot."

"Yes."

"I would advise that your cook, *myself* for instance," and Satan's Pet laughed heart-ily, "prepar[e]s a haversack of provisions for the ladies, and that they be supplied with arms, for fear of accidents, for if we do load our horses heavily in the start, the scout and I will soon get our steeds, and yours can serve as pack animals on our march."

"My friend, all shall be as you suggest; but are you competent to take this trail alone, with two ladies under your charge?" asked the Danite chief.

"I have been hunted for two years by your Danite command, and also by the Indians, and no one yet has gotten the reward for my head," was the modest reply.

"That is true, as I ought to know, having offered it at the command of the Prophet."

"And besides, I will not be alone."

"Ah, yes, you have an ally?"

"And a good one, and also the foe of the Danites."

"His name?"

"Buffalo Bill, his pards call him."

"By the Prophet! there is no better man on this frontier, though he be an enemy."

"I agree with you there, chief, and, like our friend in petticoats here, Satan's Pet, he seems to have a charmed life, and well deserves his name," said Captain Vane.

"Thank you, sir, for my half of the compliment. Now I have dinner to get, so must retire," and Satan's Pet turned away at the general laugh which his remark brought forth.

"Hold! where is your friend, this Buffalo Bill?"

"At our Salt Lake Snuggery, sir, where we always put up."

"Then I will send him word—"

"No, don't, for you won't know where to send; and if you did, he wouldn't come."

"I will go myself as soon as I've to dinner, and we'll both come back good Danites, mount two of your horses, which please have ready, join our pards, who have dis-carded their petticoats, and be ready for the trail by nine o'clock," and with a military salute, Satan's Pet departed for the culinary department.

Chapter XXVII.
A Strange Quintette.

AFTER the departure of Satan's Pet in his comical disguise of an Irish Judith, the Danite chief, his *aide* and the maidens held a short consultation in regard to what was best to be done.

Captain Vane said he could easily secure the disguises for the young ladies, and also the belts of arms, while the chief promised to give them the best horses in his stable and their equipments, adding;

"You will have to stick to your disguises on the whole trail."

This the maidens promised to do, and then they departed to their room to make all necessary preparations, while the chief and Captain Vane rode out together to reconnoiter and discover the exact whereabouts of John Leigh's spies and how many of them were on duty.

Hardly had they departed from the house, before the trusted butler and valet of the Danite chief came into the kitchen where the pretended Judith was preparing dinner with a skill that was not to be expected of him in his new calling, and at the same time, singing an Irish song.

"You is not so Irish as you look, be you?" said the butler.

"What is it yez is afther remarking, Misther Thomas?" and, ladle in hand, the cook turned upon him.

"You can speak English when you wish?" and there was a grim smile upon the man's face.

"Is it dumb, dafe or crazy I am, that I'm not afther understanding yez?"

"Oh, you understand well enough, and I'm not dumb, deaf or crazy."

"Bedad, ther man is clean gone woild."

"No, I have not; but I have ears."

"And so hes afther havin' every ither jackass, Misther Thomas."

"Do you call me a jackass?" said the man, with anger.

"Be jabers, it's not the loikes o' me that w'u'd be afther callin' ye at all, at all."

"You are a fool."

"How was it that iver ye found that out, yer h'athen Mormon spalpeen?"

"By listening at the door."

"Oho, ye war eavesdroppin'?"

"I heard enough to advise you to go in with me and let the Prophet know."

"Little profit ye'll ever git out of it."

"Yes, he'll pay well for the news."

"Take ther goods to him thin."

"I intend to; only there's some things I can explain—"

"Yer hearin' wasn't as good as ye'd loiked, maybe."

"Yes, I could not hear all, so advise you to tell what I want to know, and we'll go halves on the cash."

"Thomas, your foresight isn't afther bein' as good as yer hindsight, or ye'd never be {15} afther comin' to a dacint woman an' ax her to sell her fri'nds."

"Decent woman? You are no woman, but a man."

"Yes, a man and your master, you accursed traitor," and Satan's Pet sprung upon the fellow and grasped him by the throat.

"Hold! I am one of Leigh's spies; hands off, or you'll regret it," gasped the man, struggling fiercely.

"When I take my hands off you, thou devil, it will be when you are dead," was the savage reply, and instantly the struggle became fierce and desperate between them.

Hampered by his woman's attire, and with a desperate man to deal with, and a powerful one, it looked as if Satan's Pet had met more than his match.

But his gripe was one of iron, and his movements so rapid, that the man could not handle him with the ease that he had at first believed.

For a few moments it looked like an equal match, and then, as if to end it, Satan's Pet let go his hold, and quickly drew a knife from the bosom of his dress.

His enemy saw this, and in vain tried to ward off the blows, for once, twice, thrice, the keen blade fell, and each time the point had touched the heart.

Springing to his feet Satan's Pet glanced around him, and then hastily dragged the body to a closet and hid it away.

"Well, a pretty looking cook I am; but it's better being mussed up in my toilet than dead," and he set about arranging his attire, and then in setting the kitchen to rights, at the same time muttering:

"It looks as though there had been an Irish wake here; but certain it is that another Danite has gone—yes, number nine of the Danite Dozen.

"I knew him the moment he took off his sanctimonious look and showed himself the traitor," and he continued his work until dinner was ready and placed on the table.

"But where is Thomas, Judith?" asked the chief.

"Gone, sir."

"Gone where?"

"Discharged."

"Who discharged him?"

"I discharged him, yer riverince."

The chief looked at his quondam cook in amazement, but received a hint to say no more before the ladies.

But after the meal was over he heard the whole story.

"My God! what shall be done with the body?"

"Oh! I'll attend to that, sir."

"You?"

"Yes, sir; he's stiff as a poker now, and we'll tie him on horseback, so he'll look all right, and carry him with us.

"Once in the mountains, and I can drop him over a cliff, and tell the ladies you only sent him along to see us out of town in safety."

"But the horse?"

"He'll come back to his stable, and you can give out that your trusted Thomas robbed you and decamped."

"Young man, I do not wonder that you bear the name of Satan's Pet given you."

"Judith, yer riverince," and with a light laugh the youth turned away, while the chief went to see his daughter, for it was but a short time longer that she would be with him.

The last conversation between the Danite and his daughter was a sad one, and yet they both felt that if the escape from the Mormon city could be made in safety, the shadows on their lives would begin to pass away.

With the setting of the sun Satan's Pet, still in his female costume, left the house and wended his way to Abrams the Jew's.

There he found Buffalo Bill most anxiously awaiting the result of his masquerading as an Irish girl, a convert to the Mormon faith, and, having heard the youth's plans, entered into them most readily.

"You are a trump card, Pet, and we can soon change ourselves into good Danites," said the scout, and half an hour later the two left the Jew's house, their "snuggery," as Satan's Pet had called it, and went straight to the residence of the Danite chief.

A number of horses were already hitched at the rack and fence, and going to the stables they found the five intended for their use all ready, for Captain Vane had faithfully performed his part of the work.

Three raps at the window was the signal for the maidens to appear, and these Satan's Pet gave.

A moment after two forms came out of the kitchen door of the house, and were met by the youth, who led them to the stable.

"All ready, Bill," he whispered, and a horse was led out and Dolores was mounted upon his back, and the reins placed in her hands, her tiny feet in the stirrups.

"Next!"

Out came another steed, and Hortense was placed in the saddle.

"Who is that?" asked Dolores in an alarmed whisper, as a horseman came out of the stable.

"A man who goes a short distance with us," answered Satan's Pet coolly, and he mounted his own horse and placed himself alongside of the animal that bore the dead Danite, propped up in the saddle, and his cold hands having the reins wound around them.

Riding on the right of the maidens, Buffalo Bill gave the order to forward, and the strange quintette moved away from the stable, passed the house, at a window of which stood the form of the Danite chief anxiously awaiting and watching, and then out of the yard into the highway.

A man walking slowly by glanced up suspiciously into their faces, as they passed but said nothing, as he evidently believed them to be officers called to the council of the Danite chief.

"That is Leigh's spy," said Satan's Pet in a low tone.

No one replied, and on the quintette went through the streets, the men perfectly calm, the maidens trembling violently, but resolute to face any danger rather than remain in that hated city.

At last the lights of the town were left behind, and sharp and clear came the order: "Halt! who comes?"

With an effort Dolores and Hortense suppressed the cry that arose to their lips, while Buffalo Bill answered sternly:

"Friends."

"Dismount, friend! advance and give the countersign, or we fire on you."

"Be calm; it is the sentinel only," whispered Buffalo Bill, as he obeyed the order, walking up to the point of the bayonets of the two men who stood in his path.

"The countersign!" said one, sternly.

"Long live the Prophet."

"Correct; you can pass, friends."

With a light heart Buffalo Bill returned, mounted, and the quintette moved on their way, Dolores and Hortense drawing a long breath of relief, for they had crossed the Rubicon.

Chapter XXVIII.
On the Trail.

With the most perfect faith in their escorts, Dolores and Hortense rode on, their hearts growing lighter with every mile they cast behind them.

Fatigue, under the circumstances, they were willing to stand, and both Buffalo Bill and Satan's Pet were surprised at the unflinching fortitude they exhibited in their hard ride, for the horses were urged on rapidly.

At last the youth, who was riding by the side of his companion, silent in death, called to Buffalo Bill that the messenger would return and that he would halt an instant with him.

The scout understood what Satan's Pet meant, for they were riding alongside of a precipice; but, hearing only that the man was going back to her father, to tell him of their safety thus far, Dolores quickly halted and rode back, followed by Hortense.

"Will you say to my father, please, that so far we are safe, and that we have full confidence in those who are our protectors?"

The man made no reply, as a matter of course, but sat up straight as an arrow, gazing directly at her with his wide-open, staring eyes, from which the light had forever gone.

"Tell him, too, that I hope to one day, ere long, meet him again, and may God bless him."

Buffalo Bill was at a loss what to say or do, and for once Satan's Pet seemed nonplused.

But he quickly rallied, and said:

"Miss Moultrie, this man belongs to the Ever Silent Order of Danites, and he will never answer you."

"Ah! but he understands, so that he can tell my father?"

"The fellow understands, if he's got his wits about him; why, he hasn't spoken to me on the whole ride out."

"Then you, sir, who know the signs with which to communicate with him, kindly tell him what I say," persisted Dolores.

"I'm not wholly up in his sign language, Miss Moultrie, but I'll do the best I can; but we must not tarry here."

Buffalo Bill took the hint, and, waving his hand to the dead form, as if in farewell, moved on with the maidens, leaving Satan's Pet happy at the corpse having escaped recognition of what it was.

Quickly unfastening the props and ropes that held the body in position in the saddle, he placed it on the ground, and then drove the riderless horse back toward town.

Raising the body in his arms, he then walked to the precipice and threw it over into the dark abyss, and stood listening until it dashed with a dull thud on the rocks far beneath.

For a moment he stood in silence gazing down into the dark depths, and then, turning, bounded into his saddle and dashed on after his companions.

Overtaking them, he placed himself by the side of Hortense, and urging a greater speed, soon came to a narrow ravine, into which he turned.

A ride of a mile from this point, and over a dangerous, and seemingly a trail never before taken, brought them to the summit of a steep hill.

Here they halted, and dismounting, led their horses down the steep declivity to a valley below.

"All right, Bill; our horses are here," cried Satan's Pet, and a call brought his splendid animal trotting up to his side and following him came the steed of Buffalo Bill, the two having been turned loose for days in a little vale, from which there was but one avenue of escape, and that had been securely barricaded by trees which their masters had cut down and made into a fence.

"You've been in clover here, nags, and had the best grass and water in the mountains, and a long rest, so you'll be able to go well on the long trail," said Satan's Pet, while Buffalo Bill took the maidens from their saddles and spread a blanket upon the velvety grass for them to rest on.

A halt of several horses [*sic* – hours?], a rest, and substantial breakfast, and the party mounted once more, and started on their way just at dawn, the horses ridden out from Salt Lake by Buffalo Bill and Satan's Pet, serving as pack animals.

And thus for awhile I will leave the fugitives on the trail to Colorado, while I beg the reader to accompany me back to the city of the Mormons.

Chapter XXIX.
Thwarted.

"Well, Leigh, you have dropped in just as I wished to see you," and the Mormon Prophet turned to Major Leigh, who just then entered his private rooms unannounced.

"I always try to anticipate your wishes, Prophet."

"That's the way with you, try to get credit for coming, when you know well enough you would not be here, if it were not to further more interests of your own.

"I tell you, John Leigh, you are a sly dog."

The Danite major laughed and answered:

"I have come to prove to you that there are other sly dogs in your kennel, Prophet, and older ones than I am."

"Perhaps there are; but I told you that you were here to serve your own interests."

"If, in my endeavor to show that you have misplaced your confidence, I serve myself, then I acknowledge the truth of your accusation, sir."

"Well, who is it now, John Leigh?"

"My chief."

"Moultrie?"

"Yes."

"Well?"

"It is not well."

"You know what I mean."

"Oh! what has he done?"

"Yes."

"What I told you."

"About the two ladies?"

"Yes, sir."

"They are there?"

"Yes sir."

"Have you seen them?" {16}

"I told you I had seen a woman passing by the window, when I looked with a glass."

"Go on."

"My spies report that no woman has left the house, other than the servant girl."

"And they are there now?"

"Yes, Prophet."

"He had a council of officers last night?"

"Yes."

"You were there?"

"I was."

"What was done?"

"A plan was proposed for the better organization of the Danite Cavalry, and the strengthening of all outposts."

"Good! that Moultrie is a good officer."

John Leigh made no reply to this, but said:

"Will you pay an unexpected visit with me to the chief's house?"

"It seems to me you are very anxious to spy out your commander's faults."

"I only act for your interest."

"And your own."

"In part."

"Well, we will go, and if I catch old Moultrie deceiving me, off comes his head."

"Figuratively speaking, you mean, Prophet?"

"Yes, though as you supersede him, it would be as well, perhaps, to have him shot, so as to set you an example," and the Prophet smiled grimly.

"As you please, sir, you rule."

"And intend to do so; but what do you wish me to do for you?"

"I have a favor to ask."

"So you said, so name it."

"I am attached to the elder lady of the two—"

"Ha! you know them?"

"I have an idea that they are Gentiles who came here to become converts."

"Ah! continue, please."

"You have promised to grant me the favor I ask, and it is that you allow me to claim the one I desire?"

"Yes. Now order a platoon of guards to follow me to the chief's house."

The order was given, and the Prophet and his favorite officer departed for the house of the chief of the Danites.

Moultrie met them at the door, pretended not to see the guard within call, and bade the Prophet and his officer be seated, at the same time ordering a domestic—for he had already filled the places left vacant by Thomas and Judith—to bring refreshments, and spoke of the honor done him by the visit of the Mormon leader.

After a few wily remarks, to put his host wholly off his guard, the Prophet said, abruptly:

"Moultrie, I learn that you have taken unto yourself a wife."

"Indeed, sir, there is a mistake," was the cool reply.

"Nay, two of them."

"It is not true."

"Who, then, are the females that have been seen in your house?"

"My domestic, doubtless; there is no other here."

The Prophet looked at the major for encouragement.

He had always found Moultrie, the Danite chief, a most truthful man.

"I am sorry, chief, but certain reports of that nature were brought to me, and I was compelled to place it before our Prophet," said John Leigh in a tone meant to be regretful.

"You did right, Major John Leigh, to report me for any wrong you believed me guilty of, for the Prophet is my superior; but if I find you in any dereliction of duty, being *your* superior, I will deal with you myself."

The Danite major winced under this shot; but, confident that he held his chief in his power, he said, in response:

"We are all liable to err, sir, and pardon me if I consider that you have done so in your statement to the Prophet."

"In what respect, John Leigh?" and it was evident the chief controlled his temper with an effort.

"In saying that there are no ladies concealed in this house."

"The house is not so large, Prophet, but that it can be easily looked over."

"No, no, Moultrie. I guess you were misinformed, John Leigh," said the Prophet, hurriedly.

"I was not, sir."

The chief stepped to the door and hailed the guard.

They were Danites of the chief's command, and came quickly at his call.

"Give the officer your orders, Prophet," said the Danite leader.

"Search this house thoroughly, place guards that no one can escape, and bring any human being in it into this room," was the stern order of the Prophet, while Moultrie said, with a sneer:

"Perhaps Major John Leigh will see that the search is thoroughly made?"

"By the Mormon creed, I will," and he arose and joined the searchers.

Every crevice, closet and room was thoroughly searched by the guard, and re-searched by the anxious Danite major, and then the report was made to the Prophet, who looked sternly at John Leigh while he said:

"You were misinformed, sir; pardon me, Moultrie for my doubt, and feel that you are fully restored to my confidence."

"I thank you, Prophet."

He bowed with his words, and then turned quickly to the major, while he said:

"And you, sir, I place under arrest."

"What! do you dare—"

"Hold! John Leigh, you seem to forget Danite law, that gives me, your chief, the power of life and death over you.

"Guards, place this man in irons!"

The chief towered to his full h[e]ight, his face was white and stern, and there was that in his look that forbade interference even from the Prophet.

For a moment it seemed as though John Leigh would resist; but he thought better of it, and grimly submitted to his fate, confident that the Prophet would not see him too severely punished.

Chapter XXX.
Set Free.

When John Leigh lay in irons in a room of his chief's house, he had time to reflect that he had gotten himself into a most dangerous situation.

A reckless fellow ever, he had never cared what were the laws that held the Danites together; but now there came back to his mind a legend that he had laid upon his head the penalty of death, for his doubt of an insolence to his superior officer.

The remembrance of the chief's face too reminded him that he would not trifle with him, and he became livid with fear, for, though a man who would take fearful chances against death to accomplish an end in view, he was a coward when he felt that he must really die.

He called to his guard, while the sweat stood in beads on his forehead, intending to send a pleading note to the Prophet, begging him to intercede for him.

To his joy he saw that the guard who answered his call was one of his own special spies.

"Hunton, I am in trouble," he said, in as calm a tone as he could command.

"So it seems, sir."

"Where is Chief Moultrie?"

"He has gone up to the Death Den, they say."

John Leigh now grew to the hue of a corpse, for he knew that only one thing could carry the chief to the Danites' Death Den in the mountains, and that was his execution, or a demand for his trial by the Black Jury as the Judges are called.

"Hunton, it is not generally known that I am a prisoner, is it?"

"It is ordered to be kept a secret, sir."

"Ah! that looks worse for me."

"It does indeed, sir."

"Hunton, where are the other guards?"

"Over at the stable, sir."

"I have done you many a favor, my man."

"Yes, sir."

"Will you do me one?"

"If I can."

"Release me and go with me."

"Ah, sir, this is asking too much."

"I have plenty of money, Hunton, and we will share it."

"But where would we go, sir?"

"To my mountain retreat."

"It is there the chief has gone."

"So much the better; when sought for they will not look there, and I know plenty of hiding-places."

"Well, sir, I will go with you."

The surprise of the man's sudden determination to aid him, almost upset the Danite major, and he feared he was not in earnest.

But the guard stepped forward, took from his belt the key of the manacles, which each one on duty gave to the other when relieved, and John Leigh arose to his feet a free man.

"Come, sir, I go off duty in an hour and we must get off," said the man hurriedly, and the two instantly left the house by the way of the piazza and crossing the garden were soon in the street.

At his own house he had left his horse when he had called on the Prophet, and thither they went, and soon after were riding away like the wind.

The soldier, being a guard for the day answered the challenges of the sentinels with the countersign, and in the darkness they passed by a party of six horsemen, two in advance a short distance, riding toward the town.

"The chief and Vane, as I live! a narrow escape that," muttered Major Leigh, and he drove his spurs into his horse and rode more rapidly on, followed by the guard.

A ride of some leagues and they entered the wild grandeur of the mountains.

It was a desolate place, dark and lonely; but the Danite officer and his comrade followed the trail without difficulty, until at last they came to where it wound around an abrupt spur, and turned into a canyon.

"Hold on here, major!"

The cry came from the guard, and quickly the officer drew rein, and half turned in his saddle.

"Well, Hunton, what the devil is the matter?" he asked impatiently.

"I'll tell you what was the matter, John Leigh; *you are my game.*"

The reply came hoarse and determined from the lips of the guard, and a rifle covered the officer.

"Good God! Hunton, what do you mean?" he cried in alarm.

"I mean that you are unarmed, and my rifle covers your heart."

"But man, you do not intend—"

"I do intend to kill you, John Leigh."

"Great God!"

"Yes, for you deliberately shot down my brother one day, when in an angry mood, and I have sworn to take your life for it."

"But, my good Hunton, he was disobedient, and you know our laws."

"You were insolent to the chief to-day, John Leigh, and he intended to have you die; but that would not be *my* keeping my oath to kill you.

"Now pray, for I shall kill you, rob you, and forever give up the accursed life I lead, for I know well the horse you ride will carry me beyond pursuit."

"Mercy, my good Hunton."

"Don't ask mercy of me, for my breasts holds no mercy for you.

"Now pray, for you have just one moment to live."

"Mercy!" appealed the man almost reeling from his saddle as he saw death staring him in the face.

"*One!*"

Like the knell of doom came the word.

"Remember, at *five* I fire."

"Oh God! I will give you thousands to spare me."

"You always carry large sums of money with you, I know, so I will get your thousands, take your life, and have my revenge too—

"*Two!*"

The man bowed his head upon his breast and trembled violently, for he felt death at last had his gripe upon him.

"*Three!*"

He could not speak, he could not move.

"*Four!*"

With the word came a flash and sharp report, followed by a death-cry and a heavy fall of a body to the earth.

Chapter XXXI.
GOOD FOR EVIL.

THE shot that had been fired as Hunton gave utterance to the word *four*, had not come from his rifle, though it would have flashed at *five* without doubt.

And the fall of a body to the earth had not been John Leigh.

Nor did the death-cry come from his lips.

The flash had come, it so seemed, out of the very side of the mountain, and the bullet, {17} truly sent, found the heart of Hunton the guard, from whose lips had escaped the cry.

Surprised, shocked, stunned at the sudden change from despair to hope, John Leigh could only sit like a statue upon his horse and gaze against the black wall of the mountain.

Who had fired the shot he did not know.

Presently a rustling of the bushes was heard, and a form, clad in pure white stepped out of the dense shadows, and stood before him.

Then did his tongue find utterance in one word.

"Queen!"

"Yes, John Leigh, for the third time I have saved your life.

"For the third time, ay, many times, have I returned good for evil," said a low, yet clear and soft voice."

"Queen, from my innermost soul I thank you."

"Thanks! why they, from your lips, are as idle as the wind.

"But come, for men expect you to die to-night, John Leigh."

"To die?" he gasped.

"Yes; your chief has been here, and the Black Jury are ready to visit upon you your fate."

"By heaven! they shall not, for I am a free man!"

"Free to escape the Black Jury, never!"

"What mean you?"

"Your steps will be tracked through life."

"I will fly to the uttermost parts of the earth."

"And desert me?"

"No. You go with me."

"Then you must face the Black Jury."

"But death will surely follow."

"I have a plan to save you."

"Name it."

"No, trust to me: your chief has returned, to send you here, and ere sunrise you are doomed to die.

"But you escaped, I heard from the lips of that corpse how, and a thousand men will be on your trail at once."

"Oh heaven! what shall I do?"

"Throw that body out of the trail and come with me."

"But, Queen—"

"If you have doubt of me do as you think best."

"I will do as you say."

"Then come to the Death Den, give yourself up, and say that you have come to face your doom."

"But—"

"Obey or not, as you please."

"What am I to do?"

"Put on your black suit and mask and meet your fate."

"Death."

"If the rifles of the Black Judges have bullets in them, yes; if not, then your life is safe, for you can fall at the fire, and will be at once placed in your coffin, and laid in the vault."

"Oh, Queen!"

"I have already drawn their bullets, and I will release you from your coffin, and to give you air it has holes in the side which I have made."

"Good, noble Queen."

"Cease your hollow praise and thanks, and ride on and do as I tell you."

"There will be no mistake about the bullets?"

"None."

"There were twelve guns you know."

"And I drew out twelve bullets."

"And you did not mistake the coffin prepared for me?"

"No."

"I will trust you, Queen."

"Would to God I had never trusted you, John Leigh," broke passionately from the woman's lips.

He would have replied, but she pointed on up the trail, and dismounting he threw the body of the guard [to] one side, turned his horse loose, remounted his own steed and rode on further into the shadow of mountains.

The woman watched him for an instant, and then turning, quickly disappeared under the shelter of the lofty cliff from which she had so unexpectedly appeared and saved the life of a man who richly deserved death.

Chapter XXXII.
The Black Jury.

In one of the wildest parts of the mountains, reached only by trails that seemed almost impassable, and which could be defended by a few men against a host, was situated the Danites' Den.

The passes to the mountain caverns, for there were a score of them, were mere fissures in the rocks, which towered far overhead.

The largest of these caverns had a man pacing before it day and night, armed to the teeth, and jealously guarding the interior from intrusion.

Up to this man rode Major Leigh, and, as the revolver of the guard was leveled at him, he said:

"Hold! do you not see who I am?"

"Pardon, chief; it is so intensely dark I did not recognize you."

"Are the Black Judges in council?"

"They are, and have been since sunset."

"I will see them."

Throwing the rein of his horse to the guard, who had evidently not known of his arrest, John Leigh strode into the cavern.

The passage was large, and tunnel-like, and dimly lighted by lanterns hung along the walls of rock.

Following the passageway, the Danite officer, after a walk of a hundred yards, came to a rudely constructed doorway, that barred his steps.

He gave twelve distinct raps upon the stout door, and waited.

A footstep approaching was soon heard, and a voice asked:

"Who comes?"

"Leigh."

"The word?"

"Death to traitors."

"What faith?"

"Danite."

There was heard a chain rattling within, and the door swung open, revealing a man in a black mask and long sable gown.

He looked eagerly at the Danite through the holes in his mask, and seeing that he was alone, asked:

"Where are your guards?"

"I came alone."

"The chief trusted you?"

"I asked him not; I escaped, and have come to deliver myself up for punishment."

"Come," and fastening the door the Black Juror led the way into a large rotunda.

It was a dismal place, the walls being draped in black, and but a single lantern hanging from a cord in the center, giving light to the vast space.

In the middle of the rocky chamber was a black altar, upon which was a coffin, and upon either side were niches in the walls, in which were visible the foot-ends of boxes in which were the dead of the order who had suffered punishment for their crimes.

Back against the wall sat eleven men, clad as the one who had admitted the Danite major, and by their side that one took a seat, as soon as the visitor was brought before them.

"Judges, I know my sentence and I have come to meet it," he said in a firm voice, though he was very pale, and his hands were clasped tightly together, as if to keep his emotion in check.

"Our chief Moultrie had reported you as worthy of death; his word is law, and we have assembled to execute you, John Leigh," said one of the Judges in sepulchral tones.

"I am ready," he answered falteringly.

One of the Black Judges then arose, and going to the altar in the center of the rotunda, beckoned to the Danite major to approach.

He obeyed with as firm a step as he could.

Taking from the coffin a black gown the Judge bade him put it on.

This he did with a shudder he could not suppress.

Then one by one, he took from the sable coffin a musket, and handed them to his colleagues, reserving one for himself.

"Now, John Leigh, take your stand," he said in a low tone, and he led the doomed man to the further wall of the rotunda where a coffin was standing up on end, the open part fronting them.

"Clasp your hands, John Leigh."

He did so, and upon his wrists were placed irons.

"Get into your coffin, John Leigh."

With a shudder that shook his frame he obeyed.

Stooping down the Judge then placed irons upon his ankles, and rising, fastened three chains across the front of the coffin, as it stood on end.

"Farewell, John Leigh," said the Judge.

"Farewell forever, John Leigh," echoed his *confreres*.

But John Leigh never spoke; in fact, notwithstanding the promise of the woman he had called Queen, he was so overcome with emotion, he dared not trust himself to utter a word, for fear he would shriek out with horror and fright.

"Will she keep her pledge?"

This question his mind was revolving continuously, and he knew that he must bide his time to discover, for now there was no hope for him, did the woman fail him.

Back to his comrades, who were ranged along in a row standing behind the altar, went the Judge who had secured him in his loathsome coffin, and for full a moment the twelve stood thus in silence.

Then in chorus, and in a tone that distinctly reached his ears, they repeated as follows:

"John Leigh: by our laws doomed to die for treachery against a member of our band, be he low, or be he high in rank, you now meet, at our hands, the Black Jury, the death you have brought upon yourself.

"Thus dying, with treachery in your heart, and venom in your soul against a fellow Danite, you have no hope hereafter, as symbol of which we iron you hand and foot."

As though drilled by word, the twelve men put one foot a step backward raised their muskets, cocked them, brought them to their shoulders, and, as one gun, they were discharged.

The sound was terrific, there in that vaulted chamber of rock, and the dense smoke of powder almost darkened the room.

But the Judges, as though accustomed to such scenes, walked slowly forward and halted fronting the coffin.

The form of the Danite major had fallen forward, and was hanging limp against the chains, which prevented its falling out.

Then the coffin was lowered, the form adjusted in it properly, and the lid put on, the hammer, driving in the nails, awakening many a dismal echo in the cavern.

Raising it, they then thrust it into a niche in the wall, dropped a sable curtain before it, and slowly marched from the death-chamber.

Chapter XXXIII.
A Cry for Mercy.

The roar of the muskets, when they were turned upon the heart of John Leigh, reached the ears of a person crouching among the rocks on the side of the mountain.

It was the same woman who had fired the shot that saved the life of John Leigh from death at the hands of Hunton.

She waited for some time after the echoes of the firing had died away, and then arose from her crouching attitude, and began slowly to ascend the rugged mountain side.

Over her shoulders she carried a long coil of rope, and dress was pinned up close around her form.

At last she paused at a clump of dwarf mountain cedars, and pushing aside the foliage, entered.

Once within their shelter, she unwound the rope from her shoulders and fastened one end securely to the trunk of one of the cedars.

Then she bent over and looked down into what seemed to be a cavernous tunnel running down into the mountain.

With her head thrust forward, she listened attentively for some moments, and then muttered:

"Yes, they have gone."

Uncoiling the rope, it was now seen to be a ladder of hemp, the foot-rests being hardly more than six inches wide.

Taking up one end of it, she let it fall gently, slipping through her hands down into the hole, until the whole length had disappeared, excepting what was fastened to the tree.

Trusting herself to this she rapidly descended from sight, and, after some thirty feet through this funnel-like space, she came to a shelf of rock.

Here she rested in the intense darkness and listened.

Apparently satisfied at hearing no sound, she took up the coil of rope, for it had stopped there, and carried it a few steps, and again lowered it.

As soon as it became taut she went over the edge of the rocky shelf, and began to rapidly {18} descend—into what seemed to be a vast cavern of perfect blackness.

Suddenly she paused in her descent, hanging in mid-air upon the rope, for her ears had caught a sound.

"What? can any of them be here?"

"No, it is dark, and they therefore must have gone."

"But, I certainly heard a voice."

"Mercy! oh, God! mercy! help! help! help!

"Don't let me die here, for I am not dead, I am not dead."

The wild cry, coming from the black depths below, caused her to almost lose her hold of the rope ladder, great as seemed her nerve.

"Thank God! all went well.

"Poor boy, he fears I have deserted him," she cried, and once more she began her rapid descent and soon her foot touched the solid rock.

Then, from back against the wall came a muffled shriek and loud cries for help.

"Courage, John, poor fellow, courage, for Queen is here," she said, soothingly.

An hysterical laugh was the answer to her words, and she cried:

"Great God! I fear he has gone mad.

"Yes, John, yes."

Instantly a bright light flashed upon the scene from a dark lantern she had carried, and quickly she went toward the back wall, drew aside the sable curtain, and seized the end of the coffin.

With an effort of strength one would not believe her capable of, she drew the coffin from the niche, and lowered it gently to the rock flooring, while the moaning and laughter, mingled together, continued.

Seizing the hatchet from within the coffin on the altar, where she seemed to know that it was kept, she hastily raised the lid of the box, keeping up all the time soothing words of encouragement to the poor wretch within.

At last the lid was raised, and the livid face of the man revealed.

"Good God!"

The cry broke from her lips, for she saw that his hair had become snow-white.

Running quickly to the coffin on the altar, she seized a bunch of keys and instantly unlocked the chains and irons that held the man prisoner.

"Now, John, you are free."

"Free! yes, free; but great God! I would rather die by slow torture than pass through again the misery I have known in the days and nights I have been there," he groaned.

"Days and nights, John? Why, you have not been there half an hour."

"What!"

"It is true; not half an hour has passed since the Judges fired upon you."

"God in Heaven! it seemed weeks to me."

"Come, nerve yourself, for you have a dangerous trip before you," she said, as she placed the empty coffin back in its niche, arranged the sable folds before it, and returned the hatchet and keys from whence she had taken them.

"Come, John," and she led him to the rope ladder.

"Up here?" he asked, mechanically.

"Yes; my woman's curiosity led me to a cave above one day, and I found that it was an unknown opening in the rocky roof of the Death Den, and thus I found it and investigated its mysteries."

"Thank God that you did, Queen. Now I believe I am ready to go; but follow me closely."

"I will, John."

Up the ladder he went slowly, and evidently with an effort, and closely she followed him, cheering him with kind words all the way.

At last they reached the shelf, and she drew up the ladder, and then ascended to the tunnel-like cave above.

Coiling her rope and closing her dark-lantern, she said, calmly:

"A fourth time, John Leigh, I have saved your life; come with me."

Silently he followed her, for he seemed completely under her control, without volition to act for himself.

Chapter XXXIV.
The Mormon Wife.

A stoutly built cabin stood against the precipitous side of a mountain, and was hidden away in a little glen of Eden beauty.

There was one heavy door to the cabin, two windows, one at either end, and protected by thick shutters, and a chimney, from which the smoke curled upward against the mountain side.

To this lonely spot, and seemingly strong retreat the woman led the Danite major, opened the door, with a key she took from her pocket, and said quietly:

"Enter, John."

She soon had a lamp shedding forth a pleasant light, which showed that the room was by no means uncomfortable, for it was furnished neatly, and around the walls hung paintings executed with considerable skill, crayon sketches, and many little odds-and-ends trinkets, as if made merely to pass away time.

There were books there also, a guitar, fancy Indian worked robes and dressed skins of beasts, and a hammock that served as a bed.

Taking from a cupboard a flask of silver, she gave the man a drink of brandy, and drew a chair up near the table and urged him to sit down.

He swallowed the liquor eagerly, and sunk into the chair, while she sat down on the other side of the table, and leaning her chin in her hands gazed straight at him.

His face was haggard in the extreme, his eyes sunken, his complexion livid, while his hair was white as snow, showing but too plainly the agony he had endured.

And the woman?

A face of Madonna like beauty, and so sad and lonely in expression that she seemed hardly earthly.

White as marble and as pure was her spotless complexion, and as black as night were her eyes, while her hair was golden, and coiled in large braids about her head, serving as a covering, and looking like a turban.

She was dressed in white cloth, and had loosened the folds of her dress upon entering the cabin, for when she descended into the Death Den she had fastened them around her.

Her form was full and faultless, and there was an air of refinement about her that showed how sadly out of place she was in that drear abode.

"John Leigh," she said softly. "Have you not had a life-long lesson to-night?"

"Yes, Queen."

"*Now,* you say so; but with the bright sunshine of to-morrow, will you feel the same way?"

"Yes, Queen."

"Oh John! why will you not let this night be a warning?

"To the world you die this night; let it be that you begin a new life.

"Remember, John, years ago I told you I loved you, when you came to my home in far-away Delaware.

"It was a happy home, John, for my father and mother were there, and my darling little brother.

"You won my love, and I believed you all that man should be.

"I became your wife, John, and we left dear old Delaware for your Western home, where you said you owned a cattle ranch.

"And where did you bring me?

"To Salt Lake City.

"A Mormon yourself, you brought me West to degrade me with your belief.

"Ah, John! it was a cruel blow to me, for I shared your love and home with others—*yes, your two other wives.*

"It broke my heart, John, yet it did not turn my love from you.

"I fled from you one night of storm, caring not where I went, and you sought and found me, nearly dead in these mountains.

"And you let the world of Mormonism believe me dead, and brought me here.

"Here I reign as queen, for *they* are not here."

"You know that my other wives died, Queen," he said, in a low tone.

"So you told me, John; poor women, I do not wonder they died, if you deceived them as you did me.

"And here, John, I have lived for years, only a few of your trusted followers knowing the dread secret.

"And in my nook I have been content, for I have had sunshine in your visits now and then.

"And, John, you know that I have lived for you, and our times have saved you from death.

"Once from a foe who would have struck you in the back, had I not warned you; once from one of your wives, maddened with jealous rage; once from an Indian, whom I shot, ere he could let fly his arrow, and to-night, when that man held you in his power, I took again on my soul the stain of human blood, rather than see you die.

"Now, John, you are believed dead; you dare not return to Salt Lake, for instantly would you be recognized and die.

"Through all your crimes I have loved you, and now I beg you to go far from here with me, and let us live away from your foes; let us go to my parents, in their old Delaware home, from whom I have not heard for so long, and to whom I have not dared to write, knowing that they look upon me as having become a Mormon, and, in their minds, an outcast.

"I have money here, John, as you know, so let us by night, steal away in disguise, and seek my parents and beg them to forgive, forget, and take us to their hearts."

She dropped on her knees before him, and looked pleadingly into his face

But he said no word and stared at her as though he looked upon a ghost.

"Speak, John, and tell me if you will go?"

"Where?" he asked, huskily.

"To my home, to my kindred."

"Queen."

"Well."

She saw by his manner that he had something to tell her, and she gazed straight into his face with an appealing, hunted look.

"Queen, I cared not to give you pain, so have kept it from you."

"Kept what from me, John Leigh?" she asked, in a stern voice.

"Queen, forgive me, but I deemed it best to add no more sorrow to your life than I had brought upon you."

"John Leigh, speak! my parents; what of them?"

She was strangely calm, and he almost feared to speak.

"Speak, sir, for I know you have evil tidings of them."

"I have."

"I am listening, sir."

"Queen, for God's sake don't look so."

"John Leigh, are my parents dead?"

"Yes, Queen."

"And my brave, noble brother?"

"Dead."

"And how know you this, John Leigh?"

"They were coming West to settle, Queen, for your father met with reverses, and they had written me to meet them at a certain point, and then they would decide where to live."

"Well, sir?"

"I hoped to give you a glad surprise, by taking you to their new home some day, and so said nothing to you about their coming, Queen.

"But alas! they left their train, with two other families, and, disregarding the dangers to be encountered in these wilds, they sought to find a valley in which to settle themselves, for unavoidably I was prevented from meeting them."

"Go on, John Leigh."

"Alas! Queen, it pains me to tell you more."

"I am calm, sir."

"Too calm, Queen; but I must tell you all, now that I have begun.

"They were set upon by Indians, and—"

"I know the rest; they were all murdered?"

"Yes, Queen; but for God's sake do not look so; you fairly frighten me."

She arose with strange calmness, paced to and fro for awhile, and then said quietly:

"Come, John, we must not be here with the rise of the sun; let us go."

"But where, Queen?"

"Anywhere, so we leave here.

"In the cave you will find your horse, for I took him from the sentinel you left him with, and the three you gave me.

"There are things here we can pack on two of them, so let us be off."

She set about her work with a calmness that was distressing, and the man's heart quivered with fear as he muttered:

"Great God! not one regret, not a tear or a sigh; only this forced calmness.

"Can she suspect, I wonder?"

Chapter XXXV.
Angels' Rest.

In a lonely valley of one of the tributaries of the Grand River, a number of mining camps dotted the fair landscape, with here and there the pretentious, for that country at that time, house of a Gold King. {19}

The rich ore was wont to pan out in large quantities for the industrious miner, and each camp in the valley had become a miniature village, with its blacksmith shop, schoolhouse, which was the church, or meeting-house on Sundays, jail, hotel, dozen stores, and score of drinking saloons, which were gambling hells as well, and the shanties, cabins, tents and more extensive houses of the denizens scattered around in the most desirable localities.

Of the half-dozen villages, or camps, of this kind in the valley, Angels' Rest took the palm as the garden spot, and the richest, not to speak of its greater dignitaries, and the fact that it could boast of a score of handsome women as denizens of the place.

And the dignitary of dignitaries in Angels' Rest was Lyman Moultrie, a man who had been one of the first miners to "strike it rich" in the valley, and had had fortune pan out well for him ever since.

As the mining camp grew in importance, Lyman Moultrie had started a graveyard by killing a desperado who took it into his head to run the place; then he was made constable, and afterward justice, and finding Angels' Rest on the eve of great prosperity, he went East and brought his wife there.

She was the first woman to locate in the valley, and a refined, kind-hearted and beautiful lady, she soon became the idol of the rough miners.

But other miners sent for their wives, or took unto themselves wives who emigrated West, and Angels' Rest thrived; but still Lyman Moultrie held his position as *the* man of the town.

One day there was great excitement in Angels' Rest, for a rumor ran like a torrent down the valley, that Lyman Moultrie had adopted two lovely girls from the East, one of whom was his kin, and they had come to the place to live.

Nobody had seen them enter Angels' Rest; but they were there, and the miners who passed the really pleasant house of the Judge, as Mr. Moultrie was called, and saw them seated on the piazza, expressed themselves in the belief that the "Rest" now deserved its name, as the Angels had arrived.

Instantly all the young beaux of the valley, and many of the old ones too, began to spruce up, get shaved, buy white shirts, and try to keep clean, while the poor little tailor of Angels' Rest saw an immediate fortune ahead of him in the orders received, and raised his prices for clothes.

And moreover, young miners with a poor claim, but good looks, began to go to their "diggin's" by the way of Judge Moultrie's mansion, as the six-roomed, whitewashed log cabin was called.

It mattered not which way they had to go to work, they went round by the Judge's, until each morning and evening appeared to be a Sabbath, with Christian stragglers meandering to and from church, for they were wont to wear their "best clothes" to the mines, get into their working suit there, and change to come home with.

The result of these changes was that within a few days after the arrival of the fair guests of the Judge, half the mining population were down with colds and the doctor and the "quacks" were kept busy, while the undertaker had an occasional call for his services.

And who were those beauties who had driven Angels' Rest so mad that every young miner, and their name was legion, who owed the Judge a small sum of money, borrowed the amount from some other friend and went up to settle it in person, investing that much with a hope they would see the maidens?

They were none other than Dolores Moultrie and Hortense Harmon, who, after a long trip, in which they had passed through many hardships and dangers, had safely arrived in Colorado at their destination, guided thither, and protected by Satan's Pet and Buffalo Bill.

Long after midnight the party of four had ridden into the valley, and a late way-farer, going home from a saloon dead broke and drunk, had directed them to the home of the Judge, who, upon being aroused had given them a hearty welcome, and called to his wife:

"Come, Sue, here is poor brother's child and her friend, so hurry up and give them welcome, with the two handsome young men who have brought them to us, thank God."

Such a welcome made them feel at home at once, and when Mrs. Moultrie came in, having thrown a wrapper around her, and kissed the maidens affectionately, the lonely wanderers felt that they were no longer alone and friendless.

But Buffalo Bill and Satan's Pet would not tarry; they said they would not give it away, by their presence that they had brought the maidens there, but would run away for a hunt of a few days.

To her uncle Dolores told all, excepting her belief that the pretended Utes who had massacred the train were Danites: this she kept to herself, as Satan's Pet had asked her to let himself and the scout work up the clew in their own way.

"Well, my child, and you, too, Hortense, this shall be your home, for we have no children, and gladly will we give you our love; won't we, wife?" said the Judge.

"With all my heart, Lyman, and I believe this is the first step toward breaking your brother loose from his allegiance to those wretched Mormons," answered the good woman.

"God grant it," said Dolores, earnestly.

"Now, Suse, you'll have to look up petticoats, for these girls have worn the breech-es long enough."

"Oh, we have more clothing with us, uncle; only man's attire is so much better to travel in," said Dolores, quickly.

"I'll bet a gold claim your male attire didn't keep those handsome fellows from talking love to you."

"Yes, uncle, for they treated us with the greatest respect, and both Hortense and myself shall ever love Buffalo Bill and Satan's Pet," was Dolores's remark.

"They are noble fellows, both of them, and their fame is well known in our valley; but come, you are at home, and must have some rest."

And, with a feeling of perfect rest, the maidens laid them down to sleep in a soft bed, and where no danger threatened them.

Chapter XXXVI.
Hercules Bluff.

A few days after the arrival of Dolores and Hortense in Angels' Rest, the citizens of that festive mining village had another cause for excitement.

This, as in the former case, was occasioned by an arrival in the town.

The new-comers rode into the valley in broad daylight, and were splendidly mounted and thoroughly armed.

They were dressed with almost dandy neatness, and were certainly as handsome a pair of men as ever were seen in company.

"Riding up to The Paradise, *the* inn of the Angels' Rest, they dismounted from their horses, threw their bridle-reins to a Chinese hostler, and told him to give the game, with which the animals were loaded, to the host of the hotel with their compliments.

Upon the Register, which was a couple of quires of foolscap sewed together, and with a buckskin cover, they wrote their names as follows.

"William F. Cody—'Buffalo Bill.'
"Guide and Scout U. S. Army."

"Arnold Aubrey—'Satan's Pet.'
"*The Danites' Foe.*
Utah."

Hardly had they gotten out of sight on their way to their room, under the guidance of a Chinese servant, when two score of men, who had noted their arrival, sprung for the register.

Then their comments began:

"Buffaler Bill! waal, he are ther boss scout, or I live like a parson," said one.

"Yas, Bunk he are lightnin', I hes heer'd."

"He are oncommon young-lookin'."

"He are oncommon han'some."

"Oh! but I has heer'd thet he are some on ther shoot."

"But t'other chap hain't way back down ther lane, ef ther court knows itself."

"What! Satan's Pet?"

"Yas."

"Waal, he hain't; they do say he hev raised 'tickler Satan with ther Danites up at Salt City."

"He were one o' a gang as was lit inter by Leigh, ther Danite, I has heer'd, an' he got away; but he's been in ther killin' biz ever since."

"He's pretty as a painted picter o' Little Sam'el, as I hes see'd in Sunday schules."

"They is both screamers fer looks, an' ef ther Moultrie gals lays eyes on 'em thar'll be fun'rals and weddin's hereabouts, I'm tellin' yer."

"I guesses they'll git thar pluck tried on in Angels' Rest, fer ther boys will want ter diskiver ef they has come honest by thar names."

"They'll get it tried on ef they ges foolin' round them Moultrie gals, fer I intends ter git on tarms with one of 'em, an' ef she don't wilt, I'll try t'other," said a surly voice, and his remark seemed to close the conversation, and those in his way fell back, for Hercules Bluff was the bully and terror of the valley.

He was six feet four in his boots, weighed over two hundred, without an ounce of superfluous flesh upon him, was straight as an arrow, knotted all over with muscles, and was a dead shot and bad hand with the knife.

No man that knew him had ever seen him backed down, and many a man he had caused to pass in his checks.

His face was refined in expression and very handsome, giving the direct lie to his cruel, heartless, and quarrelsome nature, and he dressed like a dandy, wearing a blue woolen shirt, with brass buttons, a white silk scarf for a cravat, black pants, stuck in handsome cavalry boots, and a military hat.

Across his broad breast was a massive gold chain, diamond studs were in his shirt fro[n]t, and heavy gold buttons in his cuffs, while a solitaire of considerable value glittered on the small finger of his left hand.

In a bead-worked belt, with a huge silver buckle, were three revolvers and a large bowie, all silver-mounted, and they looked as though they were for use instead of show.

He was a gambler and miner combined, working his claim every Sunday, and playing cards during the week days.

Walking up to the register he glanced contemptuously at the names, and said with a sneer:

"Buffalo Bill and Satan's Pet.

"I have heerd of 'em, an' I guesses ef they stays long heur they'll heur o' me.

"I'll be sartin' ter interdoose myself, ef I catches 'em puttin' on frills up at ther jedge's, fer I hes met them leddies, an' I is dead struck on both.

"Yer hes heard me talk, pards, and yer all knows Hercules Bluff."

They did all know him, and not a word was said as he walked away.

But when he was gone a long breath was drawn, and one said:

"Pards, we is safe ontil next time."

"Yas; but yer hear me talk. Diggas, thar'll be music in ther Rest, afore long, fer them children hain't going ter be bullied, even by Hercules Bluff."

"It'll be a case o' ther right chu'ch but ther wrong pew ef he tackels 'em, I'm thinkin'," said another.

"Yas, he'll punch ther ticket o' ther wrong passenger ef he wakes 'em up."

"Pards, I camp right out heur ter see ther fun: no diggin' dust fer me, ontil I see ther meetin' called," and this last remark seemed to be the prevailing opinion of the loafers of Angels' Rest.

Chapter XXXVII.
HERCULES BLUFF'S LITTLE GAME.

As ill fortune would have it, Mr. Hercules Bluff had been on hand to render a favor to Dolores and Hortense one morning a few days after their arrival in Angels' Rest.

The Judge had been giving them, with his wife, a drive in an army ambulance he had purchased, and the two horses, wild as bucks, had become unmanageable and started to run, but were caught by Hercules Bluff, whose giant strength quickly brought them to a stand-still, and saved, without doubt, the lives of the entire party, as the road wound around a precipice a short distance ahead, over which all would have been dashed.

The Judge knew Hercules Bluff well, and though shunning him, had been careful not to offend him, as he cared for no row with the fellow.

But now, in his thankfulness, he had introduced the bully to the maidens, and accepted his invitation to get in and drive the horses home, as he was completely worn out from tugging at them.

It was Sunday afternoon, and Hercules Bluff had been working his claim all day; but willingly knocked off work and jumping in drove the horses up to the door of the Judge's home, and was of course invited to remain to supper, an invitation he promptly accepted, if the ladies would excuse him while he went to the hotel and "slicked up."

He came back in his best suit, and was certainly a splendid looking man; but heart and soul had been neglected in his composition to make the form.

He was delighted with both maidens, and it was nearly midnight before he left, and his being there, caused a dozen or more, young beaux who had dropped in during the evening, to curtail their visit to a few minutes' duration, and then poured oil on their troubled souls by standing outside in the darkness and cursing him.

But his appearance at last put them to flight, and he strolled slowly back to the hotel convinced that he was in love, had made a deep impression, and intended to marry.

As for Dolores and Hortense they had heard his character, and though thankful to him for saving their lives, they disliked and feared him; but the Judge had warned them not to anger him. {20}

One afternoon he strolled up to the "mansion," and invited the maidens for a walk.

The Judge and his wife were away on a visit, and not daring to refuse, they accepted, and Hercules Bluff led the way into the town.

As it was Sunday afternoon, he knew all the boys would be loafing about, and he determined to show them his prizes, as he called them.

It happened too, to be the day after the arrival of Satan's Pet and Buffalo Bill at the Paradise Hotel, and just as the bully and the maidens came in sight, the two friends left the hotel for a walk, intending to call at the Judge's.

They had kept their room constantly since their arrival, lying off and resting; but had now put on their best looks and were on the way to make a call.

"Does yer see them pilgrims, leddies?" asked Hercules Bluff, upon catching sight of Buffalo Bill and Satan's Pet.

At a glance both Dolores and Hortense recognized their brave protectors, and the former said quickly:

"Yes, it is Mr. Cody and Mr. Aubrey, gentlemen whom we have before met."

"Gentl'men, is they? Waal, I guesses not, fer I says they is durned gerloots, an' I'll show yer that I makes 'em howl, moppin' up ther road with 'em."

Both Dolores and Hortense were now alarmed, for they felt that it was the intention of the bully to "show off" before them.

They knew that he was a giant in strength, and a fearful hand with the revolver and loved a difficulty; but they also knew he had two dangerous persons to deal with, and of course they dreaded trouble, and Hortense cried nervously:

"Come, Dolores, let us go back, please."

"Yes, we will return, Mr. Bluff," answered Dolores.

"No you don't; I hain't thet kind o' gerloot.

"Them gerloots writes the'r names Satan's Pet an' Buffler Willi'm, an' I are Hercules Bluff, as will show yer some fun with 'em."

In the mean time all who knew Hercules Bluff's nature, felt that, his being with the maidens, would make him insult the two strangers in the valley, and they gathered quickly to see the fun.

Buffalo Bill, when they were within some fifty paces, halted to shake hands with some miner who had met him before, while Satan's Pet walked on, and, seeing that the bully was determined for a row, both Dolores and Hortense concluded not to run off, hoping that their presence might prevent trouble.

But vain the thought; they had not yet learned the true inwardness of border character.

Chapter XXXVIII.
A Border Sport's Mistake.

ALL on the principal street of Angels' Rest were now duly excited, for with frontier instinct they knew there was trouble brewing, and like veteran war-horses snuffed the battle from afar.

In fact many of them preferred to snuff it from afar, well knowing that many an innocent person got shot in a street *melee*, instead of the one who should have caught the bullet.

With a perfect understanding of how matters would go, if it came to "draw and fire," they left an open space for the bullets to fly, if they missed their intended marks.

All this neither Sat[a]n's Pet or Buffalo Bill seemed to see.

The former, smoking a cigar, came quietly along toward the ladies, before whom stood Hercules Bluff, for all three had halted.

On the bully's face was a sinister smile of anticipated triumph, and it was certain that he intended to start the fracas.

As for Buffalo Bill he still talked to the citizen of the Rest, and seemed unconscious of any excitement.

Drawing near to the maidens and the sport, Satan's Pet caught the eye of Hortense, who, anxious to prevent trouble, said quickly:

"How do you do, Mr. Aubrey, I am so glad to see you."

"And I also, Mr. Aubrey," and the two maidens advanced with extended hands.

"And so is I, Mr. Gerloot, put it thar," and ere either Dolores or Hortense could grasp the youth's hand, Hercules Bluff sprung forward, seized it with a gripe of iron, and gave him a jerk that dragged him off his feet.

Satan's Pet was possessed of remarkable strength for his size and age, for he could not be over nineteen, but with a man like Hercules Bluff, with a gripe on his hand, pulling him about, he was powerless to resist, unless he used a weapon, and this the presence of the maidens prevented.

"For shame, Mr. Bluff," cried Hortense.

"We do not care to see your brute strength, sir," said Dolores.

"Oh, let him have his fun," said Satan's Pet, pleasantly, keeping his feet in spite of the terrific jerks the huge bully was giving him.

"I'm so glad ter see yer, yer dandy gerloot," laughed the bully.

"When you get tired of using my little pard as a whip-cracker, shake me up, please."

The remark was made by Buffalo Bill, and, as if to enforce his request, he dropped his hand upon the arm of the Hercules in a style that checked the intended jerk he was about to give the youth.

"This is my circus, Bill," said Satan's Pet, cheerily.

"Well, I'm ring-master, Pet, and shall stir up the giraffe," and his grasp, still on the wrist of the bully, caused him to release the hand of the youth.

He knew by the *feel* of the scout's hand that he had a man to deal with, and attempted to drop his clutch upon a revolver in his belt; but he was dealt a blow upon his arm that benumbed it, while Buffalo Bill cried:

"No, you don't take that trick, pard, but follow suit."

As he spoke another blow, like a sledge-hammer, fell on the arm, and then with lightning rapidity the strokes rained thick and fast in the bully's face.

In vain was every effort of the bully to release his right wrist from the scout's steel gripe; he could not do it, and his left arm had received several such stunning blows as to render it almost useless, while the fist of Buffalo Bill, driven into his face one moment, and upon his chest the next, bewildered him, and the blood blinded him.

In amazement, both Dolores and Hortense shrunk back, but were held by sheer fascination to the spot, for they had believed no three men could handle Hercules Bluff.

In dumb astonishment the crowd gathered around, wondering if it was the huge desperado that was being so severely punished.

With folded arms, and an indifferent air, Satan's Pet looked on, only once remarking:

"That's your claim, now, Bill; work it all you've a mind to, for you've struck a good lead, and the claret pans out well."

This raised a laugh from the crowd, for they saw that Hercules Bluff was too blinded with blood to see who of them enjoyed the joke.

At last the bully, in utter frenzy, suddenly thought of kicking his foe, for, never having had any one dare face him before, he really knew not how to handle himself, depending wholly upon his brute strength.

But when his first kick was given, out from under him, as quick as a flash, was knocked his other leg, by a sudden movement of the scout, and the giant fell his length upon the hard earth with a force that left him breathless.

A wild yell burst from two hundred throats at the defeat of Hercules Bluff, and a rousing cheer was given for Buffalo Bill, who raised his sombrero, and walked on and joined Dolores and Hortense, who extended to both the friends a most hearty welcome.

"I'll lend you my other hand to shake, ladies, for this on got caught in a vise," laughed Satan's Pet, and the four turned back toward the home of Judge Moultrie, who just then hailed them from his vehicle, he and his wife having arrived in time to witness the punishment given the bully.

"Bravo, Cody, you've done Angels' Rest an everlasting favor in punishing its greatest devil, whom we all thought infallible.

"Come on, you and Aubrey, with the girls, and have supper, and we'll drink a toast in my best brandy to the Border Sport's mistake in waking up the wrong passenger," and, laughing heartily, the Judge drove on, leaving the young people to follow on foot.

Chapter XXXIX.
Hors de Combat.

When Hercules went down under the punishment given him by Buffalo Bill, there were plenty of his satellites ready to play the Good Samaritan and raise him up.

Not that his toadies did so from any feeling of affection for him, for there was not really one person in Angels' Rest who liked him; but the truth was, they feared him, and did not expect Buffalo Bill and Satan's Pet to make their residence there, and knew that the bully would remain.

Because he had received one thrashing, it was no sign that Hercules Bluff would allow himself to continue to be whipped, any more than was it that one swallow will make a summer.

With these personal considerations to govern them, the toadies, appointing themselves a relief committee, carried Hercules Bluff to his room at the hotel and sent for the entire medical force of Angels' Rest.

As the doctors all arrived together, they had to take the patient *en masse*, and when they caught sight of his face they concluded that a *post-mortem* was in order to decide by autopsy what he had died of.

Of their mistake, however, Hercules Bluff soon made them cognizant by a few round oaths, and they set to work to put him in shape once more.

With the cuts and bruises he had received and the swellings that followed, Hercules Bluff was by no means the handsome man he had been a couple of hours before, and this he realized when he got a glimpse of his face, and during the dressing of his wounds and plastering up of the cuts, entertained the medical fraternity with some choice profanity and threats against Buffalo Bill and Satan's Pet.

"This heur arm feels ez tho' a muel had let drive at it with his bizziness eend, doctor," he growled.

"It is only bruised," answered an M. D.

"Only be d—d; I wish you hed ther bruise, yer cussed pill pirate, an' I guesses yer'd think yer'd been blow'd up in a steam ingine."

"We'll soon bring that round all right, Mr. Bluff."

"Ef yer don't, I'll give thet old coffin artist a leetle work on your account, for ef yer don't know yer biz yer is no good, ther whole tooth-drawin', leg-sawin', pill-givin' pack o' yer.

"Now, durn yer, see ef this heur wrist o' mine hain't been swinged with a red-hot iron."

"It is where he had his gripe on you, Mr. Bluff; a powerful man, I should say."

"Then you tells ther truth now, ef yer does lie sick folks black in ther face at other times.

"*Powerful!* waal, I hain't no baby in arms, an' ef I didn't think thet hell hed bu'sted up through ther mines an' was a-rushin' red hot through Angels' Rest, yer kin call me a liar.

"I jerked thet young cuss round a leetle, jist ter git acquainted with him, and he hain't no slouch, for he comed down every time on his pins, tho' I did lift him some, as yer may hev see; but when thet steam saw-mill on stilts got a holt on me, then the devil were to pay an' no pitch hot.

"Powerful, did yer say? yer durned old terrer o' measles, he are a leetle mite more powerfuller then were thet boss o' 'em all Sampson, as I hes heerd about killin' thousands o' Ph'listines with the jaw-bone o' a jackass.

"I tell yer, pill pards, at fust I thought I were Sampson, then I got the idea I were the jawbone, ontil at last I concluded as I were the Ph'listines."

When at last the doctors had put Hercules Bluff in the best condition possible, and told him he had to remain indoors for a week, they took there [*sic*] departure amid a storm of oaths.

Then the toadies took him in charge to cheer his loneliness, and began by telling him how Dolores and Hortense had laughed while he got whipped, a story they had manufactured just to keep up the bully's spirits.

The next day Buffalo Bill and Satan's Pet left Angels' Rest, and this news was detailed by the toadies as a proof of their fearing to meet Mr. Bluff upon his arising from a sick couch.

Then hints were given that the scout and the youth stood the best show with the maidens up at the Judge's, added to which inflammatory piece of information, was given the opinions of the citizens of the valley regarding Hercules Bluff deserving the punishment he got, and the general belief that it would cow him to such an extent as to make him keep in the background.

That these stories, retailed with variations and embellishment, to the *hors de combat* bully, did not add to his peace of mind may be readily imagined, and when he at length, after weeks' illness, to allow the bruises and cuts to heal, got out upon the street, he was in the mood of a frenzied tiger, and swore vengeance against every one in general.

So determined was the desperado to show that he was not cowed, that a man, a peaceable miner, who looked at him curiously, was knocked down for it, and a friend of his interfering, was shot dead.

"Ther lion are out ag'in, pards, an' we is ter be all chawed up," was the cry that went around the town when the desperado began his murderous exploits once more.

CHAPTER XL.
THE WOUNDED DANITE.

SEVERAL weeks after the trouble between Hercules Bluff and Buffalo Bill, a horseman was riding slowly through the mountains, not many leagues from Salt Lake City, and following no trail, apparently.

Suddenly he drew rein, for, beneath a rude wicky-up, made of the boughs of trees, he saw a man lying, apparently in deep sleep.

The face was pale and haggard, the form emaciated, and there was that appearance about him and the surroundings, that showed he was ill.

Dismounting quietly, the horseman approached, and the man opened his eyes with a start, and tried to get his hand upon a pistol that lay near.

"Hold! I will not strike a man when he's down, though I recognize you."

"And I recognize you too; you are the Danites' foe, Satan's Pet," said the man in a low tone.

"That's what men call me," was the reply.

"And you deserve the name; yes, and you are right to follow the red trail you have, as I well know."

"Yes, you should know, for you are one of Leigh's Red Dozen, and, if you were not flat on your back I would kill you now, so hurry up and get well so I will feel no compunctions about it."

"Pard, I said awhile since you were right to follow the red trail you have, for I know how {21} you and yours suffered, and my brother and myself tried hard to stop that devil's work, but we could not."

"Do you speak the truth?"

"I do, pard, and to prove it, John Leigh killed my brother on account of ill-feeling started at that time from what he said.

"I have been a bad man, but I meant not to be as bad as that, and I remained with him to one day avenge my brother."

"You had ample time and opportunity."

"Not to escape after it; but the other night I tried it; he was arrested by our chief, put in irons, and was to be taken to our Death Den to die.

"I aided his escape, and in the mountains was about to kill him, for he was unarmed and I held him in my power; but a woman saved him, and gave me this wound."

"A woman?"

"Yes; she was at the roadside, and heard what I said to him."

"And shot you?"

"She did; and they both believed she had killed me, and he dragged me out of the trail."

"And John Leigh?"

"Went on to the Death Den, and the next night, as I was hiding in the bushes, I heard two men pass, talking together, and they said the Black Jury had killed him."

"No, no, no! that cannot be; no, it is not true, for John Leigh cannot die by other hand than mine.

"This has been my prayer, my belief, and my presentiment, and many a time have I spared him, knowing that in the end I would kill him.

"Yes, as soon as I killed those twelve, of whom you are one," and Satan's Pet spoke excitedly.

"I am one, only one other lives now, for Leigh killed my brother."

"I have sent nine to their door, and they all knew who was their slayer."

"Your brother was ten, and you are eleven, and I spare you from what you said; but there is one more, and then comes Leigh."

"That other is one of the guards at the Death Den in these mountains."

"Ah! then he dies soon, and then comes Leigh."

"He's dead, I told you."

"I say he is not! he will only die by my hand; no other can kill him."

"You talk as if you knew; but please help me a little, pard."

"Willingly, my poor fellow; here is my hand that my enmity toward you has ended. "This was a bad wound."

"Yes, I had to dress it myself, for I dared not let any one see me, and I hid here and have been here ever since."

"Alone in this wretched place, and almost dying!"

"Yes, pard; I had a little food and it has kept me, and you see the creek's near."

"You are a brave fellow and I will soon bring you round all right; now let me dress your wound."

Satan's Pet was a skillful hand with wounds, and he soon probed for the bullet, cut it out with almost professional skill, and dressed the wounded arm so well that the man said he already felt a hundred per cent better.

A good shelter of boughs was then made, his own blankets spread for the wounded Danite, and a meal prepared of which he ate with real relish.

"I'll camp with you Mr.—"

"Hunton is my name, sir; Edward Hunton, and I hailed from Maryland before I was fool enough to come out here and turn Mormon."

"Well, Hunton, you can turn back again; better be a turn-coat than a Mormon, and I'll look up number twelve of that Doomed Dozen, and after I have killed him, I'll find Leigh."

"You are awful cool about it."

"That's the way to be."

"And you don't think John Leigh is dead?"

"No more than I am."

"Well, sir, if you kill the guard, Chadwick, when he's on duty at the Den, then there's a way of finding out, if you don't fear the dead."

"No, nor the living; the dead certainly are the best neighbors, Hunton, so we'll find out."

"Well, sir, I know the ropes, and I'll show you as soon as I get on my pins again, and then I'll strike east again at a rapid pace, as old Ebony yonder has had a good long rest, and plenty to eat," and he pointed to his horse, lariated not far away.

Chapter XLI.
Number Twelve.

Under the attentive nursing of Satan's Pet, Hunton, the ex-Danite, for he had sworn to give up Mormonism and all connected with it, recuperated so rapidly that it was not many days before he expressed his willingness to move.

He felt anxious, even in that solitude where his camp was, for fear some one might stumble on it, and he be run down by his former comrades, for aiding the Danite major to escape, as they knew not his motive.

So, one afternoon, near sunset, Satan's Pet saddled the horses and aided Hunton to mount and they set off for the Death Den.

It was late when they arrived in the canyon that led up to the cavern in the mountains; but they rode on, Hunton knowing the signals and passwords, should they be halted.

Up the ravine to the front of the Death Cavern they went, until halted by the sentinel on duty.

"I am from the chief; is the Death Jury in reunion?" asked Hunton, keeping at a safe distance and disguising his voice.

"No, the jury will not meet for three nights!" was the answer.

"It is not the man you seek," whispered Hunton, and he turned his horse and rode down the canyon followed by Satan's Pet.

"To-morrow night your man is on duty; that much we found out," said the ex-Danite.

"I can bide my time; there is no hurry," was the quiet response, and back to their camp they went to pass the time until the next night.

But then promptly they were on hand, and up to the guard they rode, until again halted.

"I am Captain Vane," said Satan's Pet, raising himself in his saddle, and imitating the voice of that officer.

The Danite guard politely saluted, and answered:

"Have you any orders, major?"

"Major; that looks as though he had been promoted in Leigh's place," muttered the youth, while he answered aloud:

"Yes, I have orders for your special ear, my man."

Riding up to the sentinel, who wholly unsuspected wrong, he bent over and suddenly seized his throat, while he thrust a revolver into his face, and hissed forth:

"Move or utter a cry and I fire."

The man was startled nearly out of his wits, and made not the slightest show of resistance.

Slipping to the ground Satan's Pet called to his companion to fasten the horses and follow, and he forced his prisoner into the passage to the gate of the Death Den Cavern.

"Now unlock this door, sir!"

Silently and with trembling hands the man obeyed.

["]There is a lantern here somewhere?"

"Yes."

"Get it, but remember you die if you cry out; here, Hunton, take his belt of arms."

"'Sh—sir, don't call my name to him."

"It makes no difference; he will never tell," was the significant reply.

The lantern was found and lighted, and Satan's Pet said:

"Now tell me where is Major John Leigh?"

"In his coffin, where you will be for this night's work, Major Vane," was the sullen reply.

"I am not Major Elmo Vane; look at me."

He turned the lantern upon his face and the man started back, while he cried in horror:

"Satan's Pet!"

"You have named me: and you are my pet, for you are number twelve of the Red Dozen!"

"That man is another, for I see him now."

"Oh I have absolved Hunton of his sins; but you, you red-handed devil, must die."

"No, no, for you will be merciful."

"Not I; it's not in my composition against such as you.

"But first show me the coffin of Major Leigh."

The guard went to the niche and said:

"This is his shelf."

"Pull the coffin out!"

"I dare not."

"Obey!"

The motion of Satan's Pet was so significant that he thought better of his refusal and obeyed.

"By heaven! I told you so!"

The coffin was empty, and the cry broke from the lips of Satan's Pet.

In his surprise and delight he momentarily forgot his prisoner.

But the prisoner had not forgotten himself, and made a bold stroke for freedom.

Out of the hand of Satan's Pet he knocked the lantern, and it fell to the rocky flooring, and was shattered in pieces.

All was darkness, and away bounded the sentinel.

An instant Satan's Pet listened to the retreating footsteps, and then came the flash and report of his revolver.

A heavy fall and a groan followed:

"You got him, thank the Prophet!" cried the delighted Hunton.

"Thank me, not the Prophet, pard," was the cool reply, and feeling his way forward in the darkness his foot touched the prostrate form.

Bending over he laid his hand on the man's heart.

It had ceased to beat.

Searching he found the bullet wound in the back.

"It went through the heart, and I know the fate of Number Twelve," he said calmly.

"Then let us leave, sir."

"I am ready."

They found their way to the gate, passed out, locking it after them. and once out in the starlight Satan's Pet wrote on a piece of paper with a pencil:

"With the compliments of
Satan's Pet,
The Danites' Foe."

This he stuck on the bayonet of the sentinel, and then the two men rode away in the darkness. Hunton leading the way to the lonely cabin of the Danite's wife, for he knew that secret of John Leigh, having been one of the trusted few.

Chapter XLII.
A Pair of Precious Pards.

"Ef yer ha'r wa'n't so white, an' yer beard so gray an' grizzly b'ar like, I'd say the eyes were in ther head o' John Leigh."

The speaker was Hercules Bluff, and he had overtaken a man hastening from an Angels' Rest grocery-store, with a supply of provisions just purchased, and making for the mountains.

The one so addressed was dressed as a miner, was slightly bent in form, or assumed it, and had snow white hair falling on his shoulders, and a grayish beard.

He was evidently startled at the address of the Hercules, for he dropped the sack of provisions, and bundle he carried, and turned quickly with his hand on a revolver.

"Henry Hall!" he gasped, not making any attempt to use his pistol.

"Called Hercules Bluff in these parts, Pard John, so don't go back to pick me up by a name I haven't heerd fer years."

"Not since you signed it without the *junior* affixed, to your uncle's check, for whom you were named," said John Leigh.

"Lordy, that leetle biz were Sunday-school teachin' ter what I hes did since," was the unabashed reply.

"Well, that caused you to light out from our old town, Henry."

"Hirkerlees—I told yer; H-i-r-k-e-r—hirker—l-e-e-s—Hirkerlees."

"Well, I stick to my old name I had when we were boy chums."

"No need ter change it, fer it were bad enough then."

"Yer c'u'd scholar consid'ble, John, while I were a dunce on books; but yer were thet wicked yer broke yer old mother's heart; what is yer doin' now?"

"Mining."

"Thet's good, when ther dust pans out; but seems to me I hes heerd yer were up among ther Mormons."

"I was once; but what are you doing?"

"Digging, lyin', cussin', cheatin', shootin', an' doin' bad in general."

"Well, Hen—"

"Hirk—"

"All right; well, Hercules, keep dark about meeting me; call me Jack—well, I'll borrow your old name—Jack Hall, and I'll take you to my cabin in the mountains, and introduce you to my wife."

"How many?"

"One."

"Though yer were a Mormon Danite?"

"I was."

"Hain't now?"

"Not exactly."

"Yas, yer changes yer spots, I sees."

"When it suits me."

"Waal, travel me ter yer camp an' interdooce me."

"You'll not gossip?"

"Nary, on a old pard."

"Well, come along."

"Are she slick?" he asked, as John Leigh took up his bundles and walked on."[sic]

"She is beautiful, if that's what you mean."

"Seems ter me yer married life hasn't been cheerful livin'."

"Why?"

"Yer isn't more 'n seven year older nor me, an' yer hair is white as yer mother's were."

"Yes, it is prematurely gray."

"It are *durned* gray, that's what it are; but I thinks o' marryin', too."

"You?"

"Yas; hain't I a dandy?"

"You certainly are a spendid-looking fellow, Hercules, but your face looks as though you'd passed through a thrashing machine."

"I has been; it were one o' ther Buffalo Bill pattern."

"Ah! you have met that famous scout, then?"

"I hev."

"And killed him, I hope?"

"He are a purty lively dead man, I kin tell yer, Jack."

"Oh! he got away with you, then?"

"I disremembers how it were adzactly; but I hasn't been out o' bed too long ter feel perfect healthy since."

"Why, I did not believe the man lived that could handle you."

"No more did I; but I hes hed reason fer changin' my private opinion, Jack, an' mayhap ef you hed seen ther thrashin' mercheen at work, yer'd 'sperienced a change, too."

"But the matter does not rest there?"

"I hasn't rested well since."

"I mean, you intend to kill him?"

"Yas, when I kin git ther drop on him, I intends ter do it, an' also take in out o' ther wet his leetle pard they calls Satan's Pet." {22}

"Great God!" and John Leigh turned deadly pale.

"Has yer got 'em, Jack?"

"Is that fellow, Satan's Pet, here?"

"He were; he an' Bill were pards, an' they is a team, I kin tell yer."

"Where are they now?"

"Levanted."

"Where?"

"Don't know; guess they hain't lost."

"What were they doing here?"

"As near as I kin find out they comed ter see my gals."

"You are a Mormon too?"

"Not adzactly; but I are in love with two leetle gals as is lovely."

"But Bill and Satan's Pet cut you out?"

"Durn 'em, no! I'll kill both Dolores an' Hortense fust," he said savagely.

"Dolores and Hortense?" cried John Leigh excitedly.

"Yas, them's the'r handles, an' they is beauties from Beautyville, I'll sw'ar, tho' they laughed when I got licked an' I doesn't love 'em so much now; but I hadn't forgot 'em, I'll tell you, confidential like, Jack."

"Where are these ladies?"

"At ther kinfolks, old Judge Moultrie's."

"Ha!"

"Ef yer wants ter laff, laff out, and don't say *ha* and quit, same as yer had tooken cramps."

"I do want to laugh from joy, Hercules, for I am so glad I have met you."

"But, mind you, not one word about these ladies, to my wife."

"Yes, I see; she shows her claws."

"She is a devil when aroused," and the face of John Leigh became flushed with triumph, at having accidentally struck the trail of Dolores and Hortense.

Chapter XLIII.
What Satan's Pet Heard.

"Well, Cody, which is the trail?" and a party of four horsemen drew up at a spot where the trail they were following down the mountain divided.

The speaker was dressed in uniform; in fact he was none other than Captain Howland Moncrief, who had left his command at Fort Uintah, some days before, in company with Buffalo Bill, Satan's Pet, and the ex-Danite Hunton, and were on their way to Angels' Rest, where, accidentally, the young officer had heard that Dolores Moultrie then was, and the hearing of which had made him quickly ask leave of absence for a few weeks.

"This is the trail, captain," said Buffalo Bill, bearing to the right.

"I'll take this one," said Satan's Pet firmly.

"You'll wind back up the mountain then, Pet," said Cody.

"Can't help it, Bill; you go that way, and I'll come along soon, for I believe in presentiments, and something tells me I'll go right in taking this trail."

"Then we'll all go that way."

"No, Captain Moncrief; you and Bill go that way, and Hunton and myself will take this trail, and join you among the Angels of the valley," and the party divided.

For some time Satan's Pet, with Hunton following close behind, rode on, and then the trail branched off into a dozen deer-paths up the mountain.

"Cody was right; oh! there's a cabin, and I'll see who has camped in this lonely place," said Satan's Pet, and he threw his bridle to his companion, and dismounting, walked the hundred paces to the little log cabin on the mountain side.

As he approached he heard voices, and suddenly his face grew pale and then flushed with excitement.

Within the cabin he knew there were two persons, and he crept nearer and listened.

The words that had arrested his attention, and so moved him with emotion, were spoken in a woman's voice.

"Oh, John, you would not do such a cruel wrong?" she said.

Then came the answer in the voice of a man:

"It is no wrong in my eyes; I have striven hard to win promotion, and the result was that accursed old Moultrie sent me to my death.

"I know that the Prophet would pardon me, and as the first step I wish to send him those two girls.

"They already know too much, as the Prophet shall be informed, and will be summoned as witnesses of that massacre, and he would do much to have them in his power before the [United] States Government begins on him.

"Old Moultrie, he will find, did deceive him, and I was right about the women being in his house, and the result will be that I get to be chief, and Moultrie finds a berth in a coffin in the Death Den, while I am pardoned.

"Now you know my plan."

"You are keeping something back, John Leigh."

"I am not."

"I say that you are."

"Well, Hercules Bluff is to turn Danite."

"I heard you pledge him one of those maidens as a wife, and a captaincy under you, if he went to Salt Lake and got your pardon from the Prophet."

"Yes, I did; but do you think I intended to keep it?"

"What! you intended to deceive him?"

"Of course; I would use him as a tool, have him capture the two girls and carry them to the city, and I have written the Prophet a letter in cipher to have Hercules at once put to death, as he is a dangerous character."

"For shame, John."

"I do not want him there; he is too dangerous a man."

"Well, have you nothing more to tell?"

"Only that Hercules has gone after the girls; he had his plans laid to capture them in their morning ride this morning, and by noon he will be here with them."

"Well, what else?"

"That is all, Queen."

"No."

"I say it is."

"You are deceiving me."

"I am not; you are to go with me and be my Queen forever."

"There is something else."

"Don't be silly, Queen."

"John Leigh, I studied out your letter in cipher to the Prophet."

The man was on his feet, and Satan's Pet heard a savage oath, and then his words:

"Curse you! you saw then that one of the maidens was to be my wife?"

"Yes, John Leigh, and I know more."

"Well, I care not what you know."

"So I believe, when I overheard you tell that huge brute, that you intended to get rid of me.

"He asked you how?

"Your answer was, John Leigh:

"'Put my knife in her heart.'"

"Then, by the gods, I'll keep my word, Queen Conrad."

The man fairly shrieked the words.

But, with the spring that he made toward her, his knife in his hand, his whole face frenzied with passion, the door was thrown open and Satan's Pet bounded into the cabin, seized him with herculean strength, and hurled him to the floor, while he placed his foot upon his breast, and pointed his revolver down in his face.

"We are well met at last, John Leigh," he cried, in hoarse tones.

Queen, who had given a cry of alarm at her danger, and tottering back, had fainted, lay like one dead upon the floor.

The knife had fallen from the grasp of the Danite, and his revolvers were on the table out of reach, so he felt his utterly helpless condition.

CHAPTER XLIV.
A LIFE-DEBT PAID.

THOUGH John Leigh knew well he was in the power of one he had no reason to expect mercy from, he determined to brazen it out to the last, and exclaimed angrily:

"How dare you call me by the name of that accursed Danite, John Leigh?"

"Well said, thou accursed Danite, John Leigh.

"But I know you, in spite of your hair, whitened by your crimes; ay, and I know who lies there.

"And you, John Leigh, shall know that I am Arnold Aubrey Conrad, the brother of yonder poor woman; the son of the poor old couple you lured out West to kill, hoping to get a fortune thereby, which your wife, my sister, would inherit.

"But you found that misfortune had come upon my parents, and you were foiled.

"You thought that I had been killed in that massacre two years ago.

"But no, I hid away from even your red fiends, and, excepting one man whom you forced to do your black deeds, you alone live.

"But, John Leigh, the hour of your death has come."

With a corpse-like face the guilty man had listened to the words of the boy who stood over him; but, as he ceased speaking, he cried:

"Mercy!"

"I shall show no mercy," and putting his fingers to his lips he gave three sharp, shrill whistles.

Almost immediately Hunton came running into the cabin, for, alarmed at the long absence of Satan's Pet, he had approached the spot.

"Good God!"

The cry broke from the lips of the Danite, when he saw who it was that entered.

"Oh! I'm alive and glad to see you well, major," cried Hunton, when, with a start, he saw who it was beneath the feet of Satan's Pet.

"Yes, but I have diagnosed his case, Hunton, and can take oath he won't live long," was the cool reply of Satan's Pet.

"Shall we hang him, sir?"

"Yes, get my lariat."

Hunton hastily obeyed.

Quickly and scientifically this command was carried out.

Together the two raised the Danite to his feet, and he tottered with weakness from fright.

Then they led him out of the cabin, the end of the lariat was thrown over a limb and drawn taut.

"Come, old horse, you shall do the dirty work," said Satan's Pet, and he fastened the end of the lariat to the bow of his Mexican saddle.

"Now, John Leigh, you have lived your last minute on earth. Come, old fellow, do your part well!"

A chirp to his horse, and the animal followed his master, and the shriek for mercy on the lips of John Leigh ended in a choking sound, as he was lifted from his feet and hoisted in mid-air.

"Halt!"

The obedient animal obeyed, and folding his arms, Satan's Pet stood gazing calmly up at the struggling form of the guilty man who so richly deserved his fate, while a short distance apart Hunton was standing, the only other visible witness of the fearful death scene.

Until the last tremor had gone through the swinging form, Satan's Pet stood there in silence, gazing upon the victim of his hate and revenge, and then he moved toward the cabin, saying, quietly,

"Hunton, he is dead; cut him down."

Opening the door of the cabin, Satan's Pet started back.

Instead of finding the form of the woman now known to be his sister, lying on the floor still in a swoon, he beheld her crouching upon her knees, her hands clasped, her face livid, and her staring eyes gazing through the open window and fixed upon the swinging form of John Leigh, the Danite.

"Sister! Queen! I have avenged you and our parents, murdered by his hand," cried the youth, in ringing tones.

"Aubrey! my brother!"

She could say no more, but threw herself in his arms and burst into tears, for at last the fountains of her grief-haunted heart were opened, and she knew that she had a protector in her brother, and that she was not alone in the wide world.

And then for a long time these two sat hand in hand in the little cabin, while Hunton placed in the grave the body of John Leigh, the Danite.

And each told to the other the story of their past since last they had met, and from out the blank clouds of sorrow in the heart came a ray of sunshine for the future.

Chapter XLV.
Well Met.

Wondering at the strange act of Satan's Pet, in deserting them for a trail that Buffalo Bill knew led away from the valley, and chatting about the strange youth, and his determined desire for revenge, the scout and Captain Moncrief rode on their way toward Angels' Rest.

Suddenly, as they came to a point, where a fine view of the distant valley could be seen, Buffalo Bill drew rein, and hastily leveled a field-glass he always carried with him.

"Pard captain, we'll just wait here, for these rocks will hide us, and give a surprise party to some one I see coming up the hill," said the scout.

"Who is it, Bill?" asked Captain Moncrief, reining his horse back behind the bowlder.

"First, it is a man who has been in mischief: he is Hercules Bluff, whom I had to thrash some time ago—"

"Yes, Pet told me about it."

"He has a pard with him whom I do not know; but I will swear that he is a villain."

"Then there are two ladies with them."

"Ladies with such villains, Bill?"

"Yes, captain; but I guess they don't care to remain in such bad company, so we'll just take them away from Bluff and his pard."

"I do not like to interfere with women—"

"Captain, I saw them through my glass, and one is Miss Moultrie and the other, Miss Harmon."

"By the God of War! Cody, I am ready to fight it out.

"That man holds them as prisoners, for some vile purpose."

"That's true, captain; but we are well met, and we'll bluff Mister Hercules's little game.

"I'll take him for a waltzing pard, and you take his comrade and we'll sail out at the word, but don't hit the ladies."

"I'm a dead shot, Bill."

"I know that, captain; but you're in love now, and a man in that condition—"

"'Sh—! Bill. I hear their horses' hoof-strokes."

"You'll hear more than that presently, captain."

Then the two friends sat in silence, awaiting the coming of the party, who were urging their horses hard.

As they came nearer, Buffalo Bill glanced cautiously around the bowlder, and whispered:

"Hercules is in front, riding by the side of Miss Hortense, and has hold of her bridle rein."

"And Dolores?"

"Comes behind, the rein of her horse held by a black-bearded pilgrim."

And on they came, the men looking ahead of them, and the poor captives with bowed heads, seemingly in perfect despair. {23}

"*Charge!*"

The cry broke in trumpet tones from the lips of Buffalo Bill, and like arrows shot from bows, their horses sprung away from the bowlder, and were alongside of the two ruffians before they could draw a weapon.

And they came to a sudden halt, and neither dared offer resistance, as a revolver muzzle was pressed hard against their heads.

So sudden had been the charge that it startled both Dolores and Hortense at first, but recognizing their deliverers at a glance, the former spoke the name of the captain, while they both called out the name of the scout.

"We have met again, Hercules Bluff, and I warn you that my bullets are harder than my fist," said Buffalo Bill, sternly.

"Yer durned fists is too hard fer me; but I guesses I is done fer."

"And me too, pard Hercules, durn yer fer gittin' a honest man inter' sich a scrape," said the other villain.

"Yes, the devil wants just such honest men as you are for kindling-wood," said Buffalo Bill, and then he continued:

"Miss Hortense, be kind enough to take those weapons out of this gentleman's belt, for they are too heavy for him to carry."

With a light laugh Hortense obeyed, while Dolores did a like favor for Captain Moncrief.

"Now, captain, we'll lasso these gentlemen with the aid of the young ladies," said the scout.

The maidens were only too glad to be of service, and in a short while Hercules Bluff and his pard were securely bound and tied to their horses.

"Now let us make for the valley, for I know these gentlemen are anxious to go to roost in a tree."

"Durnation! yer isn't goin' ter hang us, is yer, Buffalo Bill?" cried Hercules Bluff.

"I am going to distribute you among the Vigilantes of Angels' Rest, and—"

"They'll h'ist us, sartin, Bill."

"If they don't, *I* will."

"Oh Lordy! Buck, yer'd better rastle up what scriptur' yer knows, an' sling in a doxology fer me, as all I knows is a Hallylujah."

"I'd ruther put a bullet in yer fer gittin' me in this heur scrape," growled the other villain, as he came on behind between Captain Moncrief and Dolores.

"Say, pard, don't sass me ef we hes got ter travel ther same road together," answered Hercules.

"Bluff, you've got nerve, and it's a pity such a splendid-looking man as you are should be such a devil," said Buffalo Bill.

"Ther heart weren't put in ther right place, Pard Bill, I guesses."

"But if they hang me it'll take a stout rope ter hang me, an' nary one will heur me shout."

"I believe you," frankly answered the scout, and urging their horses into a canter, they dashed on at a more rapid pace and soon after drew rein before the home of Judge Moultrie, where already a large party of horsemen, armed to the teeth, had assembled to go in pursuit of the kidnappers, for a miner had seen the maidens captured while out riding that morning.

"Gentlemen, here is the game we bring you," said Buffalo Bill pointing to the two desperadoes.

"And I guesses we'll be durned well cooked game, Pard Buck, afore they is done with us," muttered Hercules Bluff, as the band of horsemen surrounded them, and with wild cries dashed away toward the town to rouse all the Vigilantes to action.

Chapter XLVI.
Conclusion.

That the Vigilantes of Angels' Rest made short work of Hercules Bluff and his wicked comrade, the reader can well understand, knowing the wild characters of the far frontier at that time.

And the townspeople were so charmed with Buffalo Bill for having brought back, as the miners expressed it, "them boss angils ter Angil Rest," they wished to make him Grand Mogul, an honor he declined with thanks, to return to his command, where he had been promoted to chief of scouts and guides.

When next he visited the valley it was to accompany Captain Howland Moncrief, as "best man," when that handsome and noble-hearted young officer wedded Dolores Moultrie, the one-time Danite's daughter, but whose father had cast off forever the cloak of Mormonism, and accompanied the happy couple on their bridal tour East, to the captain's home, and where they were all welcomed most kindly by Mrs. Moncrief, who looked with such favor on the ex-chief, she laid her snare, and caught him in the net of matrimony, from which he did not seem anxious to escape.

And Hortense?

The Judge and his wife not only refused to give her up, but adopted her as their child, and received as her governess none other than the sad-faced woman who had been a Mormon wife.

But three years after they were compelled to resign the beautiful maiden, and her governess too, as two persons arrived one day who held a love claim against them which they had promised to pay.

These two holders of the claims were Lieutenant Aubrey Conrad, of the United States army, and once known as Satan's Pet, and the other, like his chief, a repentant Danite, Elmo Vane, who, with his beautiful Queen, sought in a foreign land to forget the sorrows they had known in their life in Deseret.

THE END.

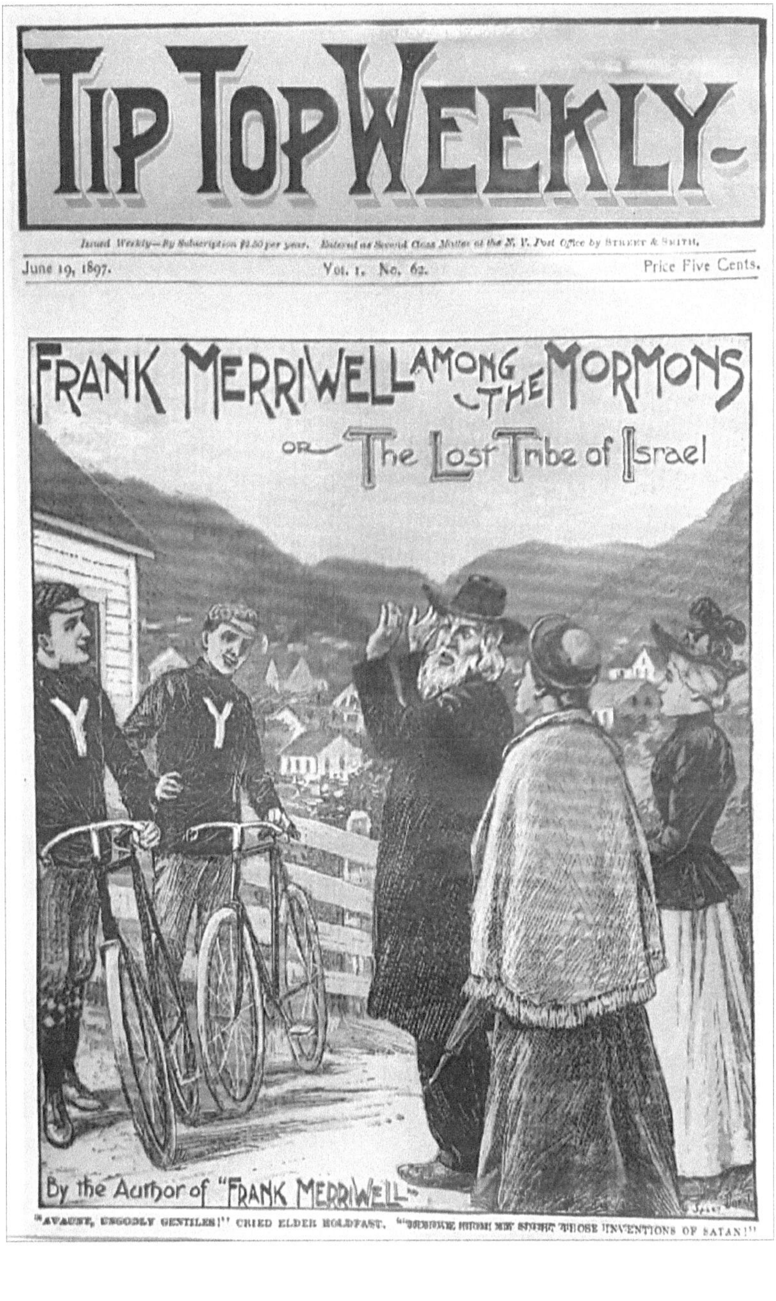

Issued Weekly—By Subscription $2.50 per year. Entered as Second Class Matter at the N. Y. Post Office by STREET & SMITH.

June 19, 1897. Vol. 1. No. 62. Price Five Cents.

By the Author of "FRANK MERRIWELL"

"AVAUNT, UNGODLY GENTILES!" CRIED ELDER HOLDFAST. "DELIVER FROM MY SIGHT THOSE INVENTIONS OF SATAN!"

Gilbert Patton. *Frank Merriwell Among the Mormons: or, The Lost Tribe of Israel.*
Tip Top Weekly, vol. 1, no. 62. New York: Street & Smith, 19 June 1897.

Frank Merriwell Among the Mormons;

or,

The Lost Tribe of Israel.

BY THE AUTHOR OF "FRANK MERRIWELL."

Chapter I

An Unyielding Father.

"Arise, daughter," said William Ayer, touching the shoulder of the sleeping girl, whose sad yet pretty face bore traces that told she had wept herself to sleep. "The morning has dawned, and this is the day that shall witness the consummation of thy happiness."

With a little pitiful cry, the girl opened her eyes and shrunk from him. Then, seeing his face, she gave a murmur of relief.

"Oh, it is you, father!" she said. "How you frightened me! I didn't know—I thought it might be that—that horrid creature."

"Of whom do you speak in such terms, my daughter?" gravely asked William Ayer. "Whom do you designate by the epithet 'horrid creature?'"

"Why, there is but one person I could possibly mean, father."

"Name that person, daughter."

"Elder Asaph Holdfast, of course."

William Ayer held up both hands, an expression of horror and sorrow on his face.

"Oh, my daughter!" he cried. "I hoped thy heart would be softened during the night and thy rebellious spirit would be bowed down with contrition, but it seems that I hoped vainly. Elder Holdfast is a chosen servant of the Lord, and a good and holy man."

"Elder Holdfast is a contemptible old wretch! Oh, how I despise and fear him!" she cried, sitting bolt upright in bed and making a wild gesture. "He has a thin, sanctimonious old face, and his hair and beard are snowy white, but his age can command for him no respect, as his evil nature is shown in his narrow little eyes. Oh, father! the look I have seen in those eyes when they rested on me—it makes me shudder with horror to think of it!" {2}

"You are hysterical, daughter!" said William Ayer, attempting to soothe her. "You are given to vain fancies and foolish thoughts. In the eyes of the good Elder Holdfast thou hast seen nothing but the tenderest regard for you and your spiritual welfare."

"Bosh!" cried the girl, sharply. "Tender regard, indeed! Such tender regard as the wolf gives the lamb it has selected for its prey!"

"Ah, but you will discover your mistake when the good elder has made thee his wife."

"Which he shall never do, father! I refuse to become the ninth Mrs. Holdfast. Asaph Holdfast already has seven living wives and one has died. Ugh!" she cried with a shiver; "it is a horrible thing to think about! And it is said that polygamy is no longer practiced in Utah!"

"That is said to deceive the wicked Gentile, who would rob our religion of all that makes it distinct and uplifting if he could."

"And do you—you, my father!—believe that polygamy makes the Mormon religion 'uplifting?' Heaven pity you if you do! Polygamy has been the shame and disgrace of the Mormons! To-day all the younger members of the church acknowledge it. Joseph Smith never believed in it."

"But there arose a greater and a wiser one than Joseph. Brigham Young was inspired of God, and he had many wives. In the old days the Brighamites suppressed and held in subjection the Josephites. It is only since the ungodly Gentile has forced himself in upon us that the doctrines of Joseph have prevailed once more. But here in this lost valley of Bethsada the Brighamites have built up a town that is shut off from the rest of the world—a town of which few outside its boundaries know anything at all. Here there are no Josephites and no Gentiles. Here the Mormon religion is practiced as it was practiced in Salt Lake City in the days of Brigham."

"And here you have dragged me, at the command of that old wretch Holdfast!"

"Hold, daughter! Thou shalt not speak thus disrespectfully of Elder Holdfast! I forbid it!"

"I don't care!" cried the girl, spiritedly. "He is an old wretch! Some day the law will reach him, and then he'll suffer. And you, father—you deceived me," she reproachfully declared. "You sanctioned my engagement to Tom Whitcomb—"

"That was before Elder Holdfast had seen thee and claimed thee, daughter."

"What evil power can that man have over you, father? Why could he, at his command, cause us to leave our pretty home in Provo and come here to this hidden town amid the mountains? And you know I would not have come here had I known at first where you were taking me."

"In this place, my child, deception was necessary in order to accomplish a great good."

"A great evil, you mean! I tell you, father, I will not marry that old wretch! Tom Whitcomb will come here and save me from him."

"It is a vain hope, daughter, for Whitcomb cannot know whither thou hast gone."

The girl was silent, but a strange look passed over her face—a look that her father failed to note.

"This is the day that thou art to be sealed to Elder Holdfast," said William Ayer. "Already the sun hath risen, and it is a beautiful morning. Array thyself in thy best apparel, daughter, and banish that sad look from thy face. Time will convince thee of thy mistake. I bid thee—nay, I command thee be gentle and respectful toward the good elder. In time thou shall learn to love him."

"Love him!" cried the girl, burying {3} her face in her hands—"love that old wretch! never! I detest him now, and I shall detest him always! Oh, father!"—and she suddenly caught both his hands—"my dear father! I beg you not to put this shame and sorrow upon me! You have told me how much you love me, and I have seen it in your eyes. Prove it now by saving me from Asaph Holdfast! You must see how much I suffer—you must know it will kill me! I cannot live through it!"

He released one of his hands and slowly stroked her hair. For a moment a light of pity shone from his eyes, but it seemed that he crushed down the pity in his heart and hardened his soul to carry out what he firmly believed was his duty.

"Daughter," he said, coldly, "thou art excited and hysterical now. You will see things in a different light very soon. It has been ordained that thou shalt become the wife of Elder Holdfast, and it is not in my power to withhold thee from him."

"Oh, you can't be so cruel—so heartless!" sobbed the poor girl, her whole shapely body wracked by the emotion that had fallen upon her. "I am your child—your own little Lona! You have held me in your arms and rocked me to sleep, and, with my head on your breast, with your arms about me, I have felt that you would shield and protect me always. I was so happy then, dear father! And now—now is it possible that you are the one to turn against me and force me into this shame! Oh, father! father!"

For a moment the man turned his face away. Then he set his teeth and, when he looked at her again, his face was cold and calm as usual.

"I tell you it is the will of one whose power I cannot deny," he declared. "It is useless for you to rebel, my daughter."

"Ah!" she sobbed, her blue eyes raining tears, "how I wish I had died when I was a happy child! How can it be you would force me to this when you know what has happened to the plural wives almost all over Utah? They have been set aside, and only the first wife remains as the true wife of the husband. Think of their wretched position—of their shame! And you would force me to this—you, my father!"

"The law may have said that none but the first wife is the legal wife of the husband," said William Ayer; "but that law was made by men and Gentiles. The law of God says all those wives are true and legal wives, and the law of God cannot err. For them there is no shame, and greater shall be their reward hereafter because of what they may suffer at present. As for you, their fate can never be yours. The people here in this beautiful valley are called the Lost Tribe of Israel, and lost they are to the outside world. No railroads shall ever come here, and Gentiles will not be permitted in this valley. Here polygamy shall continue and flourish long after you have passed away, so have no fear that the fate of plural wives in other parts shall befall you."

"You are crazy!" cried the girl. "Such a thing cannot continue! Sometime the Gentiles will pour in here, and then the railroad will come. With it shall come the putting away of the plural wives. But I'll not live to see that time! If I am forced into this by the father I have loved, it will kill me!"

"Nonsense, daughter! Let us have no further folly. Arise, as I have commanded, and don thy gayest attire. At ten Elder Holdfast will come for thee and take thee to the Endowment House, where thou shall be sealed unto him. Be ready."

Then he turned and left the chamber.

Shaking, sobbing, moaning, the girl flung herself down on the bed, burying her face in the pillows.

"Oh, Tom—Tom, my sweetheart!" she cried; "where are you now? Did you receive my letter? Will you be able to {4} find me? Will you reach me in time? If not, if you are too late, you will find me when I am dead!"

CHAPTER II.
WILLIAM AYER IS SURPRISED.

Through the pretty little Mormon town of Bethel, which stood in the Valley of Bethsada, hidden deep in the heart of the mountains, slowly and sedately walked Elder Asaph Holdfast, accompanied by one of his seven living wives, a plain, stout, matronly-looking woman.

Elder Holdfast had long white hair and a long white beard, and he seemed to be wrapped about with an air of self-conscious righteousness. At a distance there was something patriarchal in his appearance, but his face was cold and immobile, with a sternness about it that told he was a man of unbending will and unforgiving nature.

The face of the seventh Mrs. Holdfast, who accompanied him, had a meek bovine look, plainly showing the woman was not of a high order of intelligence.

Mrs. Holdfast did not walk abreast her lord and master, but kept a step to the rear, showing she fully felt her utter inferiority and unworthiness.

Not a word did the good Elder Holdfast say, but there was on his face a steady determination of purpose, and it is possible that his eyes, which were set close together, betrayed something of the pleasant anticipation that filled his soul.

For was not this the day that should see him sealed to the charming and beautiful daughter of a brother Mormon, who must feel it an untold honor to have his only and dearly beloved child become the ninth wife of one so high in the Mormon church as Elder Asaph Holdfast!

The sun was shining and the birds were singing. It seemed that all the world was filled with joy and happiness, and surely there could be nothing of sorrow and wrong in the beautiful little town of Bethel, where the Mormon religion, as expounded by the Prophet Brigham, was practiced and held full sway.

Here no Gentile had ever come to bring discord and unhappiness. The regular approaches to the valley were guarded by chosen ones, whose duty it was to turn back any suspicious persons who could not give sure and convincing proof that they were of the Mormon faith and endowed members of the church in good standing.

Elder Holdfast approached a small cottage, and rapped slowly and sedately on the door, which was opened almost immediately by William Ayer.

"Ah, Brother Ayer," said the elder, offering his hand, "you see I have come, as appointed."

"Ah, Elder Holdfast," said the other, accepting the proffered hand, but failing to give it a very cordial pressure, "I am glad to see thee, and I trust thou art well. Wilt thou enter?"

The elder entered. He did not offer to introduce the wife who accompanied him, but William Ayer placed a chair for her, and bade her sit down, which she did, after the elder had taken a chair.

Elder Holdfast's eyes were keen, and he detected a troubled look on the face of the other man. Of this he did not speak at once, but observed:

"Brother Ayer, I trust your daughter is in readiness to accompany us to the endowment house, for the appointed hour is at hand."

"Elder Holdfast," said Ayer, hesitatingly, "it saddens me to inform thee that my daughter is not well."

The cold look on the face of the Mormon elder grew colder still, and he regarded Ayer with sternness.

At last he spoke:

"I saw by thy face that something was amiss. But thou knowest, brother, that {5} this is a matter that cannot idly be put off to please the whim of a girl."

"I know, I know," said the father, hastily; "but in truth Lona is not well. You should remember as I have told you, that she had formed a foolish attachment for a young man in Provo."

"I remember that thou didst speak of it, Brother Ayer. If I remember aright, the young man's name is Whitcomb, a son of Jarius Whitcomb, who during life was a firm believer in the Mormon doctrine and a useful member of the church. Am I right?"

"Thou art right."

"Let me see," continued the elder, "it striketh me that Brother Whitcomb was at one time one of the Destroying Ones, chosen by the Prophet Brigham for a great and holy purpose."

"In that thou art right."

"But the son, I am told, hath been beg[u]iled by the false teaching of the ungodly Gentiles, and hath turned in a measure from the religion of his father."

"It is even so."

"Then," said Elder Holdfast, "there is no reason why we should give him any consideration, and certain it must be, Brother Ayer, that you could not desire your daughter to wed such a man."

"I had rather she would not," said Ayer, weakly.

"Had rather!" came sternly and reprovingly from Asaph Holdfast's lips. "My brother, I am astonished—nay, I am amazed! It is something to which, under no circumstances, you should give your consent."

William Ayer seemed to feel the sting of the good elder's reproval, and he hung his head for a moment. Then, with an attempt at self-justification, he looked up and said:

"You know she is my only child, and I love her so I hate to cause her sorrow."

"As she is thy only child, it is all the greater reason why thou shouldst have great care that she should not err in such a grave step. I much fear thou art too yielding with her, brother. It is ever for the good of an unthinking child that a stern and steady hand guideth it in the course it should pursue. But it seemeth that I came to Provo in time to save thy daughter from such a sad mistake as a marriage with a son who hath renounced the religion of his father—the true religion."

"But it was so sudden, Elder Holdfast—that is why it has shattered the poor girl's nerves and made her ill."

"Brother Ayer, it striketh me that thy daughter is shamming. I much doubt that she is ill at all."

Nor would the good elder be confined. He insisted that the girl must prepare herself at once to accompany them to the Endowment House. Ayer tried to remonstrate, in a feeble way, but all he said had no impression on the elder, and he finally gave in.

"If possible, I will bring her down," he said, as he started to leave the room.

"Tell her that she must come down, or I, myself, will come for her. Mrs. Holdfast, accompany Brother Ayer, and use thy arts of persuasion on the wilful child. Tell her plainly that I have come for her, and will not go away without her. If necessary, she shall be carried to the Endowment House in a cart."

Without a word, the woman arose and followed William Ayer to the chamber of the girl. As he lifted his hand to knock at the door, the father paused in surprise, hearing the voice of his daughter speaking within.

"She is talking to some one!" he exclaimed. "Who can it be?"

Then he abruptly opened the door.

To his further surprise, he saw that Lona had risen from her bed and was dressed. She was at the window, which opened on the front of the story-and-a-half cottage. The window was open, and {6} she leaned out as she spoke to some one outside.

"Here—now?" she was exclaiming, in a most excited manner. "Is this true—can it be true?"

"What does this mean?" cried the father, as he strode into the room.

With a little cry, the girl started back and attempted to close the window, but William Ayer reached it, and his hand held it open, while he thrust her aside.

Looking out, the Mormon saw something that caused him to stare and gasp.

Beneath that very window were two youths, attired in dust-covered bicycle suits, standing beside their wheels, which also were covered with dust.

They were looking up at that window, and it was plain that they had been speaking with the girl.

Now William Ayer, although he had been less than forty-eight hours in Bethel, knew full well that no such young men belonged there, and no bicycles had ever before been seen in the Valley of Bethsada.

The young cyclists were handsome-looking fellows, and they lifted their caps to the man at the window with a careless nonchalance that made him gasp again.

"How do you do, sir," said one of them, pleasantly. "I trust you will pardon us, but we are strangers here—in fact, we came upon this town quite by accident—and seeing the young lady at the window, we took the liberty to ask her some questions, which she very kindly answered. Will you be good enough to thank her for her courtesy. Good-day, sir."

Then before William Ayer could speak, they mounted their wheels and pedaled on into the town.

———

CHAPTER III.
A FRUITLESS APPEAL.

William Ayer let go the window, which came down with a crash.

"Breath of my soul!" he cried.

Then he looked at his daughter, who was confused and excited, with a strange flush on her cheeks.

"Tell me the truth, girl!" he commanded, as he suddenly gripped her wrist. "Who are those young men?"

"I do not know, father."

"Tell me the truth, I command thee!"

"I have told you the truth."

"And you were speaking with them?"

"I saw them come along, and their appearance caused me to look out of the window. They stopped and spoke."

"The insolent dogs!" burst from William Ayer.

"They were not insolent, father; they lifted their caps, and were very polite. I am sure they—"

"It was insolent of them to speak to you at all! And they are not Mormons! They are Gentiles!"

"It may be."

"It may be! You know they are—you know!"

"How should I know?"

"No Mormons in this town ride bicycles."

"Which shows that this town is very slow," said Lona, in a manner that caused her father to gasp for the third time.

"My daughter," he cried, "what has wrought this change in thee? A little while ago thou wert ill."

"Yes, but I am better now."

"Thou art better since speaking with those Gentiles. There is something wrong in this. How they ever got in here is a mystery, but they will not long remain. The good elder must be told what has happened."

Then he hurried down and told Elder Holdfast everything. Holdfast seldom {7} allowed himself to become excited, so he listened with affected calmness, but his face grew harder than William Ayer had ever seen it.

"There has been some reprehensible carelessness," he said. "Some one must be punished for it. But now the Gentiles are in here they will not find it so easy to get out."

"But what will be done with them?"

"Brother Ayer," said the old elder, a forbidding and sombre look on his aged face, "it is said that polygamy is not practiced anywhere in Utah. You have seen how true this is. It is also said that the Destroying Ones no longer exist. You may never know whether this is true or not, for not even all staunch and devoted members of the church know everything, but you may rest assured that any dangerous Gentiles who may enter the Valley of Bethsada will not go back to the world to tell what they have discovered."

Despite himself, the listening man shuddered and drew back. The look in Elder Holdfast's eyes at that moment was not pleasant to see, and William Ayer was chilled to the marrow.

He recovered his nerve with an effort, and hastily said:

"Is it not well that the townspeople should know whom there is in our midst, Elder Holdfast? Should not the brethren be warned not to hold communication with the two Gentiles?"

"Surely, Brother Ayer, they should be warned. Go at once through the town, and communicate to them the fact that the ungodly are with us."

"But Lona, my child—I cannot leave her."

"Be not fearful on that account, Brother Ayer; she is in good hands and safe."

Yes, safe—safe as is the lamb that is left in the care of the wolf! Safe! The word was a mockery!

William Ayer hesitated and gazed doubtfully at the good elder, and in the good elder's eyes he saw a command that he dared not disobey.

"Go!" said Holdfast.

William Ayer sought his hat, and humbly though reluctantly, he left the cottage.

Holdfast arose, and, without hesitation, he ascended the stairs to the chamber he knew was occupied by the child he had chosen for his prey.

At the door he paused to listen, and he could hear his seventh wife talking with the girl within. Then he heard Lona Ayer speak plainly and distinctly, and the words she uttered were far from flattering to the soul of the listening man.

"You say your husband is a servant of God!" cried Lona. "My poor woman, you have no husband! I pity you—indeed I do! And you would place me in a situation quite as wretched as your own. Oh, I beg of you—I entreat you to aid me in escaping that devouring monster! You are a woman—you have a woman's heart that must go out to me in pity. I tell you the truth when I say I would much rather die than submit to the fate it has been said I must meet! Don't tell me Asaph Holdfast is good and kind! He is a monster in human form! I have seen the Evil One in his eyes—his greedy old eyes!"

Then Asaph opened the door and stepped into the room.

"Sister Ayer," he said, solemnly and reprovingly, "thou hast spoken words for which thou shalt some day repent in sackcloth and ashes."

The girl fell back, uttering a cry of fear.

"Don't!" she cried—"don't come near me! Keep off!"

He did not obey, but advanced to the centre of the room, while she retreated to a corner, holding up her hands in mute appeal. {8}

"Sister Ayer," spoke the white-crowned old elder, "I have come to take thee to the Endowment House, where thou art to be sealed to me this day. Put on thy street garments, and we will start at once, for already there hath been too much delay."

"No!"

The good elder folded his hands, and a sinister, mirthless smile curled his withered lips.

"It has been ordained," he declared. "Get ready!"

There was nothing of relenting in his manner, and the girl felt that she was but a weak thing in his hands.

"No!" she cried, for the third time. "No! no! no!"

"Sister Ayer, if thou wilt not go willingly, thou shalt be carried by force. It is foolish for thee to attempt to rebel. Here in this holy valley my word is law. I have but to give the signal, and ready and waiting ones will hurry to my side to do my bidding. What is your power against mine?"

The girl was silent, and he smiled again—triumphantly.

"Prepare at once," he commanded, in a tone that told he would brook no denial. "Thou shalt go of thy own accord or thou shalt be taken by force, as thou chooseth."

Then she suddenly fell on her knees before him, and with her clasped hands uplifted, her eyes raining tears down her pretty face, she crept to his feet, begging for mercy.

It was a spectacle to move a heart of stone, but Asaph Holdfast looked on calmly, his face emotionless and unrelenting.

The words of the girl were wild and incoherent—her agony was most pitiful. Even the bovine seventh Mrs. Holdfast, with her fat, smothered nerves, could not look on unstirred, and she turned away.

But what availed tears with Asaph Holdfast! What mattered it to him that the tender heart of this girl was breaking! What cared he that she was suffering such agony and fear as few may suffer and survive!

He had looked upon her, and she was fair to his eyes. She was young, with blue eyes and brown-gold hair. She was plump, and in the bloom of perfect health. He had seen the rose-blush in those cheeks that now were so pale and tear-wet.

And had he not honored her by choosing that she should become the ninth Mrs. Holdfast! Had he not chosen this girl with the view of exalting her far above those upon whom he had not looked with such favor!

Some day she would repent of her folly; he was sure of that. Some day she would become as calm and docile and tractable as the wife who had accompanied him to the cottage.

She might not love him in the foolish way that some women fancy they love their husbands, but he would be kind and firm with her, and she would succumb.

What was earthly love at most? Vanity, vanity!

And so, convincing himself that his course was just, he remained unmoved by her frantic appeals.

She looked up, and she saw nothing in that cold face that gave her the slightest encouragement. Far from that, it crushed the hope in her heart.

But that was not all that was left to her. Hate came to her—such a frightful sensation as she had never before experienced.

She sprang up, and the look on her face startled Asaph Holdfast.

"You old monster!"

She spoke the words slowly and dis- {9} tinctly, and each word was like a blow in its intensity. They fairly moved the old elder, despite himself, but they simply made him sterner and more unrelenting, if such a thing were possible.

"Thou shalt repent!" he said. "Is it necessary to take thee to the Endowment House by force?"

"And you would seal to you one who hates you and despises you! You would make your wife one who loathes the very sight of your wicked old face—one who shudders with horror in your presence! Noble man, fit elder of the Mormon—"

"Stop! I may listen in silence as you rail about me, Sister Ayer, but I cannot hear you speak ill of the church. Shall I send for a conveyance to take you to the Endowment House?"

"No. I will walk."

"It is good," bowed Asaph, fresh triumph in his eyes. "Prepare."

———

Chapter IV.
Frank and Jack.

Frank Merriwell and Jack Diamond were the two lads who had found their way in some mysterious manner into the Mormon Valley of Bethsada.

After leaving William Ayer's cottage, they proceeded slowly, and were surprised to see a man running down by a cross path to get in advance of them.

"That is singular," said Jack. "He seems to have come from the cottage we just left."

"And, unless I am much mistaken," cried Frank, "he is the very man who appeared at the window, and with whom we spoke."

"I believe you are right!" exclaimed the young Virginian.

"Sure I am. What is the old duck up to? There is something in the wind."

"You bet! he is going to head us off."

"Well, if we get off with our heads after coming here we'll be dead lucky. That is old man Ayer, the girl's father."

"And she is a peach!" burst enthusiastically from Jack. "I don't wonder Whitcomb is stuck on her and crazy to save her from the old elder he says has selected her for a future wife."

"Steady, Jack—steady, boy!" laughed Frank. "You stand no show in this little game. Besides that, it wouldn't be a square deal to Whitcomb, after promising him that we would do our level best to help him rescue the girl, to fall in love with her and attempt to steal her from him."

"Look here, Frank," cried Diamond, somewhat hotly, "I am a man of honor, don't forget that! I would not think of doing such a thing. We have pledged ourselves to Tom Whitcomb, and we'll stand by him through thick and thin."

"Through thick and thin!" echoed Merriwell. "He seems to be a white man and all right, even if he is a Mormon."

"Do you know, I am getting a different opinion of the Mormons than I once had."

"How is that?"

"Why, the Mormons I have seen seem like other people. I believe some of the wild stories told about their religion, and their ways are a mess of lies."

"The Mormons are not what they were, Jack. They have changed in recent years, and the younger Mormons are all right. They still hold to their religion, but they have cast aside polygamy, and I believe no man has a right to say how another shall worship God. The Mormons believe they have the only true religion, and it is their privilege to think so."

"Well, we won't discuss that. You may be sure I'll stand by Whitcomb, and I'll not try to steal his girl, no matter how much I may like her appearance. What interests us most now is the man ahead of us. See, he seems to be warning the town! Look—there are other men, and they are running from house to {10} house. By Jove! we are in for a hot time here, Frank."

"Surely we are likely to find it interesting," smiled Merriwell.

As the boys proceeded, they found the cottages were closed, and they saw no signs of human beings anywhere about.

"Crawled into their holes," chuckled Frank. "They seem to be very shy."

"I don't like their shyness," admitted the Southern lad. "To me it has an unhealthy aspect."

"Let's get off and see if we can't raise somebody."

"I am with you."

They dismounted before a cottage, and Frank walked up boldly and rapped loudly on the door.

They waited a minute, and then he rapped again.

Another minute, and no one answered the knock.

A third time Frank applied his knuckles to the door, exclaiming:

"Here goes for a corker!"

But that "corker" produced no further result than had the other knocks.

"Somebody lives here, that's sure," said Jack.

"But they are not at home to us, and that's sure," smiled Frank.

"Look, there is a well. Let's get a drink."

Leaving their wheels, they went round the corner to the well, where they drew up a bucket of water, and, with the aid of a handy dipper, obtained a fresh, cooling drink.

And what tasted better to a hot, weary and dusty cyclist than a drink of clear, sparkling water from a well by the wayside? No wine, no drink prepared by man, nothing soothes and refreshes him like pure cool water.

If pure water were not so readily obtained, if it were not a free gift of nature, if it were an invention of man, all humanity would be eager for it in preference to the most costly of wines, or the finest liquors. If it were scarce and hard to obtain, it would command a fancy price, even though beer ran in rivers everywhere.

Does the boy who considers it a manly thing to drink beer and whiskey, even though the taste of the stuff may be nauseating to him, and who speaks pertly of water as "good stuff to bathe in"—does he ever pause to think what a foolish fellow he is?

He drinks beer or whiskey because he thinks it a manly thing to do; but it is far more manly to drink water, and truthfully say he does not like beer or whiskey and so will not drink anything he does not like.

The boy who will do this and stick to it is a moral hero, and he has in him the stuff that makes a successful and honored man. The more he is ridiculed and "guyed" by his friends and acquaintances, the greater hero he is, and the more he will be respected in the years to come.

Not all the heroes wear epaulettes on their shoulders. The humblest boy in the smallest and most obscure village has scores of opportunities to become a hero, although it is seldom he recognizes the fact.

He may not be regarded as a hero, but that will make him no less a hero. Let him refuse to do anything he may know is wrong, and thus he has become a hero.

The world is full of heroes and heroic deeds.

Having obtained a drink from the well, the boys went back to their wheels, which they brought into the shade of the cottage, where they sat down.

From their position they could obtain a fine view of the town, which they enjoyed greatly.

Jack was restless, but Frank seemed quite at ease.

"It's no use to get all torn up over this matter," Merriwell said. "We have to take things as they come."

"I never saw another fellow like you!" cried Jack. "I believe if you were to lose both your legs, you'd coolly observe that it couldn't be helped and that you didn't propose to cry over spilled milk."

"Well, we've got to stay here till Whitcomb comes, anyway. We made a hustle to get here before the girl was sealed to the old elder, having promised him we'd do our best to defend her and save her till he showed up."

"That's right, and it was a most remarkable chance that caused us to find {11} her immediately on entering the town. When you saw the girl at the window and asked her if she knew a Miss Lona Ayer, she nearly took away my breath by saying she was Lona Ayer."

"I came near dropping dead myself," confessed Frank.

Thus they chatted for a while till they saw three persons slowly advancing down the road. One was a man with white beard and hair. The others were a stout woman and a young girl.

"Here they come!" said Frank, rising to his feet. "The old villain is taking her to the Endowment House. Here's where we'll have to get in our work, Jack. It is going to be a warm morning."

———

Chapter V

WHITCOMB'S STORY.

Where were the others of the bicycle boys who had started from New York to ride across the continent to San Francisco? Harry Rattleton, Bruce Browning and Toots, the colored lad, were missing.

The entire party had reached Utah and were on their way to Salt Lake City when at Lehi Junction, a town north of Utah Lake, they became acquainted with a young man about twenty-one years of age.

The acquaintance came about by accident, as in crossing the railroad tracks the young man, who held a letter in his hand, became so confused that he was nearly run down by a train.

Frank Merriwell saw the stranger's peril, and, with ready wit and nerve, sprang to his rescue and dragged him from the track, just as the train swept past.

"You must be walking in your sleep, my friend!" exclaimed Frank, with a short laugh. "Certainly you had a close call that trip. If I hadn't seen you were dazed the engine would have killed you."

"It wouldn't have made any difference if it had!" came hoarsely from the lips of the rescued one. "I don't know whether to thank you or not for saving me."

Frank looked at him in amazement.

"Are you daffy, man?" he cried. "Why, you are young and strong and in the best of health. How is it that you do not care whether you live or die?"

"Oh, it wouldn't interest you. Poor little Lona!"

"Girl in it!" cried Frank. "I knew it! Always is a girl in it when a young fellow like you gets to feeling that way. Never mind, old man; get a brace on, and let her go. She's not the only one. There are others, and you are the kind of chap to take your choice."

Whitcomb was a good-looking fellow, with a fine, intellectual face, and he was well-dressed and prosperous in appearance.

"You do not understand," he said, huskily. "Never mind. I can't explain. It would take too long. Poor little Lona!"

Then Frank was struck by another thought.

"Great Scott, man!" he cried. "Something has happened to your sweetheart? I do understand now, and you have my sincerest sympathy. She is dead?"

"Worse than dead!"

"Worse? It can't be! I don't wish to pry into your affairs, but—well, I won't ask questions. I see it has hit you hard. That's why you were walking along that track as if you were in a trance. Lucky I saw you."

"Yes, I will thank you for that."

The young man dropped the letter, which Frank picked up and handed to him, saying:

"You may not care to lose this."

"No, no!" cried Whitcomb. "It is from her—the last letter I may ever receive from her! She has appealed to me to save her, but I do not know where he has taken her, and he will seal her to him before I can reach her. I might find her—I might find him—and kill him!"

Frank's interest increased.

"As long as there is life there is hope," he quoted. "If she has made an appeal to you, there may be a chance of saving her."

Whitcomb took a long look at Merriwell.

"Do you know," he said, "I like your face. It is all right. You are from the East. I can tell it by your speech. You cut the letter 'r' out of everything you say." {12}

"You are mistaken," smiled Frank, "I do not cut it out. I use the letter, but I do not gargle my throat with it, as seems to be the habit among you Westerners."

"Well, I knew you were from the East by your speech. I suppose the 'Y' on your sweater stands for the bicycle club to which you belong?"

"That 'Y' stands for the noblest institution in all the East—Yale College."

"Then you are a college man. Say, I have a desire to tell you everything. I must tell somebody. I believe you are the one. Do you care to listen?"

"Unburden your soul, old man. I'll give you my sympathy, if nothing else. Where shall we go? I presume you do not care to have anybody and everybody hear your story?"

"No. Come with me."

"Wait till I speak to my friends."

Then, for the first time, Tom Whitcomb saw Merriwell's four friends, all of whom were dressed in uniform bicycle suits.

Frank spoke a few words to Rattleton, and then followed Whitcomb to a spot where they were quite alone, and the young man told him his love story, which will not be given in full here. It is enough to say that he loved Lona Ayer, who lived with her father in Provo, and they were engaged. Tom confessed that he was a member of the Mormon church, but he did not believe in polygamy. Frank was rather surprised to hear him speak of Brigham Young in terms that were not altogether respectful.

Having told how he became acquainted with Lona Ayer, and how they were finally engaged, Tom explained that some business connected with the Mormon church had brought to Provo one Asaph Holdfast, an elder who believed in the doctrines of Brigham. Holdfast had been a guest at the home of William Ayer, and there he had seen Lona. She had written Tom about the old elder and how he watched her with his greedy eyes. She had said that she avoided him as much as possible, but that letter had not prepared him for the one that was to follow.

Her second letter had been mailed from Nephi, far to the South. It was despairing and hysterical, and it was plain she had not been given opportunity to finish it, for it was broken off in the middle. That letter told Whitcomb how Elder Holdfast had demanded her as an addition to his wives, and how the man seemed to exercise a hypnotic influence over her father, who had agreed to all his demands. Then, when she rebelled, she had been led by her father to believe she would not be forced to marry the elder, but that she must go away at once.

They started, and on the journey the girl had discovered she was being taken to a hidden town amid the mountains, where polygamy was practiced as it had once been practiced in Salt Lake City. She could not escape, but she succeeded in sending the letter to Tom, begging him to follow and save her.

"That is the story," said Whitcomb, in conclusion; "but I do not know where he has taken her, so how am I to follow?"

"You are a Mormon, and you should be able to find out where this town is located."

"At that, I might not be able to reach it in time."

"Take chances. You might."

"But what could I do?—alone!"

"Make a struggle. Tell you what I'll do!"

"Yes."

"I'll go with you."

Whitcomb was surprised.

"Why should you?" he asked.

"Because I am interested in you, old man, and I want you to save that girl and marry her. The whole crowd will go with you, if you want them. My friends will stick to me like glue."

A new light came to Tom Whitcomb's face.

"You give me a ray of hope!" he cried. "We can try it. If we can find the town—if we can!"

"It must be somewhere to the south—somewhere down past Nephi. That is a clew."

"But the railroad branches at Nephi, which is a junction."

"You must find out which branch to take. What is the good of being a Mormon if you can't find out where this polygamous town is located! Surely there are many Mormons who know all {13} about it. Make a hustle, man—get a gait on! How many of my friends shall I take along?"

"Not all of them. One will be enough. Are you a fast rider?"

"Well, excuse my blushes! I don't like to say."

"All right. Take the best rider you have as a companion. If you stick to me, the time may come when you'll have to ride for your lives. Let him be a good fighter, too, for it is not likely we'll be able to save Lona without a fight."

"Diamond is the man," said Frank. "He can ride like the wind, and he is a fighter from 'way back when he gets started. In fact, he enjoys a fight better than a square meal."

"Then he is the one. We will start for Provo at once. There I have friends who may be able to put us on the trail. Oh, if we can save her!"

"We will, old man, if she stands Elder Holdfast off a little. All we need is time."

"But how shall I be able to pay you?"

"Look here, don't you talk to us about pay. I am in this thing for the racket, and I know Jack will be ready enough to take a hand. Pay! Well, say! if you hint at such a thing again—don't do it! Elder Asaph Holdfast, we are on your trail, and you'll find us harder to dodge than bullets. We won't do a thing to you when we catch you!"

———

CHAPTER VI.
"IN THE FORBIDDEN VALLEY."

Being a Mormon, Tom Whitcomb was able to obtain full information concerning the Lost Tribe of Israel, to which he had heard Elder Holdfast belonged.

He learned the exact location of the town of Bethel, which lay in the Valley of Bethsada, and, with Frank Merriwell and Jack Diamond as companions, he lost no time in reaching the vicinity of the valley.

But the valley was guarded, and Whitcomb knew it would be a difficult thing to enter it. Still it was said there was a way of getting into it over the mountains, for an old hermit, known as Old Lonely, entered and left the valley at will.

Old Lonely was "cracked," for he believed himself a prophet, and he boasted that nothing on earth could injure him. He often entered Bethel and "prophecied," but although he was not of the Mormon faith, he was never molested, as the inhabitants of the valley believed him quite harmless.

While Frank and Jack sought to find a way of getting into the valley without the assistance of other parties, Whitcomb sought Old Lonely, hoping to obtain aid from the hermit.

Between them it was agreed that if the bicycle boys reached the town first everything was to be done to delay the "sealing" of Lona Ayer to Holdfast till Whitcomb appeared.

If Whitcomb got in first, he would try to hold things up till his friends arrived, and the trio would make a desperate attempt to carry of[f] the girl.

At a distance, it had seemed that the task of rescuing Lona could be accomplished easily, but when the boys found how hard it was to get into the valley they began to realize what kind of a job they had tackled.

Frank Merriwell, however, was not the lad to be frightened by anything, no matter how formidable it appeared, and it was mainly through his nerve and skill that he and Jack found a way down from the heights above into the valley, after obtaining a position where they could view the town.

But Merriwell was forced to confess that they could not return as they had entered. Even though they could scale those steeps themselves, where they had let their wheels down with the aid of a rope, those wheels could not be dragged up through the scraggy timber.

They had entered the "Forbidden Valley," but would they ever get out to tell of their adventures?

If so, they would be the first Gentiles to boast of such a thing.

"We'll do our best for the girl, Jack, if we can find her," said Frank.

"That's what we will," nodded Diamond, determination written on his dark face. "But it is about a hundred to one we'll not be able to find her."

Fortune favored them, however, for they saw the face of a pretty girl at the upper window of a cottage, and paused to ask if she knew such a person as Lona {14} Ayer. To their astonishment and satisfaction she informed them that she was Lona Ayer.

Then Frank Merriwell told her that Whitcomb was near, and that an attempt would be made to save her from the clutches of Holdfast. It was at this juncture that William Ayer detected his daughter in conversation with the bicycle boys.

Although the conversation was interrupted in this manner, already had the girl told them that Elder Holdfast had come to take her to the Endowment House, which they could see in the distance.

On leaving the cottage they had ridden toward the Endowment House, but had paused some distance away to obtain the drink of water from the well.

And now they saw advancing down the road Elder Holdfast, the seventh Mrs. Holdfast, and the unfortunate girl who was to be forced to become a plural wife of the Mormon elder.

The boys arose to their feet and stood by their wheels, in lively anticipation of what was to follow.

"Yes," said Frank, repeating his remark, "it is bound to be a very warm morning, Jack. Here's where we've got to get in our work."

"We can't wait for Whitcomb," fluttered Jack. "We've got to make an attempt to save that girl—at any cost."

"Oh, but you are hard hit!" murmured Merriwell. "I believe you would be pleased if Whitcomb never put in an appearance."

"Oh, don't talk of that! Quit your jollying! This is no time for fooling, Merry. What are we going to do to stop this affair."

"Well, we'll have a little argument with Elder Holdfast."

"Argument? What good will that do? Is there a bug in your head, old man? We'll have to work, not argue."

"Sometimes it is work to argue," smiled Merriwell, coolly. "If you were provided with a tandem now, we might get the girl away from the old duck and carry her off."

"But we'd not be able to get out of the valley."

"We might. We could attempt to run the gauntlet of the sentinels at the eastern entrance."

"Well, we haven't a tandem, so talk about something we can do. They are getting very near!"

"If she were a boy, one of us could carry her off on his back."

"We'll have to try it now!" exclaimed Jack, desperately. "She can cling round my neck, and I'll try it!"

"You are excited, old man. We'd never get off like that."

"Well, for goodness' sake tell what we can do!"

"Keep cool. Here they are. We'll jolly the old elder."

The girl saw them first, and a look of relief and joy swept over her sad face. They had not deserted her; they were still there.

As Elder Holdfast approached with sober step and slow, Frank and Jack pushed out to the street, and Merriwell hailed the man.

"Excuse me, my dear sir," said Frank, doffing his cap. "I wish to speak with you a moment."

Holdfast halted in surprise, turning his eyes toward them.

"Ahem!" coughed Frank, smiling sweetly. "I wish to call your attention, sir, to the latest model of the Get There Bicycle, the perfect wheel, none other like it on earth. We are agents for the Get There, and we are introducing them all th[r]ough the West, where they are giving the most perfect satisfaction. They have reinforced forks, the stoutest diamond frame in existence, the most beautiful and perfect sprocket ever made, the greatest crank-shafts ever conceived, all-bearing head, Never Pop tires, and other advantages over the ordinary wheels which I will be pleased to point out. You should secure one of these wheels for yourself, sir, another for your wife, and a third for your charming daughter."

Frank bowed low to Lona, whipping out a note-book and pencil as he did so, and continuing, before Holdfast could catch his breath.

"Permit me to take your order, sir, for your entire family. Wheels to be paid for on deliverance, satisfaction guaranteed or money refunded, all wheels to be kept in repair for one year free of charge if {15} brought to any of our regular agencies. Your name and address, sir. I will take your measure to see what height frame you require."

"Avaunt, ungodly Gentiles!" cried Elder Holdfast, uplifting his hands, with an expression of horror on his face. "Remove from my sight these inventions of Satan!"

"Eh?" exclaimed Frank, in apparent surprise. "Inventions of which? Come again. I slipped a cog and didn't quite get you that trip."

"Get behind me!" sternly commanded Asaph.

"I could do that all right on a tandem, sir," chirped Frank, pleasantly. "Perhaps you would choose to have a tandem for yourself and wife, while you purchase an ordinary wheel for your daughter. The Get There Tandem is a peach! It is a thing of beauty and a joy forever. You don't have to push it along, although it is a good thing—it goes itself. Actually you have to hold it back to keep it from running away with you—when you are going down hill. Talk about flying, why, my dear sir, the Get There Tandem has wings! Get it fairly started, and it touches the ground only in high places. I assure you, sir, I firmly believe it will be the nearest approach to flying that you will ever make."

"Come," said Elder Holdfast, speaking to the bovine Mrs. Holdfast and the girl; "we will leave these Gentiles to their own destruction, which they have brought upon their heads."

"Now, don't tear yourself away," entreated Frank. "Stop a while, and we will talk it over. It is possible you are prejudiced against a wheel, but I think I can overcome that if you will lend me your pocketbook—I mean your ear. You may not see the advantages to be derived from bicycling. Few do at first. On some it dawns slowly, while others have to have it beaten into their heads with a club. Now I'd like the job of beating it into your head if you—"

But Asaph would stop to hear no more.

"Come!" he again commanded; "we will go on."

He started, and the woman placed an urging hand on the arm of the pretty girl; but the girl shook that hand off, ran swiftly toward the boys, flung herself on her knees before them, and wildly cried:

"Save me—save me from that old wretch! he is dragging me to the Endowment House, where I am to be sealed to him!"

<hr />

Chapter VII.
A Dash to the Rescue.

"What's this?" cried Frank, in apparent surprise. "Sealed to him? Why, isn't he your father?"

"No, no! Tom must have told you about him. This is Asaph Holdfast, who is trying to force me to become one of his many wives. Save me from him!"

By this time Jack had reached the girl and lifted her to her feet, placing a protecting arm about her, as he swiftly whispered in her ear:

"We'll stand by you, don't be afraid. We knew you all the time, and Merry is chaffing old Holdfast."

"Don't let him touch me again!"

"If he does, it will be over my dead body!" came in a rather stagey manner from the lips of the young Virginian.

Frank gave the Mormon elder a reproving look, and shook his head, as he sadly said:

"Oh, Asaph, Asaph! methinks thou art an old rat! Why, I thought she was your daughter all the while—or your granddaughter. I was not clear on that point, but thought I would flatter you by calling her your daughter. And you are thinking of making her your wife against her will! My! my! Asaph, old fel., you are a sad dog, indeed!"

The old elder gasped for breath and nearly turned black in the face. No longer was he icy cool. The insolence of the young Gentile was enough to arouse a man of stone.

But what aroused Asaph more than anything else was the sight of Jack Diamond, with his arm about Lona and his face, close to hers, as he spoke some fervent vow in her ear.

"Unhand that girl, thou unholy one!" shouted Elder Holdfast. "Cease to defile her with thy polluting touch!"

He took a step toward Jack, but Frank {16} ran his bicycle between them and interposed his own body.

"Let's talk this matter over," he said, smoothly.

"Stand aside!" snarled the Mormon, with a menacing gesture.

Frank did not seem at all alarmed.

"Don't get gay with me, Asaph," he smiled. "I have a desire to respect your gray hairs, although I fear it would be difficult to do so. I am a great respecter of age, but surely nothing is more repulsive and harder to respect than a wicked old man who makes a bluff at being pious."

"Oh, thou shalt suffer for this!" fumed the old elder.

"I am willing to take chances on that. What I most wish to know is if it is quite true that you have more than one wife, and you are thinking of forcing this young and defenceless girl to marry you? Give it to us straight, old boy."

"It is none of thy business, meddling Gentile!"

"To you it may seem none of my business, but, however, nevertheless and likewise, I have an inclination to make it some of my business. It's a way I have. You may call me down and say I am too fresh and all that, but it won't make any difference. I have traveled in Europe, Eerup and Ohrup, and slipped through Greece, but travel has never seemed to cure me of my freshness to any great extent. I'm always getting into trouble by mixing into some affair where I'm not invited, but still I continue to mix, while I use arnica on my bruised and battered body and beefsteak poultices on the blackened eyes I receive."

"Get out!" cried Holdfast, with a flourish of his arms, in doing which he struck the seventh Mrs. Holdfast a smacking backhand slap in the face, nearly upsetting her.

"Gently, gently, Asaph," cautioned Frank. "If you flourish your arms like a windmill, you will be sure to damage someone."

Then the elder uplifted his voice and uttered a wild, strange cry.

Almost immediately the door of the cottage behind the two boys flew open, and out rushed two men.

Diamond did not see the men, and they were close upon him when Holdfast uttered an order.

"Take that girl from the Gentile."

Lona gave a cry of warning and fear.

"Look out!" she screamed.

As Jack turned, he received a heavy blow that stretched him stunned upon the ground.

One of the men grasped the girl, while the other faced Frank, who had cast aside his wheel, as if it were of no value.

"Here's where things commence to boil," murmured Merriwell, as he made a jump for the man.

The Mormon seemed to think it would be an easy thing to handle that young fellow, but he met with the greatest surprise of his life, for Frank gave a side swing, ducked under the fellow's arms, caught him about the body, lifted him from his feet, and threw him down upon his head and shoulders.

Elder Holdfast had started toward the man who was holding the screaming girl, but he halted in amazement when he saw how swiftly and easily Merriwell disposed of the other man.

But the elder's cries had aroused more than two men. Several others were hurrying toward the spot, as Merriwell saw.

"Ginger!" he exclaimed, to himself. "This is bad! We can't carry the girl off, and we'll be beaten by numbers. Jack seems to have been knocked out at the start."

Still he made his lunge at the man with the girl, snatched her away, and gave the fellow a thump that staggered him.

In her excitement and terror, however, the girl clung to Frank so tightly that he was not able to use his arms. Then it was that the men rushed upon him, and he received a shower of blows that felled him to the ground.

The girl was borne shrieking away, while the young bicyclists were left lying on the ground.

Frank was the first to recover and sit up. He reached over and gave Jack a shake, cheerfully saying:

"Make a brace, old man. Are you still in the game?"

Jack's eyes were open, but he was dazed by the shock of the blow and fall. He {17} sat up with difficulty, staring blankly around.

"Did I fall, or was I pushed?" he murmured.

"It seems to have been a combination of circumstances. It strikes me that I was pushed."

Then Jack seemed to realize what had happened, and he cried:

"Miss Ayer—what has become of her?"

"Elder Holdfast and his minions were too many for us, and he has carried her off."

Jack struggled to his feet, staggering dizzily.

"We—we must follow!" he hoarsely exclaimed. "We must stop him before he reaches the Endowment House. Remember our promise to Whitcomb, Frank."

"I remember," said Frank. "It'll not be our fault if we fail to keep it. We'll make another bluff. Fortunately they have not taken our wheels."

Getting on their feet, they could see a party of men far down the road that led toward the Endowment House, whither they were hurrying. In the midst of those men the unfortunate girl was being carried along, while Elder Holdfast rushed on in the lead.

"Quick, Frank!" cried Jack. "If we lose a moment, they'll reach the Endowment House ahead of us."

"We can't hold 'em up long, at most, but we'll try to hold 'em up as long as we can. Come on!"

They mounted their wheels, and away they went down the road in pursuit of the party that had carried off the girl.

Jack was wildly excited by the fear that the girl would be dragged into the Endowment House before they could reach her.

Frank was trying to think of some scheme for carrying the girl off bodily and bidding defiance to the Mormons for a time. It seemed utterly impossible to do such a thing, and he began to feel that they had attempted a task that would have appalled men of sober judgment.

Nearer and nearer the Endowment House rushed the party with the girl, the Mormon elder urging them on, as he ran along in advance.

The seventh Mrs. Holdfast was too fleshy to keep up with the others, and she had fallen behind. She saw the bicycle boys coming in pursuit, and placed herself in the middle of the street, wildly flour[i]shing her umbrella, and shouting for them to stop.

"Out of the way!" cried Jack.

"We need room!" shouted Frank.

But the woman resolutely stood her ground, unmindful of all danger.

"Look out! Do not run her down," warned Merriwell.

Both boys were spinning straight ahead, and she aimed a blow at them as they came near. Like a flash, they swerved aside and sped past, passing on either side of her.

The umbrella cut the empty air with great force, and as it met with no obstruction, the woman was thrown forward in the road by the impetus of her own blow.

Holdfast saw the boys coming, and he urged the man to hasten still more in getting the unwilling girl into the Endowment House.

The very door of the building was reached, and it seemed that Frank and Jack would be too late.

At that moment a horseman appeared, coming round the building at a mad gallop. He wore old clothes, and his long white beard was split and fanned over each shoulder by the wind. His head was bare, and his hair, like his beard, was white.

"Stop!" shouted the old man. "Unhand that girl, or feel the wrath of an avenging one!"

"It is Old Lonely, the crazy prophet!" cried the Mormons.

"Do not mind him!" came from the lips of Elder Holdfast. "Into the Endowment House with the girl!"

But the horsemen charged straight into the knot of men, who scattered before him. He stooped and caught up the girl, in doing which he accidentally tore the beard form his face, showing it was false.

The girl saw his face, and a scream of amazement and joy came from her lips.

"Lona, my darling!" he cried, as he lifted her from the ground.

"Tom—Tom, my sweetheart!" she joyfully sobbed. {18}

Then the big white horse bore them both away.

———

CHAPTER VIII.
THE MAD PROPHET.

The scattered Mormons were dumb with amazement, scarcely able to believe what their eyes had beheld.

Scores of times they had seen the old hermit come into the town, and never before had he attempted an act of hostility toward them.

The old hermit? Was this the same old man? True he had looked like Old Lonely as he came charging round the Endowment House, but the Mad Prophet had never been known to possess a horse, and the accident which had snatched the false beard from the man's face had betrayed the fact that he was not old at all, but was a young man in disguise.

Certain it was that they had not been deceived right along by the prophet. This was a person who had made himself up to look like Old Lonely, but it could not be Old Lonely.

Frank and Jack had witnessed the rescue of the girl, and they had recognized Whitcomb when he straightened up with Lona in his arms.

Off came the caps of the two bicyclists, and the Yale yell of triumph pealed from their lips.

"Hey, Whitcomb!" shouted Frank, with satisfaction.

"He was on hand, after all," said Jack, and it seemed that there was a shade of disappointment in his voice.

"Don't let it hit you like that, old chap," laughed Frank. "If he hadn't been on hand, we'd been too late."

"That's right," confessed Diamond.

"Allee samee, we held old Holdfast up long enough to give Whitcomb a chance to get here. He has us to thank for that."

"But he doesn't propose to thank us. He is going to get out as fast as he can, and leave us to hoe our own row."

"That's all right. He's got the girl, and his first thought is to save her."

"He ought to have a thought for us, after what we have done for him. We have risked our lives."

"I don't believe he'll forget us. We must follow him."

Follow him they did, but the horse bore the young man and the girl up a steep hill, and then they disappeared from view. When the boys reached the top of the ascent, nothing of the young couple could be seen.

In the meantime, the Mormons had been pursuing for pursuit.

Asaph Holdfast was dazed when he saw the false beard torn from the face of the horseman and recognized the young Mormon lover of Lona Ayer.

Asa[ph] had believed the horseman was the Mad Prophet, and his metamorphosis into a young man seemed magical.

But the old elder quickly recovered, and then he shouted:

"After him! Do not let him escape from our clutches. Lose no time. The sentries must be warned, and these intruders shall not be permitted to escape. Bring back the girl without harm, for she is the daughter of a brother Mormon, and is to become my wife. Go!"

They hastened away to obey his commands.

Horses were soon gathered, and a body of pursuers were following Whitcomb and the girl, who did not seem inclined to make for either outlet from the valley, but struck straight toward the steepest and most formidable range of mountains.

The street came to an end, and the ground grew rougher and rougher. Onward they pressed, till it seemed that horses could go no further.

Then they came upon the very same white horse on which the rescuer had appeared—the animal that had borne the young man and the girl away.

"They can't be far away!" cried the leader of the party, triumphantly. "Watch out for them. Remember, do not harm the girl. If he gives up quietly, take the man captive. If he fights—well, his blood be on his own head!"

In less than a minute a great shout went up, and one in advance was seen excitedly pointing toward something.

Looking in the direction indicated, they saw, sitting on a bowlder, an old man with long white hair and beard.

It was Old Lonely!

In a moment a dozen guns were aimed {19} at the Mad Prophet, and he was ordered to surrender quietly.

He looked at them without moving or speaking. His eyes alone told that there was life in his body, for he sat there like an image of stone.

They advanced and surrounded him.

"We have caught you, old man!" they cried, triumphantly.

Then he arose.

"What wouldst thou with me?" he asked, in a deep, full-chested voice. "I am here."

"Where are they—where have you hidden them?" fiercely demanded the leader of the Mormons. "Speak, and tell the truth!"

"I never speak anything but the truth," he declared, his eyes gleaming from beneath the shaggy eyebrows. "But the truth is something seldom heard in this forbidden valley. Down here it is that lies are upheld as the gospel of Heaven, and the weak and lowly are trodden under foot till the very rocks and hills cry out, 'How long, my Lord, how long?'"

"Oh, shut up!" coarsely commanded the leader. "You can't play that game any more. We have been fooled long enough by it. Now we know you have aided our enemies, and that settles your case. It must have been you who aided them to enter the valley, and you provided one with a disguise that made him look like you."

"How do we know that this is not the same one—the same fellow?" cried one of the party. "It may have been a trick all along. Try his whiskers."

Then a hand reached out and gave the beard of the Mad Prophet a strong sharp jerk.

It did not come off, and it was seen by those nearest that it was genuine beyond a doubt. The man who carried off the girl had provided himself with a disguise in some way, and had fooled those who saw him till the moment when he unwittingly unmasked himself as he snatched the girl up.

Fire gleamed from the eyes of the hermit, and it was plain he did not like the treatment he was receiving.

"There cometh a day of judgment," he said, his heavy voice rumbling away in the caverns of his breast—"a day in which the oppressor shall tremble, and the oppressed shall rejoice. Beware of that day! Touch me not! Let me pass!"

He made a move to leave the spot, but they crowded still closer about him, and the leader cried:

"You cannot go! We are going to hold you now, till you confess the truth. You shall be taken down into the valley and imprisoned there till—"

A hoarse, mocking laugh broke from the old man's lips.

"You cannot take me," he declared. "Place thy hands upon me at thy peril! Stand aside!"

"Grab him and hold him!" cried the leader.

They attempted to do so, and the Mad Prophet struck out with his bony fists, his arms working like piston rods, and a fierce fire blazing in his eyes. Smack! smack! smack! sounded his blows, and men reeled back before them.

"Blow, horn of Joshua, and let the walls totter and fall!" he thundered, as he struck right and left. "Smite, sword of Gideon, and let thy enemies feel thy destroying touch! Stand still, O sun in yonder sky—stand still till the battle shall be finished! As Samson smote the Philistines thus will I smite and slay my enemies!"

And it was marvellous how he beat them back and sent them reeling and falling before his blows.

At a distance, amid the rocks further up the mountain, crouched Frank Merriwell and Jack Diamond, where they had hidden. They could see the old man battling against great odds, and their hearts were filled with admiration for him. With his snow-white hair and beard, he loomed above his assailants, and the words that came from his lips were distinctly heard by the bicycle boys. It seemed that a strange soft light fell on his old face, and to Frank he was the counterpart of some patriarch of Bible times.

"Look at him!" exclaimed Diamond. "Merciful goodness! He is a wonderful fighter! It is astounding!"

"It is!" declared Frank; "and I can't stand this any longer!"

"What are you going to do?" {20}

"I am not going to keep still and see him battle against such odds. I am going down and give him a hand. Come on!"

"Stop, Frank! It's no use to—"

But Merriwell was impulsively bounding down the rocky steep, and Jack followed him as fast as possible.

———

Chapter IX.
A Battle Against Odds.

Fierce and terrible was the fight made by the Mad Prophet, but his enemies crowded upon him and beat him down by force of numbers.

Once he sunk to his knees, and they uttered cries of triumph, thinking he was conquered; but he rose again, flinging them off with his powerful arms.

"Nay! nay!" he thundered; "think not to conquer me thus easily! The strength of the Mighty One is in these arms and a holy fire burns in my heart! Thou shalt fall before me as the Philistines fell before Samson! Down! down! down!"

But he was human, and they beat him to his knees again, struck him on the head, and stretched him powerless on the ground, where they flung themselves upon him.

Then it was that, with a loud Yale yell, Frank Merriwell came charging like a wild steer right into their midst, with Jack Diamond following him closely.

Biff! biff! biff! rained the blows from the hard fists of the two young athletes, and every blow counted.

They came near creating a panic among the Mormon gang, but the leader held the men from taking to their heels, and the boys quickly found themselves in the midst of a red hot fight.

"Give it to them, Jack!" rang out Frank's clear voice. "Show them the kind of stiff Old Yale turns out!"

Never in all his life had Frank felt so strong and dauntless. It seemed to him that he had been given strength and skill for the occasion. He smashed a man in the mouth with his right, drove his left into the pit of another man's stomach, dodged several hands that were stretched out to grasp him, minded not the blows that fell upon him, and in the midst of it all he laughed!

Jack was not backward. He could fight, also, and the Mormons were astounded and amazed by the terrific onslaught of the reckless college lads.

"A thousand furies!" snarled the leader of the gang, spitting out teeth, after receiving a blow on the mouth from Merriwell's hard fist. "What ails you, men? Beat them down! Kill them!"

"If that's it, we'll die game!" flung back Frank.

"Hurrah!" shouted Diamond, his dark cheeks flushed and his eyes flashing fire. "There will be some satisfaction in making a die of it in this manner, if croak we must!"

"You're the right stuff, old man!" cried Frank. "That's the sort of stuff old Virginia turns out! They make men down in old Virginia!"

The boys clung together.

"Back to back!" directed Frank. "We'll fight as long as we can in that manner."

"The Lord of Hosts hath raised up friends for me in my hour of need!" thundered the deep voice of the Mad Prophet, as he suddenly flung off the last of those who were trying to hold him down.

He arose, and his white-crowned head towered in the midst of his enemies.

"Give it to them! We are with you!" encouraged Merriwell.

Old Lonely did "give it to them." Again he fought like a modern Hercules, and his face wore an inspired look, as he shouted these words:

"The triumph of the wicked shall be short, and in the Day of Judgment their punishment shall be great. 'Twill be then they shall hear the awful words, 'Depart from me, thou sinful ones, into the lake of fire and brimstone that burneth with an unquenchable flame!' And there shall be weeping and wailing and gnashing of teeth. They shall cry aloud for the rocks and hills to fall on them and cover them from the wrath to come, but nowhere under the face of all the heavens shall there be a hiding place for them."

His deep and thunderous voice was flung back in heavy echoes from the rocky steeps, and it seemed to reverberate amid the crags above. An eagle, wheeling {21} across the azure sky, sent down an answering scream.

The prophet caught up one of the Mormons, and, with wonderful strength, lifted him and dashed him against others of the party, sending them all down in a writhing, scrambling heap.

One of the men who had been beaten down fastened his arms about Frank's legs, and Merriwell was partly thrown. He recovered, and struck the fellow such a blow on the temple that those clinging hands relaxed, and the man lay stretched on the ground.

Jack dragged Frank to his feet, and they fought on, their blood leaping in their veins, their hats off, the warm sunlight of a perfect summer day shining on their perspiring faces.

"Oh, if the rest of the gang were here!" cried Jack. "If we had Browning's powerful arms to aid us!"

"It's no use to think of them," panted Frank. "We've got to do our own fighting, and we seem to be doing a fairly good job."

Driven mad with fury, one of the Mormons tried to drive a knife into Jack.

Frank caught the wrist of the murderous wretch, and gave it a twist that caused him to drop the bright blade.

Like a flash Merriwell caught up the knife. Then it was that the Mormons actually wavered once more.

At that moment a body of men came rushing up from below, scrambling over the rocks, and shouting encouragement to those who were trying to overcome the two boys and the Mad Prophet.

"Reinforcements!" palpitated Diamond.

"Sure!" came huskily from Merriwell.

"That settles it!"

"That settles us!"

"But we won't give up!"

"Not as long as we can wiggle a finger! Hoe in!"

They made a last desperate spurt in the fighting, but once more Frank was seized about the legs and dragged down.

The same man had repeated the trick.

Merriwell had the knife in his hand, and he could have settled the fellow with a single blow.

"No!" he gasped; "I'll not stain my hands with blood! It would be useless."

The knife was flung aside, and he grappled with the man. Over they rolled, each trying to get his hands on the other's throat. The eyes of the man glared at Frank, and Merriwell's parted lips showed his set teeth.

In the mad struggle, Frank's head struck against a rock, and his senses swam. That gave his foe an advantage, and he obtained the hold he desired.

Frank tried to breathe, but could not. He tried to speak, but no sound came from his lips. The world seemed reeling about him in a blood red mist, and there was a roaring in his brain. It grew dark.

"Good-by, Jack!" he tried to say. "We made a jolly good fight of it, but we're done up at last."

Then he lay limp and lifeless on the ground.

When Frank went down Jack's back was no longer protected, and his foes swarmed at him there.

The Mad Prophet seemed to realize the danger, and he flung them aside for a time.

But even Old Lonely was not invulnerable, and his blows began to lose their force. The men swarmed in and separated the boy and the old man.

Jack could see the white head of the strange man in the midst of the enemies who surrounded him, and he heard the prophet cry:

"Unholy mockers of the true God, what wouldst thou with me? Depart from me, or beware of the wrath to come!"

But the Mormons would not depart. They swarmed on him thicker and thicker, and they beat and dragged him down for the third time. This time they took care to make fast his hands and feet, and Old Lonely was captured at last.

This done, they turned their attention to Jack, and he was unable to resist the force of numbers. They handled him with such ease that he was amazed.

"Seems as if you might have done that before, if you had made a real try," he said. "You are a lot of cowards, and that's what's the matter with you!"

When he was secured, he looked around for Frank. He saw him, and Merriwell lay on the ground, his face dark and discolored, while his tongue seemed to protrude from his lips. {22}

"Merciful Heaven!" groaned Diamond, turning away in horror. "He is dead! Poor Merry!"

———

Chapter X.
In the Dungeon.

The Mormons were triumphant; the boys and the old hermit were overcome and captured. The leader of the Mormons gave orders that the captives should be carried into the town and disposed of as Elder Holdfast should design.

Jack had tried to creep to the side of Frank, but he was prevented from doing so. He was lifted and carried away, still murmuring:

"Poor Merry!"

The fury of Asaph Holdfast knew no bounds when he found the girl had not been found, although the Mad Prophet and the two bicycle boys had been made captives.

"To the ruined fort with them!" he cried. "Fling them into the dungeon, and there let them remain till the Black Tribunal shall decide on their fate."

They were carried onward again, and soon they saw before them a structure of stone, situated near the western entrance to the valley. Looking at this structure, Jack Diamond was filled with wonder, for plainly it was an old fortification, and it showed much skill in the construction, the walls being high and solid, capped with turrets and towers. Formidable indeed was the appearance of the old fort, and Jack wondered what hands had constructed such a marvelous piece of work in that remote and lonely valley.

He was not given much time to inspect it. Into the fort they were hurried, by way of a great gate, and soon the walls of stone were around them.

But they were not to be left there, with the open air of heaven to breathe. Across the open space they were taken, and a black opening loomed before them in the wall. Through the opening the Mormon captors bore their prisoners.

A dark passage was entered, and there the Mormons paused to light a wretched old lamp, which shed a very dim light. That light was enough to show them where to take their captives, which was all they desired.

At the end of the passage they came to a stone door. There was a clanking of chains and a clang of heavy iron bars, and then the door was opened.

Beyond that door lay a black space that was awesome enough to cause the stoutest heart to quake.

"In with them!" harshly commanded the leader.

The captives were thrust into the hole, and the door closed behind them with a sullen shock.

It was very dark in there, and the air seemed heavy. Surely it was a place to strike terror to the stoutest heart.

Jack's hands had been set free at the very moment when they flung him into the dungeon, and he lost little time in removing the rope from his feet.

"This is better than being trussed up, anyway," he muttered.

Then he spoke to the old hermit, but received no reply. He spoke again and again but the man remained silent, although Diamond could hear him breathing near by.

"I wonder where Merry is? Poor Merry!"

The young Virginian sought his friend, and his hands soon touched Frank Merriwell's body. Frank was huddled in a little heap, still lying quite motionless, as if dead.

Eagerly Jack felt for the pulse of his friend whom he loved—felt for his heart, and listened with his ear close to Frank's breast.

A great cry of joy escaped his lips.

"He lives! He is not dead yet!"

With nervous haste he tore the cords from Frank's wrists and feet, released Frank's clothes about the neck, and began to work to restore him to consciousness.

Then it was that Jack prayed. He asked God to spare the life of the friend he loved and admired, not minding or caring that the old hermit was near to hear his words.

After a time a groan and a sigh came from Merriwell's lips, and then he began to breathe hoarsely, as if his throat pained him.

"He is coming round all right—he still lives!" shouted Diamond, and the {23} sound of his voice smote on his ears painfully.

Ten minutes passed, and Frank began to understand that Jack was near—was speaking to him. After that Merry recovered rapidly.

"What makes—it—so—dark—Jack?" he slowly and painfully asked. "Is—it—night?"

"No, not night, Frank, old fellow. We are shut up in a dark hole."

"Shut up?"

"Yes. You know we had a fight."

"I know something happened, for every breath I draw seems to burn my throat, and my head is filled with a dull pain."

"You remember—we fought the Mormons—we went to the aid of the old hermit, who was fighting them all alone."

"I remember now. Well, we did the best we could. I told you it was bound to be a warm day."

"All our fighting did no good."

"Oh, I don't know! I remember getting in a few licks that must have damaged somebody's coco. It was rather lively while it lasted."

"And it landed us here."

"We'd have landed here anyway, and I didn't propose to give up without a fight. The sight of the old man, with his white head, fighting all that howling gang was more than I could endure. I was bound to go to his aid."

"Well, I think we are pretty near the end of our rope. The Mormons have us fast and safe, and our goose is cooked."

"Where is the old man?"

"He is somewhere here with us."

"A prisoner, too?"

"Yes."

"I'm sorry for him. He deserves a better fate. I wish I had a drink of water. I believe it would cool my throat. It burns so!"

"There is no water here, Frank."

"Well, we'll have to get along without it. Where's the old man? I want to talk with him."

"If you succeed, you will do better than I could. I tried to talk with him, and he would not speak to me at all."

They crept over till they found Old Lonely lying on the ground, bound hands and feet. Then they both set to work to release him, which they soon accomplished.

But, although Frank did his best, he could not induce the hermit to speak. At last Frank gave up the task.

"If he'd talk, we could find out something about Whitcomb," said Frank.

"Whitcomb!" shouted Diamond, savagely. "Don't talk to me of that fellow! I never want to hear his name again!"

Merriwell was surprised.

"What is the matter? What has struck you now?"

"Whitcomb has deserted us! We came here and risked our lives for him, but, the moment he got the girl, he skipped out and left us to our fate!"

"For which I do not blame him."

"You don't?"

"No."

"Then something must be the matter with your head! It was a cowardly thing to do!"

"It was all right."

"How do you make that out?"

"It was his place to make sure first that Lona Ayer was safe from the clutches of the Mormons, and it was our place to bother pursuers till he could get away. We did the bothering."

"And he did the getting away!"

"But, having placed the girl in a position of safety, I believe Whitcomb will return and see what he can do for us."

"By that time it will be too late to do anything but plant us."

"Oh, I don't know! I have been in tight boxes before this. Remember the old saying about the slip between the cup and lip."

"I have very little hope in slips in cases like this."

"Well, we won't give up until we have to. My throat feels some better, and my head does not ache so badly. We'll examine this place, and see how tightly we are cooped up."

As well as they could, they made an examination of the walls, feeling all round the place with their hands. From this they received no satisfaction at all.

"She seems solid," confessed Frank.

"She is," declared Jack.

"We'll have to wait till somebody comes, and then, perhaps, we'll be able {24} to find out how long they mean to keep us in here."

"We are to be kept here till we are removed to be tried before the Black Tribunal. I heard old Holdfast say so."

"Then it's no use to flutter. We may as well take it easy, and wait for the Black Tribunal to get in their work."

"I never saw a fellow like you!" shouted Jack. "You are inclined to be altogether too cool about things of this sort!"

Then he flung himself down on the ground, and they waited.

Chapter XI.
The Black Tribunal.

At last, after many hours, during which they were kept in the dungeon without food or drink, they heard someone at the door. The chains rattled and the iron bars clanked as the heavy door swung open, and a gleam of light shone into the dungeon.

Back of that light were men, whose faces were hidden by masks, and who carried deadly weapons in their hands.

"They have come to finish us!" exclaimed Jack, as the weapons were pointed at the three captives.

"Come forth!" commanded one of the masks, sternly.

"Thanks awfully," said Frank Merriwell. "We don't care if we do."

He coolly walked out, stooping to keep from striking his head, as he passed through the low door.

He was seized in a moment, and his hands were again bound behind his back.

Then Jack was ordered to come out, and he did so, being served the same as Frank.

To the surprise of all Old Lonely made no resistance, but came out when ordered to do so, and permitted them to bind his hands.

Then they were marched along the dark passage, where the light flared fitfully and the air was dense and foul.

"We are going to our doom!" whispered Jack in Frank's ear.

"Well, doom or dinner—I feel like going to one or the other," returned Merriwell. "If they are thinking of finishing us, I hope they will give us a square meal before they do the job."

"This is no time to jest."

"That's jest right, Jack; but this hunger of mine is no jest. I have a healthy and growing appetite."

"Silence!" commanded one of the masked guards.

"All right, your royal muchness," said Frank, resignedly. "We'll be still as clams."

They passed across the open space within the walls, and entered another passage, which was dark as the first. Proceeding along this passage, they came to a square chamber, which was lighted by flaring, smoking torches.

In a semi-circle at one side of the chamber sat twelve cloaked and cowled figures, their garments of sombre black. They sat there, motionless as statues, and, in truth, at first glance, the boys fancied they were images.

Slightly in advance, behind a block of stone, on which was an open book, sat another black-robed figure. This one, however, did not wear a cowl, but his head was hidden by a mask made to resemble the head of a black bear.

"Prisoners," said one of the guards, "you are standing before the Black Tribunal and the great judge of the lost tribe of Israel. Here in this chamber you shall be tried, and sentence shall be pronounced upon you."

Then the three were placed in a row before the black-robed figures, and the guards fell back a few steps.

The figure that wore the bear's head arose.

"Ye shall be judged according to thy deeds, ungodly ones," he said, in a deep and solemn voice. "Speak truly and with reverence when questioned, for much dependeth on thy words and manner."

"It is even so," came in unison from the semi-circle of dark forms.

Then the great judge read a passage from the book before him, which was the Mormon Bible. When this was finished, he addressed himself to the hermit.

"Man of the white hair and beard," he said, "grave and terrible is the charge against thee. Thou has been permitted to enter and leave the Valley of Bethsada {25} at thy will, and no one has lifted a hand to do thee harm. We felt that thou wert our friend, and we were yours. But now it seemeth thou has conspired against us. It is charged that thou hast aided Gentiles and enemies of the Mormon faith to enter the valley. Speak man; is the charge true?

The Mad Prophet drew himself up to his full height, and his eyes steadily regarded the judge, but his lips parted to utter no sound.

"Speak!" again commanded the judge.

Still the hermit was silent.

"Hast thou no defence?"

Silence.

"Thus thou condemneth thyself!" said the judge. "If you have no words of defence, the Tribunal shall pronounce thy fate, for it is useless to question thee further."

There was scorn and defiance written on the face of the old man, and it was plain that nothing could force him to unseal his lips in his own defence.

"Brothers of the Tribunal," said the great judge. "You see he hath no defence to make. What shall be his fate?"

"The pit of fire," came in chorus from beneath the cowls.

"The pit of fire it shall be," declared the judge. "He shall be utterly destroyed from the face of the earth—wiped out root and branch. Take him away."

He waved his arm, and the guards grasped Old Lonely, who did not resist as the[y] conducted him from the chamber.

It came Frank's turn next.

"It's no use!" whispered Diamond, despairingly. "The[y] mean to kill us anyway, and we may as well keep still."

Frank was singled out and the great judge said:

"Art thou a Gentile?"

"I presume that is what you would call me as I am not a Mormon," answered Merriwell quietly.

"How comes it thou wert in the Valley of Bethsada?"

"My bicycle brought me here."

"But there was a reason why thou camest here. Speak the truth."

"My dear sir, I would not be impolite enough to contradict you even if you were mistaken in anything you may assert."

The judge made a gesture of displeasure.

"Thy tongue is smooth but they [*sic*] manner is insolent," he said. "Why didst thou come to this valley?"

"Well, sir, my reason for coming was to do my best to save an innocent girl from being forced to become the plural wife of a gray-headed old wretch who should be preparing for his departure from this world, instead of accumulating more wives. There you have it straight from the shoulder, and I hope it satisfies you."

"Brothers," said the judge, "hast thou heard?"

"We have heard," came back solemnly.

"Gentile," said the judge, "didst thou know this valley was forbidden to all not of the Mormon faith?"

"I had heard so."

"And still thou didst not hesitate to enter here," came sternly from the hidden lips of the judge. "Thou hast heard, brothers. What shall be his fate?"

"The pit of fire!":

Jack Diamond uttered a cry of horror, while it seemed that Frank remained unmoved.

The judge waved his hand, and Merriwell was seized and taken away.

Then it was that Jack became desperate and furious.

"Take me with him, you murderous ruffians!" he cried, in his clear, strong voice. "I am as guilty as he! You may kill us both, but you'll not always escape the punishment you merit! You are a lot of bloodthirsty hounds! I do not believe you are true Mormons at all! I do not believe the Mormon Church would recognize you, if it knew the truth about you! You are outcasts on the face of the earth, and—"

"Brothers," came the loud, yet somewhat muffled voice of the great judge, "you have heard enough. Pronounce his fate."

"The pit of fire!" came for the third time from the Black Tribunal.

"What a farce!" shouted Diamond. "We were condemned in advance, and this pretended trial is a mockery! Miserable men! How you will shudder and quake when you stand before the last {26} great Tribunal in that day when all men shall be judged!"

Then he, too, was borne away.

———

CHAPTER XII.
THE PIT OF FIRE.

One by one the three captives were cast into a narrow space where the walls on either hand were more than twenty-five feet in height. At the top this space was open to the sky, but it was night, and a crescent moon hung low, so its light did not sift down into that grim pit.

"Well, here we are," said Merriwell, as Diamond was thrust in. "This is the pit all right, all right; but I fail to see the fire."

"It cannot be this is the place to which we were condemned!" cried Jack. "There is no fire here."

In the centre of the pit, standing motionless, his arms folded over his broad breast, was the Mad Prophet, who still remained silent.

"There is no fire here," admitted Frank; "but it is possible they mean to make a little fire for us some way. I do not think they have brought us here for nothing."

"These men are not Mormons!" declared Diamond. "At their worst, Mormons never destroyed their enemies in such a manner. They may claim to be Mormons, but I know the Mormon church to-day would not acknowledge them as such."

"It makes little difference to us what they are, they have us foul, and they mean to snuff us out. Look there!"

On the top of the wall appeared a human figure, bearing a torch. It was one of the dark robed thirteen known as the Black Tribunal.

Others followed, each bearing a torch, till the thirteen were assembled on the wall of the pit.

It was a strange and fantastic spectacle as revealed by the flaring light of the torches. High above were the mysterious and awesome ones in cloaks and cowls, looking down upon the three helpless captives confined within the narrow limits of the walled enclosure. The faces of the captives were upturned, and they looked white and despairing, with wildly gleaming eyes.

Still stood the old hermit, his white head bare, his arms folded over the beard that flowed down across his breast. There was dignity and disdain in his attitude, and it seemed that he was supported by another and higher Power than his own.

Was it possible that out of the thirteen human beings on the wall not one looked down in pity at those helpless captives whom they had doomed?

"The time hath come!" said the voice of the great judge. "Thus let all Gentiles perish from the face of the earth!"

"Now comes the fire!" muttered Frank.

"Whew!" exclaimed Jack. "It is something besides fire! What a frightful odor! Are we to be smothered?"

"It is escaping gas!" cried Merriwell. "It must be this place is connected with a natural gas well, and the gas has been turned in here! I see through their trick now!"

Then the old, white-haired hermit was seen to move. He unfolded his arms, and stretched them toward heaven, his face upturned and his lips moving.

"He is praying!" whispered Merriwell, awed by the spectacle.

From the figures on the wall mocking laughter came down.

"Laugh, O wicked ones!" thundered the powerful voice of the Mad Prophet. "The Lord of Hosts is my Lord and my God! His sheltering hand is over me! As he protected the three Hebrew children in the fiery furnace thus he will protect us!"

"Let's see how well you will be protected!" sneered a voice from the wall.

Then a torch came whirling down into the pit.

In a moment there was a burst of fire from twenty different places where the gas was pouring into the pit. The heat was scorching and awful, and it drove the boys to the very centre of the enclosure.

"It has come, Frank!" gasped Jack. "We can't stand this more than a minute! It will soon cook us!"

The jets of fire grew fiercer and fiercer, telling that the gas was being given a greater head. {27}

Once more the Mad Prophet uplifted his arms and cried aloud:

"Give me strength, Lord, as thou gavest Samson strength to pull the temple down and destroy his enemies in the ruins!"

With that prayer on his lips, he rushed to the wall between the jets of fire, and there before him was what had once been a door, but was sealed up in a crude manner with rough stones. Against these stones he placed his shoulder.

Once more those above laughed mockingly.

"Push!" they cried. "It is thy only hope!"

He did push. He set his shoulder firmly, and gave a mighty heave.

And then—wonders of wonders! The sealed doorway gave before him! From the top of the wall came loud cries of amazement. Another mighty surge, and the sealed portion burst outward, making a large opening in the wall.

A miracle it seemed, but, in truth, the sealed portion of the wall was weak and it had not required an enormous outlay of strength to burst it open.

Falling rocks rained down about the Mad Prophet, but did not seem to harm him as he burst through and disappeared.

Jack Diamond seemed stupefied by what had happened, but Frank was quick to comprehend that fortune had favored them, and there was a chance to escape.

"Come!" he cried, catching hold of the Virginian, and forcing him through the opening. "For your life, run!"

They fled from the spot, but had not gone far when they heard a voice calling to them:

"Thither—thither if thou wouldst escape! There is but one way for us to get out of the valley, and I know that."

"It is the Mad Prophet!" exclaimed Frank. "We must follow him!"

"That's right," said Jack, recovering his speech at last. "I am ready to follow him after what he has done to-night."

The tall figure of the strange man loomed before them, and they allowed him to guide them through the town and to the rocky steeps beyond, as they ran hearing faint cries of pursuers far behind them. Up the rocks he climbed, and they labored along behind him till they came to the mouth of a hidden cave.

And there at the mouth of that cave Tom Whitcomb was waiting. He was rejoiced to see them, and he said:

"I was on the point of descending into the valley to see if I could not find you, although Old Lonely had promised that he would shield you from harm."

Whitcomb was astounded when he learned what they had passed through, and he looked on the strange hermit with added awe.

"He is a wonderful man," he whispered in Frank's ear. "He told me a bit of his story. He hates all Mormons with an undying hatred, for they murdered his brother and tried to kill him. There is no doubt that he is crazy. He says he is remaining here till the time when God shall give him power to destroy all the guilty ones in the valley at a single stroke and spare the innocent. He also says that he could have destroyed them all long ago, but refrained, as the innocent would have perished with the guilty. I am inclined to think he raves when he makes such talk, as he fancies himself endowed with supernatural powers."

"Surely the manner in which he toppled down the walls of the pit of fire seemed supernatural," said Frank.

Jack was restless.

"Where is Miss Ayer?" he asked. "Is she safe?"

"She is safe," assured Whitcomb. "And your bicycles are safe, also, for I found them down amid the rocks a short time ago—stumbled on them by accident."

"Where are they?"

"I brought them up here, and they are in the cave."

"Well, say!" cried Frank; "I want a chance to sit down and rest! This turn of affairs has completely taken away my breath! It is wonderful, and I can scarcely realize it."

"Young men," said the solemn voice of Old Lonely, "you must confess that the sheltering hand of the Most High hath been over us. Thank not man for thy deliverance, but thank God."

* * * * * *

They left the forbidden valley by the road that was known so well to Old {28} Lonely, who had befriended and aided Tom Whitcomb on hearing the young man's story.

When they were outside, the hermit bade them farewell.

"Go!" he said, warningly—"go, and do not stop till far from this accursed spot. Never return here. Do not tell the tale to anyone, for it will not be believed."

"That's right," nodded Frank.

"Marry the girl as soon as possible, and guard her as a precious jewel," said the Mad Prophet to Tom Whitcomb. "Better take her out of Utah. Her father will come to thee in time, and he will rejoice that his daughter was spared from the clutches of the old elder."

Then he addressed the girl.

"Be a good wife to him," he said, "for he has risked his very life for thee. And these other young men have risked no less."

"But I cannot marry them all!" cried Lona, in confusion.

Was it possible that the ghost of a smile flitted across the face of the old man?

"No," he said; "but you can reward them with your gratitude and your admiration. Surely they deserve that. And now farewell. We shall never meet again, for I go back to watch and wait till the time comes to strike. Farewell all."

He turned and left them.

* * * * * *

It was three days later that Frank and Jack joined the others of the party, who had been impatiently waiting for them, wondering and speculating over their absence.

"Well, give a report of yourself," drawled Browning, sternly, "I am actually getting tired of hanging around and doing nothing."

"That must be a new disease for you," laughed Frank.

"Mah goodness!" cried Toots, surveying Merry critically. "I done begun teh believe I nebber was gwan teh set mah eyes on yo' face no mo'. What yo' been doin', boy? Hab yo' been gallavantin' off arter some ob dese pretty Mormon gals? Land ob watermillions! I's hit de fus' pop! I done seen de guilt in yeh eye, boy! Yum, yum! But yo' is jes' nacherally a terror, yo' is!"

"Will you steep kill—I mean keep still!" cried Rattleton. "I want to hear what Frank and Jack have to say for themselves."

"If we tell you everything, you will think we are drawing the long bow," said Frank. "Eh, Jack?"

"That's so," nodded Jack.

The boys protested that they would accept everything as literal truth, and so the story was told at last. When it was finished, Harry asked:

"Where are Whitcomb and his sweetheart now?"

"They are married, and on their way East. They are going to get out of Utah."

"I don't blame them," yawned Browning. "If I were Whitcomb I wouldn't stop this side of the Atlantic Ocean. And I rather think we had better be getting out of Utah before Frank and Jack have another fit and run off after some other pretty Mormon girl."

"We'll get a move on us in the morning," said Frank. "Hurray for the road and the spinning wheel! We're still in the ring, for all of the knockout blows that have been aimed at us."

[The End.]

[Francis Worcester Doughty]. *The Bradys Among the Mormons; or, Secret Work in Salt Lake City*. Secret Service. Old and Young King Brady, Detectives, no. 239. New York: Frank Tousey, 21 August 1903.

The Bradys among the Mormons;
or,
Secret Work in Salt Lake City.

By a New York Detective.

Chapter I.
The Man with the Roman Nose.

The Bradys, the most famous detectives in the United States, having been sent for by the chief of the Secret Service Bureau, arrived in Washington one rainy evening in the early Spring.

Taking a cab at the B. & O. station, they drove directly to the house of the chief, as per instructions.

Old King Brady wore his usual peculiar dress.

The long-tailed blue frock coat with brass buttons, the big white hat, the stand-up collar and the rest of his antique costume were all there.

Young King Brady, as usual, was dressed up to the minute.

The detectives, as they rolled over the asphalt, had not the remotest idea why they had been summoned to the capital.

They frequently received such calls from the Secret Service Bureau, and the work assigned to them never failed to prove to be of the most confidential and secret nature.

Upon reaching the residence of the chief, Young King Brady went in alone, leaving his partner in the cab.

This was also as per orders.

It was [not] desirable that Old King Brady's presence in Washington should become known.

Harry, as Young King Brady is usually called, was gone but a very few moments, when he bounced into the cab again, having given a hurried order to the driver.

"Well?" asked Old King Brady, as they rolled down Vermont avenue, "what is up?"

"Mormon business, Governor."

"Indeed! It is a long time since I have been to Salt Lake City."

"I don't know that this call will take us to Salt Lake City."

"Did you see the chief?"

"Yes, for a moment."

"What did he say?"

"Next to nothing. He asked if you were in the cab, and when I said you were he replied that you were not to show yourself without disguise upon any account. We are to go to the home of Senator Truesdell on Rhode Island avenue, where a reception in honor of the Corean minister is being held."

"We shall want dress suits in that case."

"We must get down to old man Stein, the costumer's, place at once."

"I know that also, and have already given the driver orders to take us there."

"Very good. Then there is nothing to do but to have a smoke till we reach Fifteenth street. Have you anything further to say?"

"Nothing, beyond that he said it was Mormon business."

"You got no hint as to the nature of the case?"

"No."

"Just like him. I suppose we are to report to Senator Truesdell for orders?"

"Yes. By the way, what state is the senator from?"

Old King Brady named the state, but we don't propose to. Enough to say that it was one of the newer states of the far West.

In due time the Bradys were put down at Senator Truesdell's door. {2}

They were now rigged up in dress suits and looked quite the real thing as society men.

"The Hon. Mr. Butterworth, Mr. Thomas Butterworth!" was the announcement as they entered the senator's brilliantly lighted salon.

Mrs. Truesdell, who had been given the invitation cards, handed Harry by the chief of the Secret Service Bureau, came forward to greet them with something of a disgusted look upon her face.

"I am delighted to meet you," she said, and the Bradys bowed profoundly. "You are friends of the senator? Pardon me, but I cannot recall having met you before."

"You have not, madam," replied Old King Brady. "This is the first of your receptions we have had the pleasure of attending."

"I thought so. I have sent for the senator. He will be here to receive you presently. Meanwhile I hope you will make yourself at home."

All this was said in a fashion which showed the Bradys that the early training of the senator's wife had been neglected.

Harry whispered as much as the lady moved away, but Old King Brady cut him short.

"Hush!" he whispered. "That woman is as keen as a needle. It is very possible that the senator does not wish even his wife to know that we are here."

The detectives placed themselves in a convenient corner and surveyed the guests of the crowded salon.

It was certainly a brilliant affair.

The ambassadors of nearly every foreign country were present.

Many of the costumes were fairly gorgeous.

Such a display of diamonds and gems as could be seen on all sides, adorning ladies beautiful and ladies homely, Harry had never before witnessed.

Altogether it was a very swell affair.

While he was looking from one beautiful low-necked creature to another and mentally figuring up how much her diamonds were worth in each case, a servant approached and said:

"Mr. Butterworth?"

"Yes," replied Old King Brady.

"You are to follow me, sir, if you please. Senator Truesdell desires to speak with you in his library."

This was what the detectives wanted, of course.

As they passed out of the room, a gentleman, under thirty, with intensely black hair and a Roman nose, suddenly stepped in front of them.

"Pardon me, but have I not met you in Salt Lake City, sir?" he asked of Old King Brady, at the same time extending his hand.

"No," replied the detective, not extending his hand. "You have never met me in Salt Lake City, or anywhere else."

"I hope you will excuse me," replied the gentleman, looking somewhat chagrined at being so effectually turned down. "Your face was familiar, and—"

"Pardon me, Senator Truesdell desires to see me," interrupted the old detective.

He almost had to push the fellow aside in order to pass him.

While this was going on Harry studied the man carefully.

This was part of Young King Brady's business, and he did not have to be told to do it.

The Bradys have methods purely their own and always work into each other's hands.

The servant now led them to the second floor, where they were ushered into Senator Truesdell's den.

It was elaborately furnished, evidently by Mrs. Truesdell.

It was no den in which a man could take his comfort. The hand of woman was visible everywhere.

The senator, a big, red-faced man, who had suddenly come into the possession of millions by a lucky rise in mining stocks, looked like a fish out of water.

"Be seated, gentlemen," he said, without rising. "I can give you but a few minutes. Alphonse, I am not to be disturbed."

The French valet bowed and retired.

Old King Brady looked doubtfully at the chairs with their spidery, gilded legs.

"With your permission I'll try the lounge, Senator," he said.

"Don't blame you a blessed bit," said the senator, with a frown—actually he used a more picturesque word. "There isn't a chair in this room fit to sit on except the one I am on now. I'd give it to you, only I've got the gout, and can scarcely stand, and any other one will break down with me. It's all the doings of the women folks. They must be fashionable, even if they break all our necks."

The senator was in bad humor and he showed it.

"Now then, Mr. Brady," he said, when the detectives were seated, "you have been highly recommended to me by the chief of the Secret Service Bureau. I want your help in a very delicate affair."

Old King Brady bowed, and Harry took out his notebook.

"What's that for?" demanded the senator, suspiciously. "Going to take me down in shorthand?"

"My partner usually takes notes of our instructions, Senator," the detective replied.

"I'm not giving you instructions yet. I have not even given you the case."

"Put up your notebook, Harry," said the old detective. "Senator, proceed."

"What do you know about the Mormons?" demanded the senator, abruptly.

"I've worked among them several times," replied Old King Brady.

"Are you well known in Salt Lake City?"

"Not particularly well. It is several years since I have done any work out there." {3}

"So much the better. Now, do you want to undertake a case in Salt Lake City for me?"

"Certainly, if you wish it, providing it suits me. I should have to hear all about it first."

"Of course, what we say is strictly confidential."

"Most certainly."

"The chief told me you were to be trusted. Now listen. In my earlier life I lived among the Mormons, although I never was one myself. My wife was also brought up among them. Her father was a Mormon, who later repudiated the church, and took his children away with him. My wife, while she professes to adhere to another religion, has no prejudices against her early friends. In fact, I believe she is secretly in sympathy with them. I cared nothing for all this until recently, Mr. Brady, but when it comes to marrying my only child, my daughter Grace, to a Mormon, who may have a dozen wives already for all I know, that's another thing."

The detective silently bowed.

"That is the state of the case," continued Senator Truesdell; "the man in question is Joseph Smith Podmore, a man of large means and great influence among his people. He professes to be single. You know that of late years many Mormons secretly maintain a number of wives. The church forces them to do this and aids them in presenting a false front to the world. This man is worth millions. He has proposed to my daughter, and Mrs. Truesdell insists that she shall accept him."

"Is your daughter in love with Mr. Podmore?" Old King Brady asked.

"No, but to be frank with you, she is perfectly willing to marry him for his money, providing it can be proven that he has no other wife. It has become the custom of these rich Mormons to marry one wife outside the church, especially such as aspire to get into politics, as this man does. He expects to be elected to the House of Representatives the next election. He has offered to settle half a million on my daughter if I will consent to the marriage and assist him by my influence to hold his seat in the House in case he is elected, which he surely will be. There is your case, Mr. Brady. I want you to do a little secret work in Salt Lake City and to find out how it really stands with this man. If he is already married to one or more wives, of course, I cannot consent to my daughter marrying him. If not, I am willing to let the deal go through."

"Interesting individual, this," thought Old King Brady. "He is perfectly willing to sell his daughter to this man providing he can do so legally. Still he is doubtless willing to pay well for this work, and I shan't object to a run out to Salt Lake City. I think I will take him up."

"I am willing to undertake the commission," he said aloud.

"Very well," replied the senator. "Remember, Joseph Smith Podmore is the name, and the man is present at my wife's reception to-night. It only remains for me to point him out to you. What are your terms?"

"We never make terms in a case like this. I will render you a reasonable bill."

"I understood from the chief that such was your way of doing business, so I suppose I shall have to accept. Now, to point out this man."

"It is not necessary."

"How not necessary?"

"I have already seen him. He is a man just under thirty, with intensely black hair and eyes, and a Roman nose."

"That is certainly his description. You know him, then?"

"Not at all. Such a man tried to claim my acquaintance downstairs. I should say that in spite of the dress suit I wear he evidently knows me."

"Is it possible? He is sharper than I gave him credit for, but that's the Mormon of it. Who can have betrayed my intention of engaging you[?] Tell me what occurred."

"With pleasure, in a minute, but in the meanwhile, Senator, would it not be just as well to find out who it is that is listening to our conversation at the keyhole of that door[?]"

Old King Brady dropped his voice to a whisper as he said this, and pointed to the door which communicated with the adjoining room.

Senator Truesdell's face grew dark.

"Attend to your work," he whispered. "If there is anybody spying on us drag 'em in by the neck, no matter who it is."

"Harry!" breathed Old King Brady.

Harry arose and tip-toed to the door.

Suddenly he threw it open, but he did not get the spy.

The hurry of footsteps in the hall was heard.

In a minute Young King Brady returned and closed the door.

"Well?" demanded the senator. "Who was it—did you learn?"

"Yes, I caught sight of him," replied Harry, sitting down again.

"It was the man?" asked Old King Brady.

"Surest thing," said Harry, coolly. "The man with the Roman nose."

Chapter II.
The Bradys Find Themselves up against Trouble at the Very Start.

Old King Brady moved further along on the lounge, folded his arms, put his back against the wall and never said a word.

Senator Truesdell looked immensely disturbed.

His face grew so red and his breath came so short that for a minute the old detective thought he was going to have an apoplectic fit. {4}

He managed to control himself, however, and it was with an air of indifference that he said,

"You see how things are running, gentlemen. I am being spied upon right here in my own house."

"I see," replied Old King Brady. "There is one thing about the Mormons, Senator, whatever you may say of their religious views, they are the greatest fellows in the world to 'get there,' whatever they undertake."

"Don't I know it?" flashed the senator. "Don't attempt to instruct me about the Mormons, man. Haven't I known them all my life? Don't I—I beg your pardon, Mr. Brady. My temper got the best of me for the moment. I—I am excited. This thing has unnerved me. I—"

"You have not told us all, Senator, that is it."

"But, my dear sir—"

"Oh, I know! You can't. Very well, you don't have to. I don't care to know about your private affairs. Let it rest right here. We will undertake your case if you wish."

"I do wish. I am most anxious to have you do so. I must know if this man is the husband of several Morm[o]n wives or not."

"Or even of one?"

"Or even of one, as you say."

"When would you like to have us begin?"

"At once."

"May I offer a suggestion as to the way in which I would begin this case?"

"Surely."

"Right here in your own house should be the place."

Senator Truesdell shook his head.

"I kn[o]w you are right," he said, "but it cannot be. I want you to go directly to Salt Lake City and confine your work to that place."

"Very well. It shall be as you say."

"Do you wish a retainer?"

"It would be as well, to cover expenses."

The senator hobbled to a desk, opened it and sat down to draw a check.

Usually the Bradys do not take retainers, as the old detective is himself a very wealthy man and has the command of money to almost any amount.

In this case it was different, however.

Old King Brady anticipated disclosures in this case which might concern the senator's own household, and as he looked to see his work end abruptly, he felt that it would be better to secure some portion of his money in advance.

The senator was certainly not illiberal in his views.

"I see but one way," he said at last. "I have a secret cipher code by which some of my constituents are in the habit of communicating with me by telegraph. I have no time to make a new one. I shall have to give you that."

"It is quite safe in our hands, sir."

"If I didn't think so you would not get it. I'll write it out."

Producing a card, Senator Truesdell scribbled an alphabet with a lead pencil.

It was simple enough.

It consisted of using the letter D for A and making A the last letter of the alphabet.

"That is all right," said Old King Brady. "Consider this sacred. Is there anything more?"

There was nothing more, and the Bradys announced their intention of withdrawing.

The last part of this conversation, ever since the discovery of the spy at the door, had been conducted in the lowest of whispers.

Now Senator Truesdell touched an electric bell.

His valet, the young Frenchman, responded.

"Mr. Butterworth's carriage, Alphonse," he said.

"Pardon, Monsieur, but Madam desires to see Mr. Butterworth before he leaves," replied Alphonse hesitatingly.

Again Old King Brady thought that Senator Truesdell would have an apoplectic fit.

But, as before, he said nothing until he had fully recovered himself.

"Say to Mrs. Truesdell that she must interview Mr. Butterworth here in this room if she desires to speak with him," he then said in a quiet way.

Alphonse bowed and retired.

Old King Brady expected that the senator would say something, but he did not utter a word until the valet returned with the announcement:

"Madam's compliments to monsieur; she does not desire to speak with Mr. Butterworth in this room."

"Enough," said the senator. "Call Mr. Butterworth's carriage, Alphonse."

The Bradys then withdrew.

Others were leaving when the detectives reached the door.

"Mr. Butterworth's carriage is ready," said Alphonse.

The cab made its way to the curb.

"You are not the man who drove us here?" said Old King Brady, looking suspiciously at the driver. "How is this?"

"He was taken suddenly sick, sir, and had to leave. He is a friend of mine. He asked me to take his place. I will drive you wherever you wish."

"Drive us to the Ebbitt House," said Old King Brady.

"What about our clothes?" asked Harry when they were inside. "You know we left them at Stein's."

"We will take another cab at the Ebbitt House and go after them. I don't like this sudden change of drivers. I fear there is something wrong."

"Had we not better walk, then?" {5}

"How can we in our dress suits in the rain? We can keep a close watch, though."

"Probably it is all right. I hardly see how they could tamper with our cabby and yet—"

"Never mind, Harry. We are taking chances. You have something important to tell me, I see by your face."

"You are a mind reader, Governor."

"I can read yours every day in the week. Well, what is it?"

"I made two discoveries while I was out of the room that time."

"I thought so. One we know. How about the other?"

"Here it is. It must have caught on the door knob while that fellow was listening. I found it on the floor."

"Yes, yes! That is important."

What Harry handed Old King Brady was the end of a gold watch chain.

It consisted of the bar, a bit of the chain and a sort of charm or talisman.

It was a circle of gold with a small seated lion inside; above the lion, also within the circle, was a representation of the all-seeing eye.

"That's Mormon all right enough," said Old King Brady. "That is their most sacred symbol, the lion with the eye above. Away back in the fifties these strange people issued a gold coin with the same symbols upon it, which has now become very rare and valuable. We will keep this. It may become useful later on."

"I thought best not to say anything about it before the senator, so long as we are going to handle the case," remarked Harry.

"And you did quite right. I fancy this is the emblem of some Mormon secret society, to which this man Podmore belongs."

"Very likely. In that case he will be apt to go to great lengths to get it back again."

"No doubt. You are sure it was the man who spoke to me whom you saw retreating down the stairs?"

"Absolutely certain."

"That's enough."

"Senator Truesdell's home must be rather an uncomfortable one, Governor."

"I should say so. I suspect the wife is at the bottom of this whole business. At first I thought the senator was willing enough to sell his daughter, but I have changed my mind, and bless my soul, Harry, I don't like this. We are going altogether too fast. This man must be a very reckless driver. Where are we, I wonder? It is as dark as a pocket outside."

It was not only dark, but raining hard now.

Old King Brady tried to rub the moisture from the glass and peer out of the window.

He could see but little.

The street was unaccountably dark.

"Something [is] wrong!" cried the detective.

He let down the window and shouted to the driver to stop.

The cab slowed down a trifle.

Then instantly came the crack of a whip, and the horses dashed forward more furiously than ever, the cab swaying from side to side.

"Harry, this is a plot to do us up," said the detective, with that wonderful calmness which he always assumed in emergency. "Jump forward! Careful, now! The pavement is slippery, but I guess we can manage it all right."

Trained to absolute obedience, Young King Brady unhesitatingly jumped.

He was just in time, but Old King Brady was just too late.

Quick as a flash the cab went over some sort of an embankment and the crash that followed filled Harry's heart with dismay.

Chapter III.
About the Man Who Threw a Fit in Old King Brady's Room.

Young King Brady spent one minute in staring about in the darkness.

So interested had they been in examining the talisman which Harry had picked up in Senator Truesdell's house that the detectives for once had been caught napping, shrewd as they usually were.

The place where the accident occurred, instead of being down town in the neighborhood of the Ebbitt House, was evidently on the outskirts of Washington.

There were but few houses visible and the street was insufficiently lighted.

Hurrying forward, Young King Brady at once discovered that repairs were in progress to raise the grade of the street.

The cab had gone over the end of the finished part in spite of a red danger lantern, which stood in the roadway, and now lay a wreck in the mud, some five feet below the grade.

The horse had fallen down, and the wrecked vehicle was partially on top of him.

Seizing the red lantern, Harry jumped down into the hole just in time to assist Old King Brady out through the door, which he had managed to wrench open.

"Are you hurt?" he demanded.

"Not a bit. A little shaken up, that is all," replied the detective.

"Look to the driver. If he was on the box he must have suffered all right. I don't believe you will find him, though."

"I see nothing of him," replied Young King Brady, flashing the lantern about. "I'd like to bet he jumped off that time he slowed down."

"That is my idea. No, he is not here. He jumped off, gave the horse a cut with the whip, and started him on the run {6} for our special benefit. Upon my word, boy, that rascal is bold."

"You think it is Podmore's work?"

"Undoubtedly. You see what he has done?"

"Killed the horse and ruined the cab, all right."

"Cabs cost money and so do horses. He must have bought the rig outright from our driver and paid that fellow to do this job."

"It looks so. Upon my word, this is an interesting piece of business."

"But it—listen! Is anyone coming?"

"I hear no one. This place seems decidedly lonely."

"That is what it is."

"Is the horse actually dead?"

"Seems to be. I think his neck must have been broken."

"Best thing we can do under the circumstances is to light right out."

There was no difference of opinion on this point.

Leaving the cab where it was, the detectives hurried away, the rain doing sad work with their dress suits before they reached Stein, the costumer's, and leaving Old Brady an extra bill to pay for repairs.

Having resumed their own clothes, they went to Willard's Hotel on Pennsylvania avenue, and engaged a double room for the night.

"We had best keep together until we are safely out of town," Old King Brady remarked. "This man Podmore is not only on to us, but he is evidently not the sort to let grass grow under his feet. There is no telling what move he may attempt next."

The detectives were not disturbed until after daylight, however.

Then Old King Brady was aroused from his last nap by a knock on the door.

"Awake, Harry?" he called over at the other bed.

"Yes; was somebody knocking?" was the reply.

A second knock saved the necessity of an answer.

Young King Brady, jumping out of bed, opened the door and took a card from the hand of a page.

"Senator Truesdell," he said, turning to his chief.

"Indeed!" replied Old King Brady. "Let him be shown up here in ten minutes."

The page retired, and the Bradys hurriedly dressed, and were ready for the senator when he was announced.

The senator was very pale and looked much trouble[d].

"Well, gentlemen, the axe has fallen sooner than I expected!" he exclaimed, sinking into a chair. "I sent for you too late!"

"What do you mean?" demanded the old detective. "Has this man Podmore gone?"

"He has, and my wife and daughter with him, worse luck!"

"Ah, is it so?" replied Old King Brady sympathizingly, "and does that bring the case to an end?"

"Not on your life. It now begins. Listen to me! My wife is to-day a Morm[o]n. I did not like to tell you last night, but it is so. Lately she fell under the influence of a Morm[o]n elder, who has been doing missionary work in Washington, and he converted her to her former faith. It is not necessary to go into details, Mr. Brady. I have had much trouble of late. I am all worn out with it. Let the woman go where she will, but save my daughter. She must be found and brought back."

"Can it be done before she marries this man Podmore?"

"It must be done, and done secretly. There is yet time. These Morm[o]n marriages are not consummated in a hurry. They have to receive the sanction of the church and that takes time, but there is more to the case than that; my wife has robbed me of a large sum of money, which she must keep, but she has also taken my private letter-book. In it are copies of letters which would ruin me politically if they came to light. This is the whip she proposes to hold over me. She left a threatening letter to that effect and—and there is more of it, which I can't explain."

Senator Truesdell leaned his elbows on the table and covered his face with his hands.

"Calm yourself, my dear sir," said Old King Brady. "There is always a way out, no matter how dark the future seems."

"Yes, but you do not know my wife. She is a fiend. I believe she would sooner kill our daughter with her own hands than to see her restored to me."

"The case remains just as it was before. If we can prove Podmore already married the law will interfere to save your child."

"Let us hope so, but you can hardly know Utah or you would not say so. Out there the Morm[o]n law is still the whole thing."

"Then we must fight the Morm[o]n law the best we know how. Have you any doubt that they have gone straight to Utah?"

"I know nothing as to where they have gone, but I presume that such is the case. They left the house early this morning, while I still slept. It was about four o'clock."

"By cab?"

"Yes."

"Did Podmore remain at your house last night?"

"No; he left shortly after you did."

"And your wife and daughter went away alone together?"

"Podmore came for them in a cab. They were seen at the station. This much I have learned, no matter how."

"Did you have trouble with your wife after we left?"

"Yes; we had words."

"About Podmore spying upon our interview?"

"Yes."

"It was certainly so, then?"

"Yes; she admitted it."

"She threatened to leave you?"

"Yes, but she has threatened many times before. I did not think her in earnest."

"And your daughter? Do you think she went willingly?"

"I am inclined to think she did. She is much under her {7} mother's influence. Still, I think when she learns the truth about Morm[o]n life she will fly from them in disgust, if she can."

"Ah, if she can! That is well put. But we must help her. We will start for Salt Lake City by the first train. Perhaps you are not aware that an attempt was made to kill us last night."

"Is it possible? What occurred?"

Old King Brady told the story.

"Well, there you are," said the senator. "Of course, all Morm[o]ns are not like this man Podmore, but they have a different way of doing business from ours, and when it comes to a fight with a gentile they consider themselves justified in adopting any means to down him. You are fortunate to have escaped as you did."

"What about this business. Does it get into the papers?"

"It never will. I have given out that Mrs. Truesdell and daughter have gone West on a visit. You are the only persons who know the truth."

"One question more, Senator, and that will be the last. Have you any clew as to where Mrs. Truesdell and her daughter may go when they reach Salt Lake City, or do you know any person there who could be likely to help us out?"

"No; I cannot help you in the least. You may, however, see me there in a day or two after you reach there, providing I can get away. I have an idea that if I could once see my daughter I could persuade her to return."

"And should she refuse to return with us in case you do not get there?"

"In that case nothing can be done, but get my letter-book if you can; otherwise I am entirely in the power of Podmore, and shall be forced to favor seating him in the House of Representatives in case he is elected, as he unquestionably will be."

This ended the interview.

As Old King Brady did not mention the talisman, Harry made no allusion to it either.

Waiting only to cash the senator's check, the Bradys took the first train West, and in due time reached Salt Lake City, where they went to a small hotel on Wahsatch street and registered as father and son, under an assumed name.

Old King Brady felt that he had never undertaken a more difficult case.

All was so vague and uncertain; it seemed so impossible to penetrate the secrets of Joseph Smith Podmore, who was a most influential lawyer in Salt Lake City and stood high in the Mormon councils.

For three days the Bradys, carefully disguised, prosecuted their inquiries about the man, but only to find themselves as deeply at a loss as ever as to how they ought to begin.

Podmore was in the city. They saw him on the street on two occasions.

They also learned that he left the train alone upon his arrival there.

No trace of Mrs. Truesdell and her daughter could be found, and a cipher dispatch to the senator brought back the answer that he had heard nothing further from them.

"We must shadow the man; there is no other way, Harry," said Old King Brady, on the evening of the third day, while they were discussing the situation, "and yet it is just the last way I care to undertake."

Their inquiries had told them that Podmore passed for a bachelor and occupied a suite of rooms at Wells' hotel, with an office over the Second National Bank of Salt Lake, on Utah avenue.

"I think," said Old King Brady, "that I will call on him boldly in the morning and see what comes of it. I can think of no other way."

He had scarcely uttered the words when the door of their private bedroom, in which this conversation took place, suddenly flew open, and a tall, seedy looking individual, whom they had observed about the corridors of the hotel, came rushing in, carrying a paper parcel in his hand.

"Oh, beg pardon, gentlemen! Beg pardon!" he cried. "Must have got into the wrong pew."

He seemed much confused; in starting to retreat he clumsily struck the paper parcel against the arm of a big easy chair.

The paper burst and a number of pieces of stone were strewn over the floor.

"Hello!" cried Old King Brady. "What's the matter, friend? You seem to be in trouble all around."

The man burst into a wild peal of laughter, and suddenly throwing up his hands, dropped to the floor, writhing and twisting and foaming at the mouth.

"Heavens!" gasped Harry, "the fellow has thrown a fit right here in our room!"

He started to rush forward to help the man, when Old King Brady caught him by the arm and pulled him back.

"Hush!" he breathed in Harry's ear. "Can't you see that that fellow's side whiskers are false?"

CHAPTER IV.
MAJOR MERRY TALKS MINE.

Harry stared at the writhing stranger, seeing now what Old King Brady had seen at first glance.

Still the man's disguise was cleverly arranged.

If he had kept on his feet the fraud could scarcely have been detected.

Old King Brady acted with great promptness, once he had made his hurried communication to Harry.

"The unfortunate fellow!" he exclaimed aloud, adding:

"Quick, Harry! We must help him. He is a genuine epileptic. Help me get him on the bed!"

They lifted the man up—he was no great weight—and laid him on the bed.

"Soap in his mouth, surest thing," thought Harry. "This {8} is business. The Mormons are on to u[s]. They don't wait for us to make the attack. They make it themselves."

"Hand me my little medicine case out of my grip," said Old King Brady. "I'll give him a dose that will fix him."

Evidently the fit thrower did not want to be fixed with a dose, for he promptly began to revive.

He open[ed] his eyes and made the usual remark indulged in by such persons.

"Where am I?"

"Among friends, my dear sir," replied Old King Brady. "Give yourself no concern."

"I—I am very sorry for intruding," he murmured. "I am subject to fits. Have I had one now?"

"A first-class one!" cried Harry.

Old King Brady frowned.

"There is no intrusion whatever," he hastened to say. "Remain here as long as you wish. Will you not have a little whisky?"

"Well, I don't know but what I will," replied the man. "I am not accustomed to using it, but it may do me good. Do you think so?"

"I am sure of it. Harry, ring the bell. Order a bottle of Old Mountain Dew."

Young King Brady obeyed, and as he did so, the man set about introducing himself.

"My name is Merry," he said. "Major Matt Merry. I have no card, unfortunately, but—"

"But none is necessary. My name is Primrose, Percival Primrose, of New York. You are sure you are feeling much better? Better let me fix you up a dose."

"No, no! I don't need medicine. It never does me any good. I am subject to these attacks. My coming here was all an accident. I thought I was entering my own room, which is on this corridor. I—I shall be all right when I get the drink."

"Which will be here in a minute. Ah, here comes the boy now. A bottle of Mountain Dew, Sam, and three glasses—and, Sam, don't forget the ice water."

While speaking Old King Brady purposely turned his back on Major Merry and motioned to Harry to do the same.

"The man is dying to get the soap out of his mouth," thought the old detective. "I'll get on to his curves in a minute."

Prepared for every emergency, Old King Brady slipped a little pocket mirror out of his mouth [*sic*] and so held it in his hand that what was going on at the bed was reflected in it.

It was only for an instant, but that instant told the tale.

In the mirror he distinctly saw the fit thrower take something out of his mouth and slip it into his pocket.

"Exit the soap," thought Old King Brady. And he added to himself:

"Now, we must not do another thing to excite his suspicion. He has forced his way in upon us; now let him have the full benefit of his rope and see where it lands him."

He returned to the bed and kindly inquired of the man how he felt.

"Better every minute," replied Major Merry. "Really, I feel quite ashamed of myself, Mr. Primrose, for putting you and your son to so much trouble."

"Don't mention it," replied Old King Brady. "Harry, pick up the gentleman's ore specimens and see if you can't find a paper to put them in. They are specimens of ore, I take it, my dear sir."

"Yes, and very rich ones," was the reply. "They came from a mining claim back among the mountains here, in which I am interested. Gold ore, Mr. Primrose, of the richest kind. Big thing, sir. Yes, a fortune for the parties who get in on the ground floor. Yes, that is sure."

"I see they are very rich specimens," said the detective, examining them, and they certainly were.

"It is odd," he added, "that you should have stumbled in on us when we came out to Salt Lake for the express purpose of looking up a good mine to invest in."

"Is it so? Then you could not do better than to look into my claim."

"Have you organized your company yet, Major?"

"Not yet, but I am just about to do so."

"You are a professional prospector—a promoter, or what?"

"All three, I may say. I am certainly an old prospector. I have promoted several companies, and when you come to 'what,' that means any old thing, and that has always been my business. Yes, I make a dollar whenever I can. Yes, I should like to show you my claim. Yes."

"Yes," replied Old King Brady, "I should be very pleased to have a look at it. If it should happen to suit me, Major, I am prepared to invest heavily, and why not with you as well as with another?"

"Yes," said the major. "Why not? Yes."

The whiskey came then.

Old King Brady passed the bottle.

The major poured out a modest drink.

"Oh, come, fill up, Major!" said the detective. "You need it in your present condition. You really do, my dear sir."

"I suppose I do," replied the major, filling his glass almost full. "Yes, I am not much accustomed to drinking, but—yes."

"Yes," replied Old King Brady, pouring out a small drink for himself.

Harry declined.

He was busy arranging the ore specimens on the table.

They were pieces of gold-bearing quartz, and wonderfully rich.

Having drank, Old King Brady proceeded to put on his glasses and examine them more closely.

"I never saw anything in the way of gold quartz to equal this, Major," he remarked.

"And you will look a long time before you can match those specimens," replied the major. "Dear me, it is really wonderful how much better that whiskey makes me feel. I {9} am quite myself again. But I must be going now. Young man, if you could manage to find me a piece of paper, I—you were saying, Mr. Primrose—yes."

"I did not speak, but I was just going to," replied the detective.

"Yes."

"Yes. I was about to observe that if one drink has helped you so much, that probably two would put you quite straight."

"Yes, I think it is possible. Two is my extreme limit. I never make it more than two. Yes."

"I always believe in playing the limit, Major."

"Ha! Yes! Well, since you insist—"

A second huge horn followed the first.

"That is fine stuff! Fine stuff!" declared the major, smacking his lips. "Well, I must be going—yes."

"Don't hurry yourself. We have nothing at all to do this evening. Have you interested anyone in this claim of yours as yet?"

"Yes. One of our most prominent citizens, Mr. Podmore. An influential lawyer, sir—yes."

"It is coming," thought Old King Brady, and aloud he said:

"Indeed."

"Yes, indeed," replied the major. "I am but little acquainted with Mr. Podmore myself, but he knows my record. I think he will go in with me and assist in the organization of the company. You might ask Mr. Podmore about me and the claim, which he has seen. Yes. A very approachable man, sir, and also irreproachable. Ha! Ha! Yes!"

"A Morm[o]n?" demanded Old King Brady, carelessly.

"Yes, but what of that? Our best citizens here are all Mormons. Yes."

"And you?"

"This time, sir, I say no. I am not a Mormon. I am nothing—a heathen. Ha! Ha! Yes! A heathen, but, then, sir, that has nothing to do with this mining claim."

"Oh, nothing at all," replied Old King Brady. "When it comes to that I fear I am something of a heathen myself. I shall take great pleasure in looking into this business and will certainly call upon Mr. Podmore in the morning."

Evidently Major Merry had fully gained his point.

He let go of Mr. Podmore instantly, and dropping much of his peculiar manner, began explaining points about the ore.

After a few minutes Old King Brady suggested another drink.

The man was too wary to be caught that way, however.

He pulled right out then, after apologizing to the Bradys for the trouble he had made them.

"Lock the door, Harry," whispered the old detective as soon as Major Merry had departed, taking his ore samples with him.

Young King Brady obeyed.

"Hang that towel over the keyhole," was the further order.

This done, Old King Brady felt comparatively safe from being spied upon in case the major decided to linger outside the door.

"A Mormon spy, of course?" remarked Harry.

"Certainly," replied Old King Brady, lighting a cigar.

"They are on to us."

"Of course."

"And yet you encouraged the man."

"And why not? I was right glad to see him. We have been here for several days now, and what has come of it?"

"Well, we have had a pretty good time. We have seen the Mormon temple, the tithing house, lots of pretty Mormon women and—"

"Time, Harry. This is business."

"As far as business goes, we have accomplished nothing at all."

"Right you are, and between ourselves I think we might have stopped at it a month without accomplishing anything. How could we ever hope to get next to a man of Podmore's standing without some ruse of this sort."

"That is so, also."

"Now, I'll tell you something. I had just made up my mind to go to Podmore and pretend that I wanted to buy a mine. I was going to-morrow. He has saved me the trouble. He has sent me an invitation. I go now with my eyes wide open to the fact that in spite of my careful disguise I am known."

"How sharp these Mormons are, Governor!"

"Sharp! Why, Harry, sharp is no name for it. Their spy system is the most perfect ever known, and at the same time the most secret. I shall make no further attempt to disguise myself. When Major Merry sees me next it will be with the blue coat and old white hat in their proper places. Now, let us call off for the night and go to bed and I shall sleep for the first time since we have been in Salt Lake City."

"Do you mean to say you haven't slept since we have been here, Governor?"

"I mean just that. There hasn't been a night that I have not feared a shot through the window or that if I lost myself even for a moment either you or I or both of us might wake up with a knife in the back, but now I know they will not disturb us, for they have other plans."

And, having finished his cigar, Old King Brady retired and was sound asleep in a few moments, not waking up again until morning dawned.

CHAPTER V.
THE HOUSE BEHIND THE WALL.

The first thing Old King Brady did next morning was to look up Major Merry on the hotel register. {10}

He found him there all right, but neither in the office of the hotel nor at the breakfast table did he see the major himself.

The lawyers about the office stared at the old detective in his quaint costume, and there is little doubt that many knew him.

At the breakfast table the detective announced that he proposed to visit Mr. Podmore alone.

["]It can do no good for both of us to go," he said. "Spread yourself about town, Harry, and see what you can pick up in the way of information about this man. You may inquire freely now, since we are known. I should be back by noon. If not, you may guess there is something wrong."

It was with many misgivings that Young King Brady saw his chief depart, but he knew how impossible it would be to restrain him.

As soon as he had gone, Harry started out, and, visiting different stores, made small purchases.

At each place he announced himself as a stranger in Salt Lake City, and made various inquiries about the Mormons and their ways in general, and Podmore in particular.

Now, in Salt Lake City at the present day it is not easy to tell a Mormon from a gentile.

Of course all the prominent churchmen are well-known, but there are many Mormons engaged in trade, who are very careful to conceal their connection with the church of the Latter Day Saints from strangers.

It was some time before Young King Brady found opportunity to gain the least bit of information about Mr. Joseph Smith Podmore, beyond the fact that he was a rich and prominent lawyer, which, of course, he already knew.

But at about ten o'clock his chance came.

Young King Brady had been full of curiosity to know the true nature of the charm or jewel which he had picked up in Senator Truesdell's home.

Seeing a little watch and clock repairing shop on a by-street, through which he was talking, in the window of which was displayed old coins, Masonic pins and odds and ends of cheap jewelry, he paused to have a look.

A thin, spare old man sat inside, engaged at repairing a watch; there were no customers in the store.

"That old fellow is as shrewd as they make 'em," thought Young King Brady. "I'm going in to tackle him. He'll be able to explain the nature of my charm."

A little bell tinkled as he opened the door, and caused the old man to look around.

"Well, what can I do for you, young fellow?" he asked without rising from his seat.

Harry had fixed his eyes upon a tray of plated watch chains in the glass showcase, and he inquired the price.

"Different prices," replied the jeweler. "Do you want to buy?"

"I might if I found one to suit me. Can I see them?"

The jeweler arose and took out the tray of chains.

"Three to five dollars each," he said, "and every one solid brass."

Harry laughed, because he thought it was expected of him, but the jeweler did not change his countenance.

"I wonder if he is a Mormon?" thought Harry, selecting a chain.

"I'll take this one," he said aloud, "and you take that. It is solid gold."

He threw down a five dollar piece.

"A dollar coming to you," said the jeweler, opening the cash drawer.

"Hold on a minute," said Harry, producing the charm. "I want this thing fastened to the chain by a split ring. I suppose you will charge for that, too."

He had hit it at last.

He saw the face of the old jeweler change the instant his eyes lit upon the charm.

"You want that put on your chain?" he asked, slowly.

"Yes."

"And why?"

"For ornament."

"Young man, do you know what this thing is?"

"Why, not exactly."

"I thought not. Where did you get it?"

"Really, my friend, I don't know that it concerns you. I did not steal it—that is one thing certain."

"I am not accusing you of stealing it. You are a stranger in Salt Lake City?"

"I am."

"I knew it."

"Why?"

"Because otherwise you would know the risk you run by pretending to be what you are not."

"I don't know what you mean."

"I will explain my meaning when you explain where you got that jewel."

"Then it is the jewel of some secret order?"

"Of the most secret order which ever existed in this or any other country."

"Mormon?"

"What else?"

"Are you a Mormon?"

"Indeed I am not, nor are you."

"That's right. But what order is this?"

"You have not told me yet where you got this jewel."

"I found it."

"Here?"

"No, in the East."

"How long have you been in Salt Lake City?"

"Only a few days."

"Very good," said the old man, handing back the jewel and the change. "Now, I know all I want to know. I will not put this jewel on to the chain for you because by so doing I should risk your life."

"And I have answered every question you have asked me, but you haven't told me what the jewel is yet."

"I know it, but I am going to. I wanted to first satisfy myself that you did not steal the jewel."

"Are you satisfied?" {11}

"I am."

"Then tell me."

The jeweler looked nervously out of the window, up and down the sidewalk, and across the street.

"You do not seem to have a spy at your heels, which I wonder at," he said, lowering his voice. "It is the jewel of the order of the Golden Lion of Judah, into which are admitted only the highest dignitaries of the Mormon church, who are the lineal descendants of the first prophets at Kirtland, Ohio, and Nauvoo, Illinois. For a Mormon not a member of the order to wear it means death. For a Gentile it must mean the same. I have repaired this very jewel. See where the gold band has been soldered right there, where your thumb rests?"

"I do, now that you call my attention to it. Is that your work?"

"It is."

"Then you must know to whom this jewel belongs."

"I certainly do. It is the property of Joseph Smith Podmore, one of the most influential Mormons in the city. This much I will tell you, and it is the last word I am going to say on the subject: For you to openly display that jewel on the streets of Salt Lake City means death."

"Thank you for the warning," replied Harry. "Later on, perhaps, I will let you know how I came to find the jewel. One question more: Where is the meeting place of this order?"

"That is more than I know, more than anyone knows outside of the members of the order of the Golden Lion, and now let me give you another warning and say what will positively be the last word on the subject. If you are a detective out here on business concerning Joseph Smith Podmore, the very best thing you can do is to abandon the business and take the first train east; otherwise I would not give two cents for your life."

Having said this, the old jeweler immediately sat down at his bench, took up the watch and went right on with his work, while Harry, feeling that no more could profitably be said on the subject, left the store.

He continued his walk for as much as an hour, thinking upon what he had heard, and scarcely observing what streets he passed through until he suddenly became aware that he had passed well beyond the city limits and was following a country road which now ran along the shore of the Great Salt Lake.

"I must get back," thought Young King Brady. "There can be no use in keeping on this way any further—no more than there is in trying to get a peep into the secret life of this man Podmore by such methods as we have adopted. The governor may make something out of his mining scheme, but as for me, I am merely wasting time. Shadowing is the only thing, and I have a good mind to undertake it on my own account."

But to do the shadowing act it is necessary for the detective to first locate his man.

Young King Brady determined to get back down town, but just as he had come to that conclusion he perceived ahead of him, on the side of the road away from the lake shore, a low stone house, built in the old Mormon style, and surrounded by a high adobe wall, on the top of which broken bottles and all sorts of pieces of glass were cemented in.

In olden times, before the days of the Union Pacific railroad in Utah, the Mormons' houses were all built upon one plan, which is so peculiar that it should be described.

A Mormon upon his first marriage was required by law to build himself a house, and as soon as possible to abandon the home of his parents and take possession with his wife.

This house was seldom more than one story high, although there might be as many rooms as were desired upon the ground floor.

The front was plainness itself, and the door was always at the side, a hallway opening from it communicating with the different rooms. All windows were in front and at the sides, the rear presenting simply a solid wall.

When the Mormon married a second wife he built another section to his house immediately behind the first, which was reached by another door and hallway.

If he married a third time another section was built, and another door and hallway added, and so on for as many wives as he chose to marry.

The first wife, who was the mistress of all the others under the Mormon law, always occupied the front end of the house, the apartments of the latest wife being just as invariably in the extreme rear.

Since the law against polygamy has been enacted in Utah the Mormons have built in modern style, and most of the old houses have disappeared.

Although many Mormons still have several wives, the practice is by no means as general as it formerly was, and being against the law, the plural wives are maintained in separate houses, where it is difficult to locate them.

All this Harry had heard from Old King Brady, and, although he could only see the tiled roof of the house above the wall, he knew by its length that it must be an old Mormon residence.

There was a heavy wooden gate at one end of the hall; it was all plastered over with mud thrown by boys, and the whole place wore a deserted air.

As Harry stood looking at all this, an old man with a basket on his arm passed him.

"Who lives in that place; can you tell me?" Harry asked.

"Nobody," was the reply. "Hasn't been occupied these many years."

Young King Brady walked across the street, and looked off upon the lake.

As soon as the old man was out of sight he walked all around the house, but less was to be seen in the rear than in the front, for the wall was higher there.

There was no other house nearer than several hundred yards in the direction of the city, while the other way the {12} only house Young King Brady could see was at least a quarter of a mile off.

"By Jove, I wouldn't mind a swim in the lake," thought Young King Brady. "I could undress behind those big boulders on the shore. I really could not have a better chance."

As there was nobody in sight except the old man with the basket, who was trudging on toward the distant house, Harry went behind the boulders, undressed and plunged into the lake.

He found the water icy cold, and so buoyant from excess of salt that it was next to impossible to keep below the surface.

While he was floating about, the sound of rapidly approaching wheels attracted his attention, and turning in the water he saw a handsome buggy, drawn by a span of magnificent black horses, come whirling along the road.

"By Jove, that's a spanking team," thought Young King Brady, getting down in the water as low as he could.

He looked up at the towering peaks of the Wahsatch Mountains, which, although several miles away, looked in that clear atmosphere as though one could walk to them in a few minutes.

"What a grand country this is," he said to himself. "I should just like to have a team with nothing to do but to drive around with my girl like that young fellow. I— hello! By thunder, there is someone in that old Mormon ranch, after all!"

The gate had suddenly opened, and Harry saw a man peer out.

He looked at his watch, and took his stand just outside the gate.

Taking a small whistle from his pocket, he blew it once.

In a few seconds another man appeared.

Both were lank, cadaverous looking fellows with long goat-like beards.

"Mormons, surest thing," thought Harry. "How they eye that team. Can they be up to any trick, I wonder. By Jove, the girl is a beauty. I—"

Harry caught his breath.

The team, now abreast of the gate, was suddenly reined in by the stylish young fellow who drove it.

At the same instant the two men darted out into the road on the side which the girl sat.

Without the slightest ceremony they seized the girl and dragged her out of the buggy.

The young man made no movement to help her[,] even, [*sic*] when she gave a piercing scream.

Once upon the ground, the two men dragged her, struggling, toward the gate.

"Help! Save me!" she cried.

Then turning her head toward her escort, she called out:

"You coward! This is your work! I am the daughter of Senator Truesdell! My father—"

She got no further, for one of the men clapped his hand over her mouth.

In a second the gate closed behind her.

The young man, turning his horses, drove rapidly back toward the city.

"Come, this is black work!" thought Young King Brady. "I am in for it at last. It is up to me to rescue that fair girl."

Chapter VI
Old King Brady Finds Himself
Next to Mr. Podmore at Last.

With Old King Brady matters took altogether a different turn from what he had expected, as will now be shown.

The old detective was destined to learn some of the true inwardness of Mormonism that day, and it was entirely due to his excellent judgment in resuming his usual peculiar dress.

Joseph Smith Podmore, posing as a lawyer devoted to railroad interests, occupied a suite of offices which were without their equal in Salt Lake City.

He employed numerous clerks and was up to date in every particular.

Unlike some others, he never denied his interest in the strange religion founded by the remarkable man for whom he was named, but he persistently asserted that the followers of Joseph Smith had abandoned their former stringent rules regarding marriage, and were now permitted to do just as they pleased about marrying at all, and that in no case were they allowed by the church to break the laws of the land in that respect.

Altogether, Joseph Smith Podmore posed as a good citizen, and considering that he was yet under thirty and had commanded a large fortune, he certainly was a very remarkable man.

When Old King Brady entered the outer office of the lawyer's suite he was received by a quiet, gentlemanly young fellow, who demanded his name.

"My business with Mr. Podmore is strictly personal," replied the detective. "Kindly tell me first if he is in. If not I will come again."

"He is in, sir, but he is very busy. I must have your name," was the reply.

Old King Brady produced his personal card.

He had resolved to beard the lion in his den.

The young man was gone but a moment, and returned with word that Mr. Podmore would see the detective.

Old King Brady was shown into one of the handsomest offices he had ever entered.

The man who had accosted him at Mrs. Truesdell's reception sat at the desk dictating to a female stenographer.

"Be seated a moment, if you please," he said quietly, and proceeded with his work.

He left Old King Brady waiting for at least twenty minutes, and the old detective knew why.

"He is studying my face," he said to himself. "He is trying to find out what sort of a man I am." {13}

At last the stenographer was dismissed, and Mr. Podmore, announcing to those in the outer office that he was not to be disturbed, closed and locked the door.

"Mr. Brady," he said, extending his hand to the detective, "do you know I admire you."

The old detective shook hands heartily.

"And why, may I ask?" he replied. "Certainly there is nothing very attractive about my personal appearance, if that is what you refer to."

"You know it is not. You know that my reference is to your nerve, cheek, absolute fearlessness, or whatever you have a mind to call it. You're an old man; you know all about Mormons and Mormonism, I have no doubt, and yet you dare—"

"To beard the lion in his den? Well, I am here."

"I see you are. Now, draw up a chair. I was expecting you."

"I knew it. You thought I would come here under the name of Percival Primrose to inquire about mining property, owned by one Major Merry."

"I did."

"You looked for me in disguise."

"Such is certainly the case."

"Instead of that you see me as I am."

"And I don't doubt that you know me as I am. That you know that I have but to raise my fingers in this town to have you wiped off the planet and your young partner with you."

"You tried to put us out of business once; the attempt failed.["]

"Ah! That was in Washington. It cost me the price of a cab and a horse, and something extra. As you say, the attempt failed."

"You are frankness itself, Mr. Podmore."

"And why not? You can do me no harm here."

"Pardon me; it is not my desire to do you harm. You were spying at Senator Truesdell's door on the night we received our instructions. You know exactly why I am here."

"I do. Let me tell you something. My family affairs are beyond your ken. You can never hope to succeed in your undertaking. Moreover, Senator Truesdell is now in my power. I hold copies of his own letters, which would utterly ruin him if they were made public. As for his wife and daughter, he had best learn to live without them. His wife hates and abhors him. She will never return to his home. He does not dare to accuse me of having a hand in their disappearance. Mr. Brady, be sensible; abandon this commission. You came to Salt Lake City to do secret work for Senator Truesdell. I confess here between ourselves, where there are no witnesses, no chance of any, that I would have gone even to the extent of killing you to block your game, but since you have come to me in this bold fashion, I shall assume different tactics, and I ask you now, sir, what the object of this visit is—what you propose?"

The old detective smiled.

"Mr. Podmore," he said, "I flatter myself that I am something of a reader of character. I think I have read yours. I think that you know the object of my visit well enough."

"I am afraid I don't quite understand you."

"Then let me explain further, and say that I recognize my inability to make headway in this case. I simply give it up, but somebody has to pay me for my trouble. I am not in the detective business for my health."

"Meaning that you look to me for your pay? I made some talk about cheek just now. I thought I had seen a good sample of it, but upon my word, sir—"

"You see a better one now."

"Never saw its equal, and yet—"

"Well?"

"I admire cheek."

"Glad under those circumstances to be able to exhibit the colossal variety. You were about to say?"

"Let me ask you what you propose to do in case I refuse to do business with you."

"First let me be sure that you fully understand me."

"Can there be any doubt about that?"

"Mr. Podmore, I am a plain man; I like plain talk."

"Then in plain words you are here to be bribed by me to drop the case, to give up your investigation as to the number of secret wives I may have scattered about this city and suburbs."

"Exactly; I am open for an offer."

"And if I refuse?"

Old King Brady shrugged his shoulders.

"Oh, well," he said, "there are always the newspapers. It would not help your political prospects any to have a little story come out about the disappearance of Mrs. Truesdell and her daughter Grace."

"It would not. You threaten?"

"By no means. I merely suggest that it would be cheaper to buy me than to fight me."

Mr. Podmore smiled grimly.

"Man, you don't begin to suspect my power," he whispered. "if I chose to I could crush you like glass. Know now that there are mines being worked in yonder mountain which no gentile except those who work them dream of. Know that the lives of the slaves in those mines are terrible. Mysterious disappearances in Salt Lake City often occur, Mr. Brady, but we Mormons believe in wasting nothing. If an able bodied man stands in our way—well, I think I mentioned the mines."

"Evidently Siberia is not in it with you Mormons, Mr. Podmore."

"You are right; it is not."

"Which brings us back to business. I do not fear your threats any more than you appear to fear mine. You were saying, and yet—"

"And yet in spite of your cheek I admire you. I have read much about you. I know that you seldom fail in your undertakings. I tried to prevent you from coming to Salt {14} Lake City, but now that you have come I am glad. Know why?"

"Because you have work for me to do, and seemingly think of engaging me yourself."

"You have hit it. Would you entertain such a proposition?"

"Seeing that my case for Senator Truesdell has failed, I would, providing the nature of the work suits me."

"The nature of the work is very simple."

"Name it."

"To deceive a dying woman and make her confess to you what she will not confess to me."

It was out at last.

Whether it referred to Mrs. Truesdell or her daughter, Old King Brady could only guess.

"The nature of the secret which this woman holds cuts some figure here," he said.

"It is mine until you get it. I can give you no hint."

"But—"

"But you want a retainer. We will drop the word bribe since it is objectionable. How much was Senator Truesdell going to pay you in case of success?"

"There was no bargain made."

"I understand it is not your custom to fix prices before hand."

"Such is the case."

"My check book is handy. Suppose I make a bid for your services?"

"Not by check. That would not look well."

"I have a safe outside; suppose there is money in it. How much cash would go?"

"It is for you to say."

"I say two thousand."

"And what guarantee have I that you will not kill me when you are through with me?"

"The word of a Mormon, sir, which is ever as good as his bond. If you agree to my terms and further agree to quietly leave this place after you are through with our—I mean my—business, you are as safe as though you were in your own office in New York."

"You give me your word?"

"I do."

"More money if I succeed?"

"Twice as much."

"And in case of failure I keep the retainer?"

"You do."

"It is a bargain. Now, Mr. Podmore, I am working for you."

There was a sneaky glitter in the eyes of the Mormon lawyer as these words were uttered which Old King Brady did not fail to observe.

"I am running a terrible risk," thought the old detective; "yet I see no other way."

"Now for my instructions," he asked aloud.

"You will meet me here at five o'clock this afternoon," replied the lawyer, "or stay. I have an engagement at that hour, which I had forgotten. Make it six. At six o'clock I will meet you here on the steps of this building."

"And the retainer?"

"You shall have it now."

And Old King Brady left the office of Mr. Joseph Smith Podmore with $2,000 of Mormon money in his pocket.

"Risk is no name for it," thought the detective, as he returned to the hotel. "I doubt if in all my experience I ever stood on more ticklish ground than I do at the present moment, but something had to be done. I am next to the man now, and that is what I wanted. The worst part of it is that I dare not make a confidant of the chief of police, which, were it any other city in the United States, I would surely do."

Old King Brady was greatly disappointed when Harry failed to put in an appearance at the dinner table, and still more so to find him still absent when it came time to keep his appointment.

He did not hesitate, however, and exactly at six o'clock he wound up at the bank building where he found Mr. Podmore in conversation with two well-dressed gentlemen.

The lawyer kept him waiting but a moment.

Then calling a cab, they were driven to a large and handsome ho[u]se on Deseret avenue.

"This is the residence of one of the elders of our church," announced Mr. Podmore. "I shall not tell you his name, and if you ever learn it, as you probably may, you are to disclose it at your peril. The Mormon arm is long-reaching. Even in New York mysterious deaths sometimes occur, as you will do well to remember. We will now go in."

They were shown by a servant into a snug little library.

After a brief wait, a tall gentleman with a flowing white beard entered.

He wore a handsome dressing gown of Japanese silk with embroidered slippers on his feet.

"Is this the man, Brother Podmore?" he asked.

"This is the man," replied the lawyer.

The old gentleman looked the detective over from head to foot.

"I have heard much of you, friend," he said in a soft, impressive tone. "They say you are very expert."

"I have had much experience, sir."

"So I am told. This case of ours is, however, peculiar. Do you know at all what it is?"

"I told you that he did not," flashed Podmore, looking much annoyed.

"Peace, Brother Podmore," replied the Mormon elder, raising his hand. "This is unseemly. You know my position in the church, I believe."

Podmore subsided.

"This man is surely one of the leading Mormon lights," Old King Brady said to himself, adding aloud:

"Mr. Podmore has told me nothing of the case, sir."

"Very good. You have been supplied with a retainer?"

"I have."

"In what amount?" {15}

"Two thousand dollars."

"It is well."

"You utterly repudiate your allegiance to Senator Truesdell?"

Old King Brady bowed assent.

He hardly dared trust himself to speak.

That the Mormon elder was a man of iron determination was plain to be seen.

His eyes seemed to pierce Old King Brady's inmost soul.

Podmore stood by, silent and awed-looking.

It was easy to see that he was horribly afraid of the man.

Old King Brady would have given much to know who he was, but as no introduction had been made, he did not dare to ask for one.

He could only stand by and await the outcome of his strange interview.

"It is well," the Mormon elder repeated. "You will now proceed with your work. Do you see that door facing you?"

"I do, sir."

"Pass through it, please. Brother Podmore, you will accompany the gentleman."

Every trace of color left Podmore's face.

"Brother, what does this mean?" he asked.

"Brother Podmore! Brother Podmore! You really surprise me!" said the elder, blandly. "Never before have I known you to question my will."

"But—" began Podmore, when the elder checked him by a wave of the hand.

"Since you insist upon an explanation of my motive, I will give it," he said. "I wish you to be present while this gentleman is being instructed. That is all, Brother Podmore. This business concerns you as much as it does me. Is it strange that I ask your assistance in starting right on these inquiries?"

"I am ready to obey, Brother," Podmore replied.

"Stop a moment," said the elder. "Brother Podmore, I desire to ask you a question. I observe something missing about your personal apparel—something which should be in its place, but is not."

Podmore clapped his hand to his watch-chain.

"It's the jewel," thought Old King Brady.

"It is gone, Brother," said Podmore. "I should have told you I lost it during my trip east. I have ordered another made."

"That is very unfortunate, Brother Podmore. Have you duly notified the council?"

"I have not, brother. I have been very much occupied since my return to Salt Lake City, as you know."

"Still you should have found time for a matter so important; but I will not undertake to discipline you. Let us now proceed with our work. Gentlemen, the door."

Old King Brady opened the door and saw beyond a little room without windows, and bare of furniture, save for a table and two chairs.

He passed in, Podmore following him.

He closed the door behind him, and sitting on the edge of the table, whispered:

"Mr. Brady, I do not like the tone of that man nor the look of things here. I shall depend upon you to stand by me in case—Ah, heavens! Lost! Lost!"

Suddenly a false partition, papered to match the walls of the little room, dropped from the ceiling, striking the floor with a thud.

"What is this? Treachery?" cried Old King Brady. "Does it mean that we are prisoners here?"

"Hush! Hush, for heaven's sake!" gasped Podmore. "Our lives depend upon your coolness! It means death!"

Chapter VII.
Grace.

Young King Brady swam ashore and dressed himself as quickly as possible.

Never had Harry done harder thinking than he did just then.

"That was the senator's daughter, of course," said he to himself. "If I could only rescue her and take her to the Wells House, the Mormons would hardly dare to interfere with her. It is a big chance, and I am going to make a try for it, hit or miss."

Equally as bold as his great chief, Young King Brady had determined upon a scheme which, had he been more familiar with life in Salt Lake City, he would scarcely have dared to undertake.

He was going to try to play Mormon.

It was running an awful risk.

While dressing behind the rocks, Harry had been slyly keeping his eyes on the gate as a matter of course.

Thus, when it opened and one of the two men who had seized Grace Truesdell slipped out and hurried toward the city, Harry saw him go.

"It leaves only one to deal with," he said to himself. "I don't believe there is anyone else in there. If I'm not equal to one of those old jays I should like to know the reason why."

Having finished dressing, Young King Brady skirted along the lake shore until he was well beyond the house behind the wall.

Then going upon the road, he crossed over to the opposite side and walked briskly back toward the gate.

Reaching it, he paused, and after listening a moment, gave three thunderous knocks and calmly awaited the result.

Now Yo[u]ng King Brady had not come unprepared.

As it happened, he had a split ring in his pocketbook, and by the aid of his knife he had contrived to detach the jewel from the bit of broken chain, and fastening it to the split ring, he attached it to the new watch chain.

"We will see what sort of business that jewel will do {16} for me," he said to himself. "That man can't possibly be a person of much intelligence or he would not have been chosen for such dirty work."

There was no response to the knock for a few moments.

Listening intently, Harry was just about to knock again when he heard heavy footsteps behind the gate, and it was presently opened by the man he expected to see.

He started back at the sight of a stranger, and stood staring for an instant.

"Well, what do you want here?" he demanded gruffly.

"Brother," said Young King Brady, "I have been sent to question your prisoner about certain private matters which concern only the church. I want to come in."

"My prisoner!" replied the Mormon, looking black. "I don't know what you mean."

"I think you do, brother. I refer to Senator Truesdell's daughter, who was brought here a short time ago. I need not tell you who by. You know perfectly well."

"I have no authority to admit anyone into this house," replied the man, "least of all a stranger. This is church property, as you must be aware. I am only the caretaker. I know nothing of what you say."

"Probably you want my authority, brother."

"I certainly should want it if what you say was true."

"Behold it then," said Harry, pointing impressively to the jewel on his watch chain.

Evidently the man had not seen the jewel until now.

He gave a quick start, and looked sharply at Young King Brady.

"To what does that symbol refer?" he asked.

"Need I tell you that it is the jewel of the order of the Golden Lion of Judah?"

"Can you, so young, be a member of the order of the Golden Lion?"

"I not only can be, but am. How otherwise could I have the jewel?"

"Your name?"

"My name is Miller."

"Ah! One of the Millers of Provo?"

"Now you begin to wake up. It is about time. Come, I don't propose to stand here in the road waiting for you to get sense into your head. Either let me in and conduct me to Senator Truesdell's daughter, so that I may deliver my message, or I will return to Brother Podmore, who sent me, and report your conduct. I presume you know what to expect?"

The man turned pale. "You will have to come in, I suppose," he said. "If I am making a mistake, I—but no matter. Follow me."

Young King Brady passed through the gate, which was immediately closed behind him, and secured by a heavy wooden bar.

Harry saw the full front of the old Mormon house then.

It had nine doors in a row, and he understood why the depth of the wall was so great.

The Mormon who had formerly occupied the house had had nine wives, and there were nine suites of apartments altogether, one connecting with each door.

"What is your name, brother?" Harry asked.

"Simon Sellers," was the short reply.

Having consented to do as Young King Brady requested, the man evidently did not think himself required to go any further.

In perfect silence he led the way to the ninth door, and opening it with a big iron key, pointed down the long hallway.

"Is she locked in there?" asked Harry.

"There is no lock except on this door," was the reply.

"Do you propose to lock it behind me?"

"I do. Such are my orders."

"And when I want to get out?"

"Knock twice."

"Enough. I shall probably not be very long."

The door was slammed behind him.

Through the hall, which was lighted only by a skylight overhead, Harry hurried.

He soon came to a door upon which he knocked.

"Why don't you come in?" cried a woman's voice. "You put me here. If you choose to enter I can't stop you. Come in and make no fuss."

Harry opened the door and found himself in the presence of the girl.

She started back as he stood on the threshold, bowing.

"You're a new one!" she cried. "What do you want here?"

"To have a few words with you, Miss Grace Truesdell," replied Harry. "I come as a friend. You will do well to confide in me. Brady is my name."

"Ah! You are one of the Bradys of New York?"

"I am."

"The younger of the two detectives my father employed?"

"Just so. Shall I enter and shut the door, so that we need not be overheard, or shall I go away?"

"Come right in," said the girl in a whisper. "Shut the door. Keep your back against it, so that we need not be surprised. Speak as low as possible. There are spies everywhere in this dreadful house, I don't doubt."

Harry obeyed.

He saw that Grace Truesdell was not only a very beautiful girl, but a most intelligent one.

"I'm thankful I have not got to deal with a fool," he said to himself. "That's one good thing."

"How did you get in here? How did you know I was here?" Grace hurriedly asked.

"I saw you when you were captured. No matter how. I worked my way in. Detectives don't like to tell their methods. Enough to say I heard your appeal, and here I am in answer."

"To help me to escape?"

"Nothing else."

"Thank heaven, and thank you, but you do not know the awful risk you run." {17}

"I can guess. Do you want to escape and return to your father, or do other ties hold you here?"

"I have no other ties, Mr. Brady. My one desire is to return to my father."

"But your mother?"

"My mother is dead. She breathed her last this morning in the house of John Jones, the Mormon Apostle."

The name we have given is not the name spoken by Grace Truesdell.

For obvious reasons that cannot be mentioned in this story. Enough to say that it was the name of the old gentleman to whose house Old King Brady was taken by Mr. Podmore, and we need only add that he is a man standing high in the councils of the Latter Day Saints.

"Indeed! Is it so?" replied Young King Brady. "How did it occur?"

"If you ask me what I know, I can tell you—nothing; if you ask me what I believe I shall have to say that I have not the least doubt that my mother was poisoned."

"Horrible! How dreadfully you must feel."

"Waste no time talking of that. My mother was a wicked woman. She treated my father shamefully. She would have sold me to the Mormons. Why should I regret her? There is no reason and I am no hypocrite. I am glad she is dead."

"That's enough. I have no more to say. May I ask, however, why you came west with her, knowing all this?"

"Because I was drugged and did not know what I was doing."

"Ah. By whom?"

"My mother."

"For the purpose of marrying you to Joseph Smith Podmore?"

"No; there never was any such intention, although I believed otherwise. The plan was to marry me to Dick Jones, the Apostle's son, who is my first cousin on my mother's side."

"Ah! The young man who drove you out here?"

"Yes."

"And you refused?"

"Utterly refused."

"And yet you rode with him."

"I had to. I could not help myself. Don't ask me to explain now, Mr. Brady. Later I may tell you all. You came here by my father's orders to find out if Podmore was married to one or more wives?"

"Such was part of my business."

"I can settle the question. He is not a married man. The church, contrary to their usual custom, has allowed him to remain unmarried in order that he could be elected to Congress and no charge of having many wives brought against him."

"You know this?"

"I had it from his own lips, and also from Apostle Jones."

"Can you believe either?"

"Well, it is perhaps true that neither can be believed, but I believe it. You are wasting time here. I shall never marry Podmore. If you want to save my father, free me from this house, get me out of Salt Lake City, take me home."

"There is one thing more, Miss. Your father was robbed by his wife."

"The Mormon Church has got the money; it never can be recovered."

"He does not care for the money. It is his private letter-book he wants."

"My mother took that?"

"Yes."

"I know nothing about it."

"Then it is not necessary to talk any further. You are willing to put yourself under my protection and go away with me?"

"I am if you can prove to me that you are actually Young King Brady, the detective, and not a Mormon spy."

"You must have believed that when I came in or you would not have talked to me as you have."

"I did believe it. Now I feel as though nothing was certain. Can you give me the proof I ask?"

"Easily. Look here."

Young King Brady threw back the lapel of his coat and displayed the shield.

"That is enough. Now, how do you propose to go?"

"Through the passage. I will knock on the door and if the Mormon on guard there tries to stop us I propose to knock him down and tie his hands behind him."

"He may prove too much for you."

"Then there is a better way. I have a revolver; you shall take it and hold him covered while I tie his hands."

"I can do that; and if both ways fail?"

"We will wait till that happens before we consider it."

"Good. Let me have the revolver, Mr. Brady, and we will go."

"She's just the sort of a girl I like," thought Harry. "Prompt, up to date, right in it all the time. Well, this will be great news for the governor, but he will want to stop and investigate Mrs. Truesdell's death, I am afraid. Meanwhile who is to watch this girl?"

They walked along the passage to its end.

Here Grace cocked the revolver and held it behind her while Young King Brady struck twice upon the door.

There was no answer.

After waiting a moment the detective tried it again.

Still no answer, and the third time he tried it the same silence followed the knock.

"Well?" demanded Grace.

"You see how it is," replied Harry. "Either he has gone away and left us prisoners here or he does not intend to open the door."

Grace uncocked the revolver and handed it back.

"There is another way out, Mr. Brady, if you have the courage to try it," she said.

"What! You know a way?" Harry cried.

"I do." {18}

"What is it? Why did you not—"

"Why did I not use it myself? Because I dared not do it alone."

"But with me to back you up?"

"I do dare," replied Grace, "but it is only right that I should tell you that it may lead us to our death."

CHAPTER VIII.
THE BROTHERS OF THE GOLDEN LION.

Old King Brady had started out to get next to Mr. Podmore, and he had certainly succeeded with a vengeance.

They were now both in the same boat, and a very bad boat it appeared to be, if the expression of abject terror upon the face of the Mormon lawyer meant anything at all.

"What is to be done, Mr. Podmore?" asked the old detective with all the calmness he could command.

"You must help me. You have my money, Brady. It is up to you."

"Are we really in such danger?"

"We certainly are."

"And this is all as unexpected to you as to me?"

"If you will only believe me, such is the case."

"Very well; then take back your money, Mr. Podmore. I want none of it. I only took it to help along my plans."

"Then you were playing it on me?"

"Draw your own conclusions, sir. You may be a rich man, but I am rich also. Two thousand dollars cuts no figure with me."

Mr. Podmore accepted the money and put it in his pocket.

"I trust you are not going to desert me," he said. "You are my last hope."

"Mr. Podmore, let us talk sense," said the old detective. "What do you fear? Death at the hands of the Mormon church?"

"Yes."

"And you intended that it should come to me alone? Be honest, if you want my help?"

"Since you put it that way I will not deny it—yes."

"Exactly so! I see I have made a mistake. I believed that you actually needed my help."

"Believe me in one thing, Brady. I acted under orders. For me to have refused to obey them would have meant death."

"Enough, sir. We understand each other. How much time have we got?"

"Impossible to say. It may be hours. It may be only minutes before—"

"Well, before what?"

"Before the church gets ready to act."

"And can nothing be done in the meantime?"

"Nothing whatever."

"Then where does my help come in?"

"Heaven help us both! I really don't know!"

"Is there no way out of here?"

"Try the walls and see for yourself."

Old King Brady struck against the walls all around the room.

"Solid iron," he muttered. "Well, this is certainly a bad job."

Turning toward Podmore, he coolly seated himself on the table and lit a cigar.

"Let us smoke and think," he said. "Have one?"

Mr. Podmore accepted the cigar, but his hand trembled so that he could scarcely light it.

"Why do they want to kill you?" Old King Brady asked.

"For two reasons, I suppose."

"Will you name them?"

"I have persistently refused to marry. Being a great-grandson of Joseph Smith, the founder of the Mormon religion, this has given great offence."

"Then you are not married?"

"I swear to you that I am not. This is a good time to tell the truth, Mr. Brady, and I am telling it now."

"Yet you proposed to marry Grace Truesdell?"

"That was only a blind. I wanted to get the girl to Utah and the mother, too."

"And you succeeded. Where are they now?"

"Don't ask me, Mr. Brady."

"But I must know."

Podmore dropped his voice to a whisper.

"Well, then, know," he replied. "The old woman is dead and the girl has been turned over to the tender mercies of Dick Jones, the son of that old scoundrel outside. He has her imprisoned in a house on the outskirts of the city, and he proposes to make her his fourth wife."

And right here, we may as well mention that Podmore gave the true name of the Mormon apostle.

For a moment Old King Brady sat on the table, puffing out rings of smoke, and made no reply.

He knew his full danger now.

This was to be another of those cases of mysterious disappearances which often take place in Salt Lake City.

To tell the truth, the detective saw but little hope.

"You have not mentioned the second reason why the church desires to put you out of the way, Mr. Podmore," he presently said.

"No, and I cannot do it," replied Podmore. "I am a Mormon, Mr. Brady. I am bound by many oaths. I believe in the doctrines of the church. If—er—if I have incurred its displeasure they have a right to kill me. I will not betray their secrets, but all the same, I am not prepared to die."

"Who is? If you would tell me the whole story I might see some way of getting out of this fix."

"It would do no good. I fear nothing can help us."

"Take no such despairing view of the situation. I am armed, and I propose to fight for my life. Tell me, how did Mrs. Truesdell die?"

"I cannot." {19}

"She was a Mormon?"

"Yes; at least she was the sister of the eighth wife of the man you met outside."

"Ha! Then this young man you spoke of is the girl's first cousin?"

"He is."

"Was Mrs. Truesdell married before to a Mormon husband?"

"Yes, since you are bound to know."

"He is dead?"

"Long since."

"I am reading your mind, Mr. Podmore. The woman was something to you."

"You will pump me," said the lawyer desperately. "She was my father's third wife. I am the child of the second one. Under the Mormon law it would have been impossible for me to have married Grace Truesdell."

"Then why the pretence? Why the bargain you tried to make with the senator? What does it all mean?"

"I will not tell you further than this: Mrs. Truesdell had decided to return to the fold of the Mormon church, which she deserted at the time of her second marriage. She wished to bring her daughter with her, and she succeeded at last to her cost."

"She was killed by order of the church?"

"I have nothing to say further than that she was taken suddenly ill in this house and died."

"When?"

"Yesterday."

"Then what you said about me getting her confession was all pretence?"

"Yes. Will you let up on the questions? I cannot and will not answer another one."

"I know enough for the present," said Old King Brady. "I will question you no more, sir, except in regard to our own affairs. What is the particular fate you fear?"

"It is the judgment of a certain secret order to which I belong. The Golden Lion of Judah."

"You have betrayed their secrets?"

"I hold a secret which they want me to betray to them, and when it is told I meet my doom."

"Bless my soul, man!" exclaimed the detective. "Then you are all right! All you have to do is to hold your tongue."

"Do you remember what I told you of secret mines, Mr. Brady?"

"I do, indeed. Was it true?"

"Only too true."

"And that will be your fate if you refuse to tell?"

"It may be my fate anyhow. I had rather be dead."

"Well, you Mormons are certainly a queer people," remarked Old King Brady, knocking the ashes off his cigar.

"We are a law unto ourselves, sir. I thought myself sufficiently powerful to defy the Mormon law, fool that I was! I now know that no Mormon can safely do that."

"Hark! Didn't I hear a sound over in that corner?"

"Heaven preserve us! You did. Our time has come!"

It was a hard, grating sound, like someone trying to move a rusty bolt.

"Where is it?" breathed Old King Brady; "do you know?"

"No!" was the whispered reply. "This house is honeycombed with secret passages. It is as likely to be in one part of the room as another. Can't you tell?"

"I can't locate it; the sound is not immediately under the floor, but deep down somewhere. Ha, they have shot the bolt now! Who will they be?"

"Prepare for masked men. They answer the same purpose as the old Danites. Conceal your revolver and don't think of trying to use it now. It will do not a bit of good. Later on it may."

Old King Brady made no reply.

Besides his revolver he had a pair of tiny derringers, which he sometimes carried to use on emergency. These he felt sure they would not find.

Other sounds were now heard.

They appeared to be behind the partition wall on the right.

Suddenly a narrow strip of the wall slid away out of sight, and a masked figure stepped into the room, plainly seen by the light which descended overhead.

It wore a long black robe, which descended to the floor, completely covering the form.

Over the head a queer pointed cap, like a fool's cap, was drawn. There were openings for the eyes and mouth, but other than these the whole head was concealed.

Upon the breast was embroidered in yellow silk the representation of a lion.

As the figure stepped through the opening it extend[e]d its right hand, and pointing at the lawyer, said in a sepulchral voice:

"Joseph Smith Podmore, thou hast proved unfaithful to thine oath! Behold the brothers of the lion! Look and ponder, for thy time has come."

With an inarticulate cry Podmore threw up his hands and sank fainting to the floor.

Old King Brady, still seated on the table, blew rings from his cigar, and swinging his legs, looked contemptuously at the mask.

Now it stepped forward into the room, and another and another still, glided through the opening until there were six—all attired in the same way.

All thought of present resistance left the detective's mind. There was nothing to do but to submit to whatever mandate the brotherhood of the Golden Lion might put forward.

The six stood pointing their fingers at Old King Brady, but never uttered a word.

"Say, gentlemen," remarked the detective, getting tired of the silence at last, "what's the use of all this monkey business? Why don't you come down to tacks?"

"Cease, ribald jester!" spoke the first mask. "You do not seem to understand." {20}

"The use of this ridiculous masquerading? I confess I don't. Why don't you show your faces like men?"

"We are not men. We are the slaves of the Golden Lion," the voice replied.

"Upon my word, I believe you," said the detective. "You act like slaves. If you were men you would be ashamed of yourselves. State your business here."

"Who are you, Gentile, to command one of the true faith?"

"True faith be hanged. I've got nothing to do with your faith. State what you propose to do with me, and be quick about it, too."

"Your fate will be settled by higher powers. Stand on your feet!"

"Why certainly. Anything to oblige. What's the next order, friend[?] I like to see something doing, even if it don't just suit me. Come, spit it out."

"Man," said the mask, "beware! For every ribald word you utter you will be made to pay dearly. Empty your pockets on that table."

"And if I refuse, what then?"

Instantly the six hands were thrust into the breast of the black gowns and six revolvers covered the old detective.

Podmore, who had recovered his senses by this time, was now on his knees, his lips moving as though in prayer.

"Put them up," said Old King Brady. "There is no need. I will do as you wish."

He placed a few of his belongings on the table—all that he felt would probably be discovered in case he was searched.

The two revolvers were among the rest, and also a knife.

The mask who had spoken now strode forward and ran his hands over the detective's clothes.

"I see but a small sum of money here," he said. "There was $2,000 to come. Where is that?"

"I have no more money," Old King Brady replied.

"Gentile, thou liest!" cried the mask. "Produce the money or—"

"Or thou diest, I suppose you were going to say," broke in the detective. "I should like to ever so much, but I really haven't got it."

"It is useless to press him, Brother!" put in Podmore. "I have the $2,000. He gave it to me."

"Rise and lay it on the table with any more you may have," was the reply." Empty your pockets of everything they contain at the same time."

Podmore obeyed.

He appeared to have plucked up some little courage and to be in a measure prepared to meet his fate.

There was no search made after this, much to Old King Brady's relief.

The mask nearest the secret panel now turned and blew a whistle through the opening.

Immediately there was more noise and confusion below, a rattling of ropes, and other queer sounds.

This was explained in a moment by the rising of a little elevator sent up by somebody from below.

"Enter!" said the talking mask. "Brother, you lead the way."

"Stay!" replied Podmore; "may I make one appeal?"

"Not to us. You well know how useless it would be."

"But why proceed further if I am willing to yield?"

"I have nothing to do with your affairs, brother, either one way or the other. Will you obey, or shall we force obedience—which?"

Without saying anything further, Podmore passed through the panel and stood upon the elevator, where Old King Brady joined him.

Two of the masks followed.

As there was room for no more, the whistle was blown and the elevator descended.

"What is to [be] my fate?" thought Old King Brady. "As Podmore says, the Mormon arm is far reaching! Am I going to my death?"

Chapter IX.
Caught in a Trap.

"Miss Truesdell, if you know of any way of escape, of course I am entirely at your service," said Young King Brady. "Tell me what to do."

"Let us return to the room and I will explain," said Grace.

And while they were walking through the long passage she went on to say:

"Mr. Brady, you must know that my mother was brought up a Mormon, and that in this house, as the ninth wife of the man who built it one of her sisters formerly lived. In nearly all Mormon houses there are secrets, and this one was no exception. Beneath it lies a secret passage to the lake, but the trouble is the entrance is not from the room in which you found me, but from the apartments of the eighth wife, which we are passing now."

"That's bad!" exclaimed Harry. "Can we get into them?"

"I think so," was the reply. "I am going to tell you a secret which my mother told me."

"Suppose we stand where we are while you tell it. I fear spies. In the room there would be a better chance to get in their fine work."

"You are right. What I have to say can be told in a few words: My mother's Mormon husband was a Podmore, the father of the man you know. He stood away up in the church, and was the leader of the secret order of the Golden Lion of Judah. He built this house and lived in it for many years.

"Of course, you know, Mr. Brady, that while these Mormons are very pleasant people to meet and are honest and upright upon all ordinary occasions, when it comes to a {21} case where the interests of the church are at stake they stop at nothing to gain their ends.

"As leader of the order of the lion, Mr. Podmore, the elder, had occasion to do many things which we would think questionable, but which in his eyes were all right. To help him out in this sort of business he had a secret passage built from this house over to the lake shore, where there are some large rocks—perhaps you may know the place?"

"I do. I was there to-day," replied Young King Brady. "I noticed an opening between two of the larger rocks, but I never imagined that it led anywhere."

"No doubt that is the place. My mother told me how to find the secret panel in the apartments of the eighth wife, which opened into this passage, and she told me how to get into these apartments, but to lift the trap door was beyond my strength. I tried it just before you came and failed."

"If that is all that stands in the way I guess we can manage it," said Harry; "but look here, you spoke of death and danger; what did you mean by that?"

"That is just what I am coming to. In addition to this secret passage there is another opening from it which leads to the secret meeting place of the order of the Golden Lion. The door connecting with that passage opens readily enough from this side, but once you have passed through it closes behind you automatically and cannot be opened from the other side unless you know the secret spring. This leaves the one who is unfortunate enough to get into it by mistake no alternative but to go on to the secret lodge room, to enter which means death for anyone not a member of the order."

"Indeed. Well there lies the risk. Do you know anything more about this order?"

"No. My mother knew nothing of it, more than the fact of its existence. No woman ever can."

Young King Brady determined to say nothing about the jewel of the lion.

It is one of the rules of the Bradys never to talk unnecessarily about their affairs.

"I think I understand the situation now," he said. "We will push on into the room and see what can be done. From what you tell me there should be no trouble in making our escape."

"Just a moment," breathed Grace, laying her hand upon his arm. "Did it not seem to you that someone was moving about behind that partition a second ago?"

"I did hear a slight noise, but I moved my foot just then. I thought I had trodden on a creaking board."

"It may have been that, but—"

"You don't think so?"

"It is not what I think, Mr. Brady, but what I fear. If you knew as much about the Mormons as I know, you would fear too. But let us go on. We want to act while there is still time."

They returned to the room and closed the door.

"Now for the trap door," remarked Harry, looking around.

The room was plainly furnished, and had evidently been the parlor or sitting room of the suite.

There was a heavy rag carpet on the floor, plaited together in the old style.

Grace pulled back one corner of this carpet, and disclosed a big iron ring, sunk deep in the floor.

"Yes, yes!" exclaimed Harry. "I guess we can manage that all right."

"It is very heavy, Mr. Brady. My mother explained to me that it is weighted on the under side, and that when you raise it you raise a corresponding trap in the next apartment.["]

"Made heavy, so that a woman can't raise it, I suppose," said Harry. "But let me try. I think I can manage it all right."

He raised the ring, and bracing his feet on the floor, pulled with all his strength.

The next thing Young King Brady knew the trap door stood open, and he lay sprawling on his back upon the carpet.

There had been no resistance.

Harry sprang on his feet, looking rather ashamed.

"Oh, I do hope you are not hurt, Mr. Brady!" cried Grace.

"Not in the least; but look here, there was no resistance at all to that thing."

"There is something very strange about it. I just could not move it."

"Looks like a put-up job."

"Do you think so?"

"You can see for yourself. Here is the staple to which the chain connecting with the other trap door has been attached. No doubt it was there when you tried to pull it up. We must be very careful. Let me go ahead alone."

"Indeed I will not. I started you in on this thing, and I propose to see you through with it. We will go together. Mr. Brady, do you suppose I can forget that it is on my account you are here in Salt Lake City? If there is secret work to be done it is only right that I should take my share of it. Now, let us go."

"She's the sort of girl I like," thought Harry. "I only wish there were more of her kind."

He now produced his little electric dark lantern and descended the short ladder, followed by Grace.

It took them down to a narrow passage, running under the partition wall at the end of which there was another ladder leading up to another trap door, which Young King Brady was able to push up with one hand.

They now found themselves in the apartments of the eighth wife. The room was plainly furnished in similar style to the one they had left, and the instant they entered it a discovery was made.

A narrow panel in the papered wall stood open.

"There you are!" exclaimed Young King Brady. "Is that your way out, Miss Truesdell?"

"It certainly is," replied Grace. "Somebody has opened it for us. What can this mean?" {22}

"Well, it may have been left so by accident. It may be a trap to catch us. Who can tell?"

"What shall we do?"

"The very best thing for you to do is to stay here and allow me to go ahead and investigate."

"But that I won't do, Mr. Brady, as I told you before."

"Very well; then we will secure this panel so that it can't possibly shut, and both of us shall go ahead; that is the next best thing. Step through. I will hold it. Wait a moment; let me get a chair."

Grace passed through the panel and Harry followed her, placing the chair in the opening, so that the panel could not close.

It did not move, however, and the precaution apparently was not needed.

Behind the panel was a narrow stairway, leading down.

"You are sure you are right?" asked Harry. "There were not two panels in this room?"

"I don't think so," replied Grace; "but really it is a long time since my mother told me the story of this house. Mr. Brady, I don't want to mislead you. I cannot be sure."

Harry pondered for a moment, and then decided to push on.

"We have to take chances," he said. "Now, what direction are we to take to avoid the passage which leads to the lodge of the lion?"

"We are to keep to the left when we come to two doors side by side, as I remember it."

"Again you are not sure?"

"Oh, yes; I am very sure it is the left."

Harry had his doubts, but he said no more.

Taking the chair with him to brace the door of the passage when they came to it, he passed on down the stairs and entered a narrow boarded way, leading in the direction of the lake.

Passing on, closely followed by Grace, for about half the distance across the road, as nearly as he could judge, they came upon two narrow doors set side by side, blocking the way.

"Well, here we are," said Harry. "Now it is the left hand door!"

"As I told you," Grace replied.

"There seems to be no latch or knob or anything; well, it is not needed. This thing pushes open easily enough. Pass on."

The door seemed to be set on invisible swing hinges. Harry held it back with one hand, and passing through, placed the chair against it.

"There; that will keep it from closing on us," he said. "Let us hurry on and if we find we are going wrong we can come right back and try the other door."

The passage was boarded up the same as before, and seemed to lead straight to the lake.

A hundred feet would decide the question, and Young King Brady, going ahead with his lantern, quickly covered it, but the passage continued straight on.

"This won't do, Miss Truesdell," said Young King Brady. "We ought to be at the end now."

"I know it," Grace replied, nervously. "Oh, Mr. Brady, let us go back! Perhaps, after all, I was wrong and it was the right hand door."

"We will try it a little further. I don't want to return here. We will make sure."

They advanced another hundred feet, but still the passage did not end, and Harry felt sure that it was gradually turning.

"It won't do," he said, stopping short. "We are surely going wrong."

"I admit," replied Grace. "We must get back at once."

Turning, they hurriedly retraced their steps.

Now Young King Brady began to regret that he had attempted to follow the passage at all.

He was thinking of what Grace had said about the door.

If it was closed, what then?

There would be but one conclusion to draw, and that was that they had been spied upon from the first, and every word uttered by Grace overheard.

A moment settled it.

The door was closed, and the chair stood on the inside.

"Oh, Mr. Brady, what have I done?" gasped Grace, sinking down upon it.

Harry put his hand upon the door.

It was fast.

Throwing himself against it with all his force, still it would not yield.

Again and again he tried it, but it remained as firm as a rock.

"You can't open it!" gasped Grace.

"I'm afraid I can't," replied Harry.

"And it is all my fault. We are in the passage leading to the lodge of the lion."

"It can mean nothing else."

"Nothing else! Oh, Mr. Brady, I am so sorry. I am afraid it is all over with us. It does mean something else. It means death."

Chapter X.
Old King Brady in the Lion's Den.

It [sic] its way Old King Brady's situations were worse than Harry's.

He was actually in the hands of the brotherhood of the order of the Golden Lion of Judah, while his partner had simply fallen into a trap, perhaps prepared for him, by the brotherhood, and perhaps by someone else.

The elevator continued to descend until it reached a depth of perhaps fifteen feet, when it stopped and Old King Brady and Podmore were ordered to step off.

They now found themselves in a small room, where two other masked men stood waiting for them. {23}

The spokesman in the room above, who had come down with them, did the talking still.

"Send up the elevator to bring down the brothers," he ordered, and the command was instantly obeyed.

Not until all were present did he speak again, and he then said:

"Brother Podmore, you are now about to retire from the world. As you are a man of affairs it is probable you may have some instructions which you would like to give regarding your business and the disposition of your property. Is it not so?"

"Brother, it is so," replied Podmore, who had assumed a much bolder front than Old King Brady had supposed possible with such a man.

"May I ask a few questions before we proceed?" he added.

"It is your privilege, brother. Of course, you understand that your case is quite different from that of this detective, and that one line of action will be pursued in your case and another in his?"

"I understand. Is this action against me brought by the direct orders o[f] our exalted ruler?"

"Brother, it is."

"Shall I be brought before him for judgment or have I been already judged in secret council?"

"You have already been judged, brother."

"Then from that judgment there can be no appeal?"

"None; but permit me to remind you that you do not yet know the nature of the judgment rendered."

"Then there is hope?"

"That I cannot say."

"Am I to know the charge against me?"

"That I cannot say."

"Where is judgment to be executed?"

"That I cannot say[.]"

"Am I to be taken before the altar of penitence?"

"I am so informed."

"Then, brother, as life is sweet to all of us, may I ask you to plead my cause with the high exalted ruler? May I ask that you request him to meet me at the altar and hear my plea? May I ask for the word of mercy, and for three witnesses, in the name of my revered ancestor, our holy prophet, and in the name of the church of the Latter Day Saints?"

"Brother," said the mask, solemnly, "I have known you from boyhood. I knew your father before you. I will speak the word of mercy. I, even I, will be one of the three witnesses. It is for you to find the other two."

"And in the name of mercy I thank you, brother," replied Podmore, his voice trembling.

He then kneeled before the mask, and kissed the hem of his black robe and remained kneeling, his lips moving in prayer.

It was a solemn moment.

All the masks bowed their heads and prayed with him, but the prayer was silent, and Old King Brady could not hear a word.

The spokesman, then extending his hand, lifted Podmore up.

"Rise, brother!" he cried. "Call for your witness, and may your prayer be answered."

Raising both hands, throwing his head back and rolling his eyes, Podmore shouted:

"In the name of the holy prophet, Joseph Smith! In the name of our most holy church! In the name of the Golden Lion of Judah! I call for a witness to speak for me in this, mine hour of distress!"

One of the masks stepped forward and solemnly raised his hand.

"In the name of all that thou hast invoked, brother, I will be thy witness!" he said, "and may our high exalted ruler show mercy to thy suffering soul!"

The mask stepped back, and the spokesman, stepping forward, uttered the same formula.

Then Podmore, throwing up his hands again, repeated his words.

This time there was no response.

Three times Podmore repeated the appeal, but in vain.

"You see, brother," said the spokesman, "there remains but one hope. If our high exalted ruler, meeting you at the altar, himself consents to be your witness, you may yet be saved. How little chance there is of that you well know. Therefore, I can do nothing but speak the word of brotherly coun[se]l and advise you by silent prayer to prepare to meet your doom."

Podmore's head sank upon his breast, and he groaned deeply.

"Bring paper and pen," he said, recovering himself after a moment. "I will write my instructions. That done, let me not delay the proceedings of this council further."

"It is well," replied the spokesman.

Paper, pen and ink were then brought from an adjoining room, together with a small desk and a chair.

It took Podmore some fifteen minutes to write out all he had to say.

In the meantime Old King Brady stood motionless and silent.

He felt that nothing he could say or do could possibly be of any use.

The paper written was folded up and handed to the spokesman.

"Proceed," said Podmore, stepping back beside the detective.

[F]our of the brothers now left the room, and presently returned, carrying with them two curiously shaped packing boxes.

They were low, and semi-circular in form.

The lids were removed and the spokesman sternly ordered Old King Brady to lie down in one of them.

The situation was hopeless. The detective could only obey.

The lid was then placed upon the box, and screwed firmly down. {24}

Now Old King Brady perceived that there were holes in the side of the box which gave him all the air he needed.

The sounds told him that Podmore was being served in the same way as himself.

As the detective lay there, wondering what was going to happen next, he began to catch the odor of ether.

"Do they intend to put me out of business so?" he thought. "Well, at least they are merciful in that. I was mad to undertake secret work in Salt Lake City. I might have known!"

Slowly unconsciousness crept over him.

The last Old King Brady remembered he was listening to what seemed like the ringing of a hundred silver bells, while before his eyes flashed a vision of a beautiful garden, filled with the fairest flowers.

Even then he knew what was happening to him. He kept his senses until at last came a moment when all sensibility was suddenly blotted out.

The next he knew he found himself lying upon a bed in a close, airless cell, without a window. The walls about him were of stone, and in front was an iron door with an opening guarded by heavy bars at the top.

"Thus begins chapter two," muttered Old King Brady, sitting up on the bed. "Thank heaven, I am still in the land of the living. While there is life there is hope."

The cell was not entirely dark. Somewhere outside a light was burning which penetrated between the bars.

"I'm all here," muttered the detective, feeling in his secret pockets. "Yes, and the derringers are here, too, thank goodness. Well, they may come in handy yet, and there is my hat lying over in the corner. Good! Whoever I come up against next will have the pleasure of seeing Old King Brady as he ought to be."

He put on his hat and started to pace the cell.

Probably half an hour was spent in this fashion, when footsteps were heard outside and a face appeared at the grating.

"Well, brother, I am here," said the detective. "What is the next thing on the programme? What do you want with me now?"

"Call me not brother," replied the mask, a crude looking specimen, with a long red beard. "I am not of thy kind, nor art thou of mine. Do you hunger? Do you desire food?"

"Not just at present, thank you," replied the detective. "But I would like to know what is coming next."

"Restrain your curiosity. No information will be given you," replied the man, moving away.

There was another lapse of time, perhaps twenty minutes, and then the door was opened and the same man appeared.

"You will follow me, mister," he said, "and let me give you a piece of advice: Be almighty careful what you say or do."

Old King Brady silently obeyed.

His conductor led him through a long, narrow passage which appeared to have been cut through the loose disintegrated sandstone so common in this part of the Far West, and in a few moments they came to an iron door upon which he paused and knocked twice.

"Come in," someone called.

The detective now entered into what he saw at once was a natural cave.

It was of no great size, but there were other chambers evidently opening off of it, for there were four iron doors to the place.

In the middle of the chamber was something covered over with a heavy black cloth. Behind this, upon a sort of dias, raised by three steps, was a large chair, heavily gilded, with a silver shield having upon it a small golden lion, fastened behind it against the wall.

A man, masked as the others had been, sat upon the chair in solemn state. There was nobody else in the room.

And in spite of the mask, Old King Brady felt sure he knew him, for through an opening in the hood below a few straggling hairs of snowy whiteness protruded.

"This is the grand panjandrum himself," thought the detective, and as soon as the man spoke his suspicion was confirmed, for Old King Brady recognized the voice of the man to whose house he had been taken by Podmore.

"Leave us, brother," said Prophet Jones—we propose to give this Mormon the name which we have attached to him before—and Old King Brady's conductor immediately withdrew.

For several moments the mask sat in silence, his eyes peering through the holes in the hood at the detective.

It grew monotonous.

"Neighbor," said the detective, "far be it from me to hurry you at all, but don't you think, between ourselves, that this is getting slightly monotonous? If you have any business with me why not speak it out right now?"

"Mr. Brady," replied the mask, "I have business with you of the highest importance. I am studying your countenance. I am trying to determine what manner of man you really are."

"Well, sir, I am a man whose record is pretty well known."

"I am aware of that."

"I am no Mormon."

"That I am aware of also, but it is not too late for you to become one, and save your immortal soul."

"There I disagree with you. It is hard to teach an old dog new tricks."

"I know; I shall waste no time trying to convert you; my purpose for bringing you here was quite different. You have been a long time in the detective line?"

"A great many years."

"And during that time you have solved many mysteries?"

"So many that I can scarcely remember them all."

"I understand that you seldom fail."

"I have been very fortunate in my work, sir."

"Or skillful—which?"

"That is not for me to say." {25}

"But others have said it for you. Were it otherwise my friend, Senator Truesdell, would scarcely have engaged you to undertake secret work in Salt Lake City."

"We are still beating about the bush. Why not come to the point?"

"I will do so. I have sent for you because I desire your professional skill."

"Indeed, and in what line?"

"We must settle terms first. You are wholly in my power. I have only to raise my finger to bring about your death. Therefore, I advise you to think well before you answer my questions, and see to it that you answer them truly. I also advise you not to refuse to answer any of them if you desire to live."

"Put your questions. I pay little heed to threats."

"You are bold, but boldness becomes a man of your years and experience, therefore I do not lay it up against you. Who sent you here?"

"You know."

"There is no one back of Senator Truesdell in this business?"

"No one."

"You have been instructed by no one else?"

"By no one."

"It is well. Now state your business in Salt Lake City. Omit not one iota of your instructions, as you value your life."

It came hard with Old King Brady.

To give away his private business so was entirely against his principles, but there was clearly nothing else to be done, so he quickly told all and stood awaiting the result.

"You have spoken the truth," said Apostle Jones, "and it is well for you that you have done so, for now I feel that I can trust you. In course of your work have you ever dealt with secret ciphers, cryptograms and the like?"

"Many times."

"It is well. Now I will explain. Mrs. Truesdell, whom you met in Washington, was formerly one of us. She was born and bred a Mormon, and married a Mormon. Later she fled from this city with Truesd[e]ll, who at that time lived here, and pretended to be interested in our faith.

"This misguided woman's first husband was a Podmore, the father of the man you know. He was the treasurer of our tithing house, and at the time of his death and in his latter years betrayed the trust reposed in him. In short, he robbed us of a large sum of money, taken little by little. The man was miserly to excess. He loved money for money's sake. What he stole from the tithing house he did not spend, but hid, buried it in the ground. All this we did not know until very recently when the discovery of certain papers in the house formerly occupied by Podmore gave us the clew.

"From these papers we learned, no matter how, of the existence of a cryptogram which gave the secret of the hiding place of this stolen cash, and we learned also that Mrs. Truesdell had it in her possession, and was aware of what it meant.

"Now, Mr. Brady, this was our motive for sending Podmore's son east. He went to get the cryptogram, not to marry his half sister, as we call her, as her father supposed. He failed in his purpose, but he did succeed in persuading the woman to return with him to Salt Lake City. She tried to bargain with us, Mr. Brady, and in the midst of it she was seized with heart disease, and suddenly died, but not until we knew that Podmore had conspired with her to obtain this money for himself, to be divided with her. I have the cryptogram, taken from Podmore. I cannot read it. I can find no one among my people who can. I want you to try your hand at it, and if you succeed—"

The apostle paused and the gleaming eyes behind the mask fixed themselves upon Old King Brady again.

"Well?" said the detective. "And if I succeed?"

"You will be required to take an oath of absolute secrecy about all this business; you will be liberally rewarded and set free."

"And if I refuse?"

"Mr. Brady, there was a man in this town who yesterday tried to thwart my will. His name was Joseph Smith Podmore. Would you know his fate; then raise that cloth behind you and behold!"

Old King Brady turned, seized the cloth and tore it away.

There, with his arms resting upon an altar covered with yellow silk, and his head upon his hands, his body all in a heap, lay Podmore.

"Dead!" gasped Old King Brady.

"Dead," said the mask; "as dead as you will be if you refuse to obey my will."

Chapter XI.
Simon Sellers Goes Back on the Mormons.

Young King Brady leaned against the wall.

He had given up trying the door now, for he knew that it was no use.

"Don't despair, Miss Truesdell," he said; "after all, it may not prove so bad. There is always a way out of trouble, according to my experience, and perhaps we may find one out of this."

"I am afraid not," replied Grace, gloomily. "What troubles me most is not my own danger, but the fact that I was the means of leading you into danger. That I admit preys on my mind."

"Then don't give it another thought. I am a man of action. What we want to do is to act, not to sit moping here. I can't open that door. I am satisfied of that, so let us explore the passage and see what we can learn."

Grace sat silent for a long time, so silent that Harry almost thought she had swooned with her eyes open.

"Come, Mr. Brady," she said at last, "you are right. We will go. There may be a way out of this trouble, as you say." {26}

"That's the way to talk," replied Harry. "Now the first thing to do is to explore this passage to its end and see where it leads us. It may not be at all as you imagine. We will start now."

As they walked along the passage Harry did his best to cheer the girl up.

Passing the point where they had been before, Harry saw that the passage was turning rapidly.

Still following on, and watching a little pocket compass which he produced, he found that they were describing a circle.

When at last he came to an iron door, which barred further progress, he felt certain that they had come back under the old stone house again.

Harry tried the door, and it opened readily, but when, as it swung back into place behind them, he turned and tried it again, he found it fast.

"Worse and worse," said Grace.

"No," replied Harry. "Better and better, because it is nearer the end."

He looked around to see what sort of a place they had struck, and soon discovered that they were now prisoners indeed.

Directly ahead of them was another iron door.

This, however, did not swing back on oiled hinges like the first one. On the contrary it was as firm as a rock.

"We are penned in now," said Grace. "Caught like a rat in a trap."

They could neither advance nor retreat, and right where they were they remained for hours. During that dismal time Young King Brady thought more than once that the girl would go insane.

Suddenly, when they least expected it, a grating sound was heard behind the door through which they had just passed, and it suddenly flew open.

Harry whipped out his revolver and stood ready.

"Stand right where you are, and give an account of yourself!" he cried.

It was the old Mormon with the goat's beard, with whom he had held the interview at the gate.

In one hand he held a lantern, while the other supported a large bag on his shoulder, out of which protruded the handle of a spade, and he carried also a pickaxe in the lantern hand.

"Put down your shootin' iron, boy," he drawled. "I don't mean you no harm ef you'll do as I bid ye. Put it down, and let's have er talk, you an' me and the gal. Now come!"

Young King Brady lowered the revolver. It was safe enough to do so as matters stood.

"I thought I'd find ye here," said the man, placing the bag on the floor. "You were so dead sot on coming this way I thought I wouldn't disapp'int ye, so I opened all the doors but that one ahead. Ye see I wanted ye both whar I could put my finger on ye. Now, didn't I do it pretty slick?"

"You are all right, neighbor," replied Young King Brady. "You are the slickest card I know. Now explain what you mean by all this?"

"Yaas!" drawled the Mormon; "I think I am pretty slick, and so will you think so, too, when I've told ye all. I suspicioned you from the fust, boy. I know'd that a man must be at least twenty-five years old to be let into the order of the Golden Lion, and you hain't that much yet. However, I had to let you in on order when you showed up that there jewel, wherever you got it, but I fixed it so as you couldn't get out till I got good and ready to let ye. Ha! Ha!"

"Right," said Harry. "You did all that. Let's see, you told me your name, but I forget."

"Sellers is my name. Simon Sellers, but yours hain't Miller, and you don't belong to the Millers of Provo. I know who you be now right well."

"Who?"

"Young King Brady, one of them two New York detectives what come out here to look up Podmore's record. I've looked up yourn while you've been a-waitin' here. I know you well enough, and I want to ax you something right now."

"Ask away, Mr. Sellers. I see you have got something weighing heavy on your mind. Let's come straight to the point."

"Waal, then, here. I'm a Mormon; I'm a married man. Much married, you might say, for I've got three wives. The first one is stone deaf, the second one is blind in one eye and sick abed all the time, and the third one is a regular Tartar, and too much for me. I've made up my mind to fly the coop, and go back on the church, but I don't know no more about the world than a baby, for you see, I was born and riz right here."

"What on earth is this man driving at?" thought Harry, and he put the question to Mr. Sellers.

"It's this," replied the Mormon. "I know a secret. I was put to looking for some money what was stole and hid by Podmore's father years ago. I've found it, but I never told nobody I want to light out. I want to take my wives and get to New York, where I can be somebody, and see something of life. Let me go there with you, young feller, and I'll give you a hundred dollars of this hyar money. We'll scoop it in now and light right out this very night, and the gal shall go along too. If you don't want to marry her I will when we get to New York."

Here was an astonishing proposition.

Harry nudged Grace to keep quiet.

"I'm with you," said Harry, "but I shall have to see my partner before I leave here."

"Which you won't," replied Sellers. "Now let me tell you something. Your partner has fallen into the hands of the brothers of the Golden Lion, and it's my belief that he is already dead. While you have been waiting here, him and Podmore was brung into that house you left behind you, each in a box. Waal, I've seem 'em come in that way before, but I never seen none go out again. Believe me, young feller, you have got all you can do to save {27} yourself unless you tie to me, who knows the ropes. Come, what do you say?"

"I've said it before, and I say it again," replied Harry. "I'll tie to you. Get us out of here, no matter what way."

"Right," said Sellers. "You just come along with me."

He picked up the bag, and advancing to the door ahead of them, touched a secret spring.

The door flew back and Harry and Grace followed the Mormon into a cave of considerable size.

Passing on for a short distance, they came to a running stream, beside which lay a great mass of broken rock, which seemed to have fallen from the roof.

"Now, then, young man," he said, "here we be. Right here thar's a pot of money buried; let's go fer it lively, for should we get caught by the brothers of the Golden Lion of Judah it won't mean nothing short of ruin."

Chapter XII.
Conclusion.

Old King Brady looked upon the dead body of Joseph Smith Podmore for several minutes, and then turned away without remark.

"Do you wish to know how he died?" asked the masked apostle, as the detective turned away.

"No," replied Old King Brady. "It's no affair of mine. I am not interested to know how he died."

"You agree to my proposition? You are ready for business?" asked the apostle then.

"I agree," Old King Brady replied.

"Then step here and draw up that chair at the end of the dias," said the apostle.

He arose and lighted a large hanging lamp, which hung from a bracket fastened to the wall.

"Here is the paper, Mr. Brady," he said, drawing a leather wallet from under his gown.

This he opened, and producing a folded paper, handed it to the detective.

Upon it were a few detached letters scrawled by an illiterate hand.

"This is no cryptogram," said Old King Brady, after examining it. "The thing is a simple cipher, that is all."

"Can you read it?"

"Give me a few minutes to study it and I will see."

A very brief study of the paper was sufficient to show Old King Brady what it was all about.

"Why, this is simply Senator Truesdell's secret cipher," he said to himself. "He must have got it from his wife, and she no doubt received it from her Mormon husband. Upon my word, one would think that a United States Senator would be able to invent something a little more original than that."

He laid the paper down upon his knee, and turned to the apostle.

"I can read this," he said.

"Very well; read it then," was the reply.

"Friend," said Old King Brady, "no doubt your will is supreme in this place; no doubt at the present moment I am being overlooked by those who could at a sign from you take my life; still, when a man renders a service he is entitled to all the return that service is worth. Is it not so?"

"Of course it is so," was the reply. "Who said it wasn't? What do you want?"

"To make terms with you now, while there is time."

"What terms do you propose?"

"I can impart the secret you so much desire to learn. It is for you to name the reward."

"I told you that you would be liberally rewarded and set free in case you succeeded."

"That is not enough."

"What do you want?"

"Not your money."

"What then?"

"To see the success of my secret work in Salt Lake City."

"I do not understand your meaning."

"Then, to be more explicit, I want Senator Truesdell's daughter and his private letter-book, which Mrs. Truesdell carried away from his house."

"The latter you shall have. I care nothing for it."

"And the girl?"

"In that matter I cannot help you. Do not ask it."

"But—"

"There is no but when I have spoken. You will be well paid for all you do; that should be enough."

"You can keep your money, sir. I want none of it."

"But why—"

"That is my business. For the present we will waive this question. I am prepared to read the paper now."

"Read then, and beware of the words you use to me."

"You have the privilege of threatening if you choose. Here is what the paper says:

"I have buried the money in Rigdon's cave. It lies beneath the third rock by the stream. Turn the rock over and a peg will be found driven into the ground at the exact spot."

"And the signature?"

"There is none."

"I thought the detached letters on the last line meant that."

"No; there is no signature, as I have said. Do you know this cave?"

"Perfectly well. It lies but a short distance from the one we are now in. Here there exist a series of small caves, each one bearing the name of one of the fathers of the Mormon church."

"Very interesting. What is to be done about this?"

"You will see," replied the apostle, clapping his hands.

Two masked figures instantly stepped out of the shadows and bowed before the apostle.

"Brothers," he said, "this Gentile claims to have inter- {28} preted the secret writing. Bring hither a spade, a pickaxe, and something to put the money in. We will then proceed to put his words to the test, and woe be unto him if his interpretation is false."

* * * * * * *

"That's the spot," said Simon Sellers, pointing to one of the big stones. "Underneath that rock thar's a pot of money. I seen it. I have got some of it in my pocket now. Let's go for it, Brady, and then we will light right out."

"All right," replied Harry. "I'm ready. Shall I turn over the rock?"

"I'll do that. Likely it is too heavy for a young snip like you."

"There she goes!" cried Harry, "and the young snip did it."

The stone rolled over, and there in a shallow hole in the ground lay a number of packages of greenbacks, tied up with common twine.

"Quick! Let's hurry!" said Sellers. "We are in danger of our lives here. Help me get them into the bag. Gal, you see that there white streak in the rock right across the stream?"

"I do," replied Grace. "What of it?"

"This of it. Alongside is an opening into another cave. You want to keep your eye right onto it, while we are a-working, for out of that cave our trouble may come."

Young King Brady and the Mormon went right to work.

While Harry held the bag open the latter tumbled the packages of bills into it in lively style.

They had just finished when Grace sounded the alarm.

"I see a light!" she breathed.

"Run for your life!" gasped the Mormon, dropping a bundle of banknotes.

Harry saw three masked figures come from behind the rocks with Old King Brady himself.

"Halt, there, Simon Sellers, traitor and thief!" shouted one of the men, making a rush forward, while another held up a large reflecting lantern, which shed a strong light on the scene.

Simon Sellers gave a wild cry of despair, dropped the bag and fell upon his knees.

"Spare me! Spare me!" he called out. "I was only doing it for the good of the church. The money would have been delivered to you."

"We are all lost unless this fellow can be made to take us out of here," thought Young King Brady.

Quick as thought he whipped out his revolver and covered the apostle, for it was he who had come rushing forward to the little stream.

"Hands up!" he shouted. "This is the card that takes the trick!"

And in the same breath he said to Sellers:

"Rise up, you fool, and lead us out of this, while I hold him covered. My partner will do the rest!"

Old King Brady had already acted.

Springing past the apostle, and leaping over the stream, he turned and faced the enemy from the other side.

"Hold 'em covered, Governor. Hold 'em covered!" cried Young King Brady. "This man will get us out all right."

Sellers was already on his feet, having plucked up courage at this turn of affairs.

He made a rush for the bag.

"Drop it and lead on!" said Old King Brady, sternly.

"Must we leave the money?" groaned Sellers.

"We must," said Old King Brady. "You may be a thief, but I am not. The Brady's have no use for the property of the Mormon church."

They passed through the door a moment later.

The last Old King Brady saw of the apostle he was still standing there with his companions by the little stream.

Sellers made the door fast, and they beat a hasty retreat through the secret passages, and in a few minutes emerged from the gate in the wall surrounding the old Podmore house, and stood upon the road.

"Just in time to cap the climax, governor, as you always are!" exclaimed Young King Brady.

"We must leave town at once," replied the detective, "or we shall surely find ourselves in trouble again."

"There is a train east in half an hour," said Sellers. "I go too, for my life hain't worth a cent. Anyhow, I got ten thousand dollars out of that hole."

And when the east-bound train pulled out of the station, the whole party was on board.

The Bradys dropped Sellers from that moment.

They went straight to Washington, where Grace Truesdell was restored to her father, much to his relief.

"You have done the best you could," the senator remarked to Old King Brady. "My wife has only met the fate she deserved, and as for the letter-book, I don't care for it, now that Podmore is dead."

And yet, strange to say, five days later, he received it by mail.

Then the senator reached for his check book, and the Bradys left his house richer by $5,000.

They immediately returned to New York, scarcely feeling safe until they found themselves in their own office once more.

Harry kept the jewel of the Golden Lion of Judah to remind him of the adventures of the Bradys among the Mormons.

THE END.

Also available from
GREG KOFFORD BOOKS

Boadicea;
the Mormon Wife:
Life Scenes in Utah

By Alfreda Eva Bell
Edited and Annotated by
Michael Austin and Ardis E. Parshall

Paperback, ISBN: 978-1-58958-566-9

First published in 1855, *Boadicea; the Mormon Wife* belongs to a sub-genre of crime fiction that flourished in the Eastern United States during the 1850s. *Boadicea* has become increasingly important to scholars of Mormonism because it gives us a glimpse of the Mormon image in literature immediately after the Church's public acknowledgement of plural marriage. Over the next half century, this image would be sharpened and refined by writers with different rhetorical goals: to end polygamy, to attack Mormon theology, or just to tell a highly entertaining adventure story. In Boadicea, though, we see these tropes in their infancy, through a prolific author working at break-neck speed to imagine the lives of a strange people for readers willing to pay the "extremely low price of 15 cents" for the privilege of being amazed by stories of polygyny and polyandry, along with generous helpings of adultery, seduction, kidnapping, and no fewer than fourteen untimely but spectacular deaths: people are shot, stabbed, bludgeoned, poisoned, hanged, strangled, and drowned. No other novel of the nineteenth century comes anywhere near *Boadicea* in portraying Mormon society as violent, chaotic, and dysfunctional.

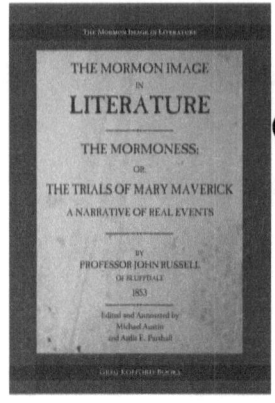

The Mormoness;
Or, The Trials Of Mary Maverick:
A Narrative Of Real Events

By John Russell
Edited and Annotated by
Michael Austin and Ardis E. Parshall

Paperback, ISBN: 978-1-58958-507-2

Published in 1853, the first American novel about the Mormons is also one of the best. John Russell, an Illinois journalist and educator, witnessed the persecution in Missouri and Illinois and generally sympathized with the Saints. The Mormoness tells the story of Mary Maverick, the heroine of the novel, who joined the Mormon Church when her husband was converted in Illinois. Though not initially a believer, Mary embraces her identity as "the Mormoness" when her husband and son are killed in a Haun's Mill-like massacre—and at the end of the novel, she must find a way to forgive the killer.

Virtually unavailable until now, Michael Austin and Ardis E. Parshall's fresh transcription, introduction, notes, and appendices enable readers to rediscover a compassionate and insightful outsider's view of early Mormonism.

"Swell Suffering": A Biography of Maurine Whipple

Veda Tebbs Hale

Paperback, ISBN: 978-1-58958-124-1
Hardcover, ISBN: 978-1-58958-122-7

Maurine Whipple, author of what some critics consider Mormonism's greatest novel, *The Giant Joshua,* is an enigma. Her prize-winning novel has never been out of print, and its portrayal of the founding of St. George draws on her own family history to produce its unforgettable and candid portrait of plural marriage's challenges. Yet Maurine's life is full of contradictions and unanswered questions. Veda Tebbs Hale, a personal friend of the paradoxical novelist, answers these questions with sympathy and tact, nailing each insight down with thorough research in Whipple's vast but under-utilized collected papers.

Praise for *"Swell Suffering"*:

"Hale achieves an admirable balance of compassion and objectivity toward an author who seemed fated to offend those who offered to love or befriend her. . . . Readers of this biography will be reminded that Whipple was a full peer of such Utah writers as Virginia Sorensen, Fawn Brodie, and Juanita Brooks, all of whom achieved national fame for their literary and historical works during the mid-twentieth century"

—Levi S. Peterson, author of *The Backslider* and *Juanita Brooks: Mormon Historian*

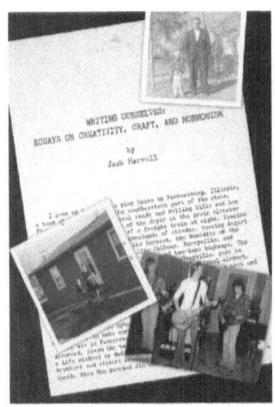

Writing Ourselves:
Essays on Creativity, Craft, and Mormonism

Jack Harrell

Paperback, ISBN: 978-1-58958-754-0

Continuing a conversation as old as Mormonism itself, Jack Harrell explores the relationship between Mormonism and the writer. Mormons see the universe in mythic proportions. Their God is a creator, their devil a destroyer. This makes meaningful conflict fundamental to their worldview, and begs the terms for religious redemption, as well as the redemptive power of art. Harrell urges writers to be authentic as they embrace the difficulties inherent in the creative process. His essays blend faithful intellectual inquiry, personal narrative, research, and application to offer insights for anyone who cares about writing, creativity, and the human condition.